"A thriller mixing fa [illegible] s
them both more fright [illegible]

"A thrilling journey around the world and into the depths of the American political machine, where all definitely is not what it seems."

—*The Santa Fe New Mexican*

"*World Order* is a fast-paced book of fiction that could have come right out of a recent front page article in your local newspaper on chemical/biological warfare. In the aftermath of the Gulf War and the hollow denial that chemical and biological weapons were released, the chances that aggressor nations or terrorist or military organizations in our own country or elsewhere would use chemical/biological weapons for their own agendas are as real as it gets.

"Goliszek's book is unfortunately very close to the truth that ordinary citizens aren't allowed to know, which makes it very informative as well as entertaining. You won't put this book down until you have turned the last page."

—Professor Garth Nicolson, Chief Scientific Officer,
The Institute for Molecular Medicine,
and Professor of Internal Medicine,
The University of Texas Medical School of Houston

"Goliszek's ghastly fiction, based on frightening fact, opens a Pandora's box of covert operations by those who believe the world would be better off without many of us. Chilling recommended reading."

—Len Horowitz, D.M.D., M.A., M.P.H., author of
Emerging Viruses: Aids and Ebola

BY ANDREW GOLISZEK
FROM TOM DOHERTY ASSOCIATES

rivers of the black moon

world order

WORLD ORDER

Andrew Goliszek

TOR®
A TOM DOHERTY ASSOCIATES BOOK
NEW YORK

WORLD ORDER

Edited by James Frenkel

A Tor Book
Published by Tom Doherty Associates, Inc.
175 Fifth Avenue
New York, NY 10010

Tor Books on the World Wide Web:
http://www.tor.com

Tor® is a registered trademark of Tom Doherty Associates, Inc.

ISBN: 0-812-56539-8
Library of Congress Card Catalog Number: 97-34389

First edition: February 1998
First mass market edition: June 1999

Printed in the United States of America

0 9 8 7 6 5 4 3 2 1

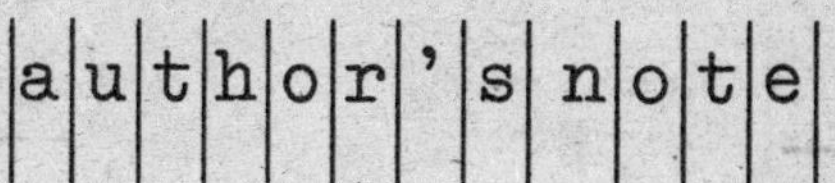

This is a work of fiction. While inspired by government records and testimony made before Congress, all names, characters, places, events, and incidents are entirely fictional and the product of the author's imagination.

To Kathy,
my wife, my best friend, and always
my first editor

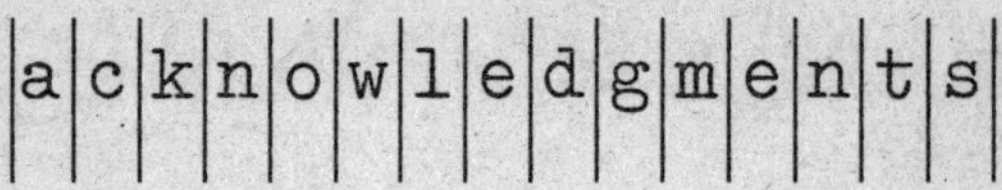

Special thanks to my editor, Jim Frenkel, and the staff at Tor Books for all their hard work. As always, I'd also like to thank my agent, Bernie Kurman, for all his help and encouragement.

During the preparation of this novel, I have drawn on information from many sources, too numerous to acknowledge here. I would like to thank, however, Dr. Garth Nicolson and Captain Joyce Riley, who first introduced me to the plight of Gulf War veterans and the possibility that we have much left to uncover.

prologue

JUNE 8, 1988, SOUTHEASTERN NEW MEXICO

In the late twilight hours, especially at that moment when the last glimmer of light mixed with dark shadows, the New Mexico desert was deceptively tranquil. On this particular evening, not a cloud was in sight. What little daylight remained fell quickly, giving way to the stark blackness of the desert night, accentuated suddenly by irregular specks of light that grew brighter by the second and, like bits of laser, pierced the violet sky.

Whatever movement of air there'd been only moments earlier was suddenly and inexplicably replaced by a lifeless stillness. As twilight painted the arid desert with a shroud of purple matched only by the richness of a fading horizon, it seemed to deepen the loneliness Joe Reed would always feel whenever he'd been away from home for more than a few days.

On evenings like this, Joe's mind inevitably would drift to thoughts of his wife, Karen, and Beth, their twelve-year-old, back home in San Diego, about Tommy, who was only six months old when they lost him to leukemia three years ago, about how much closer he was to his family since then and how many more trips like this one he'd have to make just to pay off the obscene hospital bills that had taken nearly all of their money. Today, the six-hour trance that was typically broken when KKLM, a country music station in Alamogordo, began to fade out, was interrupted by a glint of light that caught the corner of his eye.

He knew from experience that the sudden blend of twilight and dark grainy sand could play tricks on his eyes. He'd seen it before. Sometimes right there on this very desert. Especially when he drove for eight hours straight, and especially now, when the jagged dunes and humanlike figures of cactus cast eerie, ghostlike shadows that seemed to grow in stature and dance across a barren landscape that stretched as far as the eye could see. For Joe, who'd been driving this route longer than he cared to remember, this was precisely the time of night when nothing seemed quite real, when everything he saw was either imagined or just plain illusion. But this was no illusion.

Joe punched the gearshift of his eighteen-wheeler and felt a sudden chill burst through the window of his International cab. He shivered uncontrollably, wave after peristaltic wave of a strange summer coldness piercing his hot flesh like icy needles. The uncharacteristic churning in his gut told him instantly that something was wrong. Different. Like nothing he'd ever experienced during any of those 400-mile runs he'd taken at least a hundred times before.

He twisted his head in every direction, listening. Nothing. Only the roar of a diesel engine and the hollow ring of air brakes that cut sharply through the parched wasteland, bounced crisply off chiseled red canyon walls, then faded into a dead silence as if swallowed by some unseen force beneath the ashen desert floor.

Up ahead, a group of men sat safely inside a specially designed vehicle and tried to assess the damage around them. Their faces glowing red from the overhead lights, they studied the panels of computer screens and monitoring equipment in front of them.

"Whaddya think, doc?" one of the men asked. "Is decontamination gonna be a problem?"

"It might be," answered a nervous scientist as he punched buttons on the keyboard and waited for the equations he'd inputted to reassure him. "I won't know how much of a problem until I get out there and take some measurements. Right now I'd say it sure as hell doesn't look too good."

"The general will want to know ASAP."

"Tell the general it'll be tomorrow at the earliest. Are the containment suits ready?"

"Ready and waiting, sir."

"Then let's get them on and see what we've got. God help us if it's as bad as I think."

As Joe eased the large diesel to a stop, the rhythmic, almost melodic echoes seemed to dance atop the lifeless air from one end of the horizon to the other, if there was anyone out there who would even notice. But except for weathered rock that had sat untouched for a million years and the dry, overgrown sagebrush that littered the scorched earth like countless pieces of brown and gray debris, there *was* no one out there, only Joe.

He downshifted into fifth, sending blackened puffs of thick smoke upward into the darkness. And there—just over the next hill, in an area the veteran truckers who'd driven the route called hell's alley—was something Joe had never before seen on any of his previous trips.

"Breaker, breaker, this is Big Joe. I'm headin' west on old Highway Seventeen . . .'bout a hundred fifty miles east of Alamogordo. Somethin' real strange out here. Real strange. Anyone read me? Over."

The CB fell silent for a few seconds, then exploded with a garbled mix of static and broken voice signals. At the same time, a deep hum erupted from out of the blackness ahead of him.

"Your br—k—g up B—Joe. Static's too b—d. Say again. Over."

"This is Big Joe. If you can read me, I'm on old Highway Seventeen, a hundred fifty miles east of Alamogordo. Do you read me? Over."

"Y—r still break—g up—oe. Over. Can't rea—. Someth—g out there that's kill—g the signa—. Try———." As he switched between channels, he listened to the CB sizzling with static.

"Damn!" Joe muttered, throwing the microphone down, the coiled wire snapping back from the impact of metal against the hard vinyl seat next to him. He continued to downshift, all the while nervously staring ahead and listening to the strange sound that was drawing him toward it like an unsuspecting fly to a beacon in the middle of night.

Joe's chiseled forearms bulged with a tension he'd rarely experienced. His knuckles, normally hidden beneath a thick layer of grease and calluses, grew white as he clutched at the steering wheel. And as he squinted through the dust on the windshield, his steel gray eyes riveted to the faint glow emanating from behind one of the peaked dunes a few hundred yards away, not even the nocturnal desert wildlife stirred from its daytime torpor, sensing, no doubt, a danger in the air and electing to remain hidden in the safety of their lairs.

Joe felt as alone in his darkness as he'd ever been. Absolutely alone. Or so he thought. Reaching for his mic, he tried again.

"This is Big Joe. Anyone out there read me? Over."

Again, a steady crackle flowed back. Not even the garbled voices could break through the static that now echoed almost angrily through the cab as if ready to explode. Joe threw the microphone down again. He pulled his rig off the asphalt road and onto hard desert sand, staring at the faint amber glow, listening to what sounded like the heavy drone of a generator at half speed interspersed with a steady, piercing whine.

Not human, thought Joe. Couldn't be human. At least not anything human he'd ever heard before. He turned the key. The truck fell silent. Instantly, the hum grew louder, even more piercing in the still air, but different—more of a deep, guttural moan that left him sick to his stomach.

"I'll be damned," he whispered at hearing it all stop as quickly as it had begun, giving the amber glow an even stranger quality in the still, quiet air; an aurora of gaseous yellow light, flickering and oscillating, its nebulous fingerlike projections, barely visible to the naked eye, reaching far into the night sky and disappearing into the black emptiness of space. If it weren't so damned unnatural, Joe would have thought it the most beautiful sight he'd ever seen in the desert.

Swinging the cab door open, Joe worked his large, muscular frame around the steering column and stepped quietly onto the rough desert sand. His well-worn cowboy boot made an almost imperceptible crunch that to Joe may as well have been a sonic boom. Grimacing, he stopped dead in his tracks. Rivers of hot sweat poured from his unshaved face and thick neck. The pounding in his temples grew harder, more intense; and he suddenly felt an almost uncontrollable urge to relieve himself right there on the desert floor. Then, easing his other foot down from the rig in exaggerated slow motion, Joe stood there, exposed and in terrified silence.

By now, the rich purple had given way to a deep blackness, erasing from the sandy landscape any remnants of lifelike images visible only moments ago. And there, directly in front of him, penetrating the black night, was the faint glow of amber.

''Goddamn,'' Joe whispered, barely able to emit the sounds through the dust in his throat.

He took one small step after another, placing the pointy toes of his size twelves almost balletlike into the sand, just as softly putting the heels down as carefully as he could. A gust of air swirled about him, enveloping him with a musty oil smell. His nostrils flared, and he took the putrid odor deep into his lungs, trying to remember when or where he'd smelled it before, suspecting that it could have been on one of his many trips through the desert and he just never noticed it. The hum began anew, pulsating in near perfect cadence. Amplified by the stagnant atmosphere of the night desert, it seemed to reach into his throat and, like a thousand sharp needles, stab at his innards. He took several deep breaths and willed himself to go on.

He crept toward a small depression just to the right of the hill. The hum, now muffling the noise of his boots against the crusty sand, had grown loud enough to make him feel a bit more at ease as he walked.

Fifty feet . . . Ten feet . . . Five. He was there, heart pounding, hands and legs trembling, and though almost numb from fear, had to go on and see what it was that was drawing him to this place.

Straining almost painfully, Joe inched his way to the depression, peered carefully through a fissure between two rocks, then froze with the same fear he'd experienced so many times during his boyhood nightmares in which he couldn't run or escape from something that was about to get him. Instantly, he felt his heart pounding in his chest as he witnessed a scene so incredible it seemed like a brief moment of insanity that would disappear only if he closed his eyes and opened them again.

Joe closed his eyes and shook his head violently. He opened them. Nothing. Still there. The scene, unimaginable, was still there.

And then, just as his muscles began to relax enough so that he could move them, the amber glow grew brighter and moved toward him, sweeping across the desert like a searchlight hunting for unsuspecting prey. In an instant it was upon him, blinding him. Reacting, he turned, running in the direction he knew his rig was parked. The beam followed radarlike, tracking every zigzag move, getting brighter, hotter, more intense.

"Over there!" a booming voice yelled out over a speaker. "Don't let him get away!"

A deep rumbling suddenly erupted and shook the ground beneath Joe's feet, shifting sand and rock, and he felt the earth buckle and tremble as if rocked by thunderous explosions deep below its mantle. The rumbling then faded, replaced at once by a deafening roar that vibrated through his vital organs and sent him crashing to the ground in excruciating pain. Lifting himself, he began to run again.

Through his squinting eyes, Joe spotted the rig, its cab light still on. The sliver of dim green urged him on, guiding him out of the darkness like a welcome beacon. If he just got to it, he thought, he might have a chance. Might even be able to try his CB again to get help, to warn someone, anyone.

Joe ran faster than he ever thought possible. The Texas-made cowboy boots that fit him like comfortable old gloves now betrayed him, digging into the desert under his weight, throwing sand ten feet into the air behind them. It *was* like one of his boyhood nightmares. The faster he tried moving his legs, the deeper he sank and the slower he ran. He thought of quicksand and how he'd gotten stuck once and how terrifying the feeling was to want to move but be unable, no matter what. Lactic acid was building quickly in the large muscles of his thighs, making both legs feel as if they'd been set on fire. If he could only hold out another few seconds, he thought, he'd be there.

Then, less than a hundred yards from his rig, a searing pain shot through his head and shoulders, dropping him to the ground like a two-hundred-pound rock. For a moment he lay writhing like a worm that had been cut in two. Within seconds, total paralysis had overcome him. No longer able to move even his fingers, he felt himself lifted abruptly by his arms and dragged across the desert back to the hill. He could barely open his eyes, but through narrow, cracklike slits, he saw the faint, blurry image of his rig moving away from him and his boots, still attached to a pair of limp feet, bouncing lifelessly across the rough desert sand. His mouth fell open. Warm saliva dribbled down his chin and onto his neck. His tongue, nothing more than a piece of numbed flesh, bounced from side to side. Through the gauzelike mucus that was spreading over the corneas of his eyes, he could make out several large white images, grossly distorted, gesturing in slow, exaggerated movements as if trapped in some thick, milky glue.

God, please. Please make this be a nightmare. Please make this go away. This can't be real, it can't be, it can't—

His senses numbed, Joe gasped for what little air he could force into his collapsing lungs. Then slowly, as if a noose were being tightened around his chest, he felt life being squeezed from his body. His existence, his wonderful life, he thought, was coming to an end. And suddenly—like blinding flashes of light—everything he'd ever held dear in his life was before him. Fleeting snapshots of thirty-three years. His wife Karen, their daughter, Beth, their dead son, Tommy, the trip to Disneyland, the picnic last weekend. The lifelike images darted into and out of Joe's semiconscious mind, swirling violently, uncontrollably, as he prepared himself to die. What would his family do without him? How would Beth, who'd always been daddy's little girl, take it? Who would give his little girl away at her wedding? How would Karen, the only woman he'd ever loved or who'd ever loved him, cope with his death?

Seconds later, after three decades had flashed through his memory like bolts of lightning, he remembered how as a child he would look out into a deceptively peaceful desert and wonder how prey must have felt at that helpless moment when they'd looked into their predator's eyes and realized that death was inevitable. Did they even know? Could they have possibly sensed that life was about to end? He remembered the dreams, the nightmares, picturing himself as prey, shuddering at the thought of dying that kind of unspeakable death. He thought of it now.

As his eyes closed and darkness consumed him, Joe felt himself being released, his head and shoulders falling to the ground with a muted thud, the warm desert sand pricking his skin as it blew over his paralyzed body. Then, forcing his swollen eyelids apart, he found himself staring up at two identical massive figures. He felt his eyelids closing again. And as much as he tried forcing a last glimpse at what it was that had so terrified him, Joe Reed took a final slow breath and slipped into the black depths of unconsciousness.

chapter one

MARCH 14, 1996: 8:15 A.M.

Somewhere on the outskirts of the nation's capital, and long before most of Washington's ruling elite and their staff had arrived at the office complexes surrounding the Washington Mall, a frantic urgency was already infecting the movements of nearly three hundred men and women wrapped cocoonlike in knee-length lab coats. There were no nine-to-five types here; only teams of dedicated individuals whose mission it was to push the frontiers of science back as far as they could go.

Inside this secret world lay a vast, concrete labyrinth that on most days resembled a human beehive. Spreading outward in every direction, rows of stainless steel windowless rooms lined highway-sized corridors that glowed white from endless streams of fluorescent lighting. Scientists—young, old, men, women—could be seen darting about those cold, hospitallike highways. Some appeared then disappeared through sterile hallways. Others shuffled clandestinely into and out of cluttered labs that sat locked behind reinforced doors. Still others emerged from polished elevator doors, holding clipboards, papers, and piles of thick, disheveled notebooks containing secrets they alone could decipher. The unnatural glow of fluorescence cast a sickly pallor over each one of them. They seemed unreal, ghostlike; human robots in an artificially created environment, kept alive by a billion-dollar system of pumps and filters that brought life-giving oxygen to their otherwise anaerobic world.

Entombed several hundred feet below the earth's surface, and constructed during the cold war days of the 1960s as a site for the U.S. government to operate underground in the event of a nuclear attack, the complex had been gradually transformed into a scientific fortress without parallel in the industrialized world. Its focus on only one thing, one mission—to advance science beyond anything known to humankind—this fortress now housed the greatest collection of creative minds in America. With the stakes exceedingly high in this game of high-tech science, potential scientists—especially those participating in secret Pentagon projects—were regarded as a commodity as important as any high-ranking government official. Not many deserted, and among the few who had and attempted to make unauthorized use of what knowledge they'd acquired, none were ever heard from again.

The laboratories themselves, kept isolated even from one another for security reasons, were scattered throughout the vast compound. Each discipline was assigned its own area, each subdiscipline its own section: MOLECULAR BIOLOGY, BIOTECHNOLOGY, GENETICS, BIOCHEMISTRY, VIROLOGY, BACTERIOLOGY, TOXICOLOGY, PHYSIOLOGY, NEUROSCIENCE, IMMUNOLOGY. These were a few of more than forty scientific fields specifically targeted by the U.S. government as part of a top-secret program designed to maintain America's edge in virtually every field of life science. Inside the laboratories: cutting edge projects, new developments in biotechnology, ongoing experiments in genetic engineering, AIDS, cancer, gene therapy, all promising to keep the United States at the forefront of scientific advances the rest of the world could only imagine.

It was here, in the late 1970s, that work had been accelerated on genetically engineered pathogenic viruses. Later, with the help of private U.S. biotechnology firms, recombinant DNA research had intensified, and secret technology at the lab complex was used to develop strains of bacteria that would be resistant to known antibiotics or which produced deadly toxins. By 1983, the Department of Defense had funded twenty-seven recombinant DNA projects, most with outside contractors. By 1985, that number had grown to sixty. And by 1986, with more than 300 companies actively engaged in the biotechnology and pharmaceutical industries, the Department of Defense had its pick of companies that had exhausted their initial investment capital and were quite eager to cooperate with the military for a share of the lucrative grant pie, even if that cooperation meant participation in various weapons programs.

Rapid government advances in biotechnology, the Pentagon feared, would strengthen the already established Soviet germ warfare program. Thus, it became common practice to rely on commercial pharmaceutical companies to manufacture large quantities of deadly toxins and new forms of pathogenic bacteria. And at the same time that viruses were being altered to make them ineffective against naturally present antibodies, protective vaccines were being developed that could then be dispensed to the "favored" population. As one insider had put it to a visiting Pentagon official, "We've created twenty-first-century science in a twentieth-century subterranean world; no one in the world can even come close."

In a separate, almost concealed area of the complex, a brown metal door with simple gold letters running across its width, belied the covert mission of those on the other side.

Security Area
Division of Biotic Investigation
Authorized Personnel Only

It was a vaguely descriptive title, purposely designed to obscure the true function of a division that no one at the complex, other than the few involved, really knew much about; a division that maintained its own security standards and answered to no one except the Pentagon's joint Chiefs and the White House itself.

Across the hall, in one of the computer labs, Dr. Linda Franklin had been staring trancelike for what seemed like eternity, a ream of data spewing nonstop from one of the printers in front of her. When a special hotline buzzed, the cup she'd been cradling between both hands dropped instantly from her fingers. Black coffee saturated the computer paper laid neatly on the table in front of her. Shards of hot glass flew in every direction at once across the smooth tiled floor, and settled haphazardly beneath desks and printers in every corner of the room.

As a molecular biologist and senior crash site investigator with NASA's special Washington bureau, Linda knew exactly what that ring meant. Everyone in the division did. Snapping her head around, she froze, fixed in place as if every sense in her body had suddenly turned numb. It mattered little how many times she'd heard that buzz before; it was always the same. The sudden rush of adrenaline, invariably followed by the instant muscle spasm and a sudden burning in the pit of her stomach that made her feel as if an explosion had just gone off inside of her.

It hadn't always been that way, though. And it seemed that lately even the most insignificant things would make Dr. Franklin jumpy. The soft, half-moon shaped dimples that penetrated her cheeks whenever she laughed were rarely seen these days. As far as the colleagues who knew her best were concerned, the old Linda Franklin, confident, always self-assured and full of life, had been emotionally dead for eight years now, her life turned upside down by a hideous tragedy that seemed to have occurred so long ago. But despite it all, despite the anger and the growing bouts with depression, Dr. Linda Franklin remained the backbone of the division, a chief investigator who could always be called upon when anything out of the ordinary came up.

Tall, medium-boned, and well-proportioned from regular workouts at the health club she'd joined a year ago, Dr. Franklin was just beginning to show the visible signs of approaching forty. Still, she remained a stunningly beautiful woman. Her auburn hair, trimmed neatly to shoulder length, framed a set of full, rounded lips that made her look young, exotic, and when adorned with the cinnamon red lipstick that had become her trademark, as seductive as any woman ten years younger. But those eight painfully long years since the accident had taken their toll. And now, even the bright green eyes had become expressionless and melancholy, sad reminders of how even time, with all its healing power, had been unable to lessen the gnawing despair that came from losing a beloved spouse.

Snapping out of her momentary gaze, Dr. Franklin sprinted across the hall and, in almost a single motion, pushed open the brown door and jumped into a cracked oxblood leather chair next to her desk. Unread papers, coffee mugs, old books, and stacks of journals were randomly scattered everywhere. A cork bulletin board on the left wall was covered with scribbled notes and pinned-up reminders of meetings and seminars. On the right, a wall-to-wall bookcase was lined with books on everything from biochemical evolution to vertebrate neuroanatomy, all arranged in subject order. Among the books, mementos sat here and there, revealing exotic trips around the world: a gruesome shrunken head picked up in New Guinea, brain coral from the Great Barrier Reef, a carved wooden goblet from Israel. All sat untouched, collecting dust like so many pieces of long forgotten treasure.

The red phone, buried beneath a pile of unread manuscripts in the corner of her oversized metal desk, buzzed for the fourth time. Clearing some of the papers away with a swipe of her left hand, Dr. Franklin snatched the receiver and took a deep breath before answering.

"Hello. Dr. Franklin."

"Mornin', Linda . . . Adam Wesely," the raspy, froglike voice on the other end responded.

She knew at the first sound of that deep, intimidating croak that she was about to be sent on another special assignment. Adam Wesely, overall director of the SELF Project (Search for Extraterrestrial Life Forms), used the hotline sparingly. And for good reason. A top-secret investigative branch of NASA, SELF had been set up by Congress following a series of unexplained crashes in the late sixties. The fact was that SELF was designed to take over certain functions from the National Security Agency, which had originally been established in 1947 to investigate these kinds of phenomena. It seemed now that while the public was worried about UFOs, the U.S. government was busy trying to keep a lid on anything that might cause national panic or disorder.

But there was another, not so benevolent, motive for maintaining a strict code of security regarding the crash of any new aircraft or satellite. As long as the public held beliefs—even suspicions—about the existence of UFOs, the government was able to conceal top-secret test flights of state-of-the-art aircraft, knowing full well that any encounter would invariably be attributed to UFO sightings. The official policy, quite simply, was to dismiss all UFO reports as anything other than UFOs, while at the same time to spread enough disinformation to leave doubts in the minds of any eyewitnesses.

The policy worked beautifully. The growing fascination with UFOs had become an American obsession. The increased level of activity by the Pentagon just added proverbial fuel to the UFO fires. Nothing the government had ever done to keep those test flights secret had been more effective than simply allowing a public ready and willing to believe anything about UFOs to feed its insatiable appetite for extraterrestrials.

The seventies had been a UFO heyday. Everyone just knew there was something out there. Even some unlikely government officials were convinced of it. But the eighties were different. SELF was fast losing its luster, regarded by a skeptical Congress as an ancillary agency and by some of the top brass as a shameless waste of taxpayer dollars. Why it was still being funded was a well-kept secret. Talk was that SELF had survived ostensibly to reward someone's budget compromise, deliver needed signatures on pet legislation, or to satisfy some misguided notion that maybe, just maybe, there really *was* life in space. And as long as something unusual came crashing to Earth once in a while—pieces of satellite, aging space debris, foreign experimental aircraft that lost altitude and burned up within the territorial United States—there was at least a modicum of satisfaction that the government was getting its money's worth. By the mid-eighties, though, SELF had been transformed from a special UFO investigative agency to an elite group of top-secret recovery teams that it was to this day.

"Linda, we have reports of an unusual crash in Brittan, New Hampshire," Adam Wesely said.

"When?" Linda asked.

"Happened a little after three o'clock yesterday morning. My team's already up here. I have your team booked on the six A.M. flight out of Washington first thing tomorrow."

"Tomorrow morning? But I've got—"

"Put it on hold," Wesely interrupted. "This is a priority one."

As chief investigator responsible for collecting biotic evidence for DNA analysis, including human remains at classified crash sites, Linda sensed this was no ordinary call. The words *crash site* echoed violently in her head, reminding her suddenly of another major crash near Tucson, Arizona, nearly eight years ago. Only then it was her husband, Peter Franklin, also a biologist for NASA, who'd been asked to help investigate an unusual crash and who was found burned and mutilated beyond recognition. The official report had listed Dr. Franklin as the victim of a bizarre accident resulting from a fuel line explosion during the investigation.

The next eight years found Linda scrambling to dig up even a partial report and make some sense of the whole incident. There'd always been too many missing pieces, too few clues; almost as if everything had been orchestrated and pieced together all too neatly and filed away in the bowels of the Pentagon where it mysteriously vanished, together with any hope that she would ever find out what had really happened. No outside agency had ever been allowed to examine the body nor allowed to review autopsy results or detailed laboratory reports. And at the time, no one had been allowed anywhere near the scene of the crash until all the wreckage had been removed and impounded.

And now, as her mind drifted back in time, Linda could still see Peter walking down the stairs of their home, turning to kiss her good-bye, and closing the door behind him. It was the last time she would ever see his face. She recalled, as if it were yesterday, the next morning's telephone call somberly telling her of Peter's death and how she cried until there were no more tears left. She found herself suddenly reliving the same pain she'd felt during the funeral service at Washington Cathedral. And now this.

"Can you give me any more details before we get up there?" Linda asked, barely able to speak.

"Afraid not," Wesely answered. "Not until you arrive with your crew for a complete investigation. I don't like the looks of this one, though."

"Meaning?"

"It's extraordinary. Something you've not seen before. Might be Russian. We just don't know. I'm sure you'll find it fascinating, I'll leave it at that. Meet you at the airport tomorrow."

"Okay, see you then."

Linda hung up and sank back into her chair. Tears formed in her eyes, though the passage of time had long since tempered the intense sadness, transforming it more into the anger and bitterness one feels at losing part of oneself. She rubbed her eyes and her forehead as if to wrest the demons of Tucson from her mind, but as much as she tried, she couldn't. Peter's violent death, pieces of his torn and incinerated body never completely recovered, the whole damn cover-up had left her with such rage that to this day she would still find herself bristling at the very thought of it. Despite that, Linda had always believed that one day she would discover what really happened. Despair had eventually given way to hope, hope into an unyielding determination, and it was that and that alone that now kept Linda going.

chapter two

Until now, most of SELF's previous work had been anything but extraordinary: Unexplained crashes that turned out to be little more than ordinary test flights; pieces of satellite no one was supposed to know about; foreign aircraft that strayed too far, then crashed.

Of course, there was space debris. At last count, over a hundred thousand individual pieces of junk floating several hundred miles above Earth. There was so much stuff, in fact, that invariably there'd always be *something* jarred from its orbit. What didn't plunge into the ocean or burn up during reentry had to be investigated and analyzed for potentially hazardous microbes that could have mutated as a result of exposure to ultraviolet radiation and survived the return trip to Earth. It was Linda's job to provide the DNA analysis.

For the most part, everyone agreed that much of the non-field-work was crap. There was always administrative paperwork, routine laboratory analyses of odd specimens gathered from crash sites around the world, general scientific drudge work that needed to be done but that no one ever got around to fast enough until pressed by NASA or the Pentagon. So the prospect of finding something unique, something that might be similar to the Tucson crash at least gave Linda hope of discovering a clue, a vital piece of a cryptic puzzle that had eluded her for so long.

Seconds after getting off the phone with Adam Wesely, Linda's mood had suddenly changed. And as though someone had ignited a fire in her belly, she raced toward an adjoining lab.

"Jack, we need to leave for New Hampshire first thing tomorrow morning," she called out. Then, stumbling headlong into what anyone else would have mistaken for total chaos, Linda squinted through a maze of scientific equipment, searching for signs of life among the rubble.

"Yeah, I'm back here," mumbled Dr. Jackson Pilofski, a short, pear-shaped scientist wrapped loosely in faded Levi's and a frayed plaid shirt so old it looked as though it were about to come apart at the seams. The obligatory pocket protector overflowed with pens of nearly every size and color.

"Jack, I just got off the hot line with Adam. There's been a crash."

"Hang on a minute," the impatient voice yelled back.

Linda could now see Dr. Pilofski bobbing up and down behind his lab bench, intently engaged in one of those couldn't-put-down experiments that left him oblivious to everyone and everything around him.

That happened often with Jack. Graduating at the top of his class at MIT with a degree in zoology, recruited by the U.S. government after receiving his doctorate in neuropharmacology from Harvard, he never quite settled into the bureaucratic system of government science, despite the incentives.

It was on October 1, 1988, that Jack had been lured away from Lantham Pharmaceuticals, one of the companies awarded a multi-million-dollar Department of Defense research contract, and offered a position at the government's lab complex, ostensibly to fill the void left by Peter Franklin's death. Joining the SELF team a year later, when it was decided that a zoologist was needed to augment the group's specialty areas, he quickly established a reputation not only as a top-notch researcher but as someone with little tolerance for administrators or political types who as he would put it, "didn't know their asses from a test tube." But despite the unpredictable tantrums and frequent outbursts, he and Linda grew inseparable; and next to Peter she considered him the best friend she'd ever had.

As he bobbed, Linda would catch fleeting glimpses of wire rim glasses pinching a bearded, cherubic face. Curly brown hair danced and bounced in every direction like loose pieces of broken spring. As always, the distinct aroma of cherry blend pipe tobacco permeated the lab, drawing her to the wisps of smoke that drifted upward from the lab bench and circled slowly overhead like white, nebulous clouds. In this secret society, at least, the tobacco gestapo had not yet established a foothold. Not that Jack would have cared one bit, much less allowed anyone to dictate his personal behavior.

"Jack, what the hell are you doing?" Linda shouted, then followed the thin clouds that hovered above the lab bench.

"One more minute," the voice pleaded.

Brilliant but eccentric, Jack had been specifically hired as a physiological zoologist responsible for classifying organisms found on, in, and around crash sites. If a craft could not be identified by markings or other physical evidence, it was his job to trace any on-site specimen to its country of origin. From that he would determine where the craft may have originated. Just three years ago, he'd exposed the prototype of an advanced Russian fighter jet that had crashed over Alaska by identifying an on-board parasitic organism indigenous only to the northern regions of Belarus.

"Any details?" Jack asked, suddenly peering enthusiastically over his lab bench like a fat prairie dog looking out of its burrow for the first time in months. A small, curved pipe hung precariously from the edge of his lips.

Linda could hardly see Jack's ruddy face among the collection of various-sized beakers, flasks, graduated cylinders, and test tube racks that were either strewn about or stacked on top of one another like discarded piles of Legos. Wires and rubber tubing seemed to appear from nowhere and in some areas of the lab dangled in midair like long-abandoned spiderwebs. Electronic monitoring equipment filled the room. Small jars overflowed with insects, worms, mollusks, and amphibians of all sorts; larger jars contained snakes, lizards, rodents, and other small vertebrates. There were fish tanks, reptile tanks, amphibian tanks, trays spilling over with microscope slides, and cages with live research animals. To a visitor who happened by, it was a scene from the Bible:

Surely Noah must have paid a visit to Jack's lab and left him everything that wouldn't fit on the ark.

"Not really," Linda said. "No details to speak of. Just that it's not your typical crash site. Could be something real unusual up there."

Jack threw some switches and watched a pen record the EEG from one of his laboratory rat's brains.

When not investigating crash sites, team members conducted their own research projects. Linda, as the molecular biologist in the group, had been assigned the task of isolating the gene responsible for triggering a rare form of cancer that she'd later learned was found only in soldiers returning from the Gulf War. It was hoped that by deciphering its genetic code, the gene could be altered through gene therapy. Jack's work, in the area of neuropharmacology, focused on how toxins alter chemical signals in the brain. The military implications of that were rather obvious, and in military think, as it was called around the halls of the Pentagon, possibilities always existed for new defensive strategies and unique types of weapon systems that involved brain chemistry.

In fact, it was Lantham Pharmaceuticals, Jack's former lab, that initiated research on batrachotoxin, a poison secreted by a brightly colored frog found only in the remote riverbeds of western Colombia. So toxic were the frogs—lethal effects included permanent muscle contraction and heart failure—that workers had been ordered never to touch them unless fully protected. Other Department of Defense–sponsored research at Lantham had involved work on tetrodotoxin, the poison found in puffer fish, which, even in minute quantities, caused complete paralysis and respiratory shutdown.

The unofficial word in the industry was that other such top-secret projects were even now being conducted at other pharmaceutical companies. These included such things as scorpion toxin, black widow toxin, shellfish neurotoxins, and toxins from cobras, pit vipers, adders, mambas, kraits, and water moccasins. Germ warfare weapons of mass destruction had purportedly been produced secretly in Florida and Texas in a joint venture between U.S. intelligence, foreign-owned pharmaceutical companies, and other foreign agencies, some of which were suspected of being involved in international terrorism. In fact, reports had surfaced that a biological weapons facility had been financed and constructed by the builder of an international research facility at Rabta, Libya. It was at the American facility, supposedly, that Prussian Blue, a special warfare grade of hydrogen cyanide, had been tested on military gas-mask filters for "mask penetration" of biologics.

Jack turned sideways and squeezed his large frame through a small opening between two lab benches. "I think Ralphy here's had enough," he said, then lifted the large rodent by the base of its tail out of a plastic test chamber, positioned it on a lab bench, and removed a long wire that extended from a metal probe implanted in Ralphy's skull to a physiograph that monitored brain activity.

"Can we talk now?" Linda asked.

"Sure. Lemme put Ralphy back in his cage." Jack placed the 400-gram white rat carefully back into its home cage, fastened the lid, then trailed Linda back into her office. "So, we're going to New Hampshire," he said, then plunged into the couch next to Linda's desk and began loading his pipe with more cherry blend. "Let's talk."

"Adam was evasive on the phone," Linda said. "I got the impression something up there's not right . . . different from anything we've investigated."

"Meaning?"

"Don't know exactly. He said it was extraordinary, maybe Russian, and left it at that. He already had us booked on the six A.M. flight when he called."

"What do you think's going on?"

"I can't say for sure, but when I heard Adam's voice it brought back such terrible memories."

Jack, seeing the pained look in her eyes, knew exactly what she was thinking and whispered, "Hey, Linda . . . I'm sorry. I'm really sorry about that."

"I'm sorry, too," Linda answered, her voice low and trembling. "It's just that after all these years, so many questions are still unanswered, so many things just don't make sense to me. I was never allowed to tell anyone the whole story, you know. I still don't believe for a minute that Peter's death was an accident. I'm not even sure anymore if that was his body they collected from the crash site, for God's sake. I'm not sure of anything.''

Jack pushed himself to the edge of the chair, stunned by Linda's admission; for he knew that in their business, suspicions like that were best kept to oneself. Especially when they involved secret Pentagon investigations that had been officially closed and classified, and especially since there were always spies among the various agencies who'd make sure that classified information was never discussed in a way that could threaten national security. ''What the hell do you mean by that?'' he asked.

''I don't give a damn anymore, Jack. I think you should know the real story . . . what really happened before you got here.''

''Go on.'' Jack began sucking on his pipe in erratic puffs, sending streams of thick, white smoke into the air like a human chimney.

''After I graduated from Stanford,'' Linda began, ''I was right in the middle of a two-year postdoctoral fellowship at Cal Tech when I met Adam. At the time, he was recruiting for the SELF program. After a few interviews, he hired me. Shortly after I arrived, I met Peter. A year later we were married. Things were great.''

Yeah, great, Linda thought, her mind wandering back almost hypnotically to a time in her life when everything seemed so perfect, thanks to Peter. Before that, though, her life as an Irish kid growing up in a lower-middle-class section of Queens had been anything but. After four years at the Bronx High School of Science, a scholarship to Cornell, graduate school at Stanford, postdoc at Cal Tech, one would have thought Linda Connelly had it all; a high school science whiz who'd won more than her share of academic awards but very few dates, though she desperately wanted them and would have done anything to be popular rather than a nerd who could work math problems better than anyone else.

By the time she'd enrolled in graduate school, the shyness that had kept her from forming any kind of meaningful relationship gave way to a confidence that had finally allowed her room to grow emotionally. A beautiful young woman, Linda found fulfillment in her studies and a newfound happiness in her life.

But as if fate were against her, it ended abruptly during the 1980 fall semester at Stanford when she was called away from one of her classes and told that both her parents had been killed by a drunk driver on the Long Island Expressway. The driver, who ironically had been convicted of D.W.I. twice before, survived with barely a scratch and little remorse for his crime. She grew pathologically intolerant of anyone who drank, and the next several years were as painful and as empty as any she had ever experienced.

Linda thought back now to her college years, to the sociology classes that taught her how one-child families cope just as well as larger families and, in fact, spend quality time together. Having grown up as an only child and envying the kids on her block who'd fight with their siblings but who'd always seemed much happier than she, she knew better. It was all psychobabble, she would think, often wondering how many of those social scientists doing their studies and compiling their statistics were actually qualified to tell *her* how she'd felt as she sat in a lonely room with only her books.

Social scientists. Idiots, she often thought disparagingly. Getting their fat government grants and saying whatever needed to be said in order to get funded the next time around. Idiots. She knew better. And then, just when she believed there would never be an end to the loneliness that seemed to have become a part of her, she was offered a job with the government, was introduced to the most wonderful man she'd ever met, and her whole life had suddenly changed.

"I can't imagine anyone else I would want to spend the rest of my life with," Peter Franklin had told her not long after they'd begun to date and had fallen deeply in love.

It seemed almost perfect from the start; a couple that

everyone agreed had more in common than most and was destined to be together. For Peter, the love he'd discovered had ended a string of disappointing relationships with women who could never offer him the lasting emotional stability he'd been searching for. And for Linda, it was as if her life had begun only after she'd met *him*. Not only did she find a best friend who could make her laugh and cry at the same time, she'd found a soulmate who understood her fears and her dreams and who could take one look into her eyes and, in a way that seemed almost mystical, feel exactly what she was feeling. Three months after Peter had asked Linda to marry him, they were honeymooning in the Grand Caymans, talking about how much they both wanted children, and promising each other that their love would, if it was possible, only grow stonger with time.

Linda remembered every episode in her life with Peter as if they had happened yesterday. Their first night together, their first meal as husband and wife, the long moonlit walks along the beach, their first quarrel, which ended less than an hour later as they rushed into the bedroom to make love, that first trip to the doctor when Linda thought she was finally pregnant, the all-night session crying in each other's arms a month later when they'd found out she had miscarried.

If only it were the miscarriage, Linda now thought as she also recalled the strain she began to feel when Peter would come home from work and seem like a different person; distant at times and unusually evasive. Of course she knew it wasn't the miscarriage at all, but something else.

"What happened next?" Jack, noticing Linda beginning to drift off, prodded her to continue.

"It was June eighth, nineteen eighty-eight," Linda said, feeling a bit uneasy about the suspicions she'd always harbored. "The team's molecular biologist was suddenly hospitalized for something and they needed an expert right away. Peter was recruited to help investigate an unusual crash site a hundred miles or so outside of Tucson. He was ordered to be there the next day . . . to join the rest of the team . . . but he couldn't wait. I remember him telling me that he felt something especially urgent about that crash, something so important that he needed to get there as soon as he could. And that may have been a mistake.''

''You think he saw something he wasn't supposed to?'' Jack asked, puffing more furiously now.

''He must have. Peter always called me after he'd arrived somewhere out of town. That should have been around five or six. He never called that night, or the next day. And then, when I got the call about the accident, I was shocked. They told me it happened at six P.M. the next evening, nearly twenty-four hours after he got there! There's no way he would have waited twenty-four hours to call me. No way.''

''And you think something happened to Peter when he got there, or soon afterward?''

''I knew Peter. He would have called me. Something must have happened to him shortly after he arrived.''

''Why would anyone lie about when Peter died, unless they wanted to cover something up?'' Jack asked.

''Exactly. I believe there *was* a cover-up. And that was only the beginning. When I flew out to Tucson the next day, I expected to get all the details about exactly what happened and when. Especially how. All I got were censored reports and officials telling me they didn't have much information.''

''But it was the day after Peter died,'' Jack said, trying to calm Linda down. ''The investigation was in its preliminary stage. We both know how the government operates. It damn sure doesn't reveal any more than it has to until a complete investigation is done.''

''That's what I thought at first. But as the investigation lingered, I began insisting on answers; and the more I asked the more secretive everyone became. Finally, I was given a one-page summary stating that Peter was killed by a fuel line explosion during a crash site investigation. All information was classified EYES ONLY. That was it.''

''So why suspect a cover-up?''

''When I got to Tucson, I was met at the airport by a government official. He took me to a remote building away from the crash site. I wasn't allowed to go near the site itself."

"Why not?"

"They claimed the whole area was contaminated. I was told they were bulldozing trees, digging up a foot of earth around the entire site, taking everything they could out of the area. Whatever it was that crashed must have been carrying some kind of chemical or biological agent. When I asked about Peter, I was told that his remains had been contaminated and that only authorized personnel could examine them before they were permanently sealed with other contaminated items."

"What type of contamination are we talking about?" Jack asked. "Was anyone specific?"

"Classified. Everything was classified for security reasons."

"So, from what you're telling me it sounds like they had one helluva spill from something that could have been transporting a weapon of some kind. So what. What makes you think something else happened that you don't know about?"

"After I was taken back to my hotel room, I rented a car and went to the hotel Peter had checked into at five P.M. on the eighth. I questioned the hotel clerk. She claimed to have seen him leaving shortly after five-thirty that evening, dragging large equipment bags with him. She also told me that at nine o'clock that night a government official came by, asking for a key to Peter's room. The next morning the maid found his room empty. No bags, no clothes, nothing. Hotel security said it was so clean they couldn't even find a fingerprint. So I know Peter never went back that night."

"Did you ask your government friend about that?" Jack asked.

"I confronted him, but he denied it." Linda's voice now quivered with anger. "He said the government wasn't responsible for Peter's nighttime activities, whatever *that* meant. He then told me that Peter hadn't contacted anyone until eight o'clock the next morning."

"Did anyone at the hotel see Peter that morning? Having

breakfast, reading a newspaper, walking around?''

''No. I asked that, too. No one saw him after he left for the crash site.''

''So, according to the official report, what happened?''

''I was told that after Peter contacted them, they all went out to the site and spent the better part of the day investigating the wreckage. The explosion occurred at six P.M. I remember thinking it odd that if they were *all* investigating, why no one else was hurt or contaminated, just Peter.''

''Very odd,'' Jack replied, placing his pipe on a small table and leaning backward. ''You think the investigation was so sensitive they didn't want Peter to contact anyone, even you?''

''That's possible, I guess. But there's something else . . . something Peter left behind that he wanted only me to see.''

''What?'' Jack snapped forward.

''Several weeks after the crash, I found a note from Peter. It was hidden in one of my desk drawers, telling me that if anything ever happened to him, for whatever reason, to look for an old notebook he had hidden behind a loose piece of insulation near the attic fan.''

''Did Peter ever give you any indication that he was onto anything?'' Jack questioned, more a detective now, trying to pry answers from a reluctant witness. ''Did he act suspicious?''

''Yes, now that I think about it in retrospect. More paranoid than suspicious. Things he'd do or say. Little things, mostly. Being so new to the agency, though, I didn't understand then that involvement in top-secret government business was inherently risky. Now, when I think back to some of the things he'd intimate, I'm sure there were people he'd been involved with who wouldn't think twice about eliminating a threat to national security. I even found a CIA memo once—''

''CIA?'' Jack interrupted, his eyes widening. ''Did the memo contain any specific code words? MKULTRA, MKNAOMI, anything like that?''

''No. When I asked him about it, he became nervous and

agitated, denying he knew anything about it. He just wouldn't discuss it.''

Linda suddenly was trembling visibly, her skin pale. After nearly eight years, it was still so real, so frightening. And now, unable to hide it any longer, she was about to share a message she'd kept to herself until this moment.

''Was the notebook where Peter said it would be?'' Jack asked.

''Tucked behind the insulation and wrapped in plastic as though waiting for me,'' she answered. ''When I opened it, all I saw were pages of scribbling. Notes, formulas, equations. But when I got to the last page, there it was, taped to the back cover. A small piece of folded paper.''

''What'd it say?''

Linda looked down at the floor, hesitant to continue, not because the message was so revealing, but because it was not. ''When I looked at it, I didn't understand what Peter was trying to tell me.''

''What'd it say?'' Jack repeated, inching his way forward until he was in front of Linda's face.

''PTW must be stopped at any cost. A threat to the entire world. I love you with all my heart. Peter.''

Linda paused to wipe a tear from her cheek. ''That was it,'' she whispered. ''I believe he knew his life was in danger when he wrote that. He must have uncovered something he wasn't supposed to and never told me because he didn't want me involved.'' She ripped a tissue from a Kleenex box and dabbed her eyes.

Jack fell back into his chair and shook his head, as bewildered by the message and the three-letter code as Linda had been. ''I don't get it. It sounds pretty goddamn ominous, but I don't understand what the hell Peter was trying to say. You have any ideas?''

Linda shook her head. ''Those letters,'' she whispered. ''PTW. I've racked my brain trying to figure it out and I still don't know what those damned letters mean. Maybe I never will.''

* * *

Jarred from a sound sleep, Linda reached over and slapped the digital alarm clock that was flashing the ungodly hour of 4:00 A.M. Tempted for a second to roll over, she gained enough consciousness to realize that in two hours she'd be on her way to New Hampshire, and the thought of that woke her up faster than cold water being splashed in her face.

She slid her legs over the edge of the bed, barely able to push herself up with her arms. Groggy, she sat motionless for a few seconds, then opened the nightstand drawer next to her. Reaching in, she removed a small gold picture frame and brushed her fingers across Peter's face. The edges of the frame were worn smooth from the thousands of times Linda would stroke it as she'd hold it, trying to keep Peter's memory alive and praying that this was all some tragic hoax and that Peter was still alive somewhere.

What was Peter trying to tell her? Linda thought. What did PTW mean? Why didn't Peter leave more? The thoughts haunted her to the point of obsession.

She'd wrestled with every possibility countless times. And now, as she stared at Peter's face, the litany of thoughts began anew. *Was the letter* P *the first initial of Peter's name? Did the* W *stand for Wesely? Were the letters a code of some kind? Did they represent numbers or variations of numbers?* Nothing made sense. If it *was* a code, it was one she couldn't crack. As always, her inability to decipher Peter's message left her more angry than frustrated. She became furious at Peter, but mostly at herself. She clenched her fist and drove it several times into the side of the bed, as if venting her rage would somehow jar loose from her memory something that would give her the answer she'd so desperately prayed for.

And then, as quickly as her anger had erupted, it faded because she knew she was about to investigate a crash that might finally give her some insight into a three-letter code that till now made no sense. Springing to her feet, Linda rushed for the shower, vowing to find answers, determined not to allow anything to stand in her way.

* * *

She dressed quickly, slipping into khaki pants, field jacket, and Red Wing field boots. Hidden deep in the lining of Linda's jacket was a copy of the note, proof of her suspicions and the sole piece of evidence that Peter's death—if it *was* Peter who died—was more than an accident.

She carried the overstuffed duffel bag she'd packed the night before, and as she had done every other time, she walked down the stairs and stared at her wedding photographs and the English landscapes that she and Peter had collected during the short time they'd been married. The Victorian mantel clock in the next room struck a deeply resonant tone, announcing that it was five o'clock. Jack would be there any second. The drive to the airport would take at least thirty minutes.

Linda pulled the front door closed behind her. And after walking out to the curb, she glanced back at the English Tudor and recalled what it was like when Peter was there with her, thought about the wonderful life they'd shared together, how empty her life had become without him, and how at times it felt as though what little happiness she'd acquired over a lifetime had been drained so completely out of her.

Then, as those thoughts of Peter swirled through her mind, an orange '84 Volkswagen bus pulled up, beeped twice, and saved her from drowning any further. Linda opened the door and slid into the front seat next to Jack.

"Tired?" Jack asked, seeing that she'd closed her eyes the minute she leaned back almost lifelessly against the headrest.

"Yeah, just tired. Let me know when we get to the airport."

chapter three

MARCH 15, 1996: 7:30 A.M., WASHINGTON, D.C.

Dawn always broke grudgingly in Washington at this time of year, giving the city a kind of reprieve from the perpetual gloom that more than ever seemed to match the character of its inhabitants. This morning was no exception. As the sun rose above the marble and stone to the east, filtering its way through the long windows behind the Oval Office desk, it cast an early morning shadow that drifted slowly across the carpeted floor and, like a dark cloud, settled finally onto the presidential insignia.

Were it not that shadows were a natural part of each morning's ritual, it would indeed have seemed like an omen. Perhaps it should have been. For the past five hours, the mood inside the White House was as dark and as solemn as a Lenten funeral mass. The president, disheveled, unshaved, dressed casually this morning in khakis and Washington Redskin's sweatshirt, was staring somberly through one of the windows at a Washington Monument framed by the gold and green satin drapes. Only an hour earlier, he stood locked in that same position, waiting anxiously for a briefing on the crash, eyes drawn to the distant flicker of the Eternal Flame at Arlington National Cemetery.

He was a stately man, erect and perpetually somber, taller than most of his cabinet members, with a broad face that exuded the confidence of a natural leader. His eyes, though brilliant in their fiery intensity, could no longer disguise his belief that this would probably be the last year of his presidency. It didn't matter. He would leave his mark, knowing that the country would be better for it, and satisfied that his final act would carry with it the eternal gratitude of generations to come.

Not since the false ICBM scare on the evening of December 3, 1984, had an incident touched off the frantic scramble that was now occurring throughout the halls of Strategic Air Command and within the Oval Office itself. Senior White House staff had been on maximum alert since 0310 hours the morning of the crash. A communications advisory was already in effect, and the Pentagon itself had issued a Code Red Standby until further notice. Domestic White House activities had been suspended, meetings with foreign diplomats pushed back, and a State Department press conference, scheduled for noon that day, was, to the dismay of the pampered Washington press corps, unexpectedly postponed until further notice.

While the preliminary investigation was ongoing, standard government policy was to assume that the territorial boundaries of the United States had been violated by something other than a U.S. craft. Any incident involving a crash of foreign or military origin demanded—according to official government protocol—a classification of TOP SECRET. What few individuals knew, however, including those inside the privileged confines of Washington, D.C., was that the smoldering craft still lying on the outskirts of Brittan, New Hampshire, was, in fact, America's most closely guarded secret.

The president turned from the window and glanced around the spacious office, at the portrait of Andrew Jackson clinging to the wall directly across from his desk, the rose garden to his right. For him it was an almost sacred feeling being there, behind that ornately carved desk, looking proudly over the nation's capital and actually standing in a room that itself seemed to exude such immense power. He straightened himself, thinking reflectively about the men before him who'd stood in that same position, who'd lived and died knowing secrets that could have changed the world, yet like him were obliged—no, required—to keep them hidden for reasons only a few could ever know or even understand.

He knew the secrets. All of them. They weighed on him

like invisible political shackles, and the more he learned of them the greater a burden he felt. It was an awesome charge, he'd often think, tainted by the bitter realization that like every president who'd stood at a crossroads in history, he, too, would have to spend his term in the shadows of men with power far greater than any he had ever imagined.

A soft knock interrupted the president's fatigue-induced thoughts. The door swung inward. A young female staff member took one step into the Oval Office and stopped abruptly, reluctant to invade an atmosphere tense enough to hit her like a rushing wall.

"Mr. President," she whispered, afraid to disrupt him from his thoughts. "Colonel Rogers is back from New Hampshire. He's here with the initial report."

"Send him in," the president answered.

Colonel Rogers, a tall, rigid figure with thick gray hair and a trace of a narrow mustache along his thin upper lip, walked into the Oval Office and snapped a salute. "Mr. President."

"Vince, sit down, please." The president pointed to a chair next to his desk and asked, "What did you find out?"

"We don't know what happened yet, sir. This is only the preliminary report, but it's as detailed as we can be at this early point in the investigation." Colonel Rogers then placed a green folder in front of the president. "Our team will begin removing the wreckage after the field investigation and begin lab analysis as soon as they can get it to our air base in Maine."

"Were you the first?"

"Yes, sir. We're confident no one saw the wreckage prior to our arrival. We secured the area immediately."

"What about the other investigative team? The NASA people. Will they be able to uncover anything?"

"No, sir. Everything's been done to make certain nothing will be left when they arrive. The bodies—what was left of them—were removed . . . taken to Air Base Delta One. The craft itself was sanitized thoroughly. There's nothing at all anyone could find, except for the wreckage itself."

"You're certain?"

"Yes, sir. Quite certain."

The president leaned back in his brown leather chair, slipped the report out of the folder in front of him, and began to read. He stopped at page three, his eyes focused halfway down the single-spaced sheet, frozen at paragraph three, line two. "What's this?" he asked with a hint of apprehension, his eyes narrowing. "SELF is being called in on this one. Who authorized that?"

"We thought it would be a greater risk not to involve them. They would have found out about the crash eventually and would have certainly questioned why they weren't sent in to investigate. It's standard protocol, as you know. We've altered the craft markings to make it look Russian. It's better to have them go in, collect their data, and write up their report than to not get them involved at all. Too suspicious."

The president nodded and continued on to the end of the document, and when he'd finished went back to page one and began again, studying every sentence, every word. He paused once more on page three, paragraph three. Dr. Linda Franklin. He ran his finger underneath her name. "What do you know about Franklin?"

"Sir?"

"What do you know about Dr. Franklin? Is she still a security risk?"

"We've monitored her activities in the past. According to our security people she's not a threat."

"Will she become one after this?"

"We're continuing surveillance. If anything breaks, we'll know before any damage can spread."

"What about any of the others? Wesely?"

"Wesely's been under surveillance as well. We suspect he might have breached security. Our people had picked up contact with nonauthorized personnel on two separate occasions. No specific evidence, but we're checking it out."

The president tossed the report in front of him and reached for the phone sitting at the corner of his desk. "Shelly, put me through to General McKnight, Pentagon. Code One."

Colonel Rogers watched urgency blanket the president's

face. The crash had already sent shock waves through those in Washington's secret establishment who had any knowledge of it. But what had made the incident even more urgent was the classified nature of what had crashed in Brittan and how close it had come to a populated area.

The dark half-circles beneath the president's eyes were a telling sign of nearly twenty-four hours without sleep. His hands were trembling, his breathing labored, almost painful. He couldn't remember the last time he'd pumped so many stimulants into his system, but he felt the effects right down to the marrow of his bones. As he drummed his finger nervously on the Oval Office desk, phone pressed to his ear, a booming voice came on.

"General McKnight speaking."

"Ben, I'm glad I could get you. We're in a goddamn panic over here, and I need some reassurance, fast."

"Yes, sir, Mr. President. I've been anticipating your call. So far, the situation seems to be under control. Security damage assessment is negative."

"I just read the preliminary report, Ben. Colonel Rogers is here right now. Do you have any further information? Anything new from your people at the Pentagon?"

"NORAD issued a general statement regarding the crash this morning," McKnight said. "Colonel Shaffer is on his way to Washington right now. He'll be meeting with me at the Pentagon as soon as he arrives. I'll keep you briefed. As far as the crash site itself, it's completely sealed off. It'll take at least forty-eight hours for the entire area to be cleared, but every vital piece of evidence has already been dealt with. As far as the investigators are concerned, it's an experimental Russian craft that got too close to an American military base, period."

"Thanks, Ben. I expect the communications blackout to remain in effect indefinitely. Meanwhile, I want the entire incident classified eyes only. The secretary of defense will be issuing a memo to that effect today. Colonel Shaffer doesn't need to know anything other than what's already in your report. You know better than anyone what this could mean for national security.''

''Yes, sir. Understood.''

The president cradled the receiver and turned back to Colonel Rogers. ''How will this affect work on the project?''

''I suspect it's going to have some impact—as it did in eighty-nine—but I don't believe this crash will have any effect on the overall mission at all. We began this program with realistic expectations. We knew the risks . . . the dangers . . . the possibility of failure. In fact, our budget allowed for something like this.''

''Any change in test flight schedule?''

''Right now target date is April sixth. The crew is being prepped and should be ready to go on a moment's notice. The other craft is already on mission standby and should be ready to go as well.''

''How many more do they think we need?''

''The plan right now is one flight a month until December. The next five are critical because they'll be simulating real conditions, penetrating foreign air space, maneuvering around defense shields as much as possible. Those flights should really test the new radar evasion technology.''

Another knock and the door swung open again. ''Mr. President, the secretary of defense and General Bridger are here for the meeting.''

''Thanks, Shelly. Send them in.''

Colonel Rogers saluted smartly and marched quickly out the Oval Office door. Entering: Robert Marshall, the secretary of defense, accompanied by General Donald Bridger, head of the air force office of intelligence.

''Gentlemen, we have a serious problem,'' the president said the minute the men stepped inside. Without the usual pleasantries that surrounded such meetings, the president then motioned the secretary and the general toward two chairs and demanded, ''I want to know who authorized that test flight over a goddamn civilian area.''

''No one authorized it, Mr. President,'' the general responded sharply. ''Instrument malfunction, I'm afraid. From our preliminary findings, based on recordings of data and voice communications, the pilot lost radar control. Shortly following that he lost power. He was at least a hundred miles off his original course.''

''Power? Billions of dollars spent, the most advanced goddamn craft on the planet, and it lost power? It was off course? I think we need some answers right away, don't you?''

''We'll know exactly what went wrong in a few days.''

''Has the memorandum been issued?'' the president asked.

Marshall pulled a folder from his leather briefcase and slipped the memo out. ''We've issued this statement to all agencies involved in the investigation. Hopefully it'll all die down soon.''

The president snatched the memo from the secretary's outstretched fingers and held it inches from his face.

* * * * * * *

Top Secret—Eyes Only

* * * * * * *

Secretary of Defense
Washington

Eyes Only **March 14, 1996**

MEMORANDUM FOR PERSONNEL INVOLVED IN CRASH INVESTIGATION
SUBJECT: BRITTAN, NEW HAMPSHIRE, CRASH

* * * * * * *

The crash that occurred on March 13, 1996, at 0310 hours EST has been classified TOP SECRET. The wreckage will be moved from the site for inspection and analysis to determine the exact cause of malfunction. During the past twenty-four hours, there have been hundreds of reports of sightings in the area by eyewitnesses, and it is certain that widespread attention will be given to this incident by the mass media. Any questions regarding the crash or the craft itself should be answered with the stan-

> dard reply that ***"the object was a military research satellite falling out of its orbit and the information is classified for national security reasons."*** No other information is to be given, and under no circumstances should any written documentation be produced unless authorized. Consider this a communications alert until further notice.

The president stared blankly at the memo, thinking back to his first ninety-six hours in office, the time when a newly elected president is briefed on all classified information and on top-secret projects few individuals ever become privy to. As a young politician, he'd become keenly aware of how somber, almost despondent, presidents became during their first few days in office. He remembered thinking that it had to be due to the enormity of the job, the deep sense of moral responsibility. Sacred trust they'd call it, often with a tone of deep reverence. He'd watch for that look of despondency following the initial euphoria of every election. He'd see it at press conferences, in photo ops, in the off-camera whisperings to cabinet members. It became a game with him; to see how long it would take for a new president to become transformed from an optimistic, promise 'em anything candidate to a sullen, almost paranoid figure who'd learned more than he had ever bargained for.

He, himself, now knew. Presidents, he discovered soon enough, learned things—incredible things—during those first ninety-six hours in office; things that irrevocably changed the way they thought and felt about virtually everything. Never again did they look at their families or at life in the same way; for every minute of every day thereafter was spent with the newly acquired knowledge that the country they'd been destined to lead is divided into the privileged few who know and the vast majority who don't. And that 99 percent of the electorate, till the day they died, would never imagine or even comprehend the secret activities in which their elected government was engaged.

As he continued scrutinizing the memo line by line, the

president recalled vividly the 1947 top secret—eyes only Majestic-12 documents he'd been briefed on during his first twenty-four hours; documents that detailed the sightings and eventual crash of what had supposedly been an alien craft, definitive proof of the existence of UFOs. He pictured in his mind the secret memos to President Harry Truman that followed, which showed progress in the development of new air force reconnaissance craft with UFO-like properties, and other documents reporting the status of disinformation disseminated about and public reaction to the UFO phenomenon. He remembered thinking about the deception; about how the public had never been told that as early as 1947, the United States government had been responsible for every damn one of those UFO sightings and was already far along in its mission to develop extraordinary weapons that were intended to keep America the dominant military air power well into the twenty-first century.

He looked away from the memo and again at the office and he knew. The UFO secret, passed on from president to president like an Olympic flame, now was his to keep, and the time for deployment was near at hand. He thought of himself as the final bearer of that flame, the last runner in a long race whose duty it was to climb the steps and ignite the torch of what had been planned secretly as the final battle against an enemy far more subtle and dangerous than anyone could have ever imagined.

He wished it weren't so; hoped that it would have come on someone else's watch, during someone else's term, and that the world were not so unstable on his. But like it or not, he knew that international events were spinning irrevocably out of control; that America was on the brink of ruin, and that *he* was the president destined to implement a series of government missions that collectively had been code-named *WORLD ORDER.*

"Mr. President. The Pentagon is on Code Red Standby until further notice," the general reported. "As soon as the crash site is cleared, the order will be downgraded."

"Very well. Keep me briefed on anything that comes up.

And let me know as soon as you get word on exactly what happened up there."

"Yes, sir. If there's nothing else, I have a flight out of Washington within the hour."

"Nothing else. Good luck." The president saluted and waited for General Bridger to walk out of the Oval Office before turning and venting an unexpected barrage at the secretary of defense.

"Have you seen the goddamn reports this morning?" The president waved his hand in the air as if lecturing to a child who balked at comprehending the meaning of an important lesson. "The world is disintegrating before our eyes. Europe is scared shit that fighting's going to erupt again and spill across its borders. The Middle East is a powder keg. Africa hasn't seen this much civil disorder since the end of World War II. The North Koreans may be sitting on top of a shit pile of nuclear weapons they'd use in a minute if they had to. Reports are coming in that China is gearing up its military and may even threaten to go to war over Taiwan. And now, just when we need to be moving as quickly as possible to prevent an imminent global explosion, this."

"I've been getting regular briefings from our CIA analysts," Marshall responded, trying to defuse the president's obvious rage over the whole incident. "They tell us that the situations in those hot spots are just that. Hot. They're not at the point of spilling over yet. So until we're ready, we still have time to maintain at least some stability through direct negotiations, dialogue, and, if necessary, sanctions, embargoes, or UN intervention. We may not have to implement that phase of WORLD ORDER if other avenues are opened."

That bit of consolation seemed, at least for the moment, to calm down the president. But not much and not for long, because the thought of having to be the one to first implement WORLD ORDER, especially since he was rapidly losing faith in CIA analysts, had lately made him sick to his stomach. After all, he now thought, the damn fools didn't anticipate the precipitous collapse of communism, nor did they predict the sudden invasion of Kuwait by Iraq, and they certainly didn't foresee the mess that had occurred in the former Yugoslavia or Chechnya and in parts of Africa where hundreds of thousands of innocent civilians had already been slaughtered and more carnage was inevitable. Not a good track record, as far as he was concerned.

"You think those idiots at the CIA are getting it right this time?" the president asked sarcastically. "Can we depend on this information?"

"I believe so. The UN is on the verge of settlements in many of the hot spots. Our information indicates we've got time. Not much time, but enough."

The president walked over to a set of French doors that led to the rose garden and gazed out, his back turned to the secretary. He stood silently for a moment, contemplating a host of global situations that to him seemed to defy solution and a world that he sensed was poised on the verge of self-destruction. He spoke softly.

"See that rose garden out there, Bob?" He waved his finger across an immaculately landscaped lawn. "How perfectly manicured those bushes are? The grass?"

"Yes." Marshall looked quizzically at the president.

"You have any idea what it takes to keep it looking that way?"

"I can imagine. Why?" *He's going mad.*

"Ever hear of entropy, my friend?"

"Entropy? Yes. What does that have to do with—"

"Second law of thermodynamics," the president interrupted, still looking directly ahead and recalling the physics lesson he sat through in college and never thought he'd ever be able to relate to anything of any consequence. "Simple, really. Everything out there, everything in nature tends to become disordered unless a great deal of energy is put into the system to maintain order."

"I don't understand."

"It's a basic law of nature, Bob. Order is unnatural. Nothing in life remains orderly. Not grass, not hedges, not bushes. Leave that garden out there alone and in a month it'll look like an overgrown, weed-infested plot. It takes work to prevent entropy . . . disorder.''

''I still don't understand.'' *He's really going mad.*

''What makes us think human beings are any goddamn different?'' the president posed. ''Are we not a part of it all? Of nature? Isn't man a naturally aggressive, disorderly creature who needs laws and religion to keep him from destroying himself?''

''Yes, but—''

''That's one of the theories of social theology, you know, that human beings may have been created in the image of God, but without God they are basically no different than any other animal on the face of the earth. What in the hell makes us think we can keep this planet—half of which is populated by damn heathens—ordered without having to expend every ounce of energy we have to keep it that way? Hell, it's hard enough keeping that rose garden from breaking rank and going to shit. Can you imagine trying it around the world, with a thousand different cultures and ethnic groups, many of them spending most of their waking hours thinking of ways to kill each other off? We should be worrying about order in *this* country, worrying about what's happening to *us,* rather than worrying about every goddamn nation that decides to kill off its own people.''

''Superpowers, I'm afraid, have no choice,'' Marshall shot back. ''Call it destiny if you want. Or call it a duty that the rest of the world's grown to expect because everyone—regardless of whether they're enemies or not—has a stake in a world that's ordered. Certainly our allies have come to expect just that from the only superpower left.''

''Allies,'' the president mouthed with enough cynicism and condescension that the secretary could predict what was about to come next. ''Look at history, dammit. Learn from it. Today's allies are tomorrow's enemies. And tomorrow's enemies are typically more vicious and less willing to remember yesterday's friendships. Never count on allies to remain allies so long as human nature is what it is.''

Turning from the French doors, the president walked back

to his desk and picked up the file. He thumbed through it again, and in a fit of anger threw it back on his desk. "Sometimes I think we've become social Darwinists for the world, trying to change cultures a millennium older than our own, assuming that once they start thinking the way we do, everyone will forever live in peace and harmony. Well, dammit, democracy without morality doesn't exist, as far as I know. The very foundation of our system is based on morality . . . on religious values. Try shoving democracy down the throats of some of these goddamn atheists and it doesn't work. Doesn't work a damn. You know as well as I do that despite our well-intentioned meddling, nearly every third-world nation we've tried to help is, in some way, worse off now than at the beginning of this century. You call that progress? Are we just fooling ourselves? Has it come to this? Have we become *that* arrogant, or are we just so stupid that at the expense of our own nation we've taken it upon ourselves to become the world's police force?"

"That's exactly what we are," Marshall said in all seriousness. "If not us, who? Russia? Japan? UN Boy Scout troops who can't even protect women and children from a bunch of thugs with assault rifles? There *is* no one else. We're it. And everyone knows it. Most of those little shit countries out there are damned glad of it."

The president, his outbursts more a result of fatigue and sleep deprivation than anything else, resumed a more civil demeanor. "Okay, we've had a setback, but we're still on track. Colonel Rogers tells me they've got another test flight scheduled as early as April sixth. If the next nine go off without a hitch, we should be ready to go if we need to."

"I think two crashes out of forty-three test flights over the last seven years is a pretty damned good success rate," Marshall said optimistically.

"One crash was too many," the president shot back. "If the radar evading technology had failed, or worse, if the thing had crashed in a populated area, it would have been devastating. The repercussions would have been incalculable. We can't afford to be optimistic. No more malfunctions. Zero tolerance. This project is too important for anything or anyone to jeopardize it."

"There's one other concern." The secretary's tone turned even more ominous now. "I'm not sure if it's anything to worry about at this point."

"Oh? And what's that?"

"Earlier this morning, air force intelligence confirmed a message intercept coming out of the Pentagon. Sounded like a code. They couldn't trace it. Said it must have been transmitted from a nondesignated location, probably someone tapping into a telephone line with a portable unit of some kind."

"What was the message?"

"It was strange. And it lasted only about fifteen seconds. Something about timber wolf being readied. A meeting to follow. That was it."

The president stiffened as though the message had sent a chill right through him, then asked, "Have they been able to decipher it?"

Marshall shook his head. "None of our Pentagon people have ever heard of it."

"Does army intelligence have any clue? Any idea?"

"One guess is that it may have been a leak. A leftover mole—maybe KGB—who was planted in the Pentagon and just got careless."

"They place any significance on the message?" the president asked nervously.

"I don't think so. It was too obscure. Not enough information in that fifteen-second transmission to really mean anything."

"And their analysis?"

"Possibly a test of some kind . . . to see if we'd pick up the signal. They've done that before. Sent an off-the-wall message that didn't mean anything just to see how successful they'd be at getting a signal out. When I worked in intelligence, they did it from time to time just to bug the hell out of us; to let us know they were there, watching us, even inside the Pentagon."

"Make sure intelligence follows up. And I'd like you to check it out with the Pentagon."

"I'll call General Fisher this morning. He should have more information for me by now. It doesn't sound like something we need to be concerned about, though."

"I just wanna be sure there's not a connection between that message and the crash. Leave no stone unturned, clear?"

Marshall nodded, then asked, "Have you spoken with NSA yet?"

"I have a meeting with Tucker later," the president answered.

"Tucker? Jesus Christ, you think we need to be worried about biologics here?"

"I'm afraid we might."

The president thought back again to those first few days in office and recalled the biological warfare debriefing he'd received on day four. What he'd learned during those hectic first hours was that the biological weapons program, established in 1943 at Fort Detrick, had advanced under the Johnson and Nixon administrations to include top-secret viral research under the auspices of the National Cancer Institute, cross-species gene manipulation for production of synthetic immune-destroying biowarfare agents, and authorization to conduct experiments on civilian populations to test the efficacy of newly developed viral and biological agents. MKULTRA, a top secret CIA project designed to test mind control drugs and behavior modification agents on civilian populations was followed by MKNAOMI, a joint CIA-Army project to develop, test, and maintain biological agents and delivery systems for use against human beings.

Some of this information was not so surprising, given the fact that he had seen declassified reports linking part of the Defense Department's budget with various biological warfare projects, even after the ratification of the Geneva Protocol. What troubled the president now was his fear that unspeakable new classes of agents, which had been developed in the name of national security, might not be so easily contained and could threaten the United States as easily as they could its enemies.

"What is it?" Marshall asked, seeing a look of fear gelling on the president's face. "Do you know? Tell me."

"That's the problem, Bob. I don't know. Isn't it a goddamn irony? I'm the goddamn president of the United States and I don't know. But whatever it is they've created over in Fort Detrick or some of those other labs is gonna come back to haunt us. I'm afraid it may have already."

"Meaning?"

"Have you seen some of those captured Iraqi log books?"

"Yes," Marshall answered. "It was our own bioagents they were using against us. So what are you saying? That we knew we'd get hit with our own stuff before we invaded? That all this chemical weapons bullshit coming out of the Pentagon is a smoke screen to hide the real truth?"

The president just shook his head and added, "That's not the half of it, Bob. If what I've seen is true, we've done more to destabilize the world already than anyone had ever imagined. I pray to God I'm wrong."

And after seeing the secretary of defense out the door, the president walked back to his desk. He grabbed hold of the U.S. flag next to the window and squeezed it tightly, once again staring solemnly at the Washington Monument in the distance and remembering clearly what he had witnessed firsthand in virtually every city he'd campaigned in only four years earlier. The collapse of America, as he had envisioned it back then but would not admit to openly, was no longer some vague projection that paper-shuffling bureaucrats explained with the aid of their statistical charts. It was here. Ongoing. Gathering speed. On a collision course that literally threatened to extinguish the long-running engine of the world's greatest economic superpower.

The president's face appeared old, prematurely wrinkled, the bags beneath his weary eyes puffy and sagging from the weight of sleepless nights. His hair had whitened noticeably since the election. He'd aged ten years in the last six months, and where there was once a look of sadness in his keen eyes, there was now a look of total despair.

As he sat at the threshold of the twenty-first century, he realized better than anyone that no one individual, including the president himself, could direct policy—any policy—without consensus. He also realized that so much as attempting to do so would make him little more than a passing footnote in American history. So much for independent decision-making, he now thought as he reflected on his every move being carefully choreographed, his every speech crafted and shaped to reflect an agenda that, like it or not, had to be followed to the letter, his every policy decision made for him by a cadre of kingmakers who'd selected him, brought him up through the political ranks, then placed him in a seat of power that was nothing more than a pitiful charade. Who would have ever believed a democracy such as this, he thought, shaking his head.

He waved the flag aside in disgust, angry at himself for being a party to it, then fell lifelessly into his chair and closed his eyes. There was a decision to make; a decision that would at long last free the office of the presidency from the bonds of political corruption, but a decision that might just cost him his life.

Why the hell did it finally have to happen on his watch, he kept thinking. Why not before this? Why now? Why ever? All he'd ever wanted was to be president; get his name in the history books. He'd spent a career planning for it, worked his ass off, paid a high personal and political price to get it, and now that he had it, no longer wanted it.

But it was too late. He knew the time had come. He realized in his heart that regardless of the consequences, it had to come to this; that there was no other way; that he had no choice but to go forward and pray that what he was about to do would make the world a better place. And though he tried to rationalize the success this mission would ultimately bring, he wanted desperately to find another means to justify an end he would have given anything to change, if only there were another way.

There wasn't. He knew that. He had to proceed, be presidential until the very end.

But now, as if things weren't bad enough, there was something else.

"Timber wolf," he whispered, his jaw tightening as the words passed from his lips.

chapter four

MARCH 15, 1996: 8:13 A.M.

Two hours into a flight so turbulent it made everyone sick to their stomachs, the privately chartered jet broke finally through an endless cloud cover and, with a rumble that shattered the early morning stillness of Manchester, New Hampshire, touched down on the far runway of International Airport. Taxiing past a row of deserted terminal gates, it headed directly for a secured area at the north end of the airport before easing to a stop several hundred yards from the nearest public gate. As it did, two marine guards snapped to attention on each side of a small door that led to a corridor below the auxiliary terminal. Eight others immediately began spreading out evenly along the tarmac between the building and the jet itself.

Within seconds, portable metal stairs rolled into position. The door of the Boeing swung open, and Linda's investigative team emerged one by one, descending into a swirling cold morning mist that covered the tarmac in a thin, silvery blanket. Like a load of precious cargo, the group was surrounded at once by security guards who ushered them hurriedly toward the door of the airline building.

"A bit of a shock, this weather." Dr. Jeffrey Allen's nasal British accent penetrated the heavy air like a foghorn, his oversized Adam's apple rising and falling beneath the skin of his long, skinny neck. Tall and gaunt, his head at least a foot above the others, Dr. Allen shuffled behind the group with long strides, squinting like a nearsighted stork at the airport terminal barely visible through the mist. A structural engineer with a background in metallurgy, Dr. Allen possessed an expertise in experimental structural design and metallurgical composition that would enable him to determine the types of composite materials that may have been used on or in the craft.

"Sure hope it doesn't look anything like this at the crash site," added Dr. Mary Abrams, an environmental toxicologist and newest member of the investigative team. Petite, boyish looking, with short cropped hair and leathery skin that hadn't felt makeup in years, the elflike Dr. Abrams had been brought on board after a previously unknown toxin was found inside the wreckage of a North Korean aircraft that had crashed over Guam two years ago. One gram of the toxin was found potent enough to kill half the population of Wichita, Kansas. Pentagon intelligence, suspecting for the past decade that new types of deadly chemical weapons were being developed by several rogue nations, including North Korea, requested a leading expert in toxicology be made a permanent member of the team. Dr. Abrams's prior assignment: chief toxicologist with the army's Third Terrorism Investigation Unit, a top-secret group operating out of Los Alamos.

The elite four-member team, bundled heavily against the unusually bitter cold, looked more like a chorus line of hunched penguins waddling across a black ice float. Quickening their pace against a wind that slapped against them with near gale force ferocity, they marched in lock step across the slippery tarmac. The second they rushed through the small door of the auxiliary building, Linda heard the familiar croak.

"Linda . . . over here!"

Adam Wesely stood alongside a separate underground corridor some twenty feet away, waving the battered tweed hat that was his trademark. His thinning salt-and-pepper hair, caught by a sudden gust of frigid wind, drifted about his head like fine strands of gray silk. At fifty, Adam was still rather handsome, distinguished. Dark brown eyes, softened by the permanently tanned skin around them, gave Adam the West Coast–like appearance of a man who looked like he'd be more comfortable on a movie set than in a government office.

"Linda, good to see you." Adam shuffled toward her. The noticeable limp that was exacerbated by the wet cold, was a painfully acute reminder that his last days in Vietnam would be with him for the rest of his life.

"Morning, Adam," Linda replied, still groggy and trying to adjust to the shock of going from intermittent drowsiness and sleep in the stuffy airplane cabin to the chilled, mist-filled air of Brittan, New Hampshire. "Been waiting long?"

"Got here about thirty minutes ago. Took us nearly an hour to drive through this goddamm fog." He slapped his hat against the side of his leg, as if that would somehow ease the stabbing pain, then raised it toward the giant of a man next to him.

An air force colonel in full dress uniform standing alongside Adam Wesely watched each member of the team like a predator stalking its prey. He stood at least six-foot-six with steel blue eyes that seemed to float effortlessly within their sockets, shifting from Linda to Jack, over to the other two members, back again to Linda. He stood as erect as a tree, nearly as thick, his hands clasped firmly behind his back and his feet together as if at attention.

Without blinking, the stonelike figure followed the team as they approached, then fixed his sickening gaze squarely upon Linda. As he did, she sensed a gnawing uneasiness; something in those menacing eyes and hard face that made her tremble; a familiar look that suggested they'd met before and shared some terrible secret.

"Linda, this is Colonel Thomas Williams." Adam introduced the two, oblivious to the silent exchange that had just occurred.

Colonel Williams continued his intense gaze into Linda's eyes, and Linda gazed back, searching her memory, trying to remember where she'd seen that cold, penetrating stare before, feeling suddenly as if she were being violated, as if those two horrible orbs were now a thousand, a million, devouring her body like invisible fingers that tore viciously into exposed flesh.

Williams reached out and, without moving a muscle on his face, took Linda's damp palm gently into his. She felt large ropelike veins wiggle against her fingertips, then disappear into wrinkled, leathery flesh.

"I've heard good things about you, Dr. Franklin," he said with the deeply monotone Southern cadence so characteristic of career military officers. "And I'm certainly looking forward to working with you." He barely smiled. His uneven nostrils flared, revealing coarse, tangled hair that nearly sealed the entrance to his crooked nose. Small pock marks dug deeply into his face, straddling the two gaping fissures that cut downward from his cheeks to beneath his chin.

"I'm glad," she answered. She never could figure why so many military men were Southern. She could only guess that it had to do with economics or the fact that patriotic fervor ran especially high south of the Mason-Dixon line. To her, Colonel Williams seemed the classic Southern gentlemen: polite and fastidious on the outside, shallow and phony beneath. "And I'm pleased to meet you," Linda added, nearly gagging on the lie and spinning around to introduce the other members of the team before a wave of revulsion overwhelmed her. Before she could finish, though, Adam Wesely, in his usual brusque and insensitive manner, interrupted.

"I've arranged to have your bags sent to the inn and the equipment transported up to the site. Meanwhile, we can get started. I'll give you a brief rundown as we drive."

Wesely led the investigative team to the customary black van parked in a specially reserved area in back of the terminal. Colonel Williams had remained behind, positioning himself just inches from a window where he could overlook the parking lot and watch the team as they sped off.

"Why isn't Colonel Williams coming with us?" Linda

asked, dangerously close to telling Adam exactly how she felt about the man.

"He has his own transportation. But he wanted to make sure he met the investigative team personally when it arrived. He was especially curious about what *you've* been doing lately."

"Oh? And why's that?"

"You probably don't remember, but he was one of the investigating officers at that accident near Tucson eight years ago. Only then he was a major and you wouldn't have had much contact with him."

The Tucson accident! Linda's memory was jarred instantly, the words flashing before her like neon lights suddenly turned on inside a darkened room. *That's where I'd seen him. In Tucson. My God! Thomas Williams . . . TW . . . the last two letters of PTW! Is it possible? Could he be part of the message?*

Her heart was skipping beats. Instinctively she slipped her hand into her coat pocket, feeling for the flimsy piece of paper that lay hidden just out of reach. She rubbed her fingers softly against the fabric. Frantic thoughts rushed through her head. If Colonel Williams was part of the cover-up, she was thinking, and those *were* his initials in Peter's message, then she may have finally gotten hold of something. She'd cracked two of the code letters. Maybe. It was more than she'd ever had before.

As she settled into the van, Linda's mind was awash in a turbulent sea of emotions. Every possible scenario was suddenly played out, every motive considered, every reason someone could possibly have had to eliminate Peter, analyzed. And in the center of it all stood Colonel Thomas Williams, a man Linda knew nothing about, but a man who'd been there and who happened to have the initials TW. A coincidence, maybe, but a coincidence much too real to ignore.

"The site's about a half hour from here," Adam said. "There's a clearing a few miles outside Brittan in an isolated forest area. That's where it happened. We'll be staying at a secured bed and breakfast on the outskirts of town and spending most of the day at the site itself.''

The four team members situated themselves in the van and waited anxiously for Adam to brief them on the crash. In unison, they rubbed their hands and blew warm, moisture-laden air onto fingers chilled from a mist that nearly froze on contact. Linda sat in the front seat next to Adam, waiting for the van to pull out, then broke the tense silence.

''Adam, why don't you give us a rundown on the crash.''

Adam paused for a few seconds, seemingly uncomfortable—uncharacteristically so—as he collected his thoughts. ''Yesterday, shortly after three A.M., we received a report from the Jackson Astronomical Observatory near Manchester. One of their astronomers, who happened to be mapping a section of the Northern Hemisphere at the time, witnessed an unknown object streak across the sky and crash in an area near Brittan. He assumed it was a large piece of space debris because it was moving so rapidly and glowing like a meteor. When we got the coordinates and went out to the area, we found it. Markings look Russian, though I wouldn't swear to it because of the extensive damage. Damnedest thing I'd ever seen, though.''

''Any survivors?'' Linda asked.

''There was nothing. Just the craft itself. I'm hoping you and your team will come up with some answers. If there *was* something there, I want to be the first to know.''

''You mean to tell me there was nothing on or in that craft to indicate it was manned? That's hard to believe, Adam. No physical evidence at all?''

''Afraid not.''

''Could you at least tell if it was one of ours disguised to look Russian?'' Jack asked.

''If it is, it's one I've never seen before.''

''That's it?'' Linda asked skeptically. ''Anything else?''

''That's it. We can discuss this further when we get to the inn. The direction you go with this is up to you and your team. I expect you to find everything you can. Absolutely everything. And if and when you do, I want you to report directly to me, no one else. Understood?''

Linda detected an evasive nervousness in Adam she'd not seen before; and she suspected at once that he knew more than he was letting on. ''Understood,'' she said, cautious not to draw undue attention to her suspicions, but sensing in Adam's voice the telltale signs of a cover-up.

Framed gracefully by wide, hundred-year-old oaks, the stately green-and-white two-story colonial was lined along its front and sides with meticulously trimmed hedges that made the fresh coat of paint glow white through the dense fog. Encircling the inn like a foreboding wall of deep green was coniferous forest. The cold mist refused to let up and instead seemed to thicken into a white soup, drifting into Linda's nostrils like heavy smoke and searing her lungs as she inhaled the moist droplets of slime with increasingly heavy, erratic breaths.

It was precisely 8:47 A.M. when the van arrived. After disembarking, the four team members were escorted past several well-armed security guards and up the wooden porch steps of the Brittan Inn Bed and Breakfast, which two days earlier had been commandeered as mission control for as long as the investigation and cleanup detail would take.

Everything about this trip so far had reminded Linda of Peter. Everything she'd seen since stepping foot off the jet had dredged up feelings and memories she'd long forgotten. The sights and sounds of the airport, the aroma of hazelnut coffee, the scent of freshly baked cinnamon rolls blending delicately with the tangy wet smell of newly cut hedge and the pungent odor of musk lingering in the heavy air of surrounding forest, all jolted from Linda's memory vivid images as if it were yesterday, as if she were there with Peter on one of their many trips to New England, laughing with him, kissing him as they walked through the woods, caressing him adoringly in a way he'd always found irresistible. It all made her wonder if she were capable of doing this, whether the feelings she still had for Peter would affect her judgment and compromise her ability to be objective. She climbed the wooden steps almost reluctantly, took one look at Adam, and clenched her teeth in anger at the thought of it all being taken away from her.

A half hour after Wesely and the team members checked into their rooms, they regrouped in the Colony House lounge for final instructions. Linda and her team arranged themselves in a circle around a large antique table located in the corner of the room. The only illumination came from dim overhead lights that hung from a wagon-wheel chandelier and two glass-enclosed candles in the middle of the table. No one else had been allowed into the lounge. A marine guard approached with a tray of coffee, but Adam waved his arm and ordered no interruptions. The door was then closed and locked, and Adam began.

"At this point, I can't tell you much about the craft itself, other than it's unusual to say the least. Like I said, no one's ever seen anything quite like it. Nothing that could tell us where it came from was found on or in the craft, except for some identifying markings that seem to be Russian. No evidence of anything living or dead was found anywhere. It's a damn mystery, but we suspect it may be a Soviet prototype of some kind."

"If it's not, do you suspect an unmanned probe, maybe?" Linda asked. "Or one of the new hydrogen-fueled scramjets we've been hearing about?"

"Doubt it," Adam said. "As you know, that research began in the sixties. It's all been put on the back burner since the Pentagon opted for liquid fuel instead of hydrogen."

"What about the X-30 space plane project?" Linda asked. "Didn't the air force secretly fund that program in the eighties?"

"I'd seen a recent government report about the X-30 several months ago," Dr. Allen interrupted, his British accent more noticeable in the emptiness of the large room. "Could go from a dead standstill to Mach three in seconds because of some secret propulsion system. Problem with the space plane—theoretically—has always been with the heat generated by hypersonic velocities . . . up to Mach ten, from what I hear. At that speed, any metal or alloy we know of reaches temperatures higher than five thousand degrees Fahrenheit. Last I heard, they were trying to develop a new type of material for the heat shield. Some kind of carbon composite that I doubt has been developed at this point.''

''If funding even continues,'' Adam said. ''The Pentagon denies the X-30 has been constructed. It's supposed to get off the drawing board this year. First test flight is planned for ninety-eight, so the crashed vehicle can't be the space plane.''

''That's the official word out of Washington,'' Jack snapped back. ''We all know about unofficial test flights of prototypes that were supposedly still on the drawing board. And everyone around this table worth their ass has seen reports of top-secret black box programs funded by the Defense Department. Forty-six billion over the last five years by the air force alone, for Christ's sake. The TR-SA, the SR-seventy-one Blackbird, the Aurora, the TR-one. All of them supposedly nonexistent until one day, there they are. You can't tell me there's not some other secret craft out there we don't know anything about yet.''

Everyone around the table was well aware of what were referred to as black programs; programs that were secretly funded but that few individuals, including most government officials, knew anything about. They also knew of the existence of groups within the Pentagon and the intelligence community so clandestine that their covert operations were unknown even within the highest circles of government, including the White House itself. Some of these groups, it was suspected, made use of private facilities and were cofunded by organizations outside the government in order to keep the flow of money and the nature of the operations hidden from prying eyes. The rationale was that by keeping the president and most members of Congress out of the loop, these groups would be free to conduct operations that might otherwise never have been allowed to exist in the first place or, at the very least, so constrained by government interference or public outcry that their success would be compromised.

President Truman, ostensibly, had been the first to warn America of covert government agencies that he felt would eventually operate outside the laws of the United States Constitution. That warning had later been echoed by President Eisenhower when he warned U.S. citizens of what he called the growing military-industrial complex. In fact, it was long believed that the power of certain groups, especially within the intelligence community and the Pentagon, had grown to such enormous proportions that they were no longer held to the same standards of law and justice as everyone else. They simply operated as independent entities. Nations within a nation, so to speak, employing whatever means were necessary to accomplish their objectives.

"What about the Pegasus?" Linda asked. "No one knows if it actually exists, but reports claim it has a propulsion system that'll make it cruise at Mach six."

"That's right," added Jack. "As recently as six months ago, eyewitnesses in Nevada reported seeing a high-flying craft accelerating at incredible speeds, turning on a dime, moving from one end of the horizon to the other in less than ten seconds. Almost every eyewitness claimed to have heard a pulsating noise as the thing passed overhead."

"The pulsating could be accounted for by a new propulsion system," Dr. Allen said.

"Yeah, it also makes the eyewitnesses pretty damn credible," said Jack. "The probability of a hundred different people, all reporting the same exact type of pulsating noise during those sightings is too high."

"UFOs," Adam said, shaking his head. "If only they knew. The Black Wing—if it's ever declassified—is probably going to be what breaks the UFO phenomenon wide open."

"How much do you know about it?" Linda asked.

"Not much. Air force has it classified top-secret umbra."

Not even the SELF team had access to umbra, the highest classification status a project could receive, and meant that access could only be secured with the approval of the White House itself.

"It's without question the most top-secret project going right now," Adam continued. "Four hundred feet wide with white lights arranged randomly underneath to mimic stars. Perfectly camouflaged against the night sky. Supposedly made with such lightweight material it can hover slowly enough to elude Doppler, then turn on its edge and fly in a vertical position. Propulsion is generated by a new synthetic fuel developed to burn slowly yet derive maximum energy for long-range flights. The composite materials were produced using particle beam technology. Yeah, if there's a UFO out there I guarantee you that's probably it."

"Any chance that one of these top-secret craft is what crashed?" Linda asked.

"No."

Adam was quick to respond, Linda thought. Almost too quick; as though he'd anticipated the question and was ready for it.

"The size and complexity of the design argue against it," he said. "I've seen mockups of all the craft we're talking about and what's out there is different. I *do* think it was manned, though. What happened to the bodies is anyone's guess. What we need to do now is make damn sure nothing is overlooked. Nothing. If there was something or someone on that craft, I want to know, even if you have to spend the whole day picking through every goddamn blade of grass in the area."

The urgency in Adam's voice suggested that, unlike any of their previous assignments, there was something exceedingly different about this particular crash.

"Who's there now?" Jack asked, lighting his pipe and sending a cloud of smoke across the room.

"My team's there as we speak," Adam replied.

"How soon did you get there?" Dr. Allen questioned. "Surely you weren't the first to arrive at the site."

"I'm assuming we got there before anyone else. The crash occurred at three A.M. We arrived promptly at noon."

"Nine hours, man," Jack snapped, ripping the pipe from his teeth and pointing it directly at Adam's face. "You know damn well that nine hours is long enough for someone else to have gotten there first, wouldn't you say?"

"After my team members looked at the wreckage and the site itself, they were convinced that no one had arrived before we did. Anything's possible, I guess. But there was no evidence to the contrary."

"What about Colonel Williams?" Linda asked, noticing that Adam was wringing his hands as he spoke. "Did he arrive here with you?"

"Yes. We flew in together. Of course his people had to clear the area before anyone else arrived . . . set up checkpoints . . . secure the crash site."

"When was *that* done?" Jack asked, irritated still at Adam's previous answer.

"Almost immediately following the crash. Standard procedure, you know."

"Standard procedure, my damn ass," Jack spat. "That means the colonel's people had to have been there long before you arrived. You can't tell me you're certain they didn't get to the wreckage and remove evidence, can you?"

"No, I can't. I can only tell you that nothing seemed suspicious when I got to the site."

"Well it sure as hell seems suspicious to me. A major piece of wreckage and nine hours later, no bodies. I think someone has some explaining to do."

"Listen, Jack, our orders are to get in, do our job, and get out," Adam said. "The rest is up to them. There *is* no explaining to do. That's all I know and that's all I can say. Now, we really need to get going. We're expected shortly."

With that abrupt end to the meeting, Linda's team got up from the table, proceeded quickly out to the loaded van, and silently began to question Adam's explanations and whether this find would really be different from any of the others. Linda, in particular, wondered if this investigation would finally yield the answers she'd been looking for and whether

her meeting at the airport with Colonel Williams was an omen of things to come.

But before Linda could step into the waiting van, Wesely took her by the crook of her arm and led her aside. Away from the group, his tone became less strident, more cautious. A renewed warmth flowed across his eyes, though fear was evident beneath them. And for a brief moment, Linda saw the face of a worried parent, of the father she'd lost on the Long Island Expressway.

"Be careful with this one," Adam pleaded. "Don't talk to anyone about what you might find, not even to your team, and especially not to Colonel Williams, until you clear it with me first."

"I don't understand. You were lying in there, weren't you?"

"Colonel Williams reports directly to General Benjamin McKnight, Pentagon, who happens to be involved in various top-secret weapons programs."

"You mean this could—"

"Don't ever," Adam cut in without answering her question, "not even for a moment, let on that you know anything about this investigation, other than what you've been told. Promise me." He squeezed her arm and she could feel his fingers trembling through her coat.

"Why? What the hell's going on here, Adam?"

"Please, Linda. Not anyone. You know damn well the government's not some monolith. It happens to be an incredibly complex entity with agencies so secret they answer to no one. Jesus, I don't even know half of it, and I'm supposed to be on the inside. Trust me on this one. Those things I said back there about not knowing . . . about not being sure what was out there, were for the benefit of your team. They can't suspect anything. What I said to you on the phone yesterday was solely for the benefit of whoever was tapped into our conversation. I couldn't say much at that point. We're being watched very closely . . . even now, as we speak."

"Jesus Christ, Adam, what *do* you know? Tell me, please."

"Not now. Believe me, you'll know soon enough. Trust me, Linda . . . Trust me."

And with those ominous words, he released her arm, slipped quietly into the van, and turned the key.

chapter five

Be careful with this one, Linda. Believe me, you'll know soon enough. Trust me. . . . Trust me. . . . Trust me.

The words, like a desperate plea from a desperately terrified man, rattled viciously in Linda's head as she tried hard to convince herself. Trust me. . . . Trust me. . . . A shiver washed over her while she debated with herself whether to take Adam's ominous warning as strictly government issued or as a plea from one friend to another. She prayed for the latter.

Then, just as she finally began settling into her ride to the crash site, Linda's head snapped forward as the van came out of a hairpin turn and screeched to an abrupt stop in front of Checkpoint Bravo One. Three marine guards dressed in full camouflage fatigues, stood legs astride, like rigid statues in the middle of the dirt road, assault rifles draped at their sides. One of them, an enormous sergeant who seemed as wide as the surrounding trees, marched directly in front of the van, hand raised. He approached the driver's side, bent forward, and glared stonelike through the window, examining the security pass Adam was holding up just inches from his face. Satisfied that everything was in order, he snapped off a brisk salute and waved the van through.

Adam proceeded cautiously, weaving his way through a road that narrowed almost immediately and seemed barely wide enough to accommodate a vehicle, much less the military personnel that lined both sides. Linda looked on, bewildered. Though accustomed to the kind of security typical of crash site investigations, she'd not seen anything the likes of this.

"Damn, this place is like a war zone," Linda whispered almost reverently as she watched the troop movements. "What the hell's going on here?"

"I told you, the government is hot on this one," Adam said. "They've put a lid on it tighter than a missile silo, and they want it to stay that way. You better believe it'd be like a war zone."

And as he said that, the government van that till now had been bouncing erratically along the tree-lined road, emerged from the dense forest into a massive clearing. Surrounding the circular meadow was a mix of new- and old-growth forest, gnarled fir trees a hundred or more feet tall, interspersed with younger, smaller trees that cropped up at various levels within the dense stands and collectively gave the serrated canopy a wild, unrestrained appearance that added gloom to the already dark atmosphere. The nearly perfect half circle of deep green was flat and stretched for what seemed like a mile from one edge of the black forest to the other. In the middle of the stark landscape, still smoldering like the charred remnants of an extinguished forest fire, lay a craft the likes of which no one on the investigative team had ever witnessed before.

"Jesus Christ," Jack said. "Look at the damned thing."

Larger than any of the team had anticipated, it was nearly the size of a 747. Adam was right, Linda thought. It was like nothing any of them had ever seen, she was sure of that. And yet to Linda, who suddenly felt as though she were finally looking at something that may have a connection with Peter, the craft seemed eerily familiar. *Was this how it all began, my love? Did you see what I'm seeing right now? Discover something you weren't supposed to? If you did, I'll discover it, too, I promise.*

The team members jumped from the van one by one, transfixed by the sight of the hulking mass. At least on past investigations they could identify the wreckage and determine right off that it was a prototype of one kind or another. But this. This was different, a new type of craft that resembled nothing they had ever seen.

"There it is," Adam said. "Let's get everything we need from the equipment van and head out."

Nearly a quarter mile from where they now stood, the craft lay broken like some giant statue, its bottom half buried in the hardened soil, its side split open like an empty can from the sudden impact of the crash. Through the breaking mist, Linda could barely make out the members of Adam's preliminary recovery team already out there, taking measurements and photographs at every possible angle, looking more like human ants next to some enormous celestial monument.

"The size of this thing is unreal," Linda said, her eyes glued to something even *she* had not expected. "Can you believe it?"

"I can believe anything," Jack replied. "I don't like the smell of this one."

"Let's go," Adam ordered.

Linda threw her field pack over her shoulder and took the first tentative steps toward what to her seemed almost alive. The immense pieces of wreckage seemed even larger as she approached. She stopped occasionally and stared in awe, studying the thing from front to back, then top to bottom. Along the entire body of the craft were broad, seamless sheets of twisted metal, some the size of a large room, still smoking from the intense heat of ignited fuel or sudden reentry. A deafening silence, as if all remnants of life had been extinguished from even the surrounding vegetation, hovered above the entire field. The dark evergreens encircling the meadow stood noticeably still. An occasional burst of frigid wind came up, whistled soulfully through their branches, then disappeared, leaving the meadow in eerie silence again. The damp meadow grass reeked of unidentifiable chemicals, musty oil, and what smelled like charred flesh. Linda tried in vain to breathe through her mouth, but the overpowering rancid odor found its way into her nose, forcing her to stop briefly. She bent over and stared at the ground, feeling like she was about to vomit. Then, composing herself, she walked briskly over a thick layer of slime that moved like quicksand beneath her boots. Fetid pools of groundwater, too numerous to avoid, produced ghostlike shrouds of mist that spiraled up and under her down jacket and sent sharp chills through her bones.

Twenty yards from the wreckage, Linda's trained eye told her that everything about the craft—the texture, the appearance, the shape—indicated something human made. Yet the manner in which the entire structure was constructed—it had the uniform appearance of liquefied silver alloy that had been molded into a continuous sheet of incredibly lightweight metal—pointed to a technology years ahead of anything she'd ever seen. And as she walked directly toward it, her mind turned dizzy with questions as she stared incredulously at the strange craft that was now only inches from her face. She closed her eyes and smelled it; touched its warm, almost silklike skin; examined the intricate way in which the entire craft had been pieced together. She couldn't imagine how rumors of anything like this, even if it *were* part of a top-secret project, could have been kept so secret from a crack investigative agency with access to nearly every government aircraft project in existence.

"So, what do you make of it?"

Linda spun toward the raspy voice coming from out of the mist. "Adam, you startled me." She thought carefully before answering, not yet sure whether his earlier offer to trust him was indeed genuine. "I really don't know what to make of it," she said, shaking her head and visually studying every inch of the craft. "The markings *look* Russian, but there's too much burn damage for me to be absolutely certain. Dr. Allen should be able to tell us. If I find anything at all, Adam, you'll be the first to know. It doesn't look like one of ours, that's for sure. And it doesn't look like any prototype—foreign or domestic—I've seen in any of our technical reports. I just don't know." Not particularly adept at tiptoeing around controversy, she then asked, "What did you mean back at the inn? Is this the same type of craft Peter supposedly investigated? I want to know, Adam." She stared into his eyes with a look that nearly melted the fog between them.

Adam glanced nervously in both directions, then took hold of Linda's arm. "I can't say, Linda. I asked you to trust me, not only for my sake but for yours. You can't imagine the danger you'd be in if any of our conversation got out or if anyone even suspected you had information you shouldn't. I want you to continue your investigation as if you'd never talked to me, as if you'd been called in to investigate just another crash . . . and when I'm ready, which will be very soon, I promise you, you'll know everything."

Adam then turned, and as mysteriously as he'd appeared, disappeared through the curtain of mist, leaving Linda shaking her head and knowing full well that the man knew everything; probably knew everything from the very beginning.

By now, the rest of Linda's team had arrived with field packs overflowing with scientific measuring and collecting equipment, anxious to begin scouring the site for anything that would reveal the origins of the strange vehicle towering above them. The team spread out individually to different areas around the site. Linda, apprehensive still about both Adam and Colonel Williams, turned away and resumed scanning the craft. She took a deep breath and stepped toward it.

Much of the craft had already cooled considerably in the near freezing temperatures, but as she held out her hand, Linda could still feel a comforting warmth radiating from its metallic skin. Like a living body, she thought. Still breathing. Still alive. Still able to communicate, if only she knew how. She reached over and touched the silver gray of what appeared to be a smooth triangular-shaped wing, fused perfectly into the broken fuselage as if one with it. Her first impression was that the craft looked like an enormous guitar pick with three blunt corners. Near the back, detached from the rest of the craft, lay an immense, funnel-shaped mass that resembled a jet engine or a thruster with large stabilizing fins surrounded by an unusually thick shield, as if to protect something inside. A power source, maybe.

Linda peered into the thruster and saw mangled fuel lines, broken into a thousand pieces and melted into twisted, intestine-like shapes of every size imaginable. Turning to the area where the cockpit had been, Linda spotted remnants of seats—not so extraordinarily different that they could not have been found in any modern aircraft—but different still. If there was someone or something on that craft before it had crashed, she knew the cockpit would most likely hold the answer.

Climbing through a small opening, then around the charred metal, Linda reached the twisted innards of the craft, incredulous that anything would have survived a crash of this magnitude and not left some kind of physical clue for her to find: a piece of burnt flesh, a bone fragment, part of a uniform or flight suit. And the more she observed the chaos of the wreckage, the more she noticed that despite the obvious appearance of broken lines, shattered equipment, and tangled metal, there was an all-too-neat look about it. Too clean, she thought. Too sterile. Some areas looked to her as though they'd been wiped down, inside pieces of the craft that should have been among the wreckage, nowhere in sight. She noted unusual scrapings everywhere, as though someone had either tried desperately to get out or, more likely, had tried desperately to remove any last remnants of evidence before the teams had arrived. Swinging her field pack off her shoulder, she bent down and began the tedious chore of sifting through what seemed like a countless number of aircraft fragments.

Two hours later, Linda was no further along than she'd been when she started. "Son of a bitch," she whispered, stunned and angered at the thought of yet another cover-up. "Son of a bitch, Adam. What the hell do you know?"

And then, in a fit of rage, Linda reached back and with all the strength she could muster, kicked some of the debris aside. She fell backward against a broken metal column, exhausted, wondering if this investigation was nothing more than another one of the government's clever charades. She stared across the chaos, convinced now that she'd been duped for some purpose she knew nothing about, perhaps to satisfy a government directive that an investigation be done but that no evidence be found. Case closed. Another Pentagon operation classified and sealed until the middle of next century. She felt deceived, lied to, manipulated like an insignificant pawn in some giant game of chess, until . . .

Contrasted against what had been an unexposed and, thus uncharred, fragment of metal she had just kicked, Linda noticed a reddish brown spot. A blood sample! she thought. And if so, she knew that within it was the entire genetic blueprint that could tell her not only what type of organism it had belonged to but, with new, state-of-the-art techniques, could even tell her who it may have come from. Her heart began to race. Maybe it was something big, maybe not, but at least it was something.

Linda rushed over to it and threw herself down, and with a penknife that was shaking so hard between her fingers she could barely hold on to it, she carefully scraped the sample into a small glass vial, tucking it safely away in her field jacket and deciding at that moment not to share this find with Adam—at least not until she had a chance to analyze it, and certainly not until he came clean with her about whatever it was he knew.

For the next several hours, Linda searched frantically for another clue, but there was nothing else to find. Whoever had scoured the area before them did one helluva job, she thought, and the blood sample, if that's indeed what it was, was all that Linda was going to get.

"Linda," a voice cried out. Jack, who had immersed himself for the last several hours in his own field investigation, had a puzzled expression on his face as he approached. "Linda, I have a strange feeling about all this."

"What do you mean?"

"Someone's already been over this thing, I know it. Things are too neat. There's nothing here."

"I found something, Jack. When I—" Linda stopped suddenly, tilting her head upward, and made a 360-degree turn as she sniffed the foul air. "You notice anything missing," she asked as she grabbed his arm.

"Missing?" Jack looked at her as if she were losing her mind, then began looking around at the wreckage.

"No," Linda said. "Not the craft. Take a deep whiff. What do you smell?"

Jack flared his nostrils and sucked the putrid air into his lungs. "Burnt metal, pine, mildew, cow shit. That's about it."

"You sure? C'mon, anything else?"

Jack took in another lung full of air while casting a sideways glance at Linda and said, "No."

"I thought so. You don't have the typical smell of jet fuel, do you?"

Jack flared his nostrils again, this time with renewed vigor. His eyes widened, his face contorting as he searched in vain for traces of fuel in the air. "Damn, you're right. The ground should have been full of the stuff."

"Jack, this bird was flying on something other than standard fuel. And that means we can eliminate any aircraft we know anything about."

Linda removed the glass vial from her field pack and held it up between her thumb and index finger. "I think I may have found the only piece of evidence that'll tell us anything."

"What is it?"

"Looks like it might be some blood. I noticed it between some metal I kicked. I don't want Adam or the colonel to know anything about it, okay?"

Jack nodded and said, "You're as suspicious as I am."

"Did *you* find anything?" Linda asked.

"Nothing out of the ordinary. Looks like an army came by and sanitized this place. I figured they would. I took a few samples of dirt and other debris from the periphery of the wreckage and some samples from inside those containers over there." He pointed his chin toward two metal canisters hanging limply from the fuselage. "They were still sealed shut, so whatever was inside should give me a pretty good idea of where this thing may have come from."

"Jack, I'm scared. Adam knows something, but won't tell me."

"He what?"

"He knows something, Jack. He knows. And he promised to tell me everything as soon as he could."

"Did he tell you anything about this craft being similar to the one—"

"That crashed in Tucson?" Linda finished. "He didn't say. But from the way he's been acting, I'd say so. You can't say anything to anyone."

"You don't have to ask me twice. If there's anyone out there who trusts idiot government officials less than I do, I'd like to find him."

"It might get dangerous," Linda cautioned. "If the government is behind this, and knows we've identified any evidence at all . . ." Linda paused, thinking the worst. "You don't have to get involved, you know."

"Hey, since when do I keep my big nose out of anything," Jack said, looking at Linda not merely as a colleague who'd worked more closely with her than anyone else at the division, but as someone who'd been there for her during the worst times of her life, and now as her best friend. "I'm with you on this all the way."

"Thanks, Jack." Linda reached into her pocket and took out a piece of paper that wilted between her fingers like toilet tissue. She offered it to Jack.

He unfolded it and read the faint inscription. "I don't know what to say. It's just like you described."

"Do you believe me now?"

"I believed you when you first told me," answered Jack. "Seems almost too unbelievable to be real." He looked up and scanned the length of the wreckage one last time. "Place gives me the creeps. But I don't think what you're looking for is out here." Jack handed the note back to Linda and grasped her closed hand tightly. "C'mon, let's get outta here.

We've got work to do and a report to write up."

"You're right. I'll feel better once we're back in Washington."

Linda knew that nine hours was more than enough time for an expert team to have cleaned the wreckage before anyone else had arrived. If nothing else, at least she had the only sample she figured was going to be worth anything. She turned and walked from the wreckage, her hand stuck deep in her pocket, the vial, isolated from the rest of her samples, nestled tightly between her trembling fingers. And once again her thoughts turned back to Peter.

Why? Why you, Peter? Was it just a freak accident or did you really know too much? My God, Peter, what the hell did you know?

chapter six

MARCH 16, 1996: 5:17 A.M.

With the blood draining quickly from his usually tanned face, Adam Wesely's complexion turned the sickly pallor of dry bone. He'd not slept since arriving back in Washington last evening. In one hand, a telephone receiver sat pressed to his ear. In the other, a loaded .38 caliber revolver clung tenaciously to his trembling fingers. On his desk, a file marked TOP SECRET—EYES ONLY included a wallet-size photograph of a beautiful young woman, appearing to be in her late twenties and standing sullenly in front of a squalid village, her arms crossed tightly against her chest as if holding inside of her the pain of war and death.

The office lights were off except for a small green desk lamp that illuminated the exquisite face in the photograph. Adam had made it a habit to look at that picture each day, to hold it and remind himself of why it was that his life had taken such a turn and become the tangled web of fraud and deceit it was. He found himself loving and hating it at the same time, cursing the haunting image that held him so spellbound in its grip.

He stroked the smooth pearl handle deliberately back and forth with his thumb, and as if transcending a world he no longer knew or wanted to be a part of, thought back to the day when it had all begun. August 11, 1974, a time when America, still preoccupied with anything North Vietnamese, was still reeling from its embarrassing withdrawal from the quagmires of Southeast Asia. As a communications officer with a top-secret clearance and a specialty in cryptology, Adam had been offered an administrative post with a special Pentagon agency he knew little about. Told only that he was being groomed for an important career in national service, he'd suspected from the outset that that was not it at all, and that instead he'd been selected for future involvement in secret military programs of vital national interest.

He'd learned, shortly thereafter, of Pentagon links to secret black projects, witnessed firsthand intelligence reports on everything from government-sponsored terrorism and sanctioned assassinations to secret germ warfare testing conducted on American civilians and, most disturbing to him, purported sightings of POWs left behind and still living in the jungles of Vietnam and Laos. And as his position with the Pentagon grew in stature, he was eventually briefed about the government's plan to develop an advanced military weapon that promised to keep America the dominant military power well into the twenty-first century.

Three years later, his future in government service virtually guaranteed, he'd been assigned to head up the SELF project, an intentional move designed to ensure that one of the agency's own would be placed in a position of prominence and would oversee special investigations of suspected Pentagon project incidents. In the clandestine world of government operations, there was a method to the madness surrounding promotions and tenure, and it had less to do with seniority, psychological profiles, or qualifications than with the particular needs of an agency that recruited individuals it knew it could control through what was laughingly referred to as its own system of incentives. Adam Wesely, to his misfortune, met that criteria.

Because of his position and maximum security clearance, Adam had become one of only a handful of individuals within the government to know the entire truth about the Pentagon's black programs. He'd made himself indispensable, a vital part of an elite inner circle and a critical player in what was then an obscure future mission designated WORLD ORDER. The price for his loyalty and silence was an incredibly well-paid lifetime appointment, regardless of which party held the White House or controlled the halls of Congress. In his world, at least, those institutions, though ostensibly held to the highest standards by a fretful but naive public that demanded government accountability, were irrelevant. The cost of coming forward with information, as everyone in the program knew, was swift and public assassination as a warning to anyone else who may have been stupid enough to have the same idea. There were no exceptions.

He'd thought about suicide at least a hundred times before. And now, after witnessing the endless conspiracies, the assassinations that seemed to have grown almost commonplace, the subsequent cover-ups that guaranteed lifetimes of immunity for people he'd considered the scum of the earth, the treasonous activities, deceptions, and lies that grew like cancers and threatened to destroy the lives of those who'd perpetrated them, he'd finally had enough. After living more than twenty years of his life cloaked in the dirty shadows of what had become a government he no longer recognized, he was on the verge of breaking down and confessing it all. And then, after he'd lifted the burden that was slowly killing him, he'd return to his office and quickly, with bitter remorse for what he'd done to his country, place the revolver to his head and end it all. Besides, he had nothing to lose, since the recently diagnosed brain tumor he'd kept hidden from everyone he knew had added a resolve to his otherwise cowardly heart.

"Hello, Jim?" Adam spoke softly on the telephone to his newspaper source, a well respected newspaper columnist at the *Washington Chronicle*.

"Adam?" the groggy voice on the other end asked. "It's five in the morning. What the hell's going on?"

"I'd like to meet you in Virginia . . . at Tony's Restaurant in about an hour. I'm at my downtown Washington office, so it'll take me a while to get there. I have something for you that's gonna knock your socks off."

The initial silence was interrupted by a prolonged sigh. Jim had suspected for some time that Adam was involved with secret Pentagon operations, but he didn't know exactly how or to what extent. For the past two years, he'd been investigating sporadic evidence that Gulf War soldiers were knowingly exposed to biological agents in Iraq and were now passing the artificially produced organisms on to the rest of the population. He never thought it was his place to question Adam about it and, knowing Adam like he did, was certain that he'd never have been told anything anyway.

"Are we finally going public on what's going on?" Jim asked. "Whatever the hell that is." Jim knew at once that whatever *it* was had to be big if Adam was involved and was now going public.

"Yeah . . . it's finally time this was leaked. The sooner the better . . . for the good of the country."

"Sounds serious. Nasty government business?"

"Nastier than you could ever imagine."

"Go on."

"I have knowledge of a group powerful enough to be directing U.S. government policy from where they're sitting right now. They have links with people in the Pentagon and the finances to literally do what they want. Not a good combination. I'm one of the few people outside this place who even knows of their existence. Don't ask me how. I got word today that they're meeting soon, maybe as early as tomorrow. I don't know what's going on yet, but I have a bad feeling something's coming down, something I've been trying to uncover for a while. May even involve Iraqgate."

"Iraqgate? Jesus Christ, you have some concrete evidence? Classified material I can use? You know as well as I do what they'll do to me if the information is not irrefutable."

"Right in front of me. Names, addresses, documents, dates, you name it. Like I said, it'll knock your socks off."

"I thought the Gulf War material was buried under the War Powers Act."

"It was. Apparently these people were able to get to the administration before anything was made public. I intercepted some of it, and I can tell you that some ugly stuff was allowed to go on in the name of financial interests."

"How ugly?"

"Ugly enough to kill for. I'm sitting on a time bomb, Jim. Still interested?"

"I'll let you know in an hour . . . when I see what I'm getting myself into."

"Okay, it's a little after five o'clock now. I'll be there around six."

Adam hung up and placed the revolver into his top drawer. Then, swinging his chair around to face a large window overlooking the picturesque Washington Mall, his eyes swept across the massive government buildings that looked more like temples to bureaucratic gods, and the rows of cherry trees that lined the marble and stone patchwork of what he knew had become a society within a society.

Swiveling back to his desk, he picked up the sealed file, slid it abruptly into the back pocket of his briefcase, and without as much as a last glance, marched soldierlike out of his plush office. Most of the staff had not yet arrived for the day, and thus he felt safe in the deserted solitude of the building. He walked down a long, dimly lit hallway to a small private elevator, stepped in, and punched the large button marked B.

The doors slid closed, revealing a distorted, silvery reflection that was suddenly transformed from that of a distinguished government official of fifty into a young army captain startled by enemy fire. The image seemed so real, so recent, that it made him flinch. His eyes widened in terror as he reached back into his memory and continued to stare blankly into the elevator door.

"Get down! Get down! Enemy fire! Enemy fire!"

Shells rocked the surrounding trees like lightning, setting the landscape on fire and turning what had been a peaceful tropical jungle only moments earlier into a deadly furnace. Men scattered like fleeing roaches as the barrage continued unabated. The acrid stench of thick smoke filled the air, literally turning day into night and nearly asphyxiating the confused soldiers, many of whom no longer had the mental consciousness to even know in which direction to run.

"Back this way! Let's move! Let's move! Charlie's on the left!"

Two young soldiers seemed to appear from nowhere out of the smoke, dropped facedown and lay motionless in a bloody rice paddy like dull green balloons. Adam saw himself running frantically toward them, falling into the stagnant mire and picking himself back up as mortars exploded around him. There was another thud, followed by a splash. Blood and pieces of warm flesh hit his eyes and lips as he turned to see shrapnel find its mark, this time tearing violently through another soldier's arms and face, leaving him floating on his back, lifeless. Beyond him a torso with no head or arms bobbed up and down like an abandoned buoy. Hands and feet and what looked like genitals were scattered everywhere. The brackish, knee-deep swamp was turned quickly into a killing field as red as a Vietnamese sunrise. Boys, some as young as seventeen, were dropping around him, screaming, on fire, dismembered, their intestines exploding from out of their uniforms, their limbs torn apart like cheap paper dolls, dying with the most vile, monstrous expressions etched on their teenage faces as if they knew at that final moment that they were falling hopelessly into their watery graves and that for them life was just about to end thirteen thousand miles from home.

Adam flinched again, grabbing his leg this time as if reliving the shrapnel that tore through it, but continued to stare intensely into the mirrored elevator door, remembering the vividly grotesque images of young soldiers dying around him. Why? he asked himself, shaking his head and cynically thinking what a tragically stupid waste of human life it all had been.

The elevator settled smoothly as it reached its destination, then jarred to a stop. The fallen soldiers faded into the silver gray of the elevator doors, and Adam's eyes, as they always did when he thought of that day in the Mekong Delta, filled with tears. As desperately as he tried to forget those gruesome scenes of the most violent death he'd ever experienced, he knew they would forever be etched in the deepest recesses of his memory.

As the elevator bumped to a stop, Adam snapped out of his reverie. The doors opened and he was immediately greeted by a familiar face.

''What are you—''

Before he could finish his sentence, Adam's head was thrown back violently, blood and yellowish pieces of bone splattered against the back of the elevator wall, the front of his skull suddenly covered with dark blood that spurted from a jagged hole the size of a fist. Moist sections of Adam's brain lay scattered on the elevator floor, shredded by the explosive-tipped bullet that ripped through the back of his head like a miniature grenade. The crimson river of arterial blood grew larger and larger around Adam's partially severed head before thickening into a round pool of coagulated ooze.

A large, military-clad figure pried the blood-stained briefcase from Adam's stiff fingers, walked calmly away, and stepped into a waiting green sedan that now headed for Tony's Restaurant.

Jim Frazier had been pacing nervously in front of Tony's for twenty minutes, awaiting what he suspected would earn him the Pulitzer Prize in journalism he'd worked half his professional career for.

"Mr. Frazier?" a voice called out.

Jim was approached by a large, heavyset man dressed in an air force uniform. A leather briefcase was tucked under his right arm.

"Yes," Jim responded.

"I'm Adam Wesely's special assistant." The large man spoke softly, his voice cold and detached, not at all what Jim would have expected from one of Adam's people. "Mr. Wesely had an emergency meeting. He asked me to give you this briefcase and said that you would find everything you need inside. He'll call you at your home in two hours with the combination, at which time you'll be able to study the contents. Those were his only instructions." He then held out the briefcase carefully and, the minute Jim took it out of his hand, turned on his heels and walked off.

There was an abruptness to the meeting that bothered Jim. But what the hell, he figured. Those Washington military types get off on being abrupt anyway. He clutched the briefcase with both hands, watching as the hulk climbed back into his dark green sedan and drove off. Then, looking down at the briefcase, he noticed his hands shaking as if what he was holding was nothing less than the journalistic coup d'état of the century. He tried to undo the latch but it was locked, just as he'd been told it would be.

"This is fantastic," he whispered, almost laughing as he formed the words. "Finally. A Pulitzer Prize, right here in my hand."

Jim Frazier walked hurriedly across the street and disappeared around the corner to where his car was parked. He slid onto the front seat, placed the briefcase next to him, and started the engine. He looked at the briefcase again and placed his hand against it, rubbing it gently like some treasure that by this time tomorrow would make him rich and famous beyond his wildest dreams. And then, as the car inched forward and pulled away from the parking space, an explosive fireball ripped the still air, sending shock waves through nearby storefronts. Emberlike pieces of glowing metal tore through the flames like missiles, incinerating everything within thirty feet. By the time a few stunned witnesses ran to the fiery scene, the Volvo station wagon was little more than a burning shell, Jim Frazier's dismembered body just pieces of charred skeleton, the incendiary briefcase a disintegrated pile of black powdered ash.

The dark green sedan drove slowly amid the commotion, then sped past oncoming traffic toward Washington, D.C.

chapter seven

It mattered little to the stone-faced sentry that on this particular day he was seeing Linda's face for the three hundred sixteenth time since being assigned this choice tour of duty. The security ritual had to be followed precisely and to the letter: a careful examination of both the driver and the inside of the car, a computer scan of the security badge, a final suspicious look from behind the dark mirrored sunglasses that were part of the uniform, rain or shine.

A rigid snap salute was followed by the hand signal that indicated it was now safe to proceed. Steel gates swung inward, allowing Linda to ease forward and stop again thirty feet ahead in what was officially referred to as the security zone. Reinforced tunnel doors then parted, revealing an illuminated two-lane passageway that spiraled hellishly downward at a thirty-degree angle.

Linda followed the steep, cavelike enclosure for nearly a hundred yards to what looked more like a concrete-and-steel bunker than the underground parking area of the government's top-secret lab complex. She pulled into her reserved space, got out, and rushed past several rows of vehicles before stopping to face one of three sets of stainless steel double doors. She inserted her hand into a narrow metal slot to the right and waited for further instructions.

"Fingerprint and palm analysis confirmed. You may remove your hand and step in."

Linda extracted her hand. With barely a swish, the stainless steel doors slid open, revealing a cylindrical chamber the size of a large closet. The second Linda stepped in, the doors slid closed behind her at the same time an electronic voice instructed her to say her name and special security number into the speaker on the left. She did so without thought.

"Voice analysis and security code confirmed."

At that, the inner door slid open, exposing the massive corridor that led to the countless laboratories within the lab complex. Linda stepped out, oblivious to the white blur of lab coats drifting past her in both directions, then turned immediately right and headed for her lab.

Dr. Franklin's research facility, located in the far west wing of the complex, had been abuzz with excitement. The team members had already arrived for what was to be a strategy session that would determine the direction of their investigation. The scientific field equipment and samples, secured on-site and flown into Washington the night before, were to have been delivered to the Division of Biotic Investigation sometime that morning. As yet, nothing had arrived.

"Is everyone here?" Linda asked, storming into her lab as if all hell had suddenly broken loose, then stood waiting beside the rest of her team, arms draped tightly across her chest. Directly behind her marched Colonel Thomas Williams, who'd been at the lab complex receiving station for nearly an hour, waiting for her arrival. He positioned himself off to the side, his hands locked behind the small of his back.

"As soon as I'd arrived," Linda announced, "I received word from the colonel here that all official records of the crash have been classified TOP-SECRET UMBRA. None of our field notes are being returned. All our samples have been confiscated, sealed, and classified for security reasons. And we're not to discuss the crash or the wreckage itself with anyone outside this room. Apparently the Pentagon has made the decision that the investigation is over. Something about an international incident between the United States and Russia.'' She glared at Colonel Williams with venom in her eyes. As far as she was concerned, the Russian part was bullshit.

''How can they justify doing that!'' Jack shouted, flailing his arms. ''How can they goddamn do that? What the hell are we here for, if not to get to the bottom of this? Is this not a crash site investigation, for Christ's sake?'' He turned and stared directly at Williams with a steel gaze that could have stopped a charging bull dead in its tracks. ''Do they even *want* us to get to the bottom of this? Is that it? Is this something we're supposed to pretend never happened? A fuckin' UFO crashes and disappears without a trace? Is that what it's supposed to be?''

Colonel Williams stared Jack down with a look of condescension typically used to put anyone lower than lieutenant colonel in his place. ''Look, mister,'' he groaned in his Georgian accent, ''I know this isn't the direction you expected the investigation to take, but from what I understand this thing's even got the White House on maximum alert. Pentagon's issued a Code Red for Christ's sake. Now, as long as you're part of this investigative unit, part of this government organization, you'll do as you're ordered. And that order is . . . the investigation is over.''

''Code Red?'' Linda's face blanched. ''God, I remember the last time that happened.''

''Eighty-four,'' said Williams, his eyes cast upward in near reverence. ''Computer malfunction at Cheyenne Mountain. Longest three minutes of my life. We all thought the Soviets had launched ICBMs. Damn near pushed the button ourselves until the backup system kicked in and caught it.'' He recounted that as if relishing the idea of almost being a key player in an all-out nuclear war.

''What in the hell does that have to do with any of this?'' Jack demanded, his round cheeks twitching with angry disbelief at the sight of this pompous colonel pining pathetically for the long-lost days of the cold war.

''Only that this is something the government wants classified,'' the colonel answered sharply, his eyes snapping back to the group. ''And, therefore, you're not to investigate it any further. This is between the State Department and the Russian military. Case closed. Have I managed to make myself understood?''

''So I suppose that's the end of it,'' said Jack, giving Williams a final, sarcastic look directly into the pupils of his serpentine eyes. ''Understood.'' *Asshole. Russian aircraft, my ass. Thinks we're fuckin' idiots.*

Linda watched with diminished emotion as the colonel made an about-face and walked quickly out of the lab. His presence at the crash site, coupled with Adam's ominous warning to her yesterday, made her suspect all along that something like this was bound to happen. Things were beginning to fall into place. And though she feared the worst, thinking that maybe the lid was being shut as tightly on this as it had been with the Tucson crash, all she could think about was Adam's promise to tell her everything.

Jack, meanwhile, stormed out of the lab, muttering obscenities and smashing his fist into the wall so hard it made Linda jump. Temper tantrums were not exactly rare events when it came to Jack. This one was no worse than last week's or the one the week before. A minute later he stormed back, a bit less animated, and noticed the blank expression on Linda's face. ''Linda, we need to talk . . . alone.''

''Meet me in my office in ten minutes,'' Linda said. ''Where the hell's Adam, by the way?'' she added, figuring that of all people, he should have been a part of this.

''No one's seen him. His office light wasn't on this morning and his door was still locked. Security said they checked him in at eleven o'clock last night, which meant he came here shortly after flying in from New Hampshire. He checked out a little after midnight and told security he was going to his private office to take care of some unfinished business. He never checked in this morning. He'll show up, and when he does, we can both give him hell.''

One side of the leather sofa across from Linda's desk was piled haphazardly with reference books and scientific papers to be read that week. She pushed them aside like trash and sank into the soft leather. Totally exhausted, her head spinning, she couldn't get Colonel Williams's ugly face out of her mind. She remembered the sternness of Adam's warning: *"Be careful with this one, Linda."* Images of the craft, the twisted metal, the bloodstain all haunted her. And now the whole scenario had been made doubly suspicious with the sudden confiscation of everything that had been brought back from New Hampshire.

"Linda?" Jack knocked lightly on her partially opened office door and stuck his head inside. "You okay?"

"Come on in." Her voice was barely audible. Her arm, draped across her face, hung limp.

Jack sat down in the overstuffed chair next to her, leaning close enough that she could smell the tobacco on his breath when she turned to face him. "You wanna tell me what the hell just happened? What the hell's going on? What you know?"

"I'm not sure anymore, Jack. It's not like Adam to do this . . . to not be here. Maybe he'll have some answers for me when he shows up. In the meantime, we've got to continue the investigation."

"You sure you want to? You heard what colonel pineapple face just said. It's officially over."

"Wrong, Jack. It's not over. I still have the blood sample and I'm starting from that. No one has to know, not even Adam." Linda turned away and stared at the ceiling, unable to muster the enthusiasm to lift herself up.

Jack leaned even closer and whispered, "I kept some of those small sample vials myself, you know; just for the hell of it. I'm glad I did, though I'm not sure it's gonna lead to anything."

Linda bolted upright, and Jack saw fire in her eyes. There was anger, but more than that, determination. "Let's find out what that damned thing was," she said, then walked to her desk and picked up what she hoped would be the springboard into their investigation.

"You don't have much there," Jack said, looking at the small vial she was holding between her thumb and index finger. "Be extra careful with the initial DNA sequence analysis."

"Don't worry," she said. "I have enough to do a karyotype, and all I need for PCR and DNA fingerprint analysis is fifty nanograms. That should at least tell us something about our missing pilot." She knew that with PCR, polymerase chain reaction, even the smallest sample could be multiplied a million or more times to yield enough DNA for a positive identification.

Jack's initial anger at a possible government cover-up turned quickly into enthusiasm. "I'll get started on my samples right away. If those sealed containers were hiding anything, I'll find it, guaranteed."

He disappeared into the clutter of his lab while Linda entered hers, fastening the door securely behind her in case Adam decided to make an inauspicious return in the middle of her investigation. Armed with no more than a hundred milligrams of what she assumed was dried blood, and a room full of scientific instruments that could dissect entire strands of DNA and analyze the molecular composition of genes, Linda was ready to step into what she thought certain was a secret world of government intrigue and possibly murder.

Her large, well-lit lab was as sterile-looking as a hospital operating room, a total contrast to Jack's: everything in its place. Light blue metal cabinets were packed neatly with glassware, each type arranged from largest to smallest. State-of-the-art scientific instruments lined the tops of shiny black lab benches, their computerized digital control panels flashing orange numbers and programming instructions. Every square inch of available space not occupied by computers and lab gear was brimming with high-tech equipment.

In the past half decade, work at the lab complex had progressed to the point where mankind was virtually standing at the threshold of discoveries that would radically change the world. In fact, it was coming dangerously close to uncovering the elusive set of multiple genetic factors that many had suspected was responsible for the extension of life itself. Anyone stepping into Linda's lab would have been transported into another world, a world where science fiction had finally, for better or worse, been transformed into stark reality. It was in this world that Dr. Linda Franklin would analyze the molecules that make up the genes that together form all the material needed to create a living human being. And there, dried and fragmented, sitting at the bottom of that glass vial she held so tightly between her fingers, insignificant to anyone but her, was the stuff of life, the entire set of precious genes that would tell her exactly who or what it was that had left them behind.

At the very moment Linda stood clutching the only sample she had, teams of security agents, the FBI, and Pentagon investigators were busy scouring every square inch of the parking deck and the elevator where Adam Wesely's body had lain since five-thirty that morning. Three hours and already the small metal enclosure reeked of body fluids, blood, and of excrement that had found its way through loosened sphincter muscles.

The blood had dried quickly on the polished metal, transformed by the cool air into irregular, scablike mounds that were now almost black. The jagged fragments of brain—some lying on the floor, others still clinging stubbornly to the back of the elevator wall—looked more like small, dehydrated pieces of yellowish brown banana. To the investigators on the scene, it looked almost amateurish; too obvious and too suspiciously brazen. A professional killer, they figured, would have made the hit look like an accident. This one didn't. Still, the consensus among the experts on the scene was that this was no amateur hit, that what they were looking at was a grisly scene purposely orchestrated to look as grisly as humanly possible.

An hour earlier, Wesely's body had been clandestinely removed and transported by FBI agents to St. Elizabeth's Hospital, where Dr. Frederick Salter, chief medical examiner, was just now completing the preliminary examination of the body and dictating his findings into an overhead microphone.

"Nine forty-seven A.M. Official cause of death, which occurred between five and six A.M., was severe trauma to the cerebrum and subsequent hemorrhage resulting from a large caliber projectile entering the frontal bone of the skull, shattering it, then traveling at an upward ten-degree angle through the right cerebral hemisphere before exploding out from the parietal bone. A fifteen-by-eighteen centimeter section of the parietal is missing, indicating the probability of some sort of explosive-tipped bullet. Tissue and arterial damage is extensive. Based on the amount of tissue loss and the extreme severity of the wounds, death is judged to have been instantaneous. . . .

Dr. Salter continued droning into the microphone for another ten minutes before removing his latex gloves with a snap. He tossed them into a receptacle beneath the stainless steel autopsy table, then motioned for his assistant to place the body in storage for further analysis.

"Let's do serology and tissue extraction as soon as possible on this one," he said with the enthusiasm of someone who had done at least a thousand of these before. Turning, he walked briskly through the autopsy room, slapped the double doors open, and found himself standing at eye level with a chest covered with military ribbons.

"Excuse me." He looked up and stared at an imposing figure that blocked him from moving any farther.

"Colonel Thomas Williams . . . Pentagon." Williams handed Dr. Salter an identification card and impatiently waited for acknowledgment.

"One of your men, I suppose?" Dr. Salter was still examining the colonel's ID.

"That's not important. He was a very high ranking official working with the Pentagon whose death, naturally, warrants a classified government investigation. I'm sure you understand. It was a mistake for him to have been brought here. We have our own team of special investigators on the case, and of course we'll need your preliminary report. Because of the classified nature of the incident, the hospital will be required to hand over all documents pertaining to the case.

The FBI has already been notified. There's a vehicle in the back waiting to receive the body now."

"That's against hospital policy." Dr. Salter, a feisty sixty year old who didn't care much for government protocol, pressed closer, readying for battle. "We've got to keep a record of everyone and everything that comes through the door. I don't give a damn if he worked for the government or not. He was admitted here by civilian paramedics, and we have our own procedures." It was all Salter could do to keep from poking a finger into Colonel Williams's chest in order to deflate the obviously bloated ego.

"Doctor," the colonel said as calmly as if he were having a conversation with an intransigent child, "the Pentagon has issued orders to confiscate all records pertaining to this incident. If you fail to do so, I have authority to have security come in here and literally tear this place apart until we've done that. You'll be taken into custody for obstructing a United States government investigation, and we'll see to it that your career as a medical examiner is essentially over. Do I make myself perfectly clear on this matter?"

"Clear enough." Dr. Salter turned on his heel, walked over to the records desk, and brusquely ordered the clerk to hand over everything they had on one Adam Wesely. He came back and shoved the file of paperwork into the colonel's outstretched hand.

"Thank you, doctor. We'll be in touch if we need anything else. In the meantime, you're not to discuss this case with anyone, not even hospital staff. Any breach of that security—I repeat, any breach of security—and you can be sure we'll know if there is—will be a federal offense and dealt with accordingly . . . severely. Your knowledge of this ends as of this moment."

The cold figure of Colonel Williams turned and marched quickly down the hall, disappearing from sight into a waiting elevator. Two other men, dressed in hospital gowns, entered the autopsy room, placed the body into a black plastic bag, and without a word, removed from St. Elizabeth's all trace of Adam Wesely's existence.

chapter eight

Things are often not what they seem.

That axiom was especially true in Washington, where polarizing differences in social philosophy and government policy would regularly trigger power struggles that some have likened to the rivalries of big city crime families. And while the talking heads on every national network hypnotized their viewers with stories purposefully designed to keep America from thinking too much while at the same time feeling as if their elected officials were looking after their best interests, the fact of the matter was that nothing was further from the truth.

Since the post–World War II days of Dwight D. Eisenhower, and particularly since the debacle of the Carter administration, growth of competing factions within the government establishment had been unrelenting. The schism between Democrat and Republican, liberal and conservative, however, was not nearly as great as the schism between those—regardless of their philosophies—who saw America as abandoning its ideals and those hell-bent on altering those ideals to fit a changing global environment.

On this day, at this secret location, eleven of those who felt thus abandoned sat stone faced, like rigid waxen statues. Spaced evenly around a solid oak conference table nearly the length of the thirty-foot room, the men, a mix of high-ranking military and CIA officers and civilian government officials who'd become convinced that no longer could anything short of the most extreme measures save the United States from imminent disaster, followed the twelfth around the room with apprehensive eyes. They watched in silence as General Benjamin McKnight, the Pentagon's senior operations officer, paced the gray carpeted floor, all of them aware that the urgently called gathering was the last such meeting they would have before final countdown to a mission they knew would change the world.

General McKnight, one of only a handful of officers having direct access to the White House itself, was beyond suspicion, a rarity in an agency that regarded security and suspicion as one of its more sacred traditions. Stocky, well built, approaching the upper end of his fifties, he was still every bit the rugged, disciplined soldier. A three-tour Vietnam veteran with a bronze star and two purple hearts to his credit, he'd been through everything life could throw at him, though lately he was beginning to show the visible strains of twenty-hour days. TIMBER WOLF's ultimate mission was his responsibility, his obsession. Nothing he'd ever done in his life, nor ever accomplished as a lifelong career army officer, had ever come close to this.

A graduate of West Point in 1961 at the age of twenty-two, his hero had always been John F. Kennedy. But then everyone's hero back in those days had been JFK, not so much because the man was the president of the United States, but because the man, as General McKnight would often say, was a true American: the hell with blind party loyalty, the perception of JFK's attitude was, even though it may not have been true. America first. America always. *That* had become McKnight's adopted motto.

The bags that sagged beneath McKnight's tired eyes were puffy half moons that looked ready to explode. The wide and visibly worn face twitched nervously as he paced the floor, stopped to look at the door, then raked his fingers across his forehead.

"Where the hell is he? Should have been here a goddamn hour ago." McKnight's face contorted more than usual. A stream of glistening perspiration flowed from his thick, ebony-colored hair as he glanced impatiently every few seconds at his watch, waiting. He lit a slim dark cigarette, took a long, deep drag that forced his cheeks into a wrinkled skeletal pose, then let out a stream of thick smoke over his watch, as though that would make time speed up. His third skeletonlike drag was interrupted by the sound of quick footsteps behind him.

"General, we just received word from Colonel Williams," a young officer announced as he marched into the room.

"Is everything in order?" McKnight asked.

"Yes, sir. The colonel is finishing up some business and left word that he should be here within the next hour or two to present you with a full report."

"Anything else?"

"No, sir."

"Very well, then. Let me know when he arrives."

"Yes, sir."

General McKnight waited for the soundproof double doors to close and lock, then turned toward the conference table. He walked briskly to the far end of the room, leaned forward with both hands at the head of the table, and stared straight ahead with dull gray eyes that pierced the silence and showed little emotion. Directly behind him, a map of the world reached from floor to ceiling and spanned one end of the wall to the other. In front of him, eleven somber faces.

"Gentlemen," McKnight began, looking each man in the eye with the intensity of a warrior, "by now you all know about the devastating crash in New Hampshire. The final reports will be complete and forthcoming within the week. At 0800 hours tomorrow, a new craft and crew will be brought in from White Sand Air Base."

"How will that impact logistics? Final preparations?" a younger, sallow-faced man asked.

"It shouldn't have much impact at all," McKnight answered, "as long as the Pentagon stays on schedule and the administration doesn't call for an inquiry."

"What's the word from the White House?"

"McKnight shook his head. "The White House is out of the strategy loop on this one, forced to accept the inevitable. Pressure is mounting to do *something* to bring order to that goddamn mess over there in Eastern Europe, which by all accounts is on the verge of total chaos. The Middle East is a growing powder keg. South of the border, Mexico is showing signs of becoming a major player in the drug trade. And intelligence, I'm afraid, has just confirmed that the Chinese have secretly joined forces with elements inside Vietnam—now that normalizations with the United States have begun—to quadruple the production and distribution of heroin and assault weapons into the United States. Everyone here knows what the hell that means."

Everyone did. It was a well-known fact that China controlled most of the world's heroin supply coming from the Golden Triangle of Burma, Thailand, and Laos. It was also suspected that for the past decade, the Chinese government had been involved in the growing export of illegal weapons and highly addictive drugs for the express purpose of undermining the United States economy and consequently its system of government. As the economy goes, the saying went, so goes the society, and along with it, the stability of its government. Fear of exactly such a scenario had been motivation enough for the likes of McKnight and his men.

To add fuel to the fires of suspicion, intelligence agents, working both sides of the Pacific, had gathered conclusive evidence that the major Chinese triads—criminal organizations inside America's borders with close roots in China—were working directly with the Chinese government, and consequently with the Chinese military, to smuggle in weapons, drugs, and as many as one hundred thousand illegal aliens each year, many of whom were being recruited for absorption into America's hidden underground for the purpose of flooding the United States with the purest and most addictive form of heroin ever manufactured. The intended result: to destroy the most powerful economy in the industrialized world through a systematic strategy of literally destroying the minds and the bodies of its most productive citizens. It was all quite simple from the standpoint of the Chinese, and exceedingly more effective than all-out war or predatory trade, a practice of which Asia had all but cornered the market.

"All of that," McKnight emphasized with sharp raps of

his index finger against the table, "means WORLD ORDER remains the most viable option for the president right now. Unless there's a dramatic shift in global stability, I don't see any turning back at this point."

"And *our* mission? Still on schedule?"

"That's the reason I've called this meeting so urgently. The target date for TIMBER WOLF has been moved up to six April. . . . The mission must be launched during the next CONDOR test flight."

A steady murmur spread through the conference room, temporarily breaking the ordered discipline of those gathered around the table. The sudden acceleration of TIMBER WOLF was unexpected and most alarming.

"Why April sixth?" Colonel Bekker asked, snapping forward.

"Two reasons," McKnight continued. "I'm afraid there's a grassroots movement out there desperate for sweeping change. Voters believe the government's gone too far, become too damn powerful . . . too corrupt. They don't trust Washington and are too willing to turn the whole damn system upside down. We can no longer be assured of the long-term status of CONDOR because we're no longer guaranteed a political system we can manipulate as easily as we can now. Military budgets are going to be cut, monies will be shifted into God knows what, internal investigations are already being accelerated, all hell is breaking loose on Capitol Hill, and the public is ready to tear the hide off any politician who even looks crooked. The inside prediction is that some of our key people are not going to be in Washington much longer. We need to take advantage of the test flights while we can . . . as soon as we can."

"The second reason?" Bekker asked.

"At this very moment, events are taking place in Washington and around the world that make pushing the mission forward absolutely critical. Waiting another four months to deploy would be too late. I'm afraid if we don't act now, we risk losing *everything*." He emphasized *everything* with a sudden rapping of his fist against hard oak.

"Have you received a final report from security?" another government official asked.

"Yes, we have. The only personnel who actually came in contact with the craft were members of my own emergency cleanup team. They assured me that everything was stripped clean. And of course, Adam Wesely's teams were called in from Washington. Regulations, as you know, require that a special NASA team investigate any unusual craft. They had to be called in."

"You sure Wesely's teams found nothing?"

"The craft was sanitized thoroughly before anyone arrived. Any extraneous samples were confiscated and classified. Unfortunately, there was a glitch: Adam Wesely. Security reported that he was about to go public with information that would have compromised the mission. Both Wesely and the journalist he'd made contact with were . . . eliminated, the documents confiscated. No other security breach was found."

"How could it have come so close?" asked Colonel Nate Patterson, a silver-haired veteran of thirty-plus years. "Are we sure there aren't any other documents elsewhere? His house?"

"We searched his home immediately after he was terminated and found nothing. We're continuing a search, just to make certain there's not a smoking gun out there."

"What about our people in the White House?" asked Colonel Frank Nitz, seated at the farthest end of the table. "We know what the official report said. What's their report on reaction *there*? Any suspicions?"

"Negative, despite one of our transmissions being intercepted."

"Any damage done?"

"McKnight shook his head. "Negative. We've confirmed that intelligence doesn't know anything. They assumed it was some sort of KGB test, nothing more. We're monitoring the situation closely, though."

The general pushed himself from the table, picked up a wooden pointer, then walked slowly toward the wall map directly behind him. He reached for the switch, flipped it, and waited as sections of the map lit up sequentially from east to west, transformed into a maze of colors that no longer resembled individual countries but groups of nations and geopolitical regions without borders, some a patchwork of red and blue, others a uniform green.

Turning again to face the eleven men whose eyes were now studying the map, he recalled the precise moment that the U.S. government made the commitment to go forward with a development that everyone knew would forever change the face of modern history. Never mind the twenty thousand or so nuclear weapons that threatened to turn the world into an ash heap, he thought. Chances were that none would ever be used in his lifetime. Never mind chemical or nerve gas warfare. That, too, was no longer likely so long as the world had the means to identify the user nation and condemn it as an international pariah. Only the most foolhardy or suicidal would attempt such folly. Besides, everyone knew that those weapons were conceived and produced solely as a deterrent and a last resort, nothing more. But this—this was different. And now, as McKnight witnessed the United States crumbling around him, its economy precariously close to beginning the secretly predicted downward spiral from which recovery would be difficult, if not impossible, he saw the use of this new technology as his sacred duty, his destiny.

A widower with two married children who adored him and three grandchildren who meant more to him than life itself, General McKnight feared the worst for them. With apocalyptic visions of a future where life would be nothing more than mere existence, this mission—his last—was every bit as important as any he had undertaken in his thirty-five-year army career.

McKnight resumed his nervous pacing, the telltale resoluteness on his face an obvious reminder to everyone before him how monumental a task it was. The eleven men followed the general anxiously with their eyes, not one of them daring to interrupt the flow of what typically began as contemplative silence but invariably shifted into the droning monologue that had become a routine end to each one of those solemn meetings.

''Gentlemen,'' McKnight began. ''As you know, we're about to witness the beginning of a new world order. Without that order, nothing else matters. Nothing. Because if America loses its dominant position in the world, we all lose. And we simply cannot allow that to happen. We *will* not allow that to happen.''

He reached into a thin, leather briefcase, pulled out a fifty-two page plastic-bound document, and held it up, turning it front to back in his hand. ''Just two hours ago, I received this final report, compiled by our own intelligence-gathering sources and detailing what we expect will happen to every one of our key industries, including aerospace, advanced biomedical, pharmaceutical, computer, electronics, and heavy machinery. You'll be shocked at the findings.'' He tossed the document on the table in front of him and continued.

''Due largely to the direction of past and current economic policies, each one of these industries will be eliminated in its entirety in this country by the end of the decade. The report, as you'll see, reveals hidden agendas, legislation, covert treaties, agreements, contracts, deals, ongoing negotiations, and secret pacts between international bankers, government officials, and U.S. and foreign investors, all of which, in effect, will undermine our industrial base and lead to the eventual withdrawal of that industrial base from the United States to the recipient nations listed on page twenty-four of the report. Those nations, gentlemen, with the full cooperation of our own government, have been targeted as the world's new industrial centers, specifically and strategically chosen to replace the United States as the next group of industrial superpowers. We have reason to believe, based on secret communications we'd intercepted in Geneva, that following this, most of the remaining manufacturing base of the United States will be systematically eroded and transported overseas, essentially crippling us as a global power.''

McKnight nearly had tears in his eyes as he envisioned the United States drifting inexorably toward what many in the world community were already seeing as the initial death throes of a once great nation. He'd seen the signs of it himself. A creditor nation less than a generation ago, the United States had become the world's largest debtor, to the tune of more than 10 percent of GDP. United States corporations, at one time the envy of the industrialized world, were now leading the world in the flight to low-wage countries such as Mexico, Indonesia, and China. Manufacturing plants in virtually every American city were shutting down in record numbers and moving overseas; by some accounts, one factory per day and growing. Infrastructure was crumbling, trade imbalance soaring, currency on world markets plummeting, employment shifting at record levels from high- to low-wage jobs, tax base shrinking, and national debt expanding to such intolerable levels that global markets and financial centers no longer saw America as a wise or long-term investment. And while other nations were investing billions in technology to secure their futures as industrial leaders, McKnight saw America essentially writing it off as if conceding the battle to every developing nation on earth.

He'd seen the reports: the combined gross domestic product of East Asia, only 4 percent of the world's economy in 1960, expected to be at least 50 percent by 2010. And with the growth of economic prosperity and a new doctrine called East Asian Authoritarianism, not only would U.S. influence disappear, its economy would crumble rapidly under the shift of economic power and the industrialization of nations that at one time were little more than backward jungles.

It was incomprehensible to McKnight that it could have come to this, that the United States government, with full knowledge of the consequences to future generations, would continue to pursue legislation and conduct policy that would open the floodgates for American industry to move offshore. The premise that America had to move forward into the global economy as a nonindustrial nation was inconceivable, if not suicidal. As a man with keen business sense and a lifelong loyalty to his country, he realized that eventually a price would have to be paid for a strategy he considered economic treason, that price being the demise of the American way of life, its standard of living, and ultimately its society; all of which, he believed, would collectively trigger a spiral of global economic chaos the likes of which the industrialized world had not seen in this century.

He'd always believed America to be the engine that kept the entire global economy purring. Who else could have single-handedly shared with the rest of the world an industrial might unparalleled in history? And because of America's unique political and economic system, he was convinced that it and it alone could sustain an indefinitely stable industrial base. Other nations, after all, never knew from one decade to the next whether they would plunge headlong into ruthless dictatorships or be swept away in waves of violent political upheavals, never to be the same again. America, he knew, would not. At least not as long as it remained economically sound. In his mind, he was saving not only America, he was saving the world as well.

McKnight looked out above his audience, and as though transported into a world a million miles away, began again. "Standard of living is expected to tumble. Our trade deficit is expected to climb to over two hundred billion by year's end. Millions of jobs lost. For those remaining, wages will equilibrate to a level far below that of most industrialized nations. In other words, gentlemen, the end of America as we know it, orchestrated both knowingly and unknowingly, directly and indirectly by a Washington elite whose naive dreams of a global economic community is frighteningly close to becoming reality. There are some in Congress who are silent in their belief that global economics is doomed to failure, but for whatever reason, they remain fearful. They need allies. TIMBER WOLF, gentlemen, will ensure that this absurd world experiment is put to a rightful end."

General McKnight paused for a moment, tears beginning to well up in his eyes. He was a man who thought of himself more as a patriot than a military officer who'd witnessed it all during his sterling career. He continued. "As we witness this insidious assault on our nation, remember this: The history of this nation is stained red with the blood of a million men who sacrificed their lives so that we might have what we have today. If we do nothing, by the end of this decade more than two hundred years of that history will mean nothing; our political system will mean nothing; everything we've fought and worked for will mean nothing; our children will be heirs to nothing; and our grandchildren, with a hopelessness and despair unknown to any generation since the founding of this nation, will curse our graves for allowing the greatest nation on the face of the earth to be dismantled piece by piece before our very eyes.''

The general then moved quickly to a small table near the back of the room and picked up a stack of manila envelopes. Printed on each in large, red capital letters were the words TOP SECRET—EYES ONLY. He walked around the conference table, placing one envelope in front of each of the eleven men.

''The final details of our mission are sealed inside each envelope. Read them now, place the documents back into the envelopes and hand them back. The contents and the envelopes will be shredded before you leave.''

General McKnight watched silently as each man studied the final mission statement, the stillness of the large room broken only by the sharp crackle of turned pages. When they'd finished, each man returned his envelope to the general. No one uttered another word. They all knew this would be the general's last mission.

''Thank you, gentlemen,'' McKnight said, choking back emotion. ''Each of you knows full well what your responsibilities are. If there are no further questions or concerns, I'll adjourn the meeting and will be calling you individually within a week for a final briefing and a set of instructions. Until then, I expect you all to continue final preparations. After today, we shall not meet as a group again.''

General McKnight then turned from the men as they left the conference room one by one. He stared solemnly at the map before him, scanning slowly across an outline of the

United States and the vast expanse of blue ocean beyond its borders to what would ultimately be the target of TIMBER WOLF's historic mission. His eyes again grew moist.

"God help us," he whispered. "God help us if we fail."

chapter nine

Standard protocol for any collected tissue evidence was to first examine the size, shape, characteristics, and number of chromosome pairs, and second to analyze the molecular structure of those chromosomes, the helical DNA strands. Even a sample the size of a pinhead, through a DNA amplification technique called polymerase chain reaction, or PCR, would contain enough DNA for positive identification.

The techniques for DNA analysis had already been well established. DNA fingerprinting, a method of identifying a person by looking at his or her distinctive DNA banding patterns, was being used successfully throughout the world. But what had made DNA analysis so valuable to the military was that more than a decade ago, the United States government had begun establishing a master DNA file bank for pilots, high-ranking government officials, and classified personnel such as intelligence agents and was now, as a matter of official policy, doing the same for all military personnel. Since the probability of any two individuals having identical sets of DNA is one in billions, it had become a genetic identification repository equivalent to molecular dog tags. Take a blood sample of the casualty, even if the body couldn't be identified physically, and compare the unique DNA banding patterns to the master computer DNA file.

Linda knew that any U.S. pilot involved in a crash such as the one in Brittan, New Hampshire, would have to be included in the DNA master file. After working furiously through much of the morning, she had the first clue in front of her. She staggered to the lab door, barely audible and visibly worn from lack of sleep.

"Jack, come in here, quick."

"What did you find?" Jack asked, racing from his lab at the sound of her voice.

"Take a look." Linda placed a computer-generated image of a karyotype, the pattern of human chromosome pairs, on the table in front of Jack. Spread across the enhanced image of a microscopic photograph were twenty-three pair of those chromosomes.

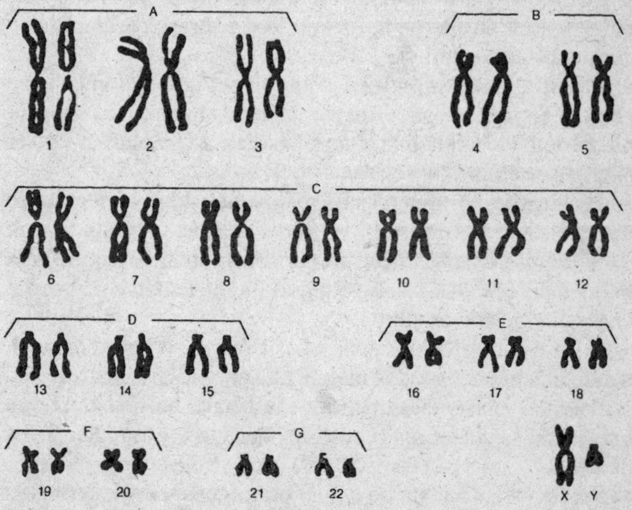

"Definitely human," Linda said. "Pair number twenty-three, X and Y."

"A human male. I would have expected that. You start the DNA work?"

Linda shook her head. "The sample was too contaminated. I'm afraid this is all we're gonna have to work from."

"Damn! You couldn't salvage enough for PCR?"

"This is it, Jack. I'm sure."

"How do you know the blood sample didn't belong to one of the goons who wiped the place clean, maybe cut himself?"

"I dug it out from between two pieces of metal that were completely twisted shut. There's no way a drop of blood could have seeped through those metal pieces. That blood had to have belonged to someone who was inside the craft and must have gotten there before or during the crash. At least we know that much."

"Shit. Means we got ourselves a new type of craft the government's gonna do anything to keep under wraps."

Linda nodded in agreement. "When we were at the site, did you look inside what looked like a thruster? You notice how thick the metal was?"

"I did . . . and I wondered about that. Figured it must have been a protective shield of some kind until I picked up a piece of it and felt like I was holding light plastic. Never handled anything like it."

"I felt it, too," Linda said. "Some new kind of composite material, like Adam said. An alloy light and strong enough to house a powerful new propulsion system. Colonel Williams's people must have gotten to the fuel source before we arrived. *You* find anything?"

"I'm not finished yet, but what I found so far were some dead parasitic nematodes indigenous only to the Southwest."

"Which means that the craft must have been stationed in one of those secret air bases out there in the middle of the desert."

"Okay, so it's gotta be a new prototype, and we know it's one of ours. But hell, do you really think it's the same—?"

"Afraid so," Linda interrupted. "We may be looking at the same damn thing as the eighty-eight crash near Tucson, except without the explosion." Linda's voice quivered as she said it.

"What the hell's going on here?" Jack asked. "No word yet from Adam?"

"I haven't heard from him since he left Brittan, but what

I'm afraid he's going to tell me is that someone—maybe the government itself—will stop at nothing to keep this thing under wraps."

"For what reason?"

"The ultimate weapon, maybe?" Linda said. "Even the most sophisticated, radar-evading aircraft has one major drawback. Range. No craft's going to carry enough fuel to fly halfway around the world and back without having to reload. A propulsion system using new, high-energy synthetics would solve the problem of continuous long-range flight. I've heard rumors, but I never figured any to be true. Developing something like that is one thing, but why it's been developed and for what reason is what scares the hell out of me."

"You've gotta be careful with this," Jack said. "You can't go around announcing that you've uncovered a new secret weapon you think may have been linked to Peter's death. First of all, you'd be violating security. Second, you have no proof. Third, you'd be dead within twenty-four hours, if not sooner."

"I'm well aware of that, Jack. We don't have to say anything to anybody. But I think we need to recruit someone who can help us dig up information from the one source that has to be behind it all . . . the Pentagon. Right now we can only get so far before hitting dead ends."

The Pentagon, as everyone knew, had a well-deserved reputation for being the one agency that got exactly what it wanted, when it wanted it, so long as it could justify its needs in the name of vital national security. Linda suspected that that included private funding sources and insidious activities few people, including government insiders, had any access to.

"Recruit who?" Jack asked, shocked that Linda would consider involving anyone else so soon. "Who the hell can you trust with this kind of information?"

"There's someone . . . a computer expert I know who works with NASA's Computer Research Center here in Washington. His name's John Peterson, and he's done work with both Peter and the Pentagon in the past. He has contacts in high places, I know that for a fact. I'll call him this evening and talk to him about it."

"Are you outta your goddamn mind?" Jack yelled. "How do you know you can trust this guy? We're talkin' about a serious breach of security here. Federal pen. No, assassination, goddammit. If they could do it to Peter, they sure as hell could do it to you . . . to us."

"He was one of Peter's closest friends," Linda replied with a resoluteness that at least seemed to calm Jack down. "Once he knows what's going on, I believe he'll want to get to the bottom of this every bit as much as I do. Yeah, I think I can trust him."

"Okay, okay, if you feel you have to, I can't stop you. But lemme know what I can do, all right? I don't want you in this by yourself."

"Thanks, Jack. Oh, I meant to tell you. I found this on my desk when we got back from New Hampshire." She handed Jack a slip of paper with the numbers 0000612084 scribbled across it. "Did you leave it?"

Jack shook his head. "Never seen it."

"You sure?"

"I would've remembered that. Maybe Adam left it."

"Maybe. I'll call you if I come up with anything."

Linda slumped lifelessly into the back of her couch, poring over in her mind exactly how she was going to explain this to someone who had once been a part of her life but to whom she'd hardly spoken in nearly a year. They'd been close friends once, but since the Tucson incident, there hadn't been much contact between them. An occasional drink, a meeting at a conference or seminar, a chance encounter along the sidewalks and jogging trails of Washington's Mall. A year seemed like such a long time. She felt awkward, but decided that she needed to trust John enough to confide in him, no matter what. Then, not sure if using her regular phone line to contact him was such a good idea, she walked over to her purse, took out her cell phone, and dialed.

"Hello?" the voice answered.

"Hi, John . . . it's Linda . . . Linda Franklin." Her voice drifted away and nearly broke. She certainly wasn't expecting a warm response. Why should she, she thought. It had been nearly a year since she'd even spoken to him.

"Linda, it's nice to hear your voice again. How are things going?"

She wasn't quite sure how to answer that without making it seem as if she were calling him as a last resort. "I'm not sure. It's been a long time. How've you been?"

"Busy. You know NASA."

"Yeah."

"John, I called because—" Linda paused to take a deep breath, trying to force the words from her lips.

"What's wrong?" John asked, at once detecting the quiver in her voice. "You all right?"

"That's why I called. I know we haven't kept in touch very much since Peter died . . . and I feel a little—no, not a little, extremely—awkward about this . . . but . . ."

"I understand, Linda. I loved Peter like my own brother. It was tough on me, too. I've missed you; missed you an awful lot."

God, she was relieved to hear those words. Linda had broken the ice more easily than she had expected, and she felt herself warmed by the sound of John's comforting voice. She remembered it as if it were yesterday; how John had held her after Peter's funeral service, trying to console her as she cried into his chest. Nothing he could have done back then meant as much to her as his solid, reassuring presence when she needed someone during the darkest period in her life.

And then she recalled how she had turned inward, how the pain of losing a husband after she'd already lost both parents had made her begin to shun those closest to her, fearing that their very presence would be a constant reminder of how lonely and miserable her life had become. She wished now that she'd done things differently, more willing to let her feelings be open.

"Actually, I'm not all right at all," Linda whispered. "Things have happened."

"Things? What kind of things? Tell me."

"We investigated a crash the other day in Brittan, New Hampshire," she said after a pause. For a second she considered forgetting the whole thing, afraid of saying too much too soon to someone she wasn't even sure would understand. "I'm not supposed to talk about it, but somehow I think it may be linked to the Tucson incident."

"How's that possible?" John asked.

"The same Pentagon investigator who was involved in the original investigation was there. I felt something I hadn't felt in a long time. It all came back like a bad dream. It was terrifying."

"Did Peter tell you anything out of the ordinary before he left? Anything at all? What he'd been working on or who he'd spoken to the day before? Tell me if he did."

Linda heard in John's voice something that warned her to be careful. "Nothing unusual," she answered, puzzled by the urgency of his tone. "Is there something I should know, John?"

"No, no, it's just that I would think he may have heard something that could help." John paused, then asked, "So what happened?"

Linda recounted the incident, cautiously revealing enough to convince John to help her, and hoping that her trust in him had not been a terrible mistake.

"It's hard to believe," John said when she'd finished a story too bizarre to be anything but real. "I had no idea. Sounds like a major cover-up you've stumbled across. You realize the danger you've put yourself in by telling me? Why *did* you?"

"I need you to help me uncover some information. Can you?" Linda tightened her grip on the receiver and hoped to God he'd say yes.

"Don't know," he said. "What kind of information are we talking about?"

"So far, we believe the craft we saw is part of some top-secret project. We suspect it might be a U.S. government black project . . . some new class of aircraft, maybe.''

''Who's we?'' John asked. ''Who's involved in this besides you?''

''That's not important right now,'' Linda said, curious that John would want to know who else was involved rather than asking about the secret project. ''What's important is that we find out why the government is even developing anything like that, what its mission is, and whether it's the same one as Tucson.''

''How do I fit in?''

Linda hesitated, her suspicions raised another notch, then said, ''I need you to look through some Pentagon computer files for me. I wouldn't ask if I didn't think it was important.''

''This isn't going to be easy, you know. If what you're looking for is so top secret, breaking into Pentagon files could be impossible.''

''For an expert hacker like you?''

''Even for me.''

''Will you at least try . . . for Peter?''

''No . . . but I'll try for you. Meet me at my office tomorrow morning at nine o'clock and we'll see what we can do.''

''Thanks so much, John. I won't forget this.''

Linda hung up, feeling as if a burden had been lifted from her shoulders and that she'd just been reunited with a long-lost friend. She immediately picked up the phone and dialed Jack's cell number. Three rings later, a familiar voice was greeting her.

''Jack, I just got off the phone with John Peterson. He's agreed to help us.''

''I'm still a little worried about trusting this guy,'' Jack said. ''You're not?''

Linda paused, trying to convince herself that there was no other choice, then said, ''Stop thinking that everyone who works for the damn government is out to get you, Jack. I'll know soon enough if we can tell him everything.''

''Okay, okay, what did he say?''

"He told me to meet him at his office tomorrow. We can at least begin by seeing if there's anything declassified in the files. If not, I think I've convinced him to look for some classified information."

"And you think he'll do that? Just break into Pentagon files and sit there, waiting for the Feds to come by and take him away in cuffs."

"I got a feeling he would. There was something there I remembered so vividly, something in his voice that told me he'd be willing to take that risk. Call it intuition, but it was there."

"Sounds like he's more than an old friend," Jack said. *Intuition, my ass. Women. I hope your damn intuition doesn't get you killed.*

"He is, Jack. I just forgot how much."

"Yeah, right. Just be careful. I don't want anything to happen to you just because you think you can trust someone who happened to be Peter's friend eight years ago. Eight years is a long time . . . and the government can change people . . . do things to people. Call me paranoid if you want, but think about everyone you knew, or thought you knew, who turned out to be a special agent who would've sold out his own mother for one cause or another. We work for a top-secret agency involved in top-secret programs, Linda. They probably have people watching us. Just be careful."

"Don't worry," Linda assured him. "If you need to contact me, you know how to reach me."

Linda pushed the disconnect button, and knowing that she couldn't allow herself to make a fatal mistake, understood exactly what Jack was saying. But at the same time she had an inexplicable sense that John could help her uncover the purpose behind a secret government project she knew was the cause of Peter's murder. Regardless of Jack's worry and her own suspicions, she had to trust her husband's old and best friend. She had to.

chapter ten

MARCH 17, 1996: 8:55 A.M.

Above a facade of white marble that framed two sets of ornately carved mahogany doors, a triangular frieze depicted images of past presidents and little known statesmen. Alongside the doors, a row of fluted columns rose thirty feet from thick granite bases. The columns, massive enough to support a building ten times as large, accentuated a set of grand stairs that flowed outward to the empty street below.

It all had given Linda the impression that she'd been transported a world away from the heart of D.C. and into a scene from *Gone with the Wind.* Oh, how she'd wished it were so. She'd found herself almost mesmerized, staring at the immense templelike building that was home to NASA's Computer Research Center and praying that her presence there was not a terrible mistake. But then, as quickly as those thoughts had flashed through her mind, they'd vanished as an irate cab driver, shouting at her to get the hell off the street, had snapped her back into the stark reality of being right there in the middle of Washington, D.C.

She climbed twenty feet up the set of enormous granite steps, then walked through the double doors and across a gray-and-white-checked tile floor. The second she stepped foot inside, her memory was jarred instantly, back to the last time she'd been there. It was at least a year after Peter's accident, and she remembered thinking how desperately she'd wanted to feel as if her life was not over, as if she still had something to live for. And now here it was, eight years later, and she wasn't even sure how seeing John would affect her.

''May I help you?'' An obese security guard pried himself

from a chair behind a large metal desk, his eyes boring straight ahead at Linda. Cinched tightly around a paunch that drooped six inches below his belt buckle was the obligatory, shiny holster. A bulletproof vest added three more inches to his bulky girth.

"Yes. I'm Dr. Linda Franklin. I have an appointment with Dr. John Peterson."

The goonish-looking guard, surrounded by sophisticated monitoring equipment, telephones, and colored switches, picked up a red telephone and punched some numbers as he continued his intimidating stare.

"Dr. Peterson, this is security," he announced in an official tone, at the same time tearing his eyes from Linda's face. "There's a Dr. Franklin here to see you." He waited a moment, thumping his meaty fingers against the hard desk, then abruptly hung up and looked back at Linda. "Have a seat. Dr. Peterson says he'll be down in a minute. Meanwhile you need to fill out this form." He handed Linda a clipboard with an attached security pass. "You'll have to wear the pass while you're here and turn it in when you sign out."

Not five minutes later, as Linda was finishing up the form, a booming voice called out.

"Linda, it's great to see you." Bounding across the lobby like a young athlete, John Peterson greeted Linda with more enthusiasm than she'd expected.

She looked at him as if the year since they'd seen each other last had been but a single day. She was surprised at how little he'd changed, at how ruggedly handsome he still was, though the tinge of gray that hadn't been there the last time she saw him told her at once that it had been too long since her last visit.

John extended his arms. Tall, six-foot-three, with broad athletic shoulders and light brown hair, his soft brown eyes had always made Linda feel as if they could see right through her.

Instinctively, Linda pressed against his chest, holding him tightly for a moment, closing her eyes and recalling the last time they had been that close. It seemed so long ago that she'd been embraced like this by anyone; and it felt warm and safe. She squeezed him tighter, afraid that if she let go she would lose the friend she'd lost once and didn't want to lose again. Tears formed uncontrollably in her eyes, trickling along the sides of her cheeks, and she felt in that firm yet tender embrace something much more than just two friends greeting each other after a long and lonely absence.

John felt her trembling. "What's wrong?" he asked, not sure why Linda was holding him so desperately, but suspecting that it had more to do with what she'd learned over the past few days than with him.

"I just missed you, that's all," she answered. "Can we go to your office and talk?"

"Sure. Let me check you in." The security guard watched the two like a circling vulture while John signed the form Linda had just filled out. "Okay, let's go."

They stepped into the elevator and faced one another, each feeling guilty about allowing so much time to go by, both unsure of exactly what to say and thinking that maybe, just maybe, there was still something there that even the years had not taken away.

"John, I know I haven't kept in touch, but it's taking me so long to get over Peter's death. Sometimes I think I never will. It scares me that I can't seem to let go."

"What about now?" John asked. "Are you okay now? Why the tears?"

"I remember how much you cared about me when Peter died, that's all. I should have told you how much that meant to me."

"You're telling me now, aren't you?"

Linda reached out to embrace John again as the elevator eased to a stop on the fourth floor. The doors opened, revealing a wide hallway that branched off in three directions. John stepped out first and pointed to his right. Linda followed. They then walked the long hallway leading to a private office and research area, and stopped to face a heavy metal door. John slipped a plastic card into the slot of a special security checkpoint and pressed a series of code numbers. Within seconds, a red digital message appeared, asking for another set of code numbers and letters. John pressed more buttons, and with a sudden whisk the door slid open.

It was nothing like she remembered. Linda crossed the threshold into what seemed like a futuristic melange of electronics and computer equipment advanced beyond anything she'd ever seen. The bridge of the starship *Enterprise*, she thought to herself, amazed at the state-of-the-art computer terminals that sat perched atop long tables like twenty-first-century television sets. Numbers, symbols, and cryptic words flashed across wide blue computer screens in secret, codelike fashion. Along the walls behind the computers and video display terminals stood a Cray T90 supercomputer, powerful enough to crunch out sixty billion calculations per second. Linked to other supercomputers in other government installations around the country, they were, at that moment, collectively solving the most complex riddles of the universe. One of those riddles: determining, from data gathered by *Voyager*, precise locations of galaxies within an expanding universe and the probability of life within those galaxies.

"What's NASA having you work on these days?" Linda asked. "Or can you even say?" She looked on as an incredible amount of data was being collected and processed at lightning speed before their eyes.

"Life."

"You mean life out there? Outside our solar system?"

"That's right. According to our latest estimates, there are roughly a hundred billion galaxies in the universe, each having up to a trillion stars, many of them just like our sun. With those kinds of numbers, the odds are pretty good we're not alone."

"Any luck?"

"We're getting some good data, especially from some of these new thinking computers. Many galaxies have areas within them that look like small solar systems. That's really what we're doing. First, trying to pinpoint solar systems that have been evolving since the beginning of the Big Bang, then, by analyzing the elements present within those solar systems, determining the probability of life.''

''Based on what?''

''Factors like gravity, temperature, proximity to a major star system that would serve as a sun, spectrophotometric analysis of the chemical makeup of the atmosphere. Things like that.''

Linda's attention drifted suddenly from John's project to what she'd really come for. ''John, I seriously need your help.''

''I figured that's why you're here. Let's go into my office.'' John led her into a neat, almost disappointingly average cubicle containing a desk, floor-to-ceiling bookcase, and two chairs. He poured them both coffee and, without asking, put just enough sugar and milk into her cup to make her smile at his remembering something so trivial.

''I see you're nervous about something,'' John said. ''What is it?''

''How did you know?''

''I'm incredibly perceptive,'' John laughed. ''Besides, you're biting your bottom lip. You need to get out of that habit if you're ever going to play poker with me.''

Again she had to smile at John's taking notice of something so insignificant about her.

''Anyway, how can I help you with your investigation?'' John asked, more serious now.

''I have to find out if there are any government projects involving new aircraft prototypes I may not know about.''

''Aircraft? Any particular reason why it's aircraft you're after?''

''Like I told you last night, Jack and I have reason to believe that the crash we investigated in New Hampshire is linked to a government project that Peter may have known about all along. I want to find out what it was he found and whether it directly led to his death . . . or more likely, his murder.''

''You *do* know that if classified files are broken into, there's a security system that tracks down the origin of the breach. They'd know it was me and they'd damn sure want to know why I needed that kind of information. Even if it's *not* classified, the Pentagon is going to suspect that I'm after something. They'll investigate, no matter what."

"No way you can override the security system?"

"There may be, but I've never tried it. Thought about it a lot last night, though."

"Could you try?" Linda pleaded with a tone of desperation.

"Yeah, I could. It'll be risky, though. For the past decade, intelligence has been bugging selected software and computer hardware for the express purpose of setting up surveillance networks. It started with a need to track financial movements around the world. Now it's routine. Every computer in every security zone—and that includes us—is wired for surveillance."

"What are you going to do?"

"If I screw up and my computer warns me that the security system is locked on, there's nothing I *can* do. I'll have to shut it down and hope to God I disengage before it tracks us down. You still want to go ahead with it?"

Linda nodded weakly.

John turned on the computer behind his desk and punched in the combination of letters and code numbers that would gain him access to the mainframe. Linda looked on anxiously, her hands clenched tightly against the back of his chair.

"I've come up with a way to disrupt the network with a complex series of commands," John continued, "at the same time, accessing the computer system in one of our Colorado offices to make it look as if it's that system that's calling up the information. Theoretically, if things work out like they're supposed to, the main security system should be fooled into thinking that someone in Colorado is the one breaking into Pentagon files. If it works, we're home free. Unfortunately, the guys at the Colorado office will be getting the third degree tomorrow morning."

"That's great!" Linda said with renewed enthusiasm, then

tempered her joy when she thought more of it. "Not about the poor guys in the Colorado office. About the security override. How soon can you do it?"

"How about now?"

John swung back around to the computer terminal and resumed typing as Linda watched. She was expert enough herself to know that what John was attempting was extremely risky, even for him. But though NASA and the Pentagon had made every effort to build in redundant security checks, she also knew John well enough to believe that if anyone could pull it off, he could.

"Got it," John said. "We're linked into the computer system at the Nelson Propulsion Labs in Mt. Jefferson, Colorado."

"You sure?" Linda asked, clenching her fingers even tighter now.

"Yeah, that was the easy part. Everything I input from now on should look like it's originating from Nelson. Now for the hard part."

John began frantically punching keys, answering a series of security probes that flashed across the blue screen. And with the final set of instructions typed in, the screen suddenly went blank. John and Linda stared, their hearts racing, waiting for something, expecting the worst. One wrong prompt and they knew the security system would pinpoint exactly where the break-in had occurred, bringing everything to a screeching end. But within seconds, a colored display flashed across the screen:

Pentagon Data File

Security Code One/Top Secret—Eyes Only
Federal Law Prohibits Access by Unauthorized Personnel

"Okay, we got it," John whispered. "Now for the real test. Let's see if we can access your information."

He pressed more keys and within seconds the computer responded.

Code Word?>

"Type in Project TW or PTW," Linda ordered.

John began the search.

Code Word?>Project TW

>Bad Command. Retry Code Word

Code Word?>PTW

>Bad command. Retry Code Word

"Nothing, Linda. Computer's not recognizing your code word."

Linda took a slip of paper from out of her wallet, unfolded it, and put it on the desk next to John. "Punch this in," she said. "I have a hunch."

John typed in the series of letters and numbers, and when the computer came alive and accessed the command, Linda froze. John sank back against his chair, surprised at what they had just brought up on the screen.

Personal Data File: Benjamin McKnight
Classified Access Code: 0000612084
File Name: Wolf
Top Secret—Eyes Only

John hastily typed in more instructions.

>Search file access code 0000612084

>Search requires file name

File name?>Wolf

>Searching

Within seconds more information:

Access Code: 0000612084
File: Wolf

Mission Code: World Order / Condor
Counter Mission: Timber Wolf / PCW
Type: aircraft / defense-evading / specs: top secret umbra
Bases: Base TWOLF-1, Prospect, ME; Base TWOLF-2, White Sand, AZ; Base TWOLF-3, Hot Rock, NM
Computer Access Limited to Authorized Personnel Only

"Christ, it's what I thought all along," Linda whispered, her eyes glued to the file. A new class of aircraft. But what the hell's CONDOR? Never heard of it." Linda reached over and placed her finger on the screen. "WORLD ORDER. God, this is insane. What the hell are Adam and General McKnight into?"

"Whatever it is," John said, "this file isn't telling us. Computer access is limited to authorized personnel."

"Can we get information from these other code words?"

"Maybe. Let's see." John typed in combinations of more words.

Code Word?>world order

>Bad Command. Retry Code Word

Code Word?>condor

>Access Denied. Eyes Only

Code Word?>timber wolf

>Access Denied. Eyes Only

"Well, we know WORLD ORDER and CONDOR are access-required classified code words."

"Meaning?"

"Meaning they're encrypted codes. No access. Let's try something else."

Code Word?>PCW

>Access Denied. Code Omega Required. Top Secret—Eyes Only

"Jesus Christ." John's voice lowered. "PCW must be one helluva secret."

"What do you mean by that?" Linda asked.

"Pentagon code omega means there's no way you're getting in unless you have a special security access code. Omega is the last letter of the Greek alphabet. Code omega means you get access only as a last resort."

"Damn!" Linda slammed her fist hard against the desk. "We've got to know what that mission code is. We've got to!"

"It's not that easy. Code omega files are what we categorize as security alpha. There's no way I can break into those right now."

"Right now?" Linda's face lit up just a bit. "You mean you can?"

"I've got a contact here in Washington. We worked together for years on a special project before he moved on to the Pentagon. I'll give him a call tomorrow and tell him I'm working on something highly classified that requires an access code. I've needed to do that before for some of our research. He'll know not to ask any questions. Besides, he owes me. The less you know the better, okay?"

John turned the computer off and whirled back around to Linda, the light from his desk lamp illuminating her face. He'd always found her attractive, and at that moment he couldn't help staring and noticing how beautiful she was. Having never found women who'd starve themselves into looking like anorexic models the least bit sensual, to him, Linda, with the healthy curviness of the college athlete she'd once been, looked absolutely perfect.

Reflexively, he reached out to her. She responded tentatively, placing her hand in his. He got up and moved closer to her until their bodies touched gently, yet just enough for John to feel the softness of Linda's faultless curves and the firmness of her breasts against him. For a brief moment, they stood there. But as though that not-so-innocent embrace should never have happened in the first place, Linda pulled away, feeling something deep within her she hadn't felt in a long time. She was confused and guilty over her excitement. What was she doing? she thought. She wasn't supposed to be feeling this way. And then, as it had last evening, a shudder went through her as she wondered again why it was that John had been so willing to put himself in danger for her.

"John, I'm really afraid," she whispered.

"Of what?"

"Everything. The investigation . . . the cover-up . . . what I might uncover. I'm not sure if I'm ready to find out."

"Then we'll find out together," John said. "And when we do, we'll figure out where to go from there."

chapter eleven

Linda couldn't recall the last time she'd slipped in a favorite CD and lost herself in the soothing sounds of the New York Philharmonic. She tossed her house keys across the top of the dresser and dropped stonelike onto her bed, emotionally exhausted but thanks to John feeling as if she'd at least cracked the door to an incredible secret. Closing her eyes she sighed deeply, listening to the crescendo of strings that broke the quiet stillness of her empty Tudor and trying to visualize Peter's face. For a moment she couldn't help thinking that it was all a lifelike dream; the way he would hold her in his arms, the way he'd kiss her face and neck, then gaze deeply into her eyes as if she were the only person he'd ever held that closely, or for that matter ever wanted to.

She wrapped her arms around herself and felt a comfortable warmth flow over her. The warmth turned into wave after wave of tingling that seemed to reach inside of her. She imagined herself with him, alive again, sensual, sexy. And then, as she pictured herself embraced in those rugged arms, her thoughts were suddenly broken by a ring that sent her racing across the bedroom and reaching for her cellular phone.

"Hello?" she answered, her heart speeding up.

"Linda, it's Jack. I've been trying to reach you all morning. Where the hell've you been?"

"With John, remember? What's wrong? You sound terrible."

"Awful news." Jack was breathing so heavily Linda could almost sense his fear through the telephone. "I'm at a pay phone a few blocks from the lab. I didn't want to risk getting intercepted. We found out about it this morning. Adam—'' she listened to heavy breathing again.

''What, Jack? What about Adam? They find him? Is he still missing?''

''Intelligence just issued a classified report. We got hold of it through security channels.''

''What, dammit! C'mon.''

''They found him in the parking deck elevator of his downtown office . . . dead.''

''My God!'' Linda's stomach felt as though it would come up into her throat. ''Who could have done something like that? Why?'' She pressed her fist into her abdomen and took deep, erratic breaths. It was all she could do to keep from vomiting where she stood.

''Official word is suicide. Said they found a gun in his hand and a note back on his office desk. I don't buy it for a minute. Not Adam.''

''But who could have—''

''No one here knows anything. The Justice Department and the Pentagon have taken over the investigation, and it's pretty much under wraps right now. Apparently, the body was removed from the hospital before anyone else had a chance to look at it, and I doubt that anyone's gonna be able to find it until they're finished doing whatever they need to do with it. From the sound of it, it was pretty bad, pretty gruesome. There's gotta be some link between this and the crash.''

''Jesus Christ, Jack, how do you know that?''

''Because there's something else. At six o'clock yesterday morning, there was a car bombing in Virginia, only an hour or so after Adam was killed. A journalist was blown up in an explosion that took half the block with it. Same journalist who wrote that series of science reports a couple of years ago about some of the Pentagon's projects. I heard he was pretty close friends with Adam. More than just a coincidence, I'd say, but not something you're gonna see plastered in the papers.''

''My God. Adam said he was going to tell me everything.

He said it would be dangerous. He said to be careful. He tried to warn me, Jack, and he may have been carrying evidence that he was probably going to show me next. Jesus Christ, I don't believe this is happening.'' Linda sat back down on her couch and began trembling.

''Can you meet me in my office in an hour?'' Jack asked.

''Yeah. I think we better find out what's going on, fast.''

Linda cradled the phone, shaking so hard she could barely walk. The body was removed from the hospital, she kept thinking; just like Peter's was removed from the crash site. There was no doubt in her mind now that Adam knew *something*, and that unless she cracked those files, the cover-ups and the killings were not going to end with this.

Jack was already at the office, waiting impatiently and filling the room with thick, nervous smoke when Linda arrived almost thirty minutes late. The radio he brought along was blaring country music loud enough to drown out any conversation that would surely be picked up if the room was wired. He wiggled his index finger at Linda and waited for her to get close to him before daring to speak.

''Linda, I'm getting a little goddamn worried about all this. If anyone suspects we know anything, I don't want either of us, especially you, ending up like Adam, the poor bastard. I was afraid to get into the elevator, for Christ's sake.''

''I know exactly how you feel,'' Linda whispered. ''I said a quick Hail Mary before I started my car.''

Linda sank into a worn couch next to her and rubbed her arms as though a cold wind had suddenly blown into the office. Jack positioned himself inches away.

''I know it was an assassination,'' Jack said. ''I know it. We have to watch every step we take from this moment on. Everything we do. Everyone we talk to. Now that they've eliminated Adam, they'll be suspecting everyone in the organization. Phones are probably being tapped right now, and I'm sure we'll all be watched very closely. So that means not even cellular phone calls, here or at home . . . and no talking to anyone about what we know. Anyone."

Linda nodded weakly, the warnings Adam had given her suddenly playing over and over in her head like a broken record. *Be careful with this one. . . . Be careful with this one. . . . You can't imagine the danger you'd be in. . . . the danger you'd be in . . . the danger . . . the danger . . .* The ominous words swirled through her mind like a vortex, and only now did she realize the extent of the danger in what Adam had been trying to tell her.

"Tell me what happened when you met with Peterson," Jack demanded. "Were you able to find out anything?"

"I found out that it had to have been Adam who left me that slip of paper with the code written on it."

"How?"

"When John punched the code into the computer, it accessed one of General McKnight's Pentagon files. PTW are code letters for some top-secret project called TIMBER WOLF. And get this, it has something to do with a new class of aircraft, one of which is stationed at an air base in Arizona."

Jack's eyes lit up. "Arizona. The crash site Peter investigated. It fits. It all fits. What else?"

"According to the data file, the prototype involves a new technology that gives it the ability to evade even the most sophisticated radar defense shields. That would explain the composite materials we saw at the crash site. There was also a three-letter code: PCW. Access for that required a Pentagon code omega."

"Code omega? Shit. A dead end."

"Not necessarily. John has a source who can get him access codes to those files."

"How the hell can he do that? No, never mind. I don't wanna know. But good lord, Linda, you think he should be screwing around with omega files? What does he have, a death wish?" Jack grabbed Linda's arms as though about to shake some sense into her, well aware of the consequences she'd face if either of them was caught breaching Pentagon security.

"It may be our last chance, Jack. And if it keeps us from winding up like Adam, I'll do more than just screw around with those files. I'll mess around with anyone involved with them and make damn sure that what we find is plastered on the front page of every major newspaper in the country."

Jack released Linda and threw himself back into the couch. "Hell, it's probably too late anyway. If the bastards are gonna get us, they're gonna get us. We might as well go down fighting."

"If we can just find out what we're dealing with," Linda said. "If we can break through and at least get some solid evidence, maybe something Adam left behind, no one's going to touch us. It'll be over. The more we expose, the more people who know, the better. That's why we've got to keep digging."

"You have something in mind?"

"No sense checking Adam's downtown office suite. It's probably the first place they looked anyway. Besides, the place is probably crawling with Feds. But I know that Adam used to do a lot of his work in his study at home. Maybe we could pay his housekeeper a visit without making it seem like we're after anything and find whatever they may have missed, something only *we'd* be able to recognize. I know Maria real well, and after we pay our respects we'd have access to the place."

"Unless someone already got there," Jack interrupted.

"There's only one way to find out."

Maria Swenson waved her thick Swedish arm in quick, tight circles, ushering Linda and Jack through the large entranceway of Adam's sweeping Victorian home.

"Dr. Franklin. It's so nice to see you again. Come right in. Come right in." Maria's eyes were red and swollen, the handkerchief she was clutching soaked with tears that obviously had not subsided since she'd heard the news of Adam's horrible death. "Thank you for coming, Dr. Franklin. It's so nice to see you," she repeated in her heavy Swedish accent.

As the door swung closed behind them, Linda paused for

a moment, the sight of the spacious wood-paneled foyer bringing her back to the last time she'd been there. It had been two years ago at least, at a Fourth of July picnic, she recalled fondly. Her memory of everything these days, it seemed, was heightened to the point that every object, every word, name, or face from her past now triggered an immediate and magnified version of past events in her life.

Adam, she reminisced, as she took in the scent of his favorite potpourri, had never been a people person. She remembered how uncomfortable he'd been with small talk, how he'd think it a waste of time and how he'd especially despised those Washington parties in which everyone shifted into beltway establishment behavior and hoped that for a few hours at least, no one noticed how phony and obsequious they really were. But she also remembered him as a kind and good-hearted man, though he hardly showed it openly and didn't much care if people knew it or not.

Maria knew. His closest friends knew. Sometimes it was only Linda who'd notice, and she remembered thinking that it was too bad more people didn't. And now, as she looked at Adam's mementos lining the shelves along the walls, many of them reminders of experiences and adventures he'd shared with her, she felt a deep and profound sense of loss for a man who more than anyone else had taken the place of the father she'd lost.

Maria escorted Linda and Jack into a spacious living room and patted the Queen Anne couch that always seemed so out of character for someone as gruff and as rugged as Adam.

"Please, sit down."

"Maria, I'm so sorry about Adam," Linda said, grasping Maria's hand in consolation and letting out tears of her own. "It was a shock to all of us."

"I can't get over it," Maria responded, wiping both sides of her tear-streaked face with her handkerchief. "How anything like this could have happened . . . to Mr. Wesely, of all people. I just don't understand it."

"We can't believe it either. Adam was such a good man. He had his rough edges, we all know that. He was under a lot of pressure lately, but no one who really knew him could ever believe he'd take his own life."

At that, Maria began to cry harder, burying her face in her hands for a few seconds, then quickly composing herself as all good Swedes are taught to do. "Most people didn't realize . . . how much Mr. Wesely had gone through during and after Vietnam. It wasn't only the injury, you know. He suffered so much emotionally. Much more than he ever did physically. All those young boys who died. He felt responsible, you know. It nearly killed him to write to each one of their parents. He'd wake up sometimes, screaming in the middle of the night, sweating all over, a look of horror in his eyes like you've never seen. And then he would cry and cry like a child. There were nights he wouldn't sleep at all. Buried himself in his work just to avoid the nightmares. Sometimes he would go away and not come back for hours. Poor Mr. Wesely. And now this. I just can't get over it."

Linda, seeing how particularly difficult it was for Maria to accept Adam's untimely death, felt guilty about having to ask her to let them rummage through his study. It seemed inappropriate so soon after his death, but time was precious. Be direct, she decided.

"Maria, I feel a bit awkward asking you this right now . . . especially at a time like this . . . but we came here for a reason. To find some important papers Adam might have brought here from work."

"Well, you're certainly welcome to look around, but I'm afraid someone's already been here."

"What! Who?"

"Three men from the Pentagon. Said they needed to confiscate some important documents that Mr. Wesely may have had here."

Linda's face turned flush, her eyes widening at the word *Pentagon.* "Was one of them a tall air force officer? A colonel?"

"Why, yes. He introduced himself as Colonel Williams. Odd-looking fellow, I thought. Ugly and a bit scary. The other two men looked more like security people . . . maybe police of some sort.''

''Did they take anything with them? Where did they look? What did they take? We need to know, damn it.'' Linda felt her blood pressure rise at the sound of Colonel Williams's name. ''I'm sorry, Maria. It's just that it's important. *Very* important.''

''They looked in the study mostly.'' Maria looked taken aback after Linda's sudden outburst. ''Spent nearly five hours in there, took a few things, but not that much, as far as I could tell. A few papers, maybe. That colonel fellow looked almost disappointed, like he expected to find something but didn't.''

''Did they look through everything?''

''I'm not sure, but they seemed very thorough.''

Realizing that Adam was too intelligent and far too careful a man to keep anything at the house that may have exposed either himself or the project to danger, Linda's demeanor changed from despair to cautious relief. ''Would Adam have kept any of his papers anywhere else?''

''He worked mainly here, but—'' Maria paused, as if trying to protect Adam's privacy, even after his death.

''But? But what?'' Linda asked.

''He *did* have a mountain cabin, you know. He went there a lot the last couple of years.''

''A cabin?'' Linda's eyebrows rose. ''I never knew anything about a cabin. He never told any of us about that.''

''I guess Mr. Wesely never told anyone. It was an escape for him . . . from Washington, especially.'' And then the embarrassing little detail that forced Maria's eyes away. ''We . . . we would go there sometimes . . . together.''

''Does anyone else know?''

''Oh, I wouldn't think so. Mr. Wesely was a very private person. He wanted that part of his life kept private, too. He ordered me never to tell anyone, and I never had reason to, anyway. Don't see much sense keeping it to myself any longer, now that he's gone.''

''Maria,'' Linda pleaded, ''you can't tell anyone else

about the cabin yet. Please. Promise me you won't."

"Of course. But why?" Maria's puzzled expression quickly turned suspicious.

"Adam may have gotten hold of some information that led to his death," Jack said. "He was going to share that information with Linda. We don't think he committed suicide at all, but was assassinated because he was about to reveal it to one of his newspaper contacts."

"The car bombing that was just on the news?" Maria asked, her hand flying to her mouth.

Jack nodded. "We're trying to find that information before anyone else does. Will you help us, please?"

"Oh, my God. Oh, my God. Poor Mr. Wesely. Of course I'll help. And you? Are you going to be okay?"

"We will be if we can find out what it was that Adam knew. We believe he had something in his possession so important he was murdered before he had a chance to reveal it. If it was that important, he must have a record of it someplace else. I'm guessing it's hidden in that cabin. The sooner we find out what that is, the better."

"West Virginia," Maria suddenly blurted. "It's along the Virginia border."

Maria then jumped up, ran into the kitchen, and a few seconds later reappeared with a map. She sat down, unfolded it and placed it on the coffee table, tracing the route from Washington to Baker, West Virginia, with a yellow felt-tip marker. "When you get to this small road"—she pointed to a gray squiggly line on the map—"turn off and go about six miles north. On the right, you'll come to a gravel road with a chain across it. There'll be a sign. No trespassing or private road or something like that. I don't remember exactly."

She jumped up again, this time rushing over to an antique secretary and pulling out two key rings from the desk drawer. One held a single key, the other a pair of keys. "The single key unlocks the padlock on the chain," she continued, walking back toward Linda. "The cabin's about a half mile up the road." She then held up the ring with the pair of keys and separated them. "This one's to the front door, this one opens the back.'' She handed the key rings to Linda and said, ''Please be careful. I couldn't stand anyone else getting hurt.''

''Don't worry,'' Linda said. ''We're not going to do anything that'll make us targets.'' Even as she said it, she realized she could only hope it was the truth.

Linda tucked the keys inside her purse, then hugged Maria as she would have her own mother. She often thought of Adam and Maria as the closest thing she had to family, to parents, and it pained her deeply to think that she had lost another one.

''Linda, over here.'' Jack was staring out the side window at a dark green sedan parked halfway down the street. ''Does that car out there look familiar to you?''

Linda ran toward the window, shadowing the wall and peeking out at the parked car. ''Not really,'' she whispered. ''But I don't like the looks of the two goons sitting in it, though. I'd bet my life we've been watched ever since we got here. Bet my life that Adam's phone is tapped as well.''

She then picked up a phone that was sitting on the table next to her and dialed the special number to the lab complex, all the while keeping her eyes directly on the green sedan. She gave Jack and Maria a nod and placed her index finger across her lips.

''Hello, DBI,'' the voice on the other end answered. DBI, for security reasons, was the code for Division of Biotic Investigation that all personnel were required to use.

''Hi, Natalie. This is Dr. Franklin. I'm calling to let you know that I'll be in my office later this afternoon. Dr. Pilofski and I are at Adam Wesely's place visiting with Maria. We came out to see if there was anything we could do to help with the memorial service.''

''I'll make sure I leave the message with your staff,'' Natalie responded.

''Thanks, Natalie. See you later.'' Linda hung up and let out a long sigh. ''If my hunch is right, someone's getting briefed right now about the conversation I just had. And if we're lucky, whoever it is will be convinced that we don't know anything.'' Again Linda peeked out the side window, this time noticing that one of the men now had the car phone pressed to his ear.

''Jesus, I hope they bought it,'' Linda whispered, then turned to Maria and took hold of her hand, squeezing it tightly. ''Maria, thanks. Thanks for everything. But can you do us one more favor?''

''Yes, of course.''

''Can you take my car and drive it toward Washington while we take Adam's?''

''I . . . I don't understand.''

''Obviously we're being followed. I'm parked on the side of the house where they can't see you getting into the car. When you pull out of the driveway, they'll follow you, thinking it's me. Jack and I will then take Adam's car and head out to the cabin. If you're stopped, just tell them I offered to sell you my car and you were taking it for a test drive. You had no idea what I had in mind. When you came back, we were gone, that's all. Can you do that for me?''

Maria wasn't sure about anything anymore, but quickly agreed. ''Please be careful,'' she finally said, her eyes growing moist once again.

''We'll keep in touch, I promise. And if we find out anything we think you should know, we'll be back. Soon. Meanwhile, if anyone asks, you haven't told us anything. All we did was visit and discuss the memorial service, that's all.''

''And if they know about the cabin and expect me to tell them where it is?'' Maria asked, no longer thinking about Linda but concerned for herself. ''What can I do?''

''Stall like hell,'' Jack interrupted. ''We should be there by . . . let's see.'' He was studying the map, calculating the mileage. ''About three o'clock. Give us an hour or two head start. If they push, pretend you're looking for directions. Tell 'em you can't find the keys. Hide the map. Anything. Just give us some time to get there, do what we need to do, and get out, okay?''

''I'll try. But please be careful.''

Maria then slipped out the side door, got into Linda's car,

and cautiously pulled out into the street. She then turned left and headed directly toward downtown Washington, D.C.

Linda and Jack watched from the window as the green sedan disappeared from sight. And after making sure no one else was anywhere in sight, took off themselves and prayed to God that what they were about to do would not get them killed as well.

chapter twelve

Throughout the urgently held briefings with the secretaries of state and defense, the head of the National Security Agency, and the Strategic Air Command, the president's mind had repeatedly drifted back to an encrypted code that even intelligence could not crack. Timber wolf. Was it a coincidence? he wondered. A red herring? There was certainly more to it than KGB, he knew that.

"Mr. President," the soft voice on the intercom announced, stirring him from an endless stream of restless thoughts. "Mr. Doyle is here to see you."

The president leaned forward and pushed the button. "Thank you. Send him right in." The one person he needed to see now more than the others was his chief-of-staff.

Sleep deprivation, combined with the steady regimen of extra-strong coffee and prescribed stimulants, was beginning to hit the president with alternate bouts of euphoria and anxiety. He wished to God the euphoria would linger. Perhaps he could slip into a temporary but debilitating delirium, he thought, and maybe then he would be forced from public office and that, mercifully, would be the end of that. Let someone else go through this hell, he figured, while he spent the rest of his days hitting golf balls around in the sunny clime of Palm Springs.

No such luck, though. The past hour had been anything but euphoria, and right now he could think of no one he'd rather see than his longtime friend and confidant, Christopher Doyle. He forced himself from his chair, walked to the door, and with a warm handshake that at least made him feel as if he was not alone, greeted the one individual inside the Washington beltway he knew he could trust.

Trust. The word, as he knew all too well, was becoming less recognized in these parts, as old-fashioned as midwestern moral values and as outdated as government ethics, if there was ever such a thing to begin with. These days it was cynically thought of as something people were supposed to have in you, not vice versa.

With Doyle it was different. Selected as chief-of-staff because of his reputation as a longtime Washington insider with a distinctly outsider philosophy, Doyle had established himself as someone who could unequivocally maintain the strictest confidence. Discretion was a commodity clearly lacking in a town infested with political sharks who held ambition and greed above trust and honesty and friendship.

"Chris, come on in."

Christopher Doyle greeted the president enthusiastically. Then, as if by some unspoken protocol, the two men immediately walked to the side door and slipped into the sanctuary of the rose garden. Here, along the covered walkway that meandered past the seclusion of the White House walls, they were always free to talk without the fear of prying ears.

"Any word on the Wesely incident?" the president began. "Intelligence come up with anything?"

"Nothing," Doyle answered. "It's officially been ruled a suicide. Despite how it looked, it was very professional. No trace of evidence anywhere. Intelligence *did* establish a connection between Wesely's murder and that car bombing in Virginia, though."

"What's the connection?"

"Apparently, the journalist involved was a science reporter for the *Washington Chronicle*. Did some stories about the Pentagon a while back, ostensibly with the help of a source no one was able to pin down."

"Wesely?"

Doyle nodded. "Intelligence placed them together on several occasions. Poor bastard must have been waiting for Wesely, who probably had something of importance for him."

"Any idea what that was?"

"Not yet."

"They mention anything about 'timber wolf'?"

"What?"

"Chris, I received a troubling report the other day. A leak of some kind from inside the Pentagon. Timber wolf. What do you make of it?"

"Timber wolf," Doyle whispered, narrowing his eyebrows and repeating the words as if trying to recall the last time he'd heard it. "Inside the Pentagon? I don't know what to make of it. Was there anything else?"

"Something about a meeting to follow, that's it. Intelligence couldn't locate the exact source and didn't have a clue either. Their initial assessment was KGB, perhaps testing a communications signal."

"What do *you* think?" Doyle probed.

The president looked down reflectively at the walkway at his feet and clasped his hands behind him. "I'm not so sure it *was* a test, Chris. I believe it was a specific transmission from someone inside the Pentagon . . . something to do with the upcoming CONDOR flights. I suspected as much the minute the secretary of defense told me about it.

"Hell, if that's true, we may have a serious problem on our hands. A leak like that could threaten national security."

"The more I think about it, the more deeply concerned I am about the whole goddamn program. We have no idea what the full impact of this could be, and I'm not so sure that what we've developed is not going to threaten our own national security. It could be devastating. I believe that, I truly do. Naturally, I can't say so openly. Feel like a damned hypocrite because I can't. But after careful consideration,

Chris, I'm convinced that the way this whole damned mission will be implemented is wrong."

"What the hell are we spending billions for if we're not going to use what we develop to ensure national security?" Doyle asked, somewhat indignantly.

"You spend it so you never *have* to use it," the president answered bluntly. "Are not our nuclear missiles a guarantee that we're never attacked, and therefore we're never forced to use them? I consider that a wise appropriation of funds, even if every one of those warheads continues to sit in the ground well after you and I are gone."

"Yes, but there comes a time when even that kind of strategy begins to break down. I'm afraid we've reached a point when action on this front is the only way to resolve the problem. I know that . . . and you know it as well."

The president then stopped and turned to his friend, the anguish in his eyes revealing his worst suspicions. "I have a legitimate fear, Chris—more so now than ever—that it may have already ended up in the wrong hands. And if it has . . . God help us."

"Jesus Christ, how do you know that?" Doyle asked.

"A few hours ago, I met with General Bridger. His people are convinced that the transmission was a coded message, encrypted as a ten-letter acronym. They're running it through NSA computers and hope to have something for me within the next twenty-four hours. This morning, when they were digging through some classified materials buried in agency files, they found an obscure CONDOR memo with the letters TW buried in the text. TW . . . for timber wolf, they suspect."

"Could they trace it?"

"Didn't have to. The memo was addressed to Colonel Thomas Williams, also having the initials TW. Could be coincidental, we're not sure."

"Williams?" Doyle stiffened. He knew Colonel Williams's Pentagon connection, and he'd heard the man's name mentioned during discussions related to black project funding.

"That's right. We're not certain what he has to do with any of this, but we've put intelligence on alert. They'd been instructed not to do anything that might put him on to us, but once they find out exactly how Williams is involved, they're sure they'll be able to get information out of him. Immunity and a new ID is better than a court-martial and life in a military prison. I'm sure he'll bite."

The president resumed his slow walk, visibly exhausted by a series of events that had swept in like a sudden storm and that now, hour by hour, were beginning to grow into a torrential whirlwind that threatened to blow at him from every direction at once.

"Have you spoken to anyone else at the Pentagon?" Doyle asked.

The president paused as if reflecting deeply on the question, then answered yes.

"Something wrong?"

"I'm not sure, Chris. When I spoke to General McKnight about it, I got the impression he'd already been briefed. The only people who knew of it at the time were intelligence, myself, and now you. We were supposed to maintain level-ten security on this one. Intelligence shouldn't have released that information to anyone else, at least not that quickly."

"Want me to check it out?"

"I'd like to know what the hell's going on here and whether I'm being left out of the loop on this for deniability purposes."

The president paused again, a distant look washing over his face. "I don't know, Chris. I'm worried that we don't have a clue as to where this'll lead . . . that we'll end up with something none of us are prepared for. I don't think we realize what we've done."

The chief-of-staff took hold of the president's arm and gently spun him around. They'd known each other a long time, and had been friends since their earliest days in local, then national, politics. And though they'd come from starkly different backgrounds—Doyle from a family of wealth and social status, the president from a blue-collar textile community that had seen its best days come and go—they'd always had similar beliefs and political philosophies. Now it was his turn to lecture his friend about the realities of being leader of the free world.

"I've had the same fears, the same doubts," Doyle said, trying to be as delicately reassuring as a chief-of-staff could be when advising his president about such matters. "But what the hell can we do about it? Right now there are thirty-five wars going on around the world. Thirty-five. CIA tells us *that's* only the beginning. By next year we could see twice that many, if you count regional conflicts in the old Soviet Union that'll end up as wars eventually. Everywhere you look—Europe, Africa, the Middle East, Asia—torture, executions, 'ethnic cleansing,' terrorism, women and children murdered on the streets, unspeakable violations of the most basic human rights. Where the hell's it going to end? And who's the only power left that has the will or is in any position to help it end?" He hoped the rhetorical questions would eliminate any uncertainty and lead to presidential answers.

Instead the president fell silent. He looked out at the dimly lit rose garden and reflected back to less volatile times. "Thirty-five wars," the president said softly, turning and starting his walk back toward the Oval Office. "You'd never know it. Seems so much more difficult selecting the ones we decide are in our national interest."

"National interest," Doyle interrupted, "is nothing more than a political game of benefit versus risk. Do we benefit from involvement? More important, do your reelection chances benefit? To what extent? Does the benefit of *not* becoming involved outweigh the risk of creating global disorder? The world's becoming smaller and more complex. So many ethnic wars. So many economic conflicts tied inextricably to our own economy and, consequently, to our holding onto the White House. We've got to shoulder some of that responsibility, if not for them, then at least for ourselves."

The president conceded the point. "It's true," he said. "But how certain can we be that we'll not undermine stability instead . . . and then watch as the world falls apart before our eyes?''

''It *is* falling apart, dammit. And don't you think that's justification enough to implement WORLD ORDER?'' Doyle asked. ''To stop this madness?''

He did once. He wasn't sure any longer. A part of him believed that his was a moral obligation, a destiny, if you will, to help achieve global stability. Part of him, admittedly, realized the economic benefit, since war-torn nations made lousy trading partners, after all. But another part of him genuinely believed that allowing this genie out of its bottle was an arrogant mistake that would cost future generations dearly.

The light drizzle that had fallen steadily over Washington throughout much of the evening had suddenly turned into a drenching rain that added a darkness to his already somber mood. At no time in his political career had the president felt the all-consuming loneliness he felt at that moment. Having overestimated his ability to use Washington for his own political gains, he'd become increasingly obsessed with his legacy and terrified that his would be an administration remembered more for scandal and corruption than for anything else. And now, toward the end of his term in office, he knew that as long as investigations about him were ongoing, as long as the evidence of his offenses mounted and the threat of indictment or impeachment loomed over his head, he could guide neither his own destiny nor the destiny of his nation, and that the only way he could ever escape the reality of his presidency was to turn inward, the only place he could find peace in the midst of torment. His despair, incomprehensible to anyone but him, was unrelenting in its tenacity and maddening in its ability to overshadow every aspect of his life.

And then, as happened so often throughout his political career, and especially since his last election, it became terribly clear to him that regardless of what one believed about the presidency, he was almost humiliatingly powerless. An elected puppet. A figurehead who, despite his political label, was in reality neither Democrat nor Republican, conservative nor liberal. He was whatever he was required to be by those who stood in the shadows of government and pulled the far-reaching strings of power. It nauseated him to think of himself in that way, but there he was . . . a man who had finally had enough and was determined to change it all.

"Intellectually, I can see your point," the president said. "Instinctually, I'm not so sure."

"Have you expressed your concerns to anyone else?" Doyle asked grimly.

"No." The president's answer was quick and emphatic. "You know I can't do that. There's too much at stake. Too many people involved. And now, with world and domestic situations the way they are, I suppose there's no turning back, even if I could. No, I feel like a lone voice on this one. A voice that's not about to go public."

"What will you do?"

"There's really only one option, I suppose. Go ahead with the mission and pray to God we're not making a catastrophic mistake."

"And you're certain you want to stay the course, even with this timber wolf thing?" Doyle asked.

"Hell, I'm not certain of anything right now. If intelligence is right about timber wolf, what we overheard may have been some sort of code, perhaps linked to WORLD ORDER in some way." As much as he hated to think that that was true, he knew that if timber wolf was a plot to misuse America's newest and deadliest technology, the world was indeed at peril.

"And if we discover what timber wolf means?" Doyle prodded.

"We'll have to make a decision then . . . regardless of how that decision affects us personally."

"Okay, I'm with you all the way on this, no matter what you decide, no matter what happens." Doyle placed his hand on the president's shoulder in an act of solidarity and saw in his friend's eyes a look of terror he'd not seen before.

"Thanks, Chris," the president said. "You know, I've often asked myself what good this new technology is going to do if the only thing it offers the world is another unspeakable method of waging war. At least nuclear weapons—unimaginably destructive as they are—could be seen. You know where the damn things are. You can count them; put your finger on them. You pretty much know who has them, though even *that's* getting more difficult. But this. How the hell is this going to be controlled once it gets out? I'm afraid we've outdone ourselves, Chris. Not because we've managed to create the most devastating weapon the world has ever known, but because the poor bastards, whoever they are, wherever they are, won't even know it's being used."

"You might change your mind about that after you look at this," Doyle said flatly, taking a sheet of paper from his jacket and handing it to the president.

"What is it?"

"CIA report. Came in this morning. If this doesn't convince you, nothing will."

The president slipped his glasses on and quickly scanned the page top to bottom. "Jesus Christ," he whispered. "Are these figures accurate?"

"Even if inflated, it's pretty damn grim."

"Jesus Christ," the president repeated, his voice quivering with anger. "It's worse than I thought. I suppose there's no other way, is there?"

He handed the report back to Doyle, shook his head at the very idea of how quickly it was all happening, and fell into a dead silence as they stepped back through the doors of the Oval Office.

chapter thirteen

Less than three hours from Adam Wesely's suburban Virginia home, Linda veered off an exit and sped onto a small winding road that angled sharply north from highway 55. Six tortuous miles later, dangling loosely from a rusted chain that stretched from tree to tree across a gravel driveway, was the sign Maria had told them to look for.

Private Road
No Trespassing

Linda pulled up just short of the chain, fumbled for the key ring stuck somewhere in the bottom of her purse, and when she'd found it, handed it to Jack. Her hands were trembling, her mouth so dry she could barely find enough saliva to moisten her lips. Since leaving Washington, all she could think about was the crash, Adam's parting words to her, and the sight of Colonel Williams walking out of her lab.

She looked out her window, then up at a leaden sky that appeared ready to open up, and prayed that there was some logical explanation for what had happened to Adam, that everything thus far would turn out to be nothing more than a fertile imagination gone wild and conjuring up distorted images of intrigue and murder. In her heart, though, she knew better.

''After you undo the lock,'' Linda said, ''better put the chain back across the road then lock it up again. I don't want anyone suspecting we're up there.'' She then shot quick, furtive glances in every direction.

Jack removed the padlock and dragged the chain across the driveway, waiting for her to drive through. He stretched it back and replaced the lock as she'd instructed. Behind him, he could see that the main road was isolated, not a sign of a car or truck evident for the past several minutes. After taking a final nervous look around, he then slid back into the seat next to Linda. "Better hurry," he ordered. "If someone else finds out about this place . . . if Maria slips up . . . God, I hope she doesn't . . . I'd hate to meet up with whoever did Adam in."

"Okay," Linda said. "If whatever we're looking for is up here, an hour should be long enough for us to find it."

The quarter-mile stretch of dusty gravel and thickly overgrown evergreen forest contrasted starkly with the filthy concrete and barren asphalt of Washington, D.C. Deep green pines, towering above the dense undergrowth of still-dormant bushes and broadleaf shrubs, lined the driveway like a dark, formidable tunnel. It was no wonder Adam had remained so protective of this place, Linda thought. It seemed to her a perfect refuge from the sterile, hectic lifestyle she knew he despised so much since arriving in Washington more than twenty years ago.

Linda hit the brake pedal abruptly and shifted the transmission into park. The sight of a cabin so isolated that it was nowhere within earshot of another human being had suddenly magnified the vulnerability she felt. How easily anyone who wanted to kill them could do so as readily as they'd killed Adam, she thought, then bury their bodies where no one would find them for months, for years, maybe never.

Jack tapped on his leg nervously, the sweat that had begun as droplets now running down his face and beard in ribbon-sized streams. "I don't think we should park out here in the open. If those guys from the Pentagon find out about this place and decide to come up here, we're dead."

Linda made a sharp U-turn and drove back to a dense stand of trees and bushes she'd seen earlier and now figured would serve as perfect cover for the dark brown car. Then, after pulling behind a row of evergreens, she and Jack covered their tracks with fallen leaves and branches and headed up to the cabin, confident that even in a worst case scenario, it wouldn't be the car that would give them away.

"You know, Jack," Linda said, still looking suspiciously in every direction, "if we get through this, I don't think I'll ever be the same. I don't think either of us will."

"If we get through this," Jack answered, "and find out that Adam was linked to or knew about some high-tech plot that got Peter and himself killed, I don't know that anyone will ever be the same."

"You're probably right," Linda sighed. "I just can't help thinking what a damn lie it all is. It doesn't matter what the hell you do, what you think, or who you vote for. Doesn't matter a goddamn bit, does it?"

"Hey, you're finally catching on," Jack replied with the typical sarcasm his voice took on whenever he spoke of government matters. "Try not to think about it too much. You might lose faith in Uncle Sam completely. You might even realize you've been living a lie all along, that people you thought you knew would rather see you dead than have you screw up their plans. Believe me, if funding in the private sector wasn't so bad, I wouldn't put up with these toads another five minutes."

"But we still don't know what any of this is all about, though; whether it's even the government that's behind Adam's death. I'm not ready to point a finger yet. And the more I think about it, the more I believe there's more going on here."

"Oh? You have a theory, do you?"

"I'm not sure what I have yet. It was a gut feeling I got when John and I were looking at General McKnight's computer files. Something I couldn't put my finger on. There was something between those words on the screen, something that was staring me right in the face that I just couldn't see."

"How do you figure?" Jack asked.

"With all the access we have to government files and research reports, don't you think we would have gotten wind of a Pentagon project called TIMBER WOLF, if it was some new prototype? We've managed to hear about everything else, for Christ's sake, why not TIMBER WOLF? And what about CONDOR? What the hell is *that* supposed to be? It doesn't make sense.''

''If this is one of those unauthorized black projects no one's ever supposed to find out about, of course it's not gonna make sense,'' Jack said. ''You think they'd let you in on something like this? Don't flatter yourself.''

''I'm telling you, Jack, there was something there.'' The resoluteness in her voice made Jack back off. ''And I'm damn sure going to find out what it was.''

The two fell silent and quickened their pace. The very notion that they may have stumbled across a black project so secret that it cost Peter and Adam their lives hit Linda like a brick. Her legs weakened at the thought, and it was all she could do to put one wobbly foot in front of the other as she forced herself on.

Hundred-foot pine trees seemed to stare down like angry sentries, following their every move and whistling mournfully as the cold forest air rushed swiftly through their gnarled fingers. The road grew narrower, winding sharply through the dense forest for what seemed like miles before ending flush against a wall of cedar logs. The two-story cabin, large and solid like a fortress, was itself as uninviting as the forest and gave the appearance of a hideaway more than a home.

''Some place, eh?'' Jack whispered.

''I feel like a rabbit caught in an open field,'' Linda whispered. ''I really don't want to stay here any longer than we have to.''

Though the wooden stairs looked firm enough, they let out a series of creaky complaints that echoed against the surrounding trees as Linda and Jack simultaneously climbed to the front porch.

Linda reached into her pocket and took out two pairs of latex surgical gloves and the set of keys Maria had given her. She handed one pair of gloves to Jack and, with a snap, slipped the other onto her fingers. She inserted the key and turned it, listening as the click of tumblers rang out like a firecracker across the wide porch. Taking a deep breath, she opened the door, recoiling at the sharp, stagnant air. Smells of aged dust, mildewed wood, and long months of emptiness and neglect suddenly engulfed her. Shaking her head, she pushed the door open enough to slip her face through the narrow fissure. Empty. Musty. And though she knew from the stench and the cobwebs that no one had set foot inside for at least a year, slid cautiously through as small an opening as possible to keep the high-pitched creak of the door to a minimum.

Jack followed, opening the door just wide enough to accommodate his forty-two-inch waist. They were now both in, and though neither uttered a word, each felt Adam's presence among the quiet of the surroundings.

"Jack, lock the door behind you. I'd feel more secure."

They agreed to work fast and stay no longer than an hour. Linda's heart was beating so hard she was nauseated, her mouth feeling as if she'd just chewed hot sand. In the middle of the cabin, a large common room surrounded them. Beneath their feet, wide wooden planks, crisscrossed with a thousand scratches and chips, indicated years of heavy pacing. Across the room, two red-and-green plaid couches faced each other, their oak legs sinking an inch into a thick, colorful Navaho rug that matched perfectly the tapestries hanging from each of the four walls.

They crept between the couches, past the stump of a redwood that served as an asymmetric coffee table and looked as if it had grown right out of the wooden floor, and stopped in front of a massive stone fireplace. Elk antlers, mounted two feet above a mantle as thick as a stout tree trunk, stretched six feet across, nearly touching the bookcases on either side.

They continued cautiously through the common room, entering a country-style kitchen lined with copper pots that hung like shiny carcasses from hooks above the island stove. A thick antique table was barely visible, piled high with dishes and cups. To the left, framing the breakfast area, a large picture window looked out on a mirrored lake that reflected a row of jagged peaks beyond it.

As Linda gazed at what seemed almost artificial in its regal splendor, there settled a deep sadness in her heart at losing a longtime colleague and a good friend. She looked at the glasslike lake, the shimmering reflection of emerald mountains, the meadow, which seemed almost lonely in its dormant stillness, and her blood boiled at the thought of Adam's life so needlessly cut short by those who thought a secret project was worth a human life.

"Come on, Linda," John said nervously, the pitch of his voice noticeably higher. "The bedrooms must be upstairs."

The two retraced their steps across the wooden planks and climbed the stairs to the second floor. A small loft overlooked the spacious common room and offered an even grander view of the massive twenty-foot beams and stone fireplace. Two rooms were set on opposite ends of the upper floor; one, a neatly organized guest room, from the looks of it, the other, a cluttered chamber of books, papers, clothes, and dusty furniture. They climbed over a stack of books and entered what they assumed to be Adam's bedroom.

"Bingo!" A reddish glow suddenly reappeared on Jack's ashen face. "This has gotta be Adam's room. Look at this place." He pointed to an early American bed, then to a matching dressing table flanked by gray metal filing cabinets on which papers and old books were stacked nearly two feet high.

"From the looks of this, we're the first ones to come up here in a while," Linda said, and with her finger wiped across the top of one of the piles, noting the clean line that was left behind. "Must be a quarter inch worth of dust."

"At least we know we're gonna have the first crack at whatever's here," Jack said. "Let's go through these files and see what we come up with."

"I'll start over there." Linda pointed at the file cabinet nearest the door. "You can start on the other one." She rushed across the room, slid open the top drawer, and began thumbing through green folders packed so tightly they felt as if they'd been glued shut.

"Remember, Linda . . . an hour . . . we need to be outta here in an hour." Jack turned and opened a file cabinet drawer that bulged with folders and loose papers stuffed haphazardly between them. "Jesus Christ. The guy was a damn pack rat. Look at this shit."

"Come on, Jack. Just look, don't complain. Remember . . . an hour. And try to put everything back as neatly as you take it out so it doesn't look like anything's been tampered with."

The two furiously picked through the maze before them, their fingers running through file after file of bureaucratic paperwork. From the sheer number, it seemed insurmountable. Two file cabinets, full. Thirty minutes had elapsed; thirty minutes left.

"Any luck, Jack?"

"Nothing. We could have found this stuff anywhere. You?"

"Nothing here either. I'm getting a feeling that if there *was* something, we'd have found it by now. I'm gonna take a walk through the house again . . . just to make sure we didn't overlook anything."

"Don't disturb anything. And be careful."

Linda wiped the sweat from her forehead and tiptoed down the stairs, still uneasy about being there in the first place. She scanned the common room inch by inch, log by log, searching for anyplace she thought Adam might have hidden something he didn't want left out in the open or buried in files. Sweeping her fingers between suspiciously wide cracks in the hefty log walls, probing behind pictures, looking under furniture, Linda eventually made her way to the bookcase and stared fiercely at the assortment of titles, thinking that maybe a particular book might be a potential hiding place. She'd reached the point of desperation. Her eyes stopped at *War and Peace*. A good place to start, she figured, snatching the Tolstoy classic off the shelf and flipping through it, nearly tearing the dulled, yellow pages. Nothing. Another promising title: *War of the Worlds*. "Yes," she whispered, flipping through that one even more violently. *Nothing. Damn.* Linda scanned frantically, tearing through title after title she thought might hold a clue or a note that could tell her something. Anything. Dostoyevski, Dickens, Shakespeare, Hawthorne, Wolfe, Poe. Master storytellers, all. Yet none who could tell her what she needed to know.

Ten minutes left. Discouraged, Linda replaced the last book and shoved it angrily into the bookcase, evoking a loud crack that echoed through the room.

"Hey, you okay down there?" yelled Jack upon hearing the book crash into its resting place.

"Yeah. I'm coming back up. Nothing here."

Linda headed back toward the stairs, this time walking along the other side of the coffee table. And then, as if her body had smashed against some invisible barrier, she froze. She cocked her head and listened. It creaked! The floor beneath the rug, in a way that sent hollow echoes through the quiet room, creaked! She rolled back and forth with the ball of her shoe and listened again. Then, dropping to her knees, she pulled the rug back and saw what looked like the faint outline of a small door. She plunged her fingernails into the crevice of the outline, trying futilely to pry it open. Trembling fingers didn't help. Her racing heart only added to the clumsiness that had suddenly infected her.

"Jack, get down here, quick!" Linda screamed in desperation, forgetting the fear she'd had a minute ago and instead scratching frantically on the door, nearly breaking her fingernails. "Down here. There's a hidden door beneath this rug. I need help getting it open."

Jack lumbered down the stairs and fell to his knees next to Linda. Flipping open a small pocket knife, he wedged it into one side of the door, pushing down on the handle repeatedly. The door moved slightly. He continued along each side until the wood became loose. Then, with a determined final push, the trap door popped open, revealing a dark space almost three feet square. Laying on the bottom was a padlocked rectangular box.

Linda stared into the pit, afraid to touch what they knew

was *it*, then gave Jack a wary, halfhearted victory smile before reaching down and removing the prize. She replaced the wooden door, tapped it down tightly with the heel of her hand, then covered the floor with the throw rug exactly as it had been before. They'd done it. They had it. Whatever it was, they knew they had it.

The metal box was black and heavy. A small padlock sealed its contents and convinced Linda that it must have contained something important to be hidden in the manner it had.

"This is it Jack. I know it. It's gotta be."

"We've been here over an hour, Linda. Let's get the hell outta here before it's too late. We can examine the box later. We can—" Jack suddenly froze, his head cocked ninety degrees to one side, listening.

"What's wrong?" Linda asked, her eyes widening as she watched the blood drain from Jack's face once again.

"Shhh. You hear something outside?" Still on his knees alongside Linda, Jack crawled clumsily over to the window, peered out, and shot back down. "Jesus Christ Almighty. There's someone here." Jack turned quickly and made his way back to where Linda was kneeling. "Let's go out the back door, fast."

Clambering to their feet, Linda and Jack remained bent forward from the waist, scurried and weaved through the common room as if negotiating a minefield, eventually making their way to the kitchen before straightening up.

Footsteps thumped heavily against the front steps, and by their sound Linda could tell there were more than two.

"Hurry, let's get out," she whispered. And as she reached for the lock, she realized in horror that she was staring at a deadbolt. No inside latch. Then, remembering the keys, she thrust her hand into her pocket and fumbled for the key ring. Empty! She listened as the footsteps, now on the porch, grew louder. She felt her body on fire. She shoved the box into Jack's fingers, which she saw were suddenly so paralyzed with fear he could barely open them. Frantically, she searched her other pocket and heard the welcome clink of metal keys. As she fished them out, Linda heard the front doorknob turn. In seconds, she knew, whoever was out there would be inside. Moving quickly, she inserted the key, turned it, and opened the door.

Jack tiptoed onto the back porch. Linda followed, holding her breath and quietly locking the deadbolt behind her. They both stood on the back porch for a second, breathing a heavy sigh of relief, but vividly aware of the danger they faced as long as they remained anywhere near that cabin.

The now familiar creak of hinges shot through the common room, and Linda's first thought was that Maria had been coerced into talking, and that whoever was there now had to eliminate any loose ends. She vise-gripped Jack's arm, pulling him toward the back stairs, then shut her eyes tightly as she saw the box shift precariously in Jack's hands.

Jack's face blanched, and his breathing turned deep and erratic as he clung to the box with both hands. "Hurry," he said, then, in totally uncharacteristic fashion, glided silently down the back stairs like a fat but agile gazelle.

Facing them was an open meadow that stretched between the cabin and the lake, that was about as inviting as an empty parking lot encircled by snipers. There were no bushes to hide in, nor trees for cover. And in a minute, more likely seconds, they knew the back door would open and they would surely find themselves eye to eye with the same .44 Magnum that blew part of Adam's head away.

"Shit," Jack whispered. "There's nowhere to go. If we go back around to the front, they'll see us for sure. If we stay *here*, we're dead."

Linda and Jack heard a crash of dishes coming from the kitchen. In a panic, they ran along the side of the cabin, looking for a place to hide.

"There! Down there!" Linda pointed to a small opening leading to a crawl space. She grabbed at Jack's arm again and dragged him kicking toward it. They hit the ground running, and with a continuous motion rolled beneath the cabin and slithered like nervous reptiles across a sheet of cold dirt that clung to their drenched skin like a magnet. Beetles and spiders, displaced from their dark resting place by the commotion, crawled across Linda's fingers and arms, then scattered in every direction. She bit down on hard grit and felt things crawling inside her mouth. And as she gagged at the tingling sensation of something trying to find its way out, reflexively stretched her tongue across her teeth and bottom lip and watched a pillbug fall into a pool of saliva and bury itself in the dirt a few inches below her face. A wave of nausea suddenly overcame her, but she recovered quickly when she heard the back door open and a voice call out.

"Colonel. Doesn't look like anyone's here."

Colonel! The word instantly made Linda nauseated again. He was there, she thought, following the same trail, looking for the same thing—a piece of loose evidence someone wanted desperately to make sure did not exist. But as she glanced over at Jack, who was still clinging tightly to the metal box, she knew it most surely did.

From where she lay, Linda could barely see what was going on. The crawl space, thank God, with a lip of earth surrounding it, was deeper than she'd expected. She held her breath and raised her head just high enough to see a pair of shoes above the mound. The toes, black and spit-shined enough to cast a reflection of the cabin, were pointing toward the crawl space.

"Let's go inside and go through the files," the voice ordered.

Linda held her breath at the sound of the distinctive southern tone.

"Want me to search the area, sir?" the other man asked.

"It's not necessary. Place looks clean. It won't take as long if we both search inside."

Linda watched the black shoes turn and march from sight. "Thank God," she whispered. "Thank God." And only then did she let out a deep sigh and drop her face to the dirt, ignoring the wetness of a large spider she'd just smashed beneath her cheek.

Jack, grimacing from the awkward position he found himself in, nonetheless turned to Linda and gave a thumbs-up sign. He moved his legs in exaggerated slow motion, careful not to stir the silence, then in relief buried his face in his hands.

"Try to stay relaxed while they're up there," Linda whispered. She saw the color returning to Jack's fat cheeks and added, "It may be a while before we can move."

As she listened to the nonstop clamor of a cabin being torn apart, Linda's mind raced with mixed emotions and thoughts of Peter. She stretched out on the cold dirt, one minute visualizing herself wrapped in Peter's warm and loving arms, the next, imagining him involved in something that may have cost him his life. She didn't understand why he wouldn't have told her and why, instead, he'd left her a note that she couldn't even decipher.

"Linda, you hear that?"

Nearly two hours after they'd hidden beneath the cabin, Jack's head popped up at the sound of footsteps above them. By now, they were both shivering from the damp earth and the icy breeze that stabbed mercilessly at them like needles. And then, just when the urge to crawl out and stretch in the warmth of the sun was so overpowering that in another few minutes they wouldn't have cared what happened to either of them, their ordeal was about to end.

"Shhh," Linda whispered as softly as she could. "Let's wait till we hear the car engine before we make a move."

Linda and Jack laid their heads back down and waited. The vibration of heavy footsteps, directly above them in the same room as the trap door, moved quickly, then stopped abruptly. A shrill creak resonated beneath the cabin like a gunshot. Linda, her heart racing, thought for sure that just as she had done, the men were now staring down at the rug, frozen by the sound of a hollow creak that rifled up at them, and surely were about to dive to the floor and discover the hidden space beneath their feet.

"Dear God, please no," she whispered. Linda waited to hear the floor panel being ripped open. It was as though time were standing still, as if Colonel Williams knew it was there and at that moment was glaring down at that throw rug with those cold eyes, relishing his find, preparing to fall to his knees to tear it back and discover the outline of a secret hiding place. But rather than hearing the thud of knees as she expected, she heard the creak again, then listened as the footsteps faded and moved toward the front door.

Linda exhaled slowly, shut her eyes for a moment, and murmured, "Thank God."

"Listen." Jack turned his head to one side, picking up the faint sound of a car engine as it idled for a moment, then sped away. "They're leaving."

Linda placed her hand on Jack's. "Let's wait a little longer . . . just in case."

Fifteen minutes had elapsed before Linda felt certain the Colonel was gone. "Let's crawl out real slow and make sure everything's okay," she whispered.

The two scientists, looking more like mounds of crawling dirt, inched their way toward the opening of the crawl space. They peeked out, inhaling deep breaths of fresh air.

"All clear," Linda announced, glancing left then right before rolling soldierlike out onto the grass. Jack followed, still gripping the metal box as tightly as if it had been sewn to his skin.

"We should split up and meet at the front of the cabin separately," Jack said. "You go around that side, I'll go this way."

Linda and Jack separated, walked slowly toward the opposite ends of the cabin, and caught a last look at each other before carefully turning the corners. Linda found herself tiptoeing, though she was certain the car she heard fade away was carrying the colonel and his assistant back to Washington at that very moment. But since locking eyes with Colonel Williams at the airport, she'd been suspicious of everything. Her stomach was tied in one enormous knot. With slow, exaggerated movements, Linda felt herself wading through an imaginary quagmire, the long muscles in her thighs and calves so stiff and heavy they were like immovable iron rods. The quagmire crept up to her chest, making her breathing more labored. But a few more steps and she knew she'd reach the front of the cabin.

She slid her fingers around the left porch railing and stopped. Holding her breath, she peered around. Empty. No trace of the colonel or the car. She'd won. She had in the metal box what she believed were copies of documents that Adam had planned to reveal, and she was convinced that Colonel Williams had no knowledge of their existence. She'd won. She walked confidently around to the front of the cabin, then felt a sudden jolt go through her at the sound of a voice directly behind her.

"Stop right there. Turn around slowly. Hands up where I can see them."

Linda's stomach was suddenly back in her throat. After all they'd gone through, to come this close, to have it all end in this way. She shut her eyes and turned to face her captor, expecting the worst. If he was going to kill her, she thought, she hoped that at least he'd make it quick. A single bullet . . . preferably in the head . . . just like Adam got. She opened her eyes slowly, afraid that once she did, she would be witness to her own execution, and found herself facing squarely down the barrel of a .44 Magnum.

"May I ask what you're doing here, Dr. Franklin?" asked a mountain of a man outfitted in fatigues and dark glasses.

Linda wondered how this military man, someone she'd never seen before, even knew her name. But from his appearance, she suspected that he was one of Colonel Williams's goons, and now that she was looking at him, pictured him waiting for Adam with that same .44 as the elevator doors opened. "We were friends of Adam Wesely's and . . ."

"We?" The human wall squinted, quickly scanning the area for signs of anyone else. "Someone else here with you?"

Linda thought quickly. "Uh . . . no. I'm alone. I meant we, like we at NASA were friends of Adam's. I came up here to find something of mine that Adam brought with him to the cabin.'' Linda dropped her head and realized at once that she looked as though she'd been digging in the dirt for the past two hours.

''I don't think so, Dr. Franklin. Now, you wanna tell me what the hell you were lookin' for? From the looks of it, something buried, maybe?'' He raised the .44 to Linda's face.

''I parked down the road and fell down an embankment on my way up here. I told you, I came up to get—'' She thought for a second. ''A copy of our annual budget report. Ours is missing.'' The lie sounded embarrassingly transparent.

The .44 drew closer to Linda's face. ''We'll see. Let's go down to my jeep. Colonel Williams already left for Washington in his car, but I'm sure he'll turn back and have plenty of questions for you the minute I call this in.''

The giant, who had to be packing at least two hundred fifty pounds on his six-foot-five-inch frame, grabbed her arm and spun her around. With a sharp poke of his thick fingers, he pushed her effortlessly toward the road.

Linda couldn't believe what was happening. Where the hell was Jack? she thought as she felt the cold metal of the gun against her back.

And then, as she began to tremble at the very idea of being lead to slaughter by one of Colonel Williams's henchmen, she heard a sickening crack followed a second later by a thud that sounded as though a tree had come crashing down to the forest floor. She spun around and gasped at the sight of Jack standing over the large, prone body, blood flowing down the side of the square face from a gash on the back of the head. In Jack's hand was a bloody metal box.

''If we don't find anything in this damn box,'' Jack said, ''at least it was good for something.''

''God, I'm glad to see you,'' Linda said, letting out a prolonged sigh of relief.

''I'll remember that,'' he said. ''We better get outta here before this bastard wakes up.''

chapter fourteen

A high-pitched buzz broke the empty silence of the conference room, and with it General McKnight's trancelike gaze at the wall map. Lurching forward, he punched the intercom button and answered sharply.

"Yes."

"General," the voice announced. "Colonel Williams has just arrived."

"Very well. Send him in."

McKnight, his mind increasingly withdrawn from everything but TIMBER WOLF, marched swiftly across a room that served him more as a refuge these days. He'd studied the mission route a hundred times, watched the flight take off in his mind at least a thousand. He'd be overtaken by near paralyzing fear over possible failure one minute and find himself laughing at his invincibility the next; weep uncontrollably at how grim a future he believed his country and his grandchildren would face if he did nothing, and admit openly his willingness to kill without mercy or remorse if threatened by anyone who dared try to stop him.

For without him, TIMBER WOLF was dead. And without a mission he was convinced would bring the country back from the brink of disaster, nothing in his life would matter any longer.

"Tom, I'm disappointed you had to miss the meeting," McKnight said as he held open the door and greeted Colonel Williams with a vigorous handshake. "Ended hours ago. Everything go okay? Any trouble?"

"None," Colonel Williams said with the satisfaction of a man who knew he had everything under control.

"Were you thorough?" McKnight probed, the smile vanishing quickly from his craggy face.

"We searched through every file in the place. There was nothing there. Not one document referring specifically to TIMBER WOLF . . . or to CONDOR for that matter."

The general paused for a moment, kneading thick, sweaty fingers. "Not one document? Not one note or file? Odd. Doesn't make sense. And you searched everywhere?" he asked nervously, the apparent distrust in his voice more obvious these days. And on this day, even Colonel Williams was not beyond his suspicions.

"Everywhere, Ben. There *was* no document."

"How'd the place look? Clean? Recently visited?" More suspicion in his voice.

"Place was a damn mess, though we *did* see some signs of activity that probably had nothing to do with this. I'm sure we'd have found a document or a report if there *was* one. One of my men remained behind to secure the area and continue a thorough search of the grounds, just in case. He'll report to me as soon as he gets back."

Something wasn't right, General McKnight kept thinking. *Not one document. Not one. In the entire place, no less.* There had to be a missing piece of evidence, he thought as he gazed intently into the Colonel's gray eyes. A report, a file, a slip of paper. Something. He knew it was out there, somewhere. Perhaps Colonel Williams had it and was hiding it, he suspected with enough paranoia to fill the room. If he was, he'd find out soon enough.

"No trace of evidence left behind here . . . in Washington?" the General then asked.

"None that we could find, Ben. Everything looked clean."

"His office?"

"Searched completely. Nothing."

"The elevator?"

"Only the body. We made certain."

"The hospital?"

"Taken care of. All records confiscated."

"And the medical examiner?"

"We explained the penalty for releasing information. I've been assured that Dr. Salter will be in full compliance."

With some relief, General McKnight extended his arm and ushered Colonel Williams into a partitioned area of the conference room where a small but formal cubicle had been reserved for the most private meetings.

They sank into a pair of brown Italian leather chairs and began loosening their ties, as though once in this sanctuary the formality of rank no longer mattered. Separating the two was a teakwood coffee table on which rested two crystal goblets, a carafe of high-priced brandy, and next to it a wooden humidor brimming with expensive cigars. Without a word, each man removed a pair of dark brown Davidoffs and initiated the ritual that had obviously been performed on many occasions before this one: clipping, lighting, taking several quick puffs, then deliberately holding and savoring the sweet taste of rich tobacco before releasing its dense, white smoke outward from puckered lips.

The smoke swirled out and up, settling like a fine mist between the general and the colonel, momentarily shielding their faces behind the gossamer veil. When the cloud dissipated, General McKnight, looking more concerned than usual, leaned forward and fixed his stare directly at Colonel Williams.

"Tom, I didn't want to mention this to the rest of the group . . . until I was sure."

"What is it?"

"There's talk around the White House that the president has serious concerns about CONDOR. First the crash in eighty-eight, which was bad enough. But now this."

"What kind of concerns?" Colonel Williams asked, the fissures in his face deepening into jagged ravines.

"We got lucky this time. It could've been much worse. We're not sure yet if the president is considering putting CONDOR on hold until more safeguards are developed."

"What does that mean for the scheduled test flights?"

"We're not certain. I have a meeting with the president tomorrow at noon. If it's true, I'll know."

"You don't seriously think he'd pull the plug, do you?" asked Williams almost disbelievingly.

McKnight shook his head, knowing full well the president's limited ability to do much of anything these days. "No, I don't think so. Too many convoluted security procedures to follow before a black program like this is touched. It's out of reach. Besides, CONDOR is critical for implementing WORLD ORDER. He damn well knows that. His people know that. He also realizes that if the plug is pulled now, the entire future of next century's U.S. military policy and readiness goes to shit. They would never allow him to do that. No, I think CONDOR's a safe bet."

"I hope the hell you're right. The last thing we need right now is a damn hit on the president of the United States."

The general shot Colonel Williams an ominous look that made the sudden silence of the room seem almost tomblike. "I'm confident we won't need to do that," he said without a trace of emotion. "But if we have to . . ."

General McKnight reached over and removed the stopper from the large crystal decanter, feeling no need to finish his sentence. He filled two goblets half full with expensive brandy, lifted one between his fingers, and placed it to his lips. He then took a long, satisfying sip and leaned back against his chair. "What about Dr. Franklin?" he asked.

"What about her?"

"Is she a threat? Do we need to be concerned?"

"I'm not sure yet. We've had our people watching her ever since the investigation in New Hampshire."

"Anything suspicious about her activities?"

"As far as we can tell, no."

General McKnight took an exaggerated drag of his cigar, then rolled it between his fingers and thumb to feel the smooth wrap of expensive tobacco. And after letting out another long, slow stream of thick smoke, said, "I've seen reports on her. That she'd tried to find out more than she needed to after her husband's disappearance back in eighty-eight. You think she's still trying to uncover anything?"

"As far as any subsequent reports we have on her, no. We believe she gave up on it long ago."

"And now?" McKnight asked. "After this recent crash?"

"I've got my people tapping her lines right now. If we get any indication she's beginning an independent investigation, we'll deal with it."

"As long as you're sure . . . and as long as you deal with it," McKnight said. "I want your people to keep close contact with anyone she associates with. I want to know everything she does, everyone she talks to or sleeps with. There's no room for error. None."

"Understood."

"Any sign of anything out of the ordinary and you take care of it immediately." The general followed the threat by placing his cigar—now sporting half an inch of gray ash from its end—between his yellowing teeth. He then grinned, looking confidently relaxed knowing that despite the setback of the crash, everything was proceeding according to plan and nothing or no one, as far as he was concerned, was in any position to stop them.

"Tom," the General continued, his mouth curling downward into a sardonic scowl as he pulled the cigar from his face. "Nothing interferes with this. Nothing. I want it understood that so much as thinking about coming forward with information will be regarded as a threat to our national interest."

"I think Wesely put an end to that," the colonel replied. "The assassination sent shock waves through the system. I wouldn't worry about defectors. Certainly we can maintain security for another three weeks."

The general's eyes narrowed into reptilian slits as he leaned forward and phrased a question that hinted more of mistrust than curiosity. "Are you sure, Tom? When I spoke to General Bridger today, he asked me if I'd ever heard of something called TIMBER WOLF." He waited for a reaction.

"What! How could he know?" Colonel Williams tensed

up, his face turning to stone. "Who would have leaked that?"

"That's what I'm trying to get to the bottom of. Apparently someone got careless. Too careless." McKnight watched Colonel Williams's face the entire time, looking for any trace of nervousness that might give him away. "The president was briefed, and now there's a full goddamn investigation. Our intelligence people have their best experts trying to track it down."

"Anything so far?"

"They're guessing it's an acronym, but without anything else, there's no way they'll be able to crack it . . . unless there's something out there . . . something Wesely may have left behind."

General McKnight, though he'd tried to remain optimistic, was fearful that *something* was still out there. The thought of it consumed him as nothing else did. And though he wouldn't say so openly, he believed that it might even have been Colonel Williams who'd gotten careless. He settled into his seat and, for now, quickly changed the subject.

"Times have certainly changed, my friend." The general, when not discussing the mission, relished talking politics, particularly when it involved domestic policy. These days, the talk was increasingly laced with a cynicism that seemed to reach inside of him and rip away whatever hope he had left of working within the system to change the course of human events. He thought back to the time he'd considered retiring from the military and running for public office. But the more he'd thought of it, though, the more he had realized that his would be one insignificant voice among an endless sea of corrupt politicians, and that he could do more to change the direction of policy from where he sat than he could from inside the halls of Congress.

"It's not like it used to be, is it?" he went on almost nostalgically. "When all we had to worry about were the goddamn Soviets. Hell, now we have to worry about our own damn government. Idiot legislators who just don't care or are too damned stupid to realize they're giving it all away."

"You're right," Colonel Williams agreed, nodding his head obsequiously. "Times *have* changed, but as long as America exists, it'll have enemies. It's always had enemies. You know that as well as anyone."

"It's never had enemies like this," McKnight lashed back. "They're inside our borders . . . our institutions . . . some of 'em sitting on their asses in Congress right now, selling out, selling their souls because they're either too scared not to or too goddamn greedy to even care."

General McKnight, a hardened veteran of two wars, had long grown weary of what he considered baby boomer politicians who'd spent the sixties smoking pot and burning flags and were now telling him—*him*—someone who'd half a dozen times nearly died for his country—that it was *theirs* to govern and do with as they damn well saw fit. Pukes, he'd call them disparagingly. Toadies who, by some fluke of the democratic process, or because no one gave a shit during the last few elections, had blown into office with their perverted idealism and had no idea what the hell they were doing.

"You know, Tom, I was a fool thinking that maybe things would change. Nothing changes unless you change it. Apathy is the one thing history and governments can always rely on. Everyone gets sick of getting screwed and being lied to. Problem is they get used to it. Government *makes* 'em get used to it. And as long as people are spoon-fed lies by liberal do-gooders and think they can get by, they don't give a shit. Just hand 'em a welfare check and promise 'em they'll be taken care of. A six-pack, a foreign-made television set, some food stamps, a goddamn football game once a week to make 'em forget they're out of work and that's all it takes. Zombies. Goddamn zombies. Have no idea what the hell's happening to them."

"Ah, but they *do* know," Williams said. "They just accept it, that's all."

McKnight, a scowl spreading across his face, shook his head at the explanation, and as if the colonel needed to be educated, asked, "You ever cook a frog?"

"What does that have to do with anything?"

"Everything," McKnight snapped. "Did you know that if you drop a frog in a pot of hot water, its natural survival reflexes makes it jump out immediately? Drop that same frog into cold water, then slowly turn up the heat, and that frog doesn't sense what's happening to it until it's too late. Damn thing'll just sit there, becoming hotter and hotter, dying slowly but surely, a little bit at a time, because as long as its body can adjust to the rise in temperature, it gets used to it. That's what's happening to *us*. We're dying a little bit at a time. Just slowly enough to make it seem as though everything is normal, that nothing is happening. But it is. It's just that we're being so conditioned that we never see the changes around us. Our survival instincts are dulled. We get used to it. And day by day, moment by moment, we die a little bit at a time until we end up exactly like that damn frog."

The general took another prolonged drag and exhaled with a sigh, frustrated to the brink of near delirium at what he considered the blissful ignorance of the American people. NAFTA, GATT, Pacific Rim Initiative, Caribbean Basin Initiative, secret agreements, international treaties, every one of them arrogantly proposed and secretly negotiated without public knowledge or understanding, all of them, as far as McKnight was concerned, nothing less than a way to sell out America, to replace the Constitution with a set of covert agreements he believed would undermine America's sovereignty and take it away piece by piece until there was nothing left.

His lone fear, which lately had developed into a recurring nightmare that would send him running for alcohol in the middle of the night, was that he would wake up one day and find it all gone. It wasn't war that General McKnight feared. It wasn't even death. It was economics. And it sickened him to the point of vengeance to think of all the three-piece-suited bastards on Wall Street who'd secretly dealt themselves lifetime corporate pensions and Swiss bank accounts and all the while watched their country rot before their very eyes.

The conference room remained silent except for the sounds of two voices that spoke as one. Smoke continued to spew upward and encircle them in a thin haze. General McKnight and Colonel Williams, as they'd done so often since the creation of the TIMBER WOLF project, remained together throughout much of the evening, drinking brandy, smoking cigars, discussing politics, and for the most part pondering the implications of a mission that had finally become reality. Neither was sure what success would bring. But after witnessing what they both believed to be the continued destruction of America before their eyes, neither could bear the consequences of failure.

chapter fifteen

Like a lighthouse glimmering through the late winter sky, the Washington Monument had always been a welcome reminder that home was just across the Potomac. But now, as she visualized one of Colonel Williams's men with a gash in his head the size of a large finger, Linda knew it would be only a matter of time before they'd be wanted fugitives, and there was no way she could risk going back now. And so, turning north on Fort Myer Drive to Key Bridge, she headed straight across the Potomac to John's town house in Georgetown, where she hoped no one would be watching or waiting.

A light drizzle had begun to fall. The asphalt streets shimmered elegantly beneath the illuminated Washington landmarks, making the urban D.C. landscape look so deceptively tranquil that for a moment Linda had nearly forgotten where she was.

"You know, Jack, we may not have anything at all," she said. "All this may have been for nothing."

"I don't believe that." Jack patted the top of the box with his hand, certain that it was holding the answers to something, if not everything. "This thing wouldn't have been hidden like it was unless there was something hot in it."

"We'll find out soon enough," Linda said. "John lives down that street." She pointed left then made a sweeping turn, deliberately driving past John's apartment and pulling around the corner. Then, waiting several minutes to make certain no one had followed, she made a sharp U-turn, drove back to the middle of a narrow street that was lined with attractive two-story brownstones, and slipped between two parked cars.

Jack clung to the metal box, pulling it into his chest and looking in every direction at the deserted street. "This is too quiet, Linda. I don't like it."

"Don't worry," she said. "Why would anyone suspect we'd come *here*? It's late and it's raining, that's all."

"What if you were followed when you went to see John. What if he told someone about your meeting with him. What if—"

"Jack, I told you. He wouldn't do that. I know him. And besides, I made sure I wasn't followed, okay? I doubt if they're gonna stake out every person I've ever known. No, I'm pretty sure we'll be all right."

Reassured for the moment, Jack climbed out of the car, still clutching the box like some valuable treasure he'd just unearthed.

Linda shut the car door and took a final glance in both directions. Nothing. The light streaming down from the sidewalk lamp filtered its way through a wall of continuous drizzle and cast distorted images onto the shiny black asphalt. And except for the soft rustle of rain against the metal of nearby parked cars, it was unnervingly quiet. Almost too quiet. She walked around to Jack's side of the car and pulled him along.

"C'mon. This way." Linda cut across the slick street and climbed six oversized steps to a set of locks and an intercom system positioned next to the door. She pressed a button and waited.

"Yes? Who is it?"

Linda's heart skipped a beat at the familiar sound of the voice. "John, it's Linda," she said.

"Be right down."

The intercom clicked off, and within seconds John was at the door. "What the hell happened to you?" he asked. "You two look like hell. What's going on?"

"We'll tell you when we get inside."

They climbed the narrow stairway and entered what looked more like a carelessly ransacked library than the cozy living room she'd remembered. Books and computer printouts were stacked one on top of another like leaning towers about to come crashing to the floor if anyone breathed too heavily. With hardly a clearing in sight, John pulled a La-Z-Boy through and around the mess. He positioned it next to the couch and threw its contents aside.

"Sorry about the mess," John apologized. "I've been trying to organize some of my stuff. Unsuccessfully, I'm afraid. Seems there's never enough time . . . or enthusiasm. So tell me, what's going on?"

"Adam Wesely was killed yesterday," Linda said, throwing herself down into the couch.

"What!"

"Assassinated, we believe . . . before he had a chance to tell me or anyone else what it was that crashed in New Hampshire and what it was supposed to be used for. When we went to his house to see if we could dig something up, his housekeeper told us of a cabin he'd had in West Virginia. No one was supposed to know about it. We just came from there. Apparently someone else found out about it shortly after *we* did. Colonel Williams showed up with one of his men, searched the place while we hid, didn't find anything, and left. We didn't know the other guy stayed behind. He caught me and was about to make contact with Williams when Jack smashed his head in." She looked down at the blood that had already dried into a thin crust along the edge of the box.

"You killed him?" John asked, turning toward Jack, his voice thin with apprehension.

"No," Jack answered. "Though I should have. Just knocked the bastard unconscious. I'm sure he came to and reported in before we even got back. He didn't see who hit him, so Linda's the only one he could identify for sure. We found this before we left." He placed the box carefully on the rectangular coffee table. "It was hidden under a floorboard beneath the carpet. We're sure there must be something important in it."

John leaned forward, and holding the box down with one hand, pulled back with all his strength on the heavy lock with the other. "It's gonna take some doing getting this thing open. Lemme get something."

Linda lifted the box and placed it next to her on the couch, then waited for John to come back from the kitchen with a hammer and chisel. She looked on as he positioned the chisel against the lock, tapped the top of the chisel once with the hammer, then lifted his arm high above his head. A sharp crack filled the room as the box, sinking deep into the soft couch from the sudden impact, bounced back up, the lid, free of the lock, flying open and revealing a thick bundle of paper wrapped tightly in rubber bands, several manila folders, and some loose documents.

Linda lurched forward, grabbing the box and setting it carefully back on the coffee table. She stared into it, at the tightly bound bundle of papers, at the important-looking manila folders, the loose, tattered sheets of yellowing documents, all having the appearance of being the evidence they'd been searching for. She reached into the box and removed its contents.

The thick bundle, heavily crisscrossed with wide rubber bands, was first. The manila folders beneath them had all been marked TOP SECRET and stapled closed as if to seal their contents, even from Adam. The loose documents, variously sized, some old and faded a dull yellow, were scattered haphazardly on the bottom.

Linda removed one of the sealed manila folders and pried the heavy staples out with a pair of scissors she found lying on the coffee table. She threw the folder onto the couch, shook her head at finding nothing of significance, then pried opened another, then another, searching, reading, analyzing. And when she got to the fourth, sank back into her chair, transfixed at what she was now holding in front of her.

"What is it?" Jack asked. "Linda? You find something?"

"Yeah . . . I found something, all right."

Linda handed the contents of the folder to Jack, whose eyes widened as he scanned the page from top to bottom.

"This is incredible. This is it. When it all began."

"This is what?" John, who'd been preoccupied rereading what Linda had been discarding, tore the paper from Jack's fingers and stared at what no doubt was a copy of the original top-secret memo detailing the beginnings of a project code named CONDOR.

* * * * * * *

Top Secret—Eyes Only

* * * * * * *

Eyes Only **Copy *One* of *One***

SUBJECT: PROJECT CONDOR BRIEFING FOR PRESIDENT RICHARD NIXON
DOCUMENT PREPARED: NOVEMBER 1973
BRIEFING OFFICER: GEN. PHILIP T. BOOKER

NOTE: This document has been prepared as a preliminary briefing only. It should be regarded as introductory to a full operations briefing to follow.

* * * * * * *

As directed, we've begun preliminary studies on the production of a long-range aircraft, code name CONDOR. Our scientists at Los Alamos are developing new materials that are lighter and significantly stronger than conventional aircraft metal currently in use and that we feel would be more than adequate to house engines that will use the new synthetic fuels. Design of the craft, together with the new composite materials, will give it the desired defense-evading capabilities. Test production is scheduled for late 1978. Actual flight tests will begin sometime in 1980.

Construction of base sites in Prospect, ME, White Sand, AZ, and Hot Rock, NM will begin early next year. Any unauthorized witnessing of test flights will be classified and leaked as unsubstantiated UFO sightings. Actual encounters with any craft will be subject to security procedures. We will update you periodically on progress.

* * * * * * *

Top Secret—Eyes Only

"Goddamn," John whispered. "If I didn't see it with my own eyes, I wouldn't have believed it."

"Believe it," Linda said.

"But exactly what does CONDOR accomplish that any of our other new weapon systems don't?" John asked.

"That's what we've been asking ourselves ever since we learned of it," Jack answered. "We know, obviously, that the government's been working on it for more than twenty years. And we know from the data files—and now from this memo—that it's some sort of advanced aircraft with defense-evading capabilities. What we don't know is why something like this has been developed. Some of these other documents could tell us more."

At that, Linda picked up several more manila folders, hoping, almost expecting. She opened each, and as if the world had suddenly come to a standstill when she came to the last one, began to cry.

"What the hell is it?" Jack asked.

Linda held the folder out to Jack and let it drop from her fingers. Inside, a copy of another top-secret memo was addressed to the Pentagon's chief operations officer.

* * * * * * *

Top Secret—Eyes Only

* * * * * * *

The Pentagon

Washington

Eyes Only **May 15, 1988**

MEMORANDUM FOR PENTAGON CHIEF OPERATIONS OFFICER
SUBJECT: CONDOR TEST FLIGHT
MISSION: WORLD ORDER

* * * * * * *

CONDOR has been cleared for test flight. Two test flights are being scheduled for 1988. One on June 7, 1988, from the White Sand Air Base, the other on July 10, 1988, from the Hot Rock Air Base. The latest propulsion tests were promising and we don't anticipate any further problems. The original fuel leakage problem has been resolved with stronger composite materials. Because of new containment devices on the engine, a crash "would not" cause contamination. However, for purposes of national security, any crash site would be classified a top-secret area, a special recovery team would secure the site, and all crash site materials would be classified and sealed.

We will be giving you periodic updates from now until the first test flight is underway. The biotechnology systems are in place and fully operational. We will also be giving you an update on the status of the new PCW payload, which we expect to be fully tested and ready to go within the next calendar year.

* * * * * * *

Top Secret—Eyes Only

"Jesus, this must have been the crash of the Tucson test flight Peter investigated." Jack looked over at Linda, who'd buried her face in her hands. "Of all the ways to find out. Linda, I'm sorry. I'm really sorry."

"I can't believe I'm acting this way over a stupid memo," Linda whispered, straightening herself and trying as best she could to get over it. But there it was. Peter's test flight staring up at her from that memo; *his* crash site in 1988, *his* breach of security that led to his death. "I'm sorry. It's just that there's something so final about this. I know I should be able to put it to rest, but it's so hard. I've got to find out what was so important about all this that Peter had to die for it."

John was staring down at the memo, almost in disbelief at what he was seeing. "Look, there it is again. PCW. And what the hell is 'world order'?" He shook his head as if ascribing to those last words an entirely new meaning that till now he figured was little more than a hollow presidential sound bite. He now envisioned something more, something he never imagined possible. "I had no idea. I never suspected 'world order' would be this."

"This? We still don't know what *this* means," Linda said in frustration. "We know there has to be a connection between CONDOR and a government mission code named WORLD ORDER. That's obvious. But what is it?"

"Look at the date in the first memo," Jack cut in. "November 1973. Doesn't that tell you something?"

"Post Vietnam," Linda answered. "Everyone was scrambling to justify the devastating loss; military brass was in shock."

"That's right. Think about it. Until Vietnam, we pretty much called the shots. The world was looking to *us* to halt the spread of communism and keep the free world from falling apart. Well, on one count at least, we failed. Failed miserably, if you ask me. And so, CONDOR was born . . . to make sure we never lose another war, never again lose our ability to control global events. According to this memo, CONDOR is a long-range vehicle . . . that means it's global. You were right, Linda. Range was the key they were looking for. And obviously CONDOR is it. WORLD ORDER may be any damn thing they want it to be."

John, who'd begun digging furiously through the pile of loose papers, was now staring curiously at a tattered newspaper clipping from the *Albuquerque Gazette*, dated August 6, 1988. He handled it as if it were tissue paper, careful to avoid tearing it into pieces and wondering why a newspaper article would be packaged in the same box with top-secret classified messages to the president of the United States and the Pentagon's chief operations officer. But it was precisely for that reason that he knew a connection had to exist.

UFO SPOTTED NEAR ROSWELL

According to several eyewitnesses, an unusual craft was sighted about 15 miles east of Roswell at 7:43 early yesterday morning. David Bruner, a local rancher in the area, was driving his pickup into town when he spotted what he'd described as a large silver cylinder with triangular wings. Bruner claims to have witnessed the cylinder flying at incredible speed very low to the ground before disappearing over the horizon seconds later. Other eyewitness reports are now coming in and are being investigated by the Defense Department.

John placed the newspaper clip on the table in front of him and slid another next to it, this one taken from the *Hot Rock Inquirer*, dated August 11, 1988.

TRUCKER MISSING FOLLOWING
UFO SIGHTINGS

A tractor trailer was found abandoned along highway 17 today following several reports of UFOs the night before. The driver, Joe Reed of San Diego, is reported missing. An eyewitness in the area, Dorothy Smith of Hot Rock, claimed to have seen an unusual craft flying a few miles from where the truck had been found. By the time Smith drove to the area she thought she'd seen the craft hover then land, it was gone. She reported seeing the truck with its cab light on but no sign of the driver. Unusual markings along the ground resembled burn marks. The case has been turned over to both the local sheriff's office and the Department of Defense for further investigation.

"What do you make of these?" asked John.

Linda picked up the Roswell clip and pointed immediately

to the second sentence. "Triangular-shaped wings," she read. "The craft we investigated was silver gray and had triangular-shaped wings. Incredibly high speeds. The new propulsion system would explain that. Jack, these UFO sightings are CONDOR test flights."

"Yeah, imagine that," Jack said. "All those crackpots who'd been witnessing UFOs were really seeing UFOs. *Our* goddamn UFOs."

"Exactly," Linda shot back. "And for the past eight years, all those crackpots have been systematically discredited to the point that any CONDOR sighting was all but ignored. It's perfect. Test a new secret aircraft, and if anyone happens to see it and reports it, it's filed away as either mass hysteria, illusion, or publicity. A perfect way to keep something top secret."

As Linda and John pored over several more clippings of UFO sightings, Jack picked up the stack of bundled papers and with a snap broke the two heavy rubber bands. The bundle contained envelopes, folded sheets of paper, index cards with faded notes scribbled haphazardly across them, and copies of fax messages. He began picking through the suspicious papers for further clues, but much of it contained nothing of the kind.

Linda continued staring at those UFO reports, trying to imagine what David Bruner and Dorothy Smith must have seen, what Joe Reed must have witnessed in the desert that made him disappear. In frustration, she tossed the clips down and turned to Jack. "Anything?"

"Nothing. Looks like some things that may have been important to Adam, but from what I can tell there's noth—"

"What is it?" Linda asked, seeing Jack's eyes widen.

"A travel itinerary."

"What about it? Adam traveled quite a bit."

"It's not Adam's."

"Whose?"

"General McKnight's."

Linda snatched the sheet of paper away and held it inches

from her face. ''According to this, he flew out of San Diego on March 15, 1986, spent a day in Hawaii before flying to Manila, flew on to Malaysia on the eighteenth. Return flight on the twenty-second. Four days in Malaysia. What the hell's in Malaysia, other than sweatshops for American companies?''

''How about the U.S. Tropical Research Center?'' John said, now staring at another document from the bundle, this one a copy of an official letter addressed to General Benjamin McKnight himself.

United States Tropical Research Center
Kuala Lumpur, Malaysia

February 10, 1989

Dear General McKnight:
Looking forward to your official visit here next month. Our work on the agent is complete, albeit somewhat behind schedule. We apologize for the delay. As you know it was necessary to alter the original G, and due to unexpected and troublesome side effects, to develop the natural binary system, which should make the agent impossible to detect. We plan to have several containers of the agent ready for you to bring back to the States next month for final testing and analysis.

If you have any questions until then, please call.

Sincerely,

Abraham Vijan

Abraham Vijan, Ph.D.
Chief Toxicologist

''I never heard of the U.S. Tropical Research Center,'' Linda said, stunned at the prospect of a secret government laboratory outside the United States producing unknown chemical or biological agents. "And why Malaysia?"

"Could be in a strategic area," Jack answered. "Could be that Malaysia is one of those out-of-the-way hellholes no one gives a shit about or would ever suspect. Or there could be something in Malaysia not found anywhere else, and that *something* is critical to the agent. If I were laying odds, that's what I'd bet on. You find out what it is the government needs in Malaysia, and I'll find out how that agent's gonna work."

"How do you know it's a government facility at all?" John proposed. "Just because it's named the *United States* Tropical Research Center doesn't mean anything. Federal Express isn't federal, is it? The Federal Reserve isn't a government bank at all; has nothing to do with the federal government."

"Of course," Linda said. "A black project."

"A black project made even more secret because it's being developed outside the country," Jack added.

"You think what's going on in Malaysia has anything to do with this new biotechnology mentioned here?" John asked, pointing to the bottom of the Pentagon memo addressed to General McKnight.

Jack grabbed the memo and examined it more closely. "Damn, this could be a front for a biotechnology installation," he said.

"Figures," Linda said, shaking her head as though she now knew exactly what they were up against.

"Whaddya mean, 'figures'?" John asked. "And what exactly do they mean by new biotechnology?"

"Its a way to manipulate DNA," Linda said. To use living organisms to produce products like hormones and other chemicals through recombinant DNA."

"Genetic engineering of bacteria," Jack interrupted.

"That's right," Linda said. "We're now able to engineer bacteria to make everything from drugs to vaccines. It's the technology of the future."

"How do you engineer a bacterium to do *that*?"

"During the last decade, we've developed the technology

to literally splice human genes, or even genes from other organisms, directly into bacterial DNA. Since bacteria have only a single strand of DNA, it makes things easy. Lets say you want to make insulin. All you have to do is remove the single DNA strand from an *E. coli* bacterium, cut it, splice a human insulin gene into the open bacterial DNA, put the DNA strand that now contains the insulin gene back into the bacterium, and let it reproduce. Since bacteria reproduce asexually, pretty soon you have billions, all of them producing insulin. Seems impossible, but we've managed to figure out a way to literally transform one of the simplest life-forms on the planet into microscopic chemical factories.''

''Incredible. Where's this technology going?''

''Gene therapy, for one. Now that we've developed the technology for engineering genes in bacteria, we're now beginning to alter genes in higher animals, fix defects in genetic structure, repair genetic diseases. Everything about us, from our height to our eye color to the shape of our ears to the number of hair cells between the knuckles on our fingers, is determined by genes. Our bodies are nothing more than a storage container for those genes, all located on the forty-six chromosomes or strands of DNA that shape who and what we are; our humanness and even our behavior. And for the next ten years, the Human Genome Project will be mapping out every one of our 80,000 genes so we know exactly where they're located and where we can look to fix the 4,000 or so human genetic defects.''

''It's incredible,'' John said. ''But how's all this linked to WORLD ORDER? What would biotechnology or recombinant DNA be used for? I still don't see the connection.''

''I could give you two connections,'' Jack said. ''One, with recombinant DNA, the Defense Department has the ability to create new organisms that would be harder to defend against. In fact, back in the late seventies and early eighties, they had at least fourteen recombinant DNA research projects going full bore.''

''Yeah, I remember back in nineteen-eighty,'' Linda said. ''The Army was even advertising in *Science* magazine for grant proposals on recombinant DNA work."

"That's right. Recombinant DNA makes it easier to develop agents that can mimic symptoms of disease and, therefore, can't be identified. I read a May 1986 report issued to Congress on one of those projects. A naturally occurring but artificially produced group of biological substances that would have powerful regulatory effects on sensory perception, organ function, and enzyme production. Since the substances are required in only minute quantities, any imbalance could cause devastating effects."

"And since they could be naturally occurring," Linda said, "death would be attributed to natural causes."

"Unbelievable," John muttered, incredulous. "What else?"

"Ethnic weapons."

"What!"

"You heard right. With genetic engineering, microbes could be transformed into weapons that target hereditary differences between human populations."

"How, for Christ's sake?"

"The whole principle behind the army's secret ethnic warfare program," Linda said, "was based on the little-known fact that ethnic groups exhibit hereditary differences and genetic predispositions that could be exploited with weapons that discriminate on the basis of race."

"Exactly," Jack said. "Certain populations have enzyme deficiencies that make them susceptible to certain agents. For example, *Coccidioides immitis* is a fungus that causes valley fever. Blacks are ten times more likely to die from it than non-blacks. Epstein-Barr virus causes Caucasians to get infectious mononucleosis, whereas blacks and Southeast Asians can develop two different forms of cancer. I can go on and on. I know for a fact that a search is currently under way for pathogens that would disproportionately affect members of specific ethnic groups. Research is also ongoing on two fronts: one, to modify existing pathogens so that they'll more likely infect members of particular ethnic populations and two, to manufacture pure antibodies that would attach to protein molecules found only in cells of certain individuals. These antibodies could be armed with toxins specifically designed to kill cells on contact. All sounds so lovely, doesn't it? You wanted world order? There you go.''

''Jack, I think I know,'' Linda said as if it just hit her.

''Know what?''

''I think I know what's in Malaysia.''

''Go on.''

''I remember Peter talking about a novel technique to use recombinant DNA to produce pharmaceuticals. It was odd, now that I think about it, that just when a unique breakthrough was imminent, the research stopped. And while reports were still coming out about recombinant biological weapons research, nothing about this was ever reported again. I'd always assumed it was funding. There's got to be a connection, I know it. If the U.S. Tropical Research Center is really a recombinant DNA installation, then what's being produced in Malaysia—whatever that is—has to be linked to WORLD ORDER. Look at Vijan's memo. The letter *G* is an abbreviation for gene. It was necessary to alter the original *gene*. The binary system referred to is a type of weapon system requiring two separate neutral components to be mixed together to produce a third toxic product, which then becomes the actual weapon. Certain classes of nerve gas are binary, and the reason they're so easy to hide is because each neutral chemical is produced at a different location and is usually harmless by itself; might even be used for commercial products. My hunch is that the agent they keep referring to is some new kind of binary chemical or toxin produced by recombinant DNA. And God only knows what that means.''

''I don't know, Linda,'' Jack said. ''Something doesn't make sense. There's something missing.''

''I'm telling you, Jack, CONDOR is nothing more than an incredibly sophisticated delivery system. An aircraft by itself is useless, harmless. It's what it delivers that makes it deadly. It's the agent we should be worrying about. And the source

. . . Malaysia. The answer may be in one of these other documents.''

The three then began ripping open envelopes, tearing out contents, picking through every document and letter, searching for a word, a phrase, a sentence, symbol, or code that might tell them something about WORLD ORDER or CONDOR or how Malaysia or biotechnology fit into the whole scheme. They plowed through every inch of every last document that lay scattered before them, and when they'd finished could find nothing more that would explain how it was all tied together.

''That's it. There's nothing else here,'' Linda said. ''And we still don't know what the hell it is we're looking for, how it's tied in with WORLD ORDER, and why they would need CONDOR.''

''Linda, something's wrong here.'' John suddenly found himself in a frenzy, shuffling through the rubble of papers and documents for something so obvious they had all overlooked it.

''What?'' Linda asked.

''It's not here.''

''What's not here?''

''TIMBER WOLF. We've been so preoccupied looking through all this stuff that we forgot about TIMBER WOLF. Not one of these documents or papers even refers to it.''

Linda and Jack looked at each other, then dove into the pile, going back over every piece of paper, every sentence, every word, searching. Even the letters *TW* would have reassured them. They searched for words they suspected may have been scrambled, encrypted messages, anything. There was nothing. No mention of TIMBER WOLF in any of it.

''My God, John, you're right.'' Linda shook her head at what she was thinking. ''TIMBER WOLF must be a separate mission.''

Jack, not nearly as surprised, said, ''Don't you remember, Linda? You suspected as much this afternoon, when we talked about McKnight's computer files. This just confirms it.''

Linda turned to John, her voice strong with renewed determination. "When do you think you can get that access code?"

"Tomorrow. Once I get in, I'll be able to scan for everything, even top-secret files."

"You know the Pentagon's gonna have a security lock on anyone trying to get access to omega," Jack warned.

"That's why we're not going to use my office computer," John countered. "I was able to bypass security last time, but this is different. No one cracks Pentagon omega files without triggering some kind of security alarm. We'll be breaking in at a remote location. They won't know who's breaking in or be able to trace where the break-in is originating from. At least I hope they won't."

"Sounds risky as hell," Jack said. "Especially with the surveillance network. How can you be sure it's fail-safe?"

"Can't say it is completely, but it's a helluva lot safer than sitting in my office, waiting for the Pentagon to break through the door and find us staring at a top-secret omega file. That's why we're going to an isolated site, getting the information, and getting out as quickly as possible."

Linda, managing a weak smile for the first time that night, felt another step closer to a plot that was becoming more sinister and more bizarre each time she put another piece of the puzzle in place. She was more hopeful than ever. Tomorrow, she was convinced, would bring her that much closer to discovering the truth behind all the lies.

chapter sixteen

MARCH 18, 1996: 7:12 A.M.

The aroma of freshly brewed coffee wafted through every room in the house, stirring Linda from the soundest sleep she'd had in days. Her eyes closed, she arched her back and unconsciously rolled across the flannel sheets to the empty side of the bed. Then, forcing her eyelids open, she momentarily panicked when she saw the strange furniture next to her, until she suddenly remembered. Jack had taken a cab back to the lab last evening. She'd remained behind, exhausted, not daring to set foot anywhere near her home and intending to make it an early evening after discussing final details of the next day's computer break-in with John. The discussions had ended shortly after they'd begun; the early evening had turned into a late-night session of small talk and recollections. And John, after finally giving in to exhaustion himself, had offered to spend what was left of the night on his pull-out sofa.

Linda ran her fingers through a mat of tangled hair as she sat up and looked around the typical bachelor pad that, as far as she could tell, included nothing feminine in sight.

The dark paneled walls were plastered with richly colored posters of European cities, giving the room the look of a cheap travel agency. A porcelain bust of Albert Einstein, wrapped in one of John's plaid scarves and topped with a brown fedora, sat perched atop an antique walnut dresser. Around the bust, mounds of dusty books and magazines tilted precariously and, from their appearance, hadn't been touched in months. In the corner of the room, a small, rolltop desk overflowed with unfinished paperwork, the narrow cubbyholes stuffed tightly with papers and envelopes that flared outward like rows of white-and-yellow fans.

As she glanced at a pile of old computer journals and magazines that lay scattered about the top of the desk, Linda's eyes were drawn to the sudden flicker of something that had caught the incoming rays of the morning sun. She jumped out of bed, walked over to the desk, and, pushing a few of the tattered journals aside, removed from their midst a small gold-embossed photo album. She wiped the fine layer of gray dust from its cover and, when she opened it, found herself staring down at an old photograph of John and Peter taken on one of their camping trips.

She flipped quickly to the next photo, then the next, and the next one after that, her fingers seemingly forced into turning the pages and making her relive a time in her life when everything was so perfect. And then, as though her subconscious would not allow her to forget how much she still missed him, that sense of loneliness she thought would have left her by now was suddenly overcoming her and, as happened so often whenever those thoughts of Peter would drift into her mind, tears began to well in her eyes.

"Linda, you awake?" John asked from outside the bedroom door, startling her.

Linda swung around at the sound of John's deep voice and said, "I'll be out in a minute."

For a moment she stood there in the oversized pajamas John had given her last evening. She clutched the photo album in her trembling hands, pressing it to her chest so tightly she could feel the outline of the hard leather against her soft breast. When she came out, she lowered the album and held it out for him to see. "I was looking at these and started thinking of—" She didn't want to say it, afraid of burdening John with her feelings.

John hesitated, wishing to God he'd thrown the damn thing in a box somewhere, then said, "I'm sorry if it brought back memories for you." There may have been more beautiful women, he thought as he watched her place the album on a small table next to the door, but at that moment, Linda, tears and all, was the most beautiful, sensual woman he had ever seen. "I fixed us some breakfast. Hungry?"

"Famished," Linda said, then followed John through the clutter of the living room and into the kitchen.

"You know, I couldn't help thinking about our conversation last night," John said after sitting down and pouring Linda a cup of coffee.

"Which part?" she asked. Still groggy, Linda scooped some scrambled eggs into her dish, then took a long sip of coffee.

"The stuff about biological agents and DNA. It's scary for me to think that we've come so far . . . that we're capable of doing what you said."

"We're capable of more than you think," Linda said almost nonchalantly.

"Oh?" John placed his cup in front of him and leaned forward as if to prod her into continuing. "Did you and Jack leave something out last evening?"

"There are things about the biological weapons program most people would be shocked to learn . . . things that I have a hard time dealing with myself."

"Such as?"

Linda hesitated, averting her eyes as if sorry that she'd brought it up.

"You okay?" John asked.

"Yeah. I was just thinking," Linda whispered. "When I started work with SELF, I'd heard things about bio weapons research I found hard to believe. Since then I've learned more than I wanted to."

"Tell me," John insisted.

"When Fort Detrick was first commissioned," Linda began, "it was used primarily as a facility that developed defensive countermeasures against biological weapons intended for use against us. That changed quickly. Offensive weapons research intensified. And by the early seventies, when Fort Detrick was taken over by the NIH and the National Cancer Institute, we started developing what were referred to as slow viruses . . . pathogens designed to cause all sorts of cancers and opportunistic infections.''

''I've never heard of slow viruses,'' John said. ''What are they exactly?''

''They're pathogens that invade the body, but instead of acting quickly like typical biological agents, they act over a long period of time in order to avoid detection . . . like AIDS.''

John froze for a moment, realizing now why Linda seemed so ill at ease with his questioning, then asked flatly, ''Were we experimenting with something similar to HIV at Detrick?''

''I can't say for sure,'' Linda answered, ''but it wouldn't be that hard to create an immune destroyer if we wanted to. There's all kinds of evidence pointing to it.''

''I've suspected as much, but most researchers disagree. What kind of evidence are we talking about?''

''It wasn't much longer after the Defense Department received funding for research on immunity-destroying viruses in 1970 that they began experimenting with a T-cell attacker called bovine lymphocyte virus, or BLV,'' Linda said. ''They also started working with VISNA, a sheep virus that destroys T cells. That's precisely what they were looking for. Something that would first attack T cells and then destroy them. When you look at the molecular structure of HIV, it's very similar to BLV.''

''I know that HIV attacks T cells,'' John said. ''But we're talking about a virus from a different, nonprimate species. Wouldn't that present a problem when using it as a *human* T-cell attacker?''

''Not if you incubate it in human tissue,'' Linda explained. ''When you take a foreign virus and grow it in human tissue, it adapts to human beings fairly quickly. We do it all the time with vaccines. Articles in *Science* and *Nature* have reported unusually close similarities between HIV, BLV, and VISNA; and a close friend of mine at one of the universities that worked with the Defense Department believes that HIV may actually be bovine visna virus, or BVV.''

"Was the molecular technology in place back then to do it?" John asked.

"Yes," Linda answered. "Gene cutting and splicing were already being used by the early seventies. Experimental agents were flowing between the DOD and research labs all over the country. And retroviruses were a hot research topic."

"Retroviruses?"

"A single strand of RNA rather than a double-stranded DNA helix. Normally a section of DNA gets transcribed into a piece of RNA, which is then used as the code for a protein. Retroviruses work in exactly the opposite way. They get into the cell, are copied into DNA strands, then migrate into the cell's nucleus, where they're incorporated into the host DNA. Because they become a part of the DNA, they can become dormant for years until something triggers them to reproduce. There's your slow virus."

"And that's why it can take years for symptoms of AIDS to occur," John added.

"Exactly."

"It's still hard to believe that that kind of retroviral research was going on since the early seventies," John said.

"Not only was it going on," Linda countered, "but the entire program was headed up by one of the men who first reported about HIV . . . Dr. Edward Davis."

"What!"

"That's right, John. Davis was one of the government's top retrovirologists. His early experiments included splicing synthetic RNA and cat viruses to human viruses and he'd been creating cancer-causing and AIDS-like viruses for the NIH, NCI, and DOD for more than a decade. In fact, if you read some of his early articles you can see references to T-cell-destroying viruses that act very much like the AIDS virus."

John shook his head, not believing that Linda was actually suggesting that HIV may have been the result—accidental or intentional—of biological warfare research. But in light of recent developments, he no longer questioned that possibility as strongly as he would have. "Is there other evidence to link HIV with anything else out there?" he asked.

"Besides being so similar to BLV and VISNA?"

"Yes."

"How about other human retroviruses such as the human T-cell leukemia viruses? HTLV I, II, III, IV, V, VI, et cetera, all seemed to have appeared together with the appearance of HIV I and II. Isn't that odd? To say that all these new cancer-causing retroviruses appeared or mutated at the same time in order to start infecting humans spontaneously is too much of a coincidence."

"And you really think, in spite of all the denials we've been hearing, that the government is still experimenting with deadly bacteria or engineered viruses as part of their biological warfare program?"

"I do," Linda said. "You know as well as I do that some of the Department of Defense's biological weapons projects were planned, funded, directed, and controlled by the CIA."

"You're talking about MKULTRA and MKNAOMI, aren't you?" John said.

"Yes, especially MKNAOMI, which I believe is still in existence as a project to create immune-destroying viruses. In fact, since its discovery, HIV has been used in both military and civilian research as an effective vector for introducing other agents into cells. I also think it's gone beyond that by now. I believe we're developing new agents that are even worse, if you can imagine it."

After a breakfast that ended with Linda trying to come up with a scenario that would help her make sense of the government's almost pathologic urgency to create new biological agents, she showered and dressed quickly. John, meanwhile, had finished packing a portable IBM computer and modem between thick layers of clothing that lined a canvas equipment bag. The secret access code was tucked safely away in the hidden lining of his jacket, a precaution in case he was caught and searched, and in the event the code could be traced back to the source who had given it to him.

Linda slipped her boots over thick woolen socks, anxious to begin the investigation again. But today it was different somehow, she thought as she looked at John and realized that there may be an entirely new motivation for her pursuing this. No longer did she feel the same need to *do this* for Peter; and for the first time it didn't make her feel guilty. *But did she really need to go through with it?* she debated with herself. *Couldn't she just go on with her life and put it all behind her? Did she really want to end up like Adam? Or worse, put John in danger as well?*

Linda's flurry of thoughts left her bitterly confused. And then she remembered. TIMBER WOLF, WORLD ORDER, CONDOR. The words flashed repeatedly through her mind like a set of brilliant neon signs. Something about it was all so diabolical, she thought, so sinister, that it had to be investigated and uncovered. As much as she wished she could simply forget everything and go on with her life, she knew that that was not possible.

"John, you almost ready?" Linda's voice broke with tension.

"Yeah, lemme make sure we have everything." John checked his equipment for the third time. Computer, modem, power packs, wires, clips, access code. He zipped the canvas bag and threw on an old Atlanta Braves baseball cap. "Let's do it. Now or never."

They gathered whatever else they needed, tossed that into Linda's field pack, and headed out John's apartment door. They stopped at the bottom of the stairs. John opened the front door just a crack, peeking outside to make sure there were no suspiciously occupied cars parked along the busy street.

The upper-middle-class Georgetown suburb had been transformed by the light of midday. Last evening's drizzle had given way to a brilliant sun that shone on the row of old but neat and well-kept brownstones that lined sidewalks already bustling with activity.

The architecture, a conspicuous blend of nineteenth-century Georgian and English traditional, for a moment made

Linda feel as if she'd been taken someplace far from the hustle and bustle of Washington, D.C. She took a deep breath and caught the scent of hot dogs and sauerkraut coming from a corner vendor nearly a block away. Turning in its direction, she watched as an overweight Middle Eastern woman, hunched beneath her colorful pushcart umbrella, slapped mustard across a frank.

"You see anything?" Linda asked.

"Nothing out of the ordinary."

"Is it always this busy around here? Doesn't anybody work anymore?"

"It's Friday. A lot of the people who live in this area sometimes work four-day weeks. Some of them put in ten-hour days so they can get three-day weekends. I'd do it in a heartbeat if NASA let me."

John's eyes tracked laserlike from one end of the street to the other, looking for anything that he didn't think belonged in the neighborhood. He knew that the hustle and bustle of the street would have made it easy for someone to follow them without being noticed. "I don't see anything suspicious. Just to make sure, though, let me go out to my car alone and drive around the block. Watch from the hallway. If you see anyone following, stay inside. If I don't see you, I'll know I'm being tailed. If not, come out to the street."

Linda watched as John started his cherry red Alfa Romeo and pulled away from the curb. The sports car jumped forward, sped down the street, and turned the corner. Linda cocked her head and listened as the gears shifted and the whine of the straining motor faded away. Not another vehicle was anywhere in sight, she noticed. She waited. If someone was going to follow, she thought, they would have done so by now. They didn't. Besides, she was now confident that no one could possibly have known where she was or that John was involved in any of this.

Swinging the building door open, Linda darted out and down the stairs, waiting for John to drive around the corner. Seconds turned to minutes. She looked at her watch, growing suspicious, thinking that maybe someone had been waiting on another street.

Then, three minutes later, Linda heard the purr of a small engine and saw the shiny red hood jutting out from the stop sign on the corner. As John pulled around and screeched to a halt next to the curb, Linda jumped in and slammed the door. Her head jolted backward as John punched into first and burned rubber toward a destination she still knew nothing about.

chapter seventeen

It was an election year. He'd already been told, in no uncertain terms, that refusing to seek reelection was not an option. His advisers, though painfully aware of the controversies surrounding his embattled personal life, were confidant that those controversies would eventually fade away, and if they didn't, meant little anyway.

It was so much simpler in the old days, he'd often think. The country, fresh from its victories over Germany and Japan, was destined to achieve a greatness that would be envied by the rest of the free world. He wasn't sure when it was that things began to change; just that some fifty years later, the country was teetering on a precipice and pretty damn close to falling straight in.

There was no longer much doubt in his mind that if decisive action was to be taken, it had to be taken outside the system. For he knew that while Congress spent its days and nights pompously arguing irrelevant and often ludicrous policy, the world outside the beltway was imploding. From hemisphere to hemisphere, he saw governments unraveling and allies overtaken by an enemy that had literally exploded like cancer, spilling relentlessly across borders and threatening global stability. Waiting much longer, he believed, risked accelerating a worldwide domino effect that would end on America's doorstep.

The more he thought of it, the more he realized that implementing WORLD ORDER was, in reality, the only way. And despite the respect he'd once held for those who had sealed his election, no longer could he ignore the profound and overriding loyalty he now felt to those who, with their votes, had entrusted their lives and their country to him.

The intercom, reverberating loudly through the solitude of the Oval Office, jolted the president from one of the few moments he'd had to sit alone and reflect on the events of not only the past twenty-four hours but the past four years.

"Mr. President," the voice announced. "General Bridger, intelligence, line two. Says it's urgent."

"Put him through," the president answered sharply.

He'd already spoken to General McKnight the previous day, briefing him on the discovery of the memo addressed to Colonel Thomas Williams and the possibility of a connection between Williams and a transmission originating somewhere within the Pentagon. General Donald Bridger, as head of air force intelligence, had initiated an investigation of Colonel Williams immediately upon discovery of the encrypted message containing Williams's name. With little to go on but the classified memo, Bridger was convinced that he would at least be able to identify the source of their leak and break the code.

"Mr. President." The urgency in the voice was chilling.

"Don, I'm surprised to hear from you this soon. The investigation?"

"It's Colonel Williams."

"Yes? Is he in custody? Being questioned?"

"Afraid not."

"What's wrong?"

"We found him in his apartment this morning. He was dead."

"Damn!" The president sank into his chair and, after a moment of stunned disbelief, banged his closed fist against the desk, furious that he hadn't given the order to place Williams in custody as soon as the memo was found. "What in the hell happened?"

"We're not sure. The body's being transferred to Walter Reed for autopsy."

"Any signs of violence?"

"None. From the initial look at the body, it seems he died of natural causes. We found him slumped over in his chair, watching TV. No signs of forced entry. No evidence of foul play. The place looked clean. The body appeared untouched when forensics arrived."

Bullshit, thought the president as he rubbed his forehead vigorously. Too much of a coincidence. Just when the colonel was being sought for questioning . . . dead. The process of elimination was unfolding in his head. *Bridger, McKnight, Doyle*—no, not Doyle—*maybe one of Bridger's people, or McKnight's.* As far as he was concerned, it could have been anyone in a network as secret and as bizarrely convoluted as any in the western world. It was impossible. No way the president could even begin to guess who had been behind this. He abandoned the mental checklist and refocused his mind on the call.

"Natural causes, you say?" The words rolled incredulously across his lips in a prolonged whisper. He shook his head. Bullshit, he thought again. "Anything else?"

"Nothing right now. I'm on my way to Walter Reed."

"Keep me apprised of everything. And call me as soon as the autopsy is complete."

"Yes, sir. Should be several hours at the very least."

The president dropped the receiver in disgust, convinced that someone had gotten to Colonel Williams first in order to keep him from revealing what he'd known of TIMBER WOLF. "Goddamn bastards," he whispered. He spun around and sat looking out the window, rubbing his temples this time and contemplating the series of all-too-coincidental events that had occurred during the ninety-six hours since the crash. His head felt ready to explode. And then—

"Mr. President," the voice on the intercom blurted. "General McKnight is here."

The president reached over and punched the middle button. "Send him in."

General Benjamin McKnight marched directly into the Oval Office. The president stood and composed himself, and as he greeted McKnight with a firm handshake, the mental checklist was suddenly back. For a second, McKnight was right there at the very top.

"Ben, sit down. I just received the bad news."

The two men faced off. General McKnight, certain that no one could possibly suspect it had been him who'd given the order, looked confidently into the president's eyes and, as was his custom, searched for a hint of anything that might be revealing or suggestive. No way anyone could know, he thought. Besides, it was daxonol they used, a new drug that mimicked heart failure by blocking nerve transmission from the SA node into the right atrium. A tiny, undetectable amount placed in the colonel's coffee grounds the evening before as he slept was all that was needed to accomplish the job with virtually no trace of evidence.

"It's hard to believe," McKnight said grimly. "I spoke to him only yesterday. He seemed fine. His medical records didn't indicate any serious health problems."

No, there was no way anyone could know, he figured, more confident now the more he thought about it. It was a perfect hit; a potentially damaging leak eliminated so cleanly that he caught himself beginning to turn the corners of his mouth into a satisfied grin, then thinking better of it, snapped quickly back into his most solemn expression. Everything was still on schedule, he thought. And no one, not even the president himself, could possibly know.

"Can you tell me anything air force intelligence hasn't reported already?" the president asked, glaring back at the general every bit as intently as the general was examining him.

The cozy but vital relationship between the Pentagon and the White House—cultivated by decades of previously hawkish administrations—was on the verge of being eroded by this one. It was evident to anyone in the know that there was an intense dislike and a bitter suspicion on both sides between the military and the current administration. This general was no exception. He, the seasoned warrior, the president, a new and unwelcome intruder, feeling each other out, testing to see if there'd be a slip of the tongue, an unspoken signal, each waiting for the other to say something that would give some secret away.

"All I know at this point is that Williams apparently died of natural causes," McKnight said. "Preliminary physical symptoms indicated possible heart attack. Coroner suspected it as soon as they wheeled him in."

"And the house? Was it searched completely?"

"Went over it with a microscope," the general said. "Don't have any reason to think the colonel had anything to do with the message . . . or with that timber wolf code, whatever it was." He watched the President's expression. No change. A good sign.

"How do you explain the initials TW in that memo?" the president asked. "Coincidence, maybe? Referring to something other than timber wolf, perhaps?"

"Perhaps. Could be anything, though. Could be nothing. Could have been the initials of Thomas Williams. We're just not sure yet."

"Well, I suppose we'll have to wait for the coroner's report before we come to any conclusions."

General McKnight couldn't care less about the coroner's report. He knew the cause of death and he knew precisely what the autopsy report was going to say: heart failure. The only thing he was the least bit interested in at that moment was how the president was about to respond to his next question. The wrong answer would determine whether or not daxonol would need to be used again.

"What's the status of CONDOR?" McKnight asked bluntly. "We've heard rumors at the Pentagon that a delay, even a suspension of operations, was being considered because of the crash. Any truth to that?"

"No." The answer was unequivocal. Sitting behind the Oval Office desk, he found it extraordinarily easy to be convincing, to deceive without hesitation. Hell, as long as vital national interest was at stake, he thought, or as long as he could convince others that national interest was at stake, it was easy as hell to lie about anything, even easier to rationalize or justify it out of hand as a matter of national security.

"You know that WORLD ORDER without CONDOR is impossible," McKnight stated flatly. "And from the new CIA reports coming in, we can't afford a delay in the test flight schedule, much less a suspension of the mission."

"I'm well aware of that, Ben. There's no plan for a delay, as far as I'm concerned."

The general allowed himself to smile for the first time since walking into the Oval Office. "I'm glad to hear that. I was afraid our efforts were going to be derailed because of one unfortunate accident."

"Which is one of the reasons I wanted to see you," the president interrupted. "We need a complete report on CONDOR and the upcoming test flights. Can you have that to me within the week?"

"I see no problem with that."

"How's the crash investigation going?"

"Our people are examining every inch of that craft. They'll have a full report to me within the next several weeks. Meanwhile, the other CONDOR bases are on full alert and ready to go at a moment's notice."

"Has the new test flight crew arrived from Roswell?"

"Last night."

"Any problems?"

"None. They flew over every military base from Arizona to Maine without being picked up on radar. It was an excellent flight. A good indicator of its capabilities, I'd say."

"What about the ground crew?"

"They're with CONDOR now, going over it with a fine tooth comb. Damn good team, I assure you."

General McKnight's hand-picked crew was first-rate; the very best pilots and crew members he'd been able to recruit, each one a seasoned veteran who asked few questions and demanded even fewer answers; the kind who dies for his country but who kicks ass and wins wars in the process.

The crew had been told only that the top-secret test flight they'd been preparing for was of vital national security; and the fact that CONDOR would be used as the ultimate global peacekeeping weapon was enough to keep their patriotic enthusiasm at fever pitch. Their loyalty was unquestionable. General McKnight had chosen his crew well.

But what the crew was not privy to was that the upcoming test flight would be replaced by something called TIMBER WOLF. The plan was diabolically simple and would end with an unexplained but devastating accident that would insure that any evidence of the mission vanished with CONDOR itself.

"Let's go over the specifics once again, Ben."

McKnight leaned forward, placing his elbows and large folded hands on the Oval Office desk. He paused to gather his thoughts, then began the litany of events that would constitute the first and most ambitious in a series of secret test flights ever undertaken by the United States military; an actual series of simulated attacks on overseas foreign targets, designed to fully test CONDOR's defense-evading and attack readiness capabilities.

"At 2300 hours, April sixth, CONDOR takes off from the Prospect Airbase, canisters filled with a substitute chemical that has nearly the identical molecular weight as the actual agent. That will simulate the weight of the canisters as closely as possible and give us an idea of flight stability and maneuverability. The flight path will take it directly west by southwest to Hawaii. It should land at our secret base on Niihau shortly before dawn at 0530 hours, which allows a ground crew twelve hours to check it over before it takes off for its final target destination . . . the Philippines."

"And we're still certain, based on the latest strategic information, that the Philippines is the most appropriate attack test zone?" the president broke in.

McKnight had to answer with another lie. "We selected

it because there's enough sophisticated U.S. radar and tracking equipment on that island to test anything we throw at it without having to worry about enemy fire, if it should come to that. Get by *them* and you know you can get by anyone. If they lock on radar, if there's even one blip on Doppler, we abort the mission. If not, simulated attacks begin at 2100 hours and continue until predawn at 0500 hours. Return flight path takes CONDOR over the South Pacific, across Mexico, and into Hot Rock, New Mexico. Mission accomplished in less than forty-eight hours.''

''Does any of the crew suspect what happens in the event CONDOR is forced down outside U.S. Territories?'' The president's eyebrows lowered, his eyes narrowing in anticipation of an answer he really didn't care to hear.

''No. After what happened in Brittan, CONDOR's internal computer system has been programmed to initiate self-destruct as soon as crash conditions exist. There would be very little left. Nothing at all that anyone could use to identify the craft or trace it back to the United States. We've put enough Russian markings on it, though, to keep 'em guessing, just in case. Crew members wouldn't know what hit them. Cleanup would be minimal and confined to a limited area.''

And that was exactly what General McKnight saw as a fitting end and a flawlessly executed cover-up to a mission he was convinced would not only change the world but, more important, America herself.

''Listen, Ben. If anything on CONDOR doesn't check out, I want this test flight suspended. There's too much at stake here to start getting careless.''

''I've got my people working on it day and night. It'll be ready and it'll be on schedule.''

The two men sat in silence for a moment, only one thing on both their minds: April 6th. For the president, it was the first in a series of dangerous overseas test flights that would pave the way for his plan to achieve world order and thus save the country. For the general, it was the beginning of an alternate mission that in his mind would accomplish the same goal but, in a much different way, change the course of global history.

McKnight looked at the president and grinned. He knew that, despite what the president thought, WORLD ORDER was dead.

chapter eighteen

A black Lincoln weaved back and forth through the traffic, crept closer, then pulled away, leaving a puff of diesel smoke in its wake. Seconds later, another sedan, this one a navy blue Cadillac, appeared from nowhere and trailed for several miles, only to turn off sharply and disappear from sight. Each had all the signs of being too official, too suspicious; and virtually any car or truck following for more than half a mile had U.S. government plastered all over it.

His eyes were darting almost spastically to and from the rearview mirror as he watched the blur of asphalt speed away. His stomach had gone beyond queasy and started to burn as though he'd swallowed a piece of hot metal. The burning turned quickly to nausea. Never in his life, he was thinking, had he ever experienced anything the likes of this.

''I can't stand this, Linda,'' John blurted. ''I'm visualizing every damn car on the road pulling up and blowing us away. You've gotten yourself in one helluva mess.''

He meant us, Linda thought. *He said you, but he meant us; just didn't want to say it.*

''I'm really sorry I got you involved,'' she said. ''I never meant for any of this to happen.'' She waited for his response, not certain herself that she wanted to sink neck-deep into an investigation that had gone beyond a search for Peter's killers and was turning into a hunt for a plot she believed was behind Adam's death and now threatened both their lives.

"Hey, I wouldn't want it any other way," John said, trying to break the suffocating tension that had him wondering if they would even make it. "Besides, I was getting bored. Until yesterday, all I did was spend my life trying to crack the secrets of the universe. Felt like I was invading God's privacy. But this. Hey, this is what it's all about. Government plots, world domination, assassinations, genetic engineering. You've given me reason to get up in the morning. It's great."

"Yeah, thanks, smarty." Linda sensed the strain in his voice, and she figured the attempt at humor was more for her sake than for his. "Joke about it if you want," she said, "but I couldn't have gotten through all this without you."

John placed his hand on hers and, feeling that it was wet and cold from fear, squeezed warmth into it instantly, reassuring her that he would be with her, no matter what. Then, glancing over at her, he couldn't believe that at thirty-eight, with little time for anything but a career that seemed to fill the emptiness of his own life, he would actually be on his way to break into Pentagon files, knowing the consequences he'd face if caught.

Extremely precocious as a child, he was a borderline genius, according to the developmental psychologists who'd tried convincing his parents that the sometimes odd behavior and temper tantrums were nothing more than his way of coping with what they'd euphemistically referred to as a fertile mind. In high school he'd been given the dubious title of "class nerd." It was a distinction that caused him a great deal of pain and, because of his already fragile self-esteem, to retreat even further from his schoolmates and friends.

By his junior year, John sensed something happening to him that made him believe he was truly going mad. Afraid to come forward, convinced that revealing his problem would only make his life more miserable than it had already been, he said nothing. The undiagnosed epilepsy, which in his case had manifested itself as bouts of extreme inattentiveness that grew progressively worse as he became older, forced him to postpone college for two years until he'd discovered the magic of computers and the facility at which he was able to manipulate numbers and symbols, despite a disorder that at times made him question his own sanity.

There'd been few relationships in college, and little hope that he would ever settle into one that would ever be meaningful. The inattentiveness grew worse, the terrifying belief that his mind was gradually slipping away gnawing at him to the point of near suicide. And then, with the eventual diagnosis of his epilepsy came a renewed zest for life and, a few years later, an opportunity to work on research projects with a brilliant scientist who eventually became his best friend.

As John felt Linda's trembling hand in his, he found it hard to keep from talking about the man he'd been closer to than anyone else except her. "Did Peter ever talk about some of the work he did?" he asked.

Linda shook her head. "Hardly," she answered. "Sometimes he'd get upset if I'd bring it up." She looked over at John with a puzzled expression. "The night I called you, you asked me if Peter had told me anything before he left for Tucson. I remember you sounding kind of nervous about that."

"Nervous? I don't think so."

"I know you did some classified work with Peter years ago," Linda continued. "I won't ask you to tell me about it if you feel you'd be breaking security."

"Believe me. I'd tell you if I could," John answered. "But all I ever received from Peter was encrypted data to analyze without knowing exactly what it was that I was analyzing. The work was coded in such a way as to remain classified. None of us knew."

"What is it?" Linda then asked, noticing a change of expression on John's face.

"I never wanted to say anything because I didn't know for sure. I still don't."

"What?"

"The reason I was so interested in your discussion about

biological agents last night and this morning is because I think Peter may have known about some illegal virus research that was being conducted secretly.''

''No, he couldn't have,'' Linda said. She shifted her body until it was facing his. ''He would have told me, and he would have reported it. The idea repulsed him.''

''I'm not saying he did, Linda. I'm just saying that shortly before he died, there was some data from his lab that were encrypted in a similar fashion to data I'd received from Fort Detrick. For all I know, someone else was working on something that even *he* didn't know the full details about.''

Linda thought back and tried to recall anything about Peter's behavior that would have revealed his involvement in research she thought for sure he would never have agreed to. ''I'm scared,'' she whispered. ''And I'm not sure what scares me more, finding what we're looking for or finding out that Peter may have known or been involved in something like this.''

''Yeah, I'm scared, too,'' John said. ''Scared as hell, if you wanna know the truth.''

Once they'd left Georgetown and pulled onto highway 395, they'd felt as if they had finally left it all behind them. The suspicious vehicles seemed to have disappeared since they'd turned off Constitution Avenue and onto Seventh Street.

John, less nervous but still cautiously searching for murderous faces looking out from tinted glass, slowed the shifting of his eyes from highway to mirror from every five seconds to every minute now. It seemed clear enough, he thought, and unless the Feds had a chopper tracking them—

''Linda, quick, look outside above us.''

''What?''

''Just indulge me, please. See if there's a chopper overhead.''

''God, I didn't think about that.'' Linda squinted into the bright sunlight and searched the sky. Nothing in any direction, not even birds. ''There's nothing out there, John. Now quit being so paranoid. Where are we going anyway? Or should I even ask?"

"Quantico."

"Quantico!" Linda wanted to reach over and slam her foot on the brake, her body snapping around a full ninety degrees. "Are you nuts? That's a marine corps base. Why are we going *there*?"

"Don't trust me, do you?" John smiled at Linda's outburst, but turned serious when it became apparent that she was seconds away from wrapping her fingers around his throat. He shifted his eyes upward, still watching the sky and, without moving his head, glanced anxiously in the rearview mirror.

"There's a remote site just outside Quantico, where we already have a setup."

"A setup? Who? Who the hell has a setup?" She dug her fingernails into John's thigh so hard he grimaced.

"Ow! Take it easy."

"Tell me. What kind of setup am I getting myself into?"

"Several years ago, a good buddy of mine with the National Security Agency—"

"The NSA?" Linda questioned, cutting him off. She knew the NSA was the most secretive of all the intelligence agencies, and she stiffened when John seemed inadvertently to have let slip a part of his background she knew nothing about till now. "How were you involved with the NSA?"

"Like I said, Linda, a buddy of mine wanted help accessing some files he really wasn't supposed to have access to. It was a national security thing, and he was desperate. And since I was the best computer expert with a top-secret clearance he knew, he recruited me for that one assignment with guaranteed immunity. That was it. We'd become good friends, and I established a pretty valuable contact."

"If you're into something I should know about, I want to know right now," Linda demanded, still skeptical.

"Don't panic, Linda. It's nothing like that. I swear. It was all legit, from an intelligence standpoint. He needed me to set up a computer piggyback. You know, use our equipment to break into the line without being detected.''

''Why Quantico?''

''Jeff—forget you heard that name—being a military insider, knew of an old abandoned communications bunker that accessed underground telephone cables leading directly into the Pentagon. It was used extensively during the sixties and seventies. The site's actually in Prince William Forest Park now, adjacent to the base. When the government decided to close down part of Quantico to expand the park, they left the bunker intact. Records of its existence were probably buried alongside all the other bureaucratic crap they had in government files. Hard to believe Uncle Sam can't even keep track of things like that.''

''You sure it's safe?''

''Absolutely.'' John felt free to smile again, sensing that he'd at least reassured Linda he wasn't leading her straight into enemy fire. ''Don't worry. I've been there several times and always felt safe.'' He pressed Linda closer to him and held her tightly. ''I told you before, I wouldn't do anything that would put you in any danger.''

Route 395 turned into 95 South, and once past Springfield, the traffic had eased enough to make being followed without notice nearly impossible. They'd stopped occasionally, pulling off the highway and into a service station, just to be sure, then got back on the road and searched the line of vehicles behind them for one they thought may have looked a little too familiar or too suspicious. Every five miles or so, a green sign filled with bold white lettering would catch Linda's eye. QUANTICO U.S. MARINE CORPS RESERVATION. And though everything had seemed to be going perfectly, the idea of heading straight for a marine corps base had begun to make her more than a little edgy.

Now, twenty-five miles and four dirty Texaco stations later, they'd arrived. The Alfa Romeo eased up as John read the sign and downshifted.

Prince William Forest Park
Next Exit

To them, the chocolate brown national park service sign was an oasis in the middle of a Virginia desert. It had taken nearly two hours to get there. It felt more like five. John pulled into the exit lane and followed the white arrows pointing toward their final destination.

"Almost there," he said, at last breaking the latest stretch of silences that had been getting noticeably longer with each pit stop.

John turned into the park's main entrance, drove almost a mile, then turned left, heading south on an unmarked and isolated road that was lined perfectly on both sides with enormous white oaks and red maples. Their twisted limbs, still bare from the unusually cold winter, reached across the two lanes and touched one another, occasionally swooping down and slapping the top of the Romeo with wind-driven fingers as if warning Linda and John to turn back before it was too late.

"How much farther?" Linda asked, rubbing her chilled arms with nervous fingers.

"Not far. A few more miles and we should see a service road. We take *it* to the site."

The heavily shadowed road began to curve sharply and grew dark as the sun disappeared behind the gray of thickening clouds. And except for mounds of crusty brown leaves that swirled tornadolike along the edges of the road, nothing on either side of them stirred. The purr of the engine, amplified by the tree-lined corridor that now enveloped them, was the only sound that broke through the crispness of cold air.

Afraid even to whisper, Linda imagined a gunman leaping from out of those woods, envisioned a roadblock around the next turn, and it was all she could do to keep from grabbing the steering wheel and insisting that John head straight back to Washington, that they forget the whole damned thing and return to their lives as if none of this had ever happened.

"There it is." John slowed down when he saw the small, one-lane service road to his left. "It's about a half mile down this way."

Linda let out a sigh of relief at seeing that the road hadn't been used in years; it was so overgrown with shrubs and overhanging limbs that the Alfa Romeo had to break through the brush like a Land Rover on a jungle safari. That was good, she thought. The less the road had been used, the greater the odds that no one else knew about the bunker. She felt herself sinking back into the soft leather seat.

John pulled the car into a clearing and stopped, waiting a good minute before he cut off the engine. When he did, the comfort of the purr was gone, replaced by the sounds of his erratic breathing and the rustling of stiff leaves battered by a suddenly unrelenting wind.

"We walk from here," John said.

They slipped out of the car and stood for a moment, their heads cocked to one side, listening. John swung the large canvas equipment bag around his shoulder. The sad moan of the wind grew louder now, the crisp air blowing dust and small leaves into their faces with increasing fury. Linda pulled her jacket up around her face and thrust her hands deep into her pockets. She trailed John across a brown grassy knoll and watched him disappear into a dense cluster of tall bushes. She followed. An obscure but noticeable path was in front of her, hidden by a thornlike wall of thick dormant vegetation that at one time had been maintained when the area was a part of Quantico but which now belonged to an uncaring public.

Linda stuck her hands in front of her face, ignoring the branches that snapped cruelly back against her. The words swirling about in her mind made her oblivious to everything around her.

WORLD ORDER, CONDOR, TIMBER WOLF. She couldn't shake the feeling. She couldn't help thinking that nothing was what it seemed. Something about TIMBER WOLF was not right. Maybe today she'd find out. Suddenly, she was terrified of dying.

"Over this way." John stopped and pointed straight ahead to what looked like an old grave marker in the midst of a small clearing.

"Where?"

"That slab of cement."

"That's it? Looks like a tombstone with overgrown weeds all over it, for Christ's sake."

"Looks can be deceiving, Linda. C'mon."

Urgently, John started toward the slab, turning his head ninety degrees in either direction. He glanced backward, sure now that they were the only ones in that secluded area of the park and, from the looks of it, perhaps the only ones who'd come to the bunker since John had been there over two years ago.

When they reached the rectangular piece of cement, Linda looked down and scanned the worn printing etched across its top. It was simple. Nothing that could identify it as government property. CB-1748 Quadrant 4. The CB stood for communications bunker.

John walked over to a clump of bushes, dug through them, and retrieved a thick five-foot metal rod. He inserted one end into a hole near the edge of the slab and pushed down, straining and grunting from the weight of concrete.

The slab popped up. He leaned against the rod with one leg, braced with the other, and moved the rod forward, positioning the cement lid so that its corner now rested on the ground and left a two-foot gap that partially revealed a set of metal steps leading down into a dark pit.

chapter nineteen

It was a massive steel and blue-tinted-glass edifice that spanned an entire city block and reached twenty-two stories into the late afternoon sky. Shielding much of the light that could otherwise have found its way to the busy streets and crowded sidewalks of Connecticut Avenue, it was one of several hundred such buildings casting its gray and ominous shadows across home to the world's last remaining superpower.

On the seventeenth floor of the Perkins Building, in a palatial room the size of a tennis court, a dozen men sat hunched anxiously around a glass-covered conference table. Mahogany paneled walls surrounded them, the deep rich grain reflecting the light from crystal chandeliers that hung like diamond pendants from a twelve-foot ceiling, itself crisscrossed with ornately sculpted mahogany beams.

The table, rimmed with polished gold borders an inch thick, concealed alligator and Italian leather shoes; the watches, all identical gold Rolexes, adorned fat wrists like high-priced symbols of greed and power; the cuff links, bracelets, and rings, either diamond or gold or flawless Oriental jade, sparkled against the clean glass and lit up the room like a thousand specks of light. The ostentatious display of wealth was typical for these men, but today it seemed especially vulgar and overdone.

One of the men rose and tapped his fourteen-karat gold pen gavellike on the glass. Every last eye focused immediately on the immense gray suit and gold chain that draped tightly across the vest, then moved up to look at a wide face that spread outward from the shirt collar like soft clay. Gregory Morris removed a silk handkerchief from his breast pocket and wiped the river of sweat that flowed from his forehead and cheeks. His eyes stared straight ahead, unblinking. He nodded in acknowledgment at the instant quiet, but did not smile.

In the midst of this blinding glitter sat the powerful elite: retired, high-ranking military men, former intelligence officers, and former administration officials; the men who at one time had pulled the strings and shaped destinies; who had dictated foreign and domestic policy and determined the direction of world governments with little more than words and promises and the bold strokes of a pen.

This was the inner circle. The Vanguard. A name fittingly chosen to signify the group of men who saw themselves standing at the forefront of economic battle; the men who had served their country and would now forge a new order out of what was predicted to be the inevitable shift of global economic power. And today, in this room, their only agenda was how they could reverse that shift and disrupt the further creation of a global economic community without international borders.

"Gentlemen," Gregory Morris said, his voice booming across the vast expanse. "I'm pleased to see all of you here and trust that everything in Geneva went well. I'm sorry I couldn't be with you, but I'll expect a full report by week's end."

He then flipped open a file folder and shuffled through a stack of documents and papers, adjusting his glasses downward. "Let's quickly begin with a report on congressional status," he ordered. More shuffling, followed by, "How many congressmen do we currently have and how many potential legislators are there out there to be had?" His brown slicked hair and beefy face made a half circle around the table as it searched for an appropriate answer.

As a major stockholder in Universal Biomedical Corporation, a pharmaceutical conglomerate with plants throughout the world and a net worth of nearly twenty billion, he'd been selected as head of a group whose principal mission was to ensure the survival of America's economy.

Morris himself was a typical Washington insider. A former NSA and CIA officer with close ties to the Pentagon, he'd spent the last decade cultivating deals, exchanging politically explosive information, and extending his cancerlike influence throughout each branch of government. It was Universal Biomedical that had helped develop both germ warfare weapons and vaccines against the world's most lethal nerve and biological agents. And in the current climate of global hostilities, a man like Gregory Morris and a company such as Universal were of immeasurable worth to the Pentagon and, thus, to the nation. His ability to divert funds from both the government and domestic corporations to black projects was another reason for his position with the Vanguard. There was no one of any significance Morris did not know, no one in Washington who didn't know him by name, and certainly few who'd managed to escape his grip of power once he chose to exert it.

"One hundred forty-seven," answered Marvin Watkinson, a thin, balding former colonel in his early fifties, who was looking through his own stack of documents, which included the number of the Swiss bank accounts of every legislator in Washington. "We bought the office for sixteen of them in the last election. Rookies, but good ones, I think. Eight senators, as well. Number one hundred forty-eight'll be on board as soon as he deposits the three million we offered him yesterday in his Swiss account."

"Three million?" Morris's eyebrows formed thick arches beneath the three folds of his wide forehead. "I don't recall authorizing three million."

"He's currently on the finance committee. He's a leading Democrat, has seniority, and we expect him to have quite a bit of influence. Three million was a good deal for someone with those kinds of credentials. And three is what it took to get him. Once he makes the trip to the bank, he's ours."

"Any chance it may be a setup?" Morris asked. "How sure are you of him?"

Half a lifetime of martinis and gin and tonics gave Morris that alcoholic look; bulgy eyes and veined, shiny skin. The bulgy eyes looked straight ahead without blinking. Cynical, more from a lifetime of dealings with political adversaries than by nature, he'd always figured politicians could either be bought or coerced. Everyone, ultimately, had a price. The older ones he'd known were greedy bastards who'd realized they couldn't do much else in office but sign their names to useless, sometimes idiotic and even dangerous legislation, line their pockets before the next election in the event they lost, and get out rich beyond even their own wild expectations. So why not line their pockets with *his* money, he'd rationalized, be signatories to *his* legislation. Hell, if the bastards had no minds of their own, he'd figured, if they couldn't be bothered reading the laws they were putting their own names to, then at least he'd be there to help point the fools in the right direction.

NAFTA and GATT proved to Morris that he was needed now more than ever. Though everyone from the president to his advisers to the State Department and members of Congress had serious doubts about legislation they knew would send economic shock waves through American industry, the agreements—several thousand pages of jargoned legalese that few, if any, legislators had the time to read—passed easily. But with Morris's resources, other such legislation was unlikely. "Like working with greedy children," he would say disparagingly, though he'd have it no other way.

Morris preferred buying these politicians, but didn't blink an eye at coercion. Sometimes, he figured, coercion was more certain, especially with the younger, more idealistic punks who initially believed they were in it strictly for public service but who were impressionable enough to be addicted quickly to the intoxicating lure of political power.

Some years back, a story had circulated around Washington about a young, newly elected senator who'd stumbled across irregularities in the powerful ways and means committee. Something about bribes and influence peddling and secret deals with dictators in Central and South America, some of which had involved the highest reaches of power. The story was that the young senator was about to testify before Congress when he had a sudden change of heart, and after a series of probes into his allegations was found in a nearby hotel room with a gun in his hand and a hole through his temple. Rumors had it that he'd been seen with a man by the name of Gregory Morris only days before. The rumors were never confirmed, and as in so many other cases involving national security or vast sums of money, this one was closed as an apparent suicide.

"A couple of pictures of him making a coke buy and grabbing his girlfriend's ass in the parking lot before nailing her in a cheap Motel 6 make us damn sure it's not a set up," Watkinson answered with a smile on his face. "The Feds and his wife would get a kick out of the eight by tens and a tape of him screwin' her eyeballs out, all the while telling her how much better she is than his wife. He probably would've taken less than three. Three at least makes him think he'd lose a lot more than he'd gain."

"How about our current lobbying efforts? Are we making any further inroads with any of the more intransigent House members?"

"So far our lobbyists have been more successful than we'd anticipated. In fact, we've been able to turn several key pieces of legislation around our way. Hell, these guys in Washington are getting easier with every election. Even the bleeding hearts seem to be more willing to step over the edge. Especially with their president and his inner circle having more damn skeletons in their closet than the Mafia, and the chances of their reelection dropping with every damn indictment. These people are running scared."

Morris smiled, his fleshy cheeks spreading outward. "Okay, we've got quite a few key legislators on board and right now it's looking good for the next election, regardless of who gets in. We've bottled up several key pieces of legislation that would have accelerated the movement of factories offshore. And we've made arrangements with our people in Geneva to consolidate our international holdings in order to maximize our influence and purchasing power. So far everything seems to be on schedule. Congress, for its part, has been pretty tenuous about making any rash legislative decisions at this point."

He stopped and removed his glasses, looking out over the group. "There's a problem, however, that has me somewhat concerned."

"And that is?" Watkinson asked.

"I'll let Mr. Anthony Lambino here give us an overview of his two-day investigation."

Morris sat down and placed his hands across his enormous gut. He nodded at an olive-skinned man as wide as he was tall with a square head and body hair that looked more like dense fur.

A former CIA operative, Lambino, head of intelligence

and investigation for the Vanguard, stood up and opened a one-inch brown folder packed with pages of reports and a stack of black-and-white photographs. He slid a pair of black glasses over ears that resembled broccoli and looked down his flattened nose at page one. His neck thickened as it bent forward until it was two inches wider than his head. As he spoke, he formed his words carefully to minimize the lisp that blended harshly with the New York accent.

"For the past forty-eight hours," he began, "we've been investigating the activities of Adam Wesely and Dr. Linda Franklin, a NASA scientist in Washington, D.C., in connection with the CONDOR crash."

The dozen silk suits began squirming in their noisy leather chairs. They all knew. They looked at one other and grimaced as if CONDOR or NASA or Adam Wesely were key words that collectively triggered their dulled nerves into action.

It was the November following the 1976 election that a cartel of elite and powerful men had offered to help fund a long-term, top-secret Pentagon black project. The project would ultimately serve two separate purposes. For the government, it would keep America at the forefront of military technology well into the next century through development of advanced chemical and biological agents and a new class of long-range aircraft, later named CONDOR. Since the public and most elected officials at the time would never have agreed to such a weapons program, private funding sources were critical. General Benjamin McKnight had been selected as the caretaker of the project, a move that had placed him in the unenviable position of pledging allegiance to both the Pentagon and the funding source for a weapons system he knew America desperately needed to survive the next century. For the Vanguard, it would guarantee that a threat to America's industrial base, and thus to its national security, would be met with intervention in the name of vital national interests.

It was quite simple. By arranging for the diversion of tens of billions of dollars—all in the name of vital national interest, of course—the Vanguard had successfully insured that the U.S. government would protect the financial interests of the United States instead of Wall Street and foreign corporations.

The investment, with or without CONDOR, proved exceedingly wise. Not only had the group gained access to Pentagon secrets, it bought access to valued legislators on Capitol Hill, and by the early nineties to members of the administration itself. Legislation, which had to pass through vital committees bought and paid for by the Vanguard, was either assured of passage or would languish indefinitely, never allowed to see the light of day.

There was urgency in these actions, for free trade was the catchword of the day, embraced as a way to interconnect the global business community and, at the same time, stabilize a fragile cold-war peace. "Global competitiveness," a term bandied about frequently when comparing labor forces among nations, was used often and unapologetically to rationalize the movement of factories offshore in order to exploit slave labor and cost-cutting production without regard for what that would do to social structures. Eventually, with the realization that power was inextricably linked to economics, and economics to global stability, the principal goal of Washington's elite had become one of sacrificing an entire nation—if that's what it took—for the good of the global economy and ultimately for the benefit of those who had crowned themselves caretakers of this new economic order.

It was no small coincidence, according to Morris's sources, that during the past decade, every international crisis responded to by the U.S. government, from the war in Kuwait to the financial bailouts of Mexico, had somehow involved the rescue of America's investment bankers or the industrial elite. It was also no small coincidence that each piece of trade legislation that passed through the House and Senate, every trade agreement negotiated, every treaty signed, was designed to make the transition of America's industrial base from domestic to international as simple as moving a factory from Kansas to Nebraska.

But Morris and his group also recognized that the die had been cast even before the Reagan years. No longer satisfied with obscene profits that exceeded their wildest expectations, the barons of global trade had seen a window of opportunity that mesmerized even the most patriotic in the bunch. As one such globalist frankly admitted, "I'd have to be insane or a goddamn fool to pay 208 million dollars a year in labor costs in New York when I can pay a little over 4 million dollars in Indonesia."

He was right. By all accounts, an American corporation employing ten thousand men and women at an average salary of just ten dollars an hour would increase its annual profit margin by over two hundred million dollars simply by moving offshore and paying its workers twenty-five cents an hour. And that, regardless of the creative accounting system one used, was incentive enough to begin driving corporate America from shores of the land that had offered it the freedom and opportunity to grow into the greatest financial empire in the modern world.

And now, thanks largely to an unrelenting, decade-long campaign to convince the public that America's future lay not in manufacturing but in service and telecommunications, the final stage had begun. The plan, Morris knew, was ingeniously simple. By the year 2000, the dismantling of the U.S. industrial base would essentially have been complete. And the architects of this new industrial revolution will have charted the course for American history with little regard for where that course would ultimately take it, simply because they had the money and the power to do so. The Vanguard would have none of that.

But before they could continue with their plan, they knew they'd have to deal with another problem. If Linda Franklin was dangerously close to uncovering the secret of CONDOR, she would also be close to exposing the Vanguard's involvement and the major players behind them. And that, they feared, would create the ingredients for disaster. For there were secrets that had to be kept at all costs, not so much because their revelation would threaten the security of the

United States, but because they would ultimately destroy the Vanguard itself.

"We initiated an investigation once we learned that Dr. Franklin continued an active interest in this particular crash," Lambino continued, "even after the Pentagon pulled the plug on it."

"Since when do we worry about someone's interest in a crash?" asked James Hamid, a former official with the Carter administration.

The remaining men turned from Hamid back to Lambino. They suspected that if Lambino thought an investigation was in order, it more than likely was. His track record for sniffing out potential problems was perfect, his sixth sense uncanny. Linda Franklin worried him. And for him, that meant only one thing.

Lambino spread several pages of the report in front of him. He picked up page three with cigar-sized fingers and lowered his glasses to help him focus on the list of events he was about to read.

"We became concerned when we picked up communications between Wesely and Dr. Franklin," he lisped. "That's when we decided to resume monitoring."

"Monitoring?" Hamid asked, his deep brown eyes narrowing into devillike slits. "You've watched her before?"

"Yes. Her husband was involved in the investigation of the last crash in eighty-eight and we wanted to make sure nothing was found. Fortunately, an explosion made that unnecessary."

"Ah, *that* was the other Franklin."

"Dr. Peter Franklin," Lambino said. "Linda Franklin's husband. We'd ceased monitoring when it became apparent she no longer posed a security threat."

"What makes you suspect she is now?" Hamid interrupted again.

"At nine-ten A.M. on the seventeenth, we followed her to the NASA Computer Research Center. She met there with John Peterson, a computer expert." Lambino pushed two eight-by-tens, one of John and another of Linda, to his right.

Morris examined them and passed them on. "She was there until ten-twenty. At ten forty-six she arrived home, but ten minutes later headed urgently back to the lab complex. We suspect she received a call about Wesely and took off. When she left, we were able to break in and tap her phones."

Lambino flipped quickly to page four, studied the handwriting, and began again. "At eleven twenty-four, she arrived at the lab and left seven minutes later with Dr. Jackson Pilofski. By noon, they were at Adam Wesely's home. It seemed like unusual activity for a busy scientist who had a lot of other things she could have been doing at the time. While at Wesely's, Franklin made a call to her lab and informed her secretary that she'd be in later that afternoon . . . that she was helping with the memorial service. Unfortunately, our surveillance team made an error in judgment."

"What do you mean error in judgment?" Watkinson asked angrily.

"Franklin never showed up at the lab," Lambino answered. "She hasn't been seen since. And we think we know why."

Lambino positioned a small tape recorder on the glass table and punched the rewind button. The tape whistled as it sped backward and stopped. "At seven forty-five P.M. on the seventeenth, there was a message left for her by Maria Swensen, the housekeeper they visited at Weseley's home that afternoon." Lambino pushed play, while twelve faces looked on in suspended animation and listened to the Swedish accent.

"Linda, some men were here a few hours after you left," the voice on the tape said with a tone of dire urgency. *"They asked questions. I didn't tell them anything. I didn't tell them what you told me about Mr. Wesely. Please be careful. Don't come here again. I'm afraid."*

The men sat in stunned silence, frozen at the sound of the ominous words. *"They asked questions. I didn't tell them anything. I didn't tell them what you told me about Mr. Wesely."*

Lambino pushed stop. "Obviously, Swensen was trying to

warn them,'' he said. ''She wouldn't have done that if she didn't know something was going on.''

''Did anyone go back to Weseley's house to question her?'' Watkinson asked, more nervous now than angry.

''Yes, but she wouldn't talk. Nothing would make her cooperate.''

''You tried everything?''

''Everything.''

''Did you eliminate the problem?''

''We had to.''

''Where's the body?''

''In storage, until the Kramer office building is started next month. Our crew will make sure she becomes a part of it.'' Lambino said that and went on as casually as if he'd lost track of every other body part lying beneath buildings and inside bridge posts throughout the city. ''I have a team of men searching for Franklin and Peterson now. Both their homes are under twenty-four-hour surveillance, as is the lab complex and the computer center. The minute they show up, we'll apprehend them. In the meantime, some of my people will be questioning Pilofski to see what he knows.''

''Thank you, Mr. Lambino.''

Gregory Morris pushed his black Italian leather chair back and rose again. Lambino gathered his reports and photographs and slipped them back into the folder. Twelve pairs of eyes followed him across the large room and out the door. The eyes focused quickly back on Morris.

''I assure you, gentlemen, Mr. Lambino will make every effort to ensure that any loose ends are taken care of as expeditiously as possible.'' Morris's cheeks spread out again as he now smiled. ''Nothing will interfere with this.''

''What if Franklin and Peterson can't be located?'' Hamid asked. ''What if they'd already discovered something and are reporting it to government agencies or getting ready to expose everything at this moment?''

''Why would they do that?'' Morris asked. ''They suspect it's the United States government behind everything to begin with. If they *are* on the run, it's because they think the Pentagon or the White House or both has given the order to find them and to eliminate them. No, I'm confident they won't try anything at this point. In the meantime, we'll find them. Believe me, Anthony will find them.''

chapter twenty

Linda fell to her knees and pushed with every ounce of strength she could gather. White clouds condensed in front of her face as she exhaled with a prolonged grunt, then fought to catch her breath. John was kneeling beside her, his temples a deep purple, straining against the metal bar. Cement grated against cement, sending a strident rumble through the cold air. Between the two of them, they managed to shift the lid several feet, creating a gap just wide enough for a body to fit through.

John threw the rod down, switched on his flashlight, and quickly descended the stairs. He looked up and waved his arm for Linda to follow. After a moment of hesitation, she slid down into thé earth, and with her head barely above the ground, took one more look around before disappearing into a hellish blackness interrupted only by the sliver of John's light.

Neither uttered a word. Their panting quickly gave way to heavy breathing that hissed as it left their lips then echoed through the pit. A few feet down, the narrow beam illuminated a small metal door to their right. John focused the beam on an iron handle, which he grasped and forced to the right. As he pushed, the door let out a chilling creak, inching forward unyieldingly as though held back by years of rust and built-up corrosion. The stream of light broke through the crack and searched the inner chamber, a concrete tomb containing little else but rusted metal panels along two of its battleship gray walls. A thin layer of transparent goo covered every square inch of the place and appeared hardened from the frigid moisture trapped beneath at least five feet of earth, metal, and reinforced concrete.

"Not much to look at, is it?" John asked, looking straight ahead as he entered the bunker and extended his hand for Linda to grab onto.

Linda nodded in agreement but remained silent, terrified at the prospect of being trapped inside this hell. She let go of his hand and immediately wrapped her arms around herself.

John placed his equipment bag next to the middle panel and removed a battery-powered lantern. He threw the switch and instantly lit up the entire wall.

"This is your basic underground government cable exchange," John said. "They have these set up at various locations for security reasons. To tap into phone lines, acquire vital information, investigate leaks. Things like that. This one was supposed to have been decommissioned before Uncle Sam gave the land to the state park system. More often than not, though, the government manages to screw up. Lucky for us."

"Yeah, lucky." With a piercing creak that sent a rattle through their teeth, John pried open the panel, exposing rows of tangled color-coded wires. He dug his fingers into the thick bundle of whites, greens, and blues and pulled out the only red one in the bunch.

"Yes, come to papa," John said, his face displaying animation for the first time since their conversation in the car. "It'll take me a few minutes to set this up." He positioned the portable computer carefully on the damp floor and flipped open the display terminal.

As she looked on, Linda's breathing grew labored. Beads of sweat dripped from her forehead, despite the wet cold. Her fingers were shaking visibly, the stifling tension sickening her to the point of nausea.

From the bag, John retrieved two long wires that had alligator clips attached to both ends. Working as deftly as if defusing a nuclear device, he first attached two of the alligator clips to the red telephone cable, then to a set of wires coming out from the back of the computer. He then disconnected a section of red wire that had obviously been disconnected before. Bypass complete.

"Almost there," John said, patting the computer and giving Linda a half-hearted thumbs up sign and a weak smile that didn't look very reassuring from where she was sitting.

Then, after switching the computer on and punching in a ten-digit telephone number, John waited for what seemed like eternity. He nodded his head at the sight of the screen illuminating, then slid his fingers into the lining of his jacket. Out came a small slip of yellow paper with a series of letters and numbers that hopefully would get him into the most classified and sophisticated computer system inside the Pentagon.

Linda was on her knees, paralyzed. If this didn't do it, she thought, nothing would. They might as well give it up; live out their lives as fugitives; probably get killed anyway.

The computer screen glowed, lighting up the tomb in an eerie shade of blue as it cast grotesque shadows against its metal walls. Linda watched as a series of instructions flashed across the screen. John continued punching keys methodically but with incredible speed, trying to bypass the encryption devices that since the early eighties had become a routine part of every government computer system. The screen suddenly went blank, then lit up again, this time displaying the message Linda had anticipated since yesterday.

U.S. Government—Eyes Only
Pentagon Omega Files
Access Code Required

Type in omega access code>

Linda and John stared at each other, frozen, and for a brief, silent moment debating if what they were about to do was worth the risk. They both knew that breaking into accessed

Pentagon omega files meant ten to twenty in a military prison. Twenty for John, since he was the one actually breaking in with an unauthorized access code.

Neither breathed a word, realizing they were beyond the point of debating the issue. They'd witnessed far too much, knew too much, and if they didn't uncover *something*, would probably end up like Adam anyway. Whoever assassinated Peter, they both agreed, had probably assassinated Adam as well and was no doubt deliberating at that moment whether to eliminate anyone else who may have had access to the same information.

With a tenuous nod, Linda urged John to punch in the access code, though for a split second, as he moved his fingers toward the keyboard, she thought seriously about grabbing them and pulling them back.

He clicked off the code and paused a few seconds before hitting return. Done. The screen went blank again. Seconds later, a message appeared that made John's head snap forward until it was only inches from his face.

Searching files . . . access being monitored . . . searching files

"Shit!"

"What's wrong?" Linda asked, looking at the words on the screen as she clutched onto John's arm, unsure of what it was that had him so riveted. "What's going on?"

"This shouldn't have happened. I bypassed encryption, I know I did."

"What! Tell me, dammit!"

"We're being traced. Access being monitored is their way of saying they got you; they know you're in the files. Must be a new security system, a sensing device I didn't know about. Shit, I was afraid of this."

"How can they possibly know where the break-in is?"

"Their computers must have picked up a change in the cable resistance along the route. Any break in the circuit, even for a fraction of a second, is picked up by the security system and pinpointed to the exact location of the break. It must have happened when I bypassed the cable with my wires.''

''Oh, God. What now?''

''It'll take a little time before the computer analyzes it and actually targets the location, but we better move like hell.''

John chewed on a fingernail as he waited for the computer to finish the file search. ''There!'' He tore his finger from his mouth. The computer screen lit up with another message.

Pentagon Data File: Omega-one
Top Secret—Eyes Only

CODE WORD?>

''Type in TIMBER WOLF,'' Linda insisted.

Code word?>TIMBER WOLF
>Bad command. Retry code word

''Damn. It doesn't make sense. Why wouldn't it be in Pentagon files? Type in PCW''

Code word?>PCW
Searching

''Got it, Linda.''

And when the computer had finished its search and the series of messages appeared on the screen, John and Linda froze as they looked at something neither had expected.

Pentagon Omega File: PCW
Top Secret—Eyes Only

File entries: Psychochemical warfare
Mission target(s): Executive directive
Mission date: Standby
Weapon system: Condor/5-HTP-5-HT/Combat operational Omni-range aircraft/Deliver biological agent to target areas/

Select populations will be depleted as a result of agent effect/Use restricted by executive order.
Code name: WORLD ORDER
Press C to Continue>

"Damn, look at that. Psychochemi—"

The words suddenly vanished, replaced by another message:

Access revoked . . . access revoked . . . access revoked

"My God, Linda, they've located the break-in already." John ripped the two long wires out of the panel and started throwing everything in the bag. "Let's get the hell outta here before they complete the trace!"

John grabbed the flashlight and made his way to the stairs. Linda was close enough behind to keep her hand on his back, pushing him along, as if he weren't going fast enough. John poked his head out the opening, twisting it in every direction and seeing that the area was still as deserted as when they'd first arrived.

"All clear. Let's go," he ordered, jumping out onto the grass and extending his hand down to Linda, who grasped it and quickly pulled herself up. "Forget the slab. It's over. They know where it is and they'll be here any minute."

Leaving the bunker exposed like an unearthed grave, John and Linda made a frenzied beeline for the car. Back through the branched wall, thorns and spindly bushes tore into their flesh like spikes, ripping at their hair and faces as they raced from the hole in the earth.

"This way." John broke through the brush and headed straight for the car, exposed and vulnerable.

Linda searched the sky, imagining a military chopper swooping down on them any second. "Hurry! I hear something!" she yelled.

They reached the car and jumped in. John started it up and peeled out, leaving deep tracks in the muddy ground. When he reached the main road he turned right and, without slowing down, threw the car into third and floored it. The engine rumbled, rocketing the lightweight sports car up to fifty miles per hour.

"You hear it, Linda?"

"Yeah. Sounds like it's getting closer. There's the park entrance. Hurry."

"Not yet. I better pull over and wait. Last thing we want is to get spotted hightailing it out of here."

Linda cocked her head to one side and listened to the thumping of rotors slicing the air above them. As John swerved to the side of the road, positioning the small car beneath the branches of a dense evergreen, she saw what looked like a camouflaged grasshopper fly overhead and head directly to the area they'd just come from.

"A marine chopper," Linda said. "I don't think it spotted us. It's heading straight for the bunker, though."

John pulled back onto the road and sped ahead through the park gate. He hung a wide left and merged with the sparse traffic heading north to D.C. As he settled into his seat, another marine Blackhawk circled overhead and flew into the park. And then, in his rearview mirror, flashing lights approaching in the distance!

"Shit! Military vehicles behind us. Shit!" John held his breath, gripping the steering wheel with one hand, the clutch with the other in preparation for a chase. "Get ready, Linda. I may have to do some serious driving."

He watched the lights zoom closer, then abruptly veer left. In his rearview mirror, he saw a line of vehicles forming a semicircle, blocking the front of the park entranceway, then several more speeding past the impenetrable blockade and through the gate.

"Thank God," he sighed. "They're surrounding the park. Must think we're still in there. Right now they're probably scaring the shit out of every camper in the place."

Linda thought about what almost happened and didn't know whether to laugh or cry. They got out this time, she thought, but at a price. She knew that when it came to national security, there existed only one unwritten rule: Any action, legal or otherwise, would be justified in the event that the United States government was under attack or if its national security was threatened. And by invoking those two words—national security—the government, with total immunity, held absolute power over any citizen of the United States.

"There's no way we can go back to your place," Linda said. "By the time we drive back to Washington, everyone's going to be looking for us."

"Right. We'll have to figure out a way to get a hold of Jack . . . tell him what's going on."

"Jack!" Linda, who'd been so preoccupied by what was happening to *them*, suddenly remembered that Jack was still in Washington and just as vulnerable as they were, if not more so. "Poor Jack. I hope he's okay."

Linda stopped and held her breath, suddenly recalling glimpses of what they'd seen on that computer screen. "Psychochemical warfare," she whispered. "My God, John, what's going on? I'm pretty familiar with most of the chemical and biological weapons systems we have, but what the hell is psychochemical warfare. And what in God's name are they trying to do with it?"

"It could all be linked somehow," John said. "The genetic engineering facility, CONDOR, WORLD ORDER. God only knows what TIMBER WOLF is and why it's not even coded in top-secret Pentagon files."

The Alfa Romeo sped along I95 North. Once again John resumed his nervous study of the rearview mirror while Linda searched the sky and exit ramps for signs of any suspicious activity. They were at least ten miles from Prince William Forest Park by now and decided that if anyone was going to pursue them, they would have noticed it by now. The road was unnervingly quiet, the sky empty except for an occasional commercial flight coming into and leaving Washington International. The one obstacle left was getting into D.C. without being seen by what they both knew would surely be an army of security people having descriptions of the car and the two of them. Escape seemed damn near impossible.

"Linda, I think we should get off and rent another car. Something less flashy. This thing's too easy to spot and they've probably ID'd it by now anyway."

"Good idea. But where?"

"We're close to Alexandria. There's a small airport near town. We can park the car in the long-term lot, bury it out of sight, and rent a small heap that'll get us around town without notice."

The I95 North signs led them around a seemingly endless maze of construction work and back onto the highway. John had parked the Alfa Romeo in the most obscure spot he could find, under an airline terminal overpass, and drove out of the Avis lot in a 1995 light brown Chevy Cavalier.

Linda sat expressionless, deep in thought, praying that all this insanity would soon end and that somehow it would all just go away. No such luck, she thought. She gazed out the window as though in a trance.

"What're you thinking, Linda? You look like you're on to something."

"I'm trying to remember what it was I saw on that computer screen before we lost it. I remember reading psychochemical warfare and was so stunned that I didn't look carefully enough at the rest of the file."

"I remember looking at the line for weapon system. There was something about a biological agent, and right after CONDOR, letters of some kind."

"What kind? Think, John; it may be important."

"I know there was a number five, then some letters. Didn't make sense."

"Jesus. Biological agent. What were those letters? Think."

"I'm trying to visualize the screen, Linda. Gimme a break." John stared ahead at the increasingly heavy traffic going into and out of D.C. Their Chevy Cavalier blended inconspicuously with the mass of cars and trucks that would have looked like dull trash next to John's bright red Alfa Romeo. He was glad now that he'd made the switch.

"I believe there was an H and a T," he said. "It's coming to me, Linda. A five, followed by a dash, I think . . . then HTP . . . another dash, followed by another five . . . another dash, and HT. Yeah, I think that was it, but I can't say for sure. Five-HTP-five-HT."

"I don't know, John, but it must be important if they had it in the same file with CONDOR. If it's psychochemical, it has to involve a chemical that somehow affects the brain. Five-HTP-five-HT may be a code or the chemical itself. We need to see Jack. He'd know for sure."

"We have a problem, then. How're we gonna find Jack without *them* finding us?"

"We call him," Linda said matter-of-factly. "If Jack's at the lab, I'll be able to tell him where to meet us in code, in case the phones are tapped."

"Code? What is this, a James Bond movie now? A code?"

"Yeah. Jack and I made arrangements to meet at an out-of-the-way diner off Florida Avenue if either of us ever suspected we were being followed or watched. Just pull off at the next gas station and let me use a pay phone."

A short while later, John eyed one of those hundred-foot Exxon signs high above the treetops. He swung off the exit and pulled up next to a dirty telephone booth that had nothing left but the metal frame and the phone itself. Linda jumped out of the car and yanked the receiver off the hook. She threw some coins into the slot, punched numbers, and waited, hitting the metal shelf impatiently with the side of her clenched fist.

"Hello, is Dr. Jackson Pilofski in, please?" Linda spoke with a disguised voice and a western drawl she'd gotten fairly good at after starring in her college play, *Oklahoma*. She looked at John, her eyes glassy from fear and exhaustion. "This is Dr. Virginia Bannister," she continued. "I'm returning Dr. Pilofski's call. He gave me this number and asked me to call him."

C'mon Jack, she thought, her hand clenched harder now.

Be there. She waited almost a minute for a response. "He's busy? Said to call him back in two hours? Thank you." She hung up and jumped back into the car.

"What happened?" John asked. "The guy too busy to even take your call?"

"He'll meet us at the diner in two hours."

"He what? That's not what I just heard."

"I know. Chances are all the phones are being monitored, so we couldn't make any kind of contact. The name Virginia Bannister was a code. As soon as Jack heard it, he knew it was me trying to get in contact with him and he knows to meet us at Bennie's drive-in."

"Damn, this *is* a James Bond movie. Did whoever answer the phone recognize your voice?"

"It wasn't Natalie, thank God. If it was, she might have. Rhonda answered, and I don't talk to her very much. I'm sure she didn't have a clue."

John got on the entrance ramp and saw the familiar sights of Washington in the distance. "I'm beginning to feel like a fugitive, Linda. But at least we're heading back to familiar territory."

"Familiar, yeah. I'm not sure how friendly."

chapter twenty-one

"They're gone."

"What the hell do you mean, gone?"

"I'm sorry, Mr. Morris. They're just gone. We—"

"How the fuck could they be gone?" Morris was staring straight into Lambino's dull eyes, shaking so hard he had to grab hold of his desk to continue. "Have your people covered every security checkpoint? Every possible location?" *Goddamn assholes.*

"I had four men stationed at every position: the lab, Franklin's home, Peterson's home. McKnight had his own security people search the entire complex and then some. I'm afraid they either know or found out something, and they're on the run."

Morris plummeted into his oversized chair and ran both sets of heavy fingers through his slicked hair. He closed his eyes in anticipation of an answer he didn't want to hear, but asked anyway. "Does McKnight have any clue . . . any clue at all as to where the two might have gone?" His eyes remained closed, prepared to burst open and fire into Lambino with a ferocity that would make even Lambino quiver.

"His sources tell him Franklin was talking about leaving Washington for a few days. Virginia Beach, maybe. His people are scouring the area right now."

"McKnight's people?" Morris's eyes popped open. "Jesus Christ! Those fools wouldn't think twice about pulling an assassination in the lobby of a crowded hotel, for God's sake. Look what they did with Wesely. Nothing subtle about their tactics. Take a couple of men—very unobtrusively—and see what you can find."

"Do you want them back here, Mr. Morris?"

"Of course not," Morris snapped as though the question was too incredibly stupid to deserve an answer. "Leave them somewhere in Virginia Beach, and make sure no one finds them this century."

Lambino turned and lumbered out the door. Morris, his face twitching, snatched a private phone out of his bottom desk drawer and punched some numbers. Sweat trickled profusely down his jowls, adding a shine to the skin that was paling by the second.

"Ben. Greg Morris here. What the hell's going on? Lambino tells me you've lost track of Franklin."

"We've lost track of them for the time being," McKnight answered. "We're sure they'll turn up."

"What makes you so confident?" The twitching intensified. "Wesely damn near slipped through your security net and Williams would've spilled his guts if they got to him before you did."

"They didn't, did they?"

"Damn lucky!"

"No. Damn good. I have my security people checking out every lead, searching every suspected location in Washington and Virginia. If they're around, we'll find them."

"And what if they're *not* around? What if they suspect they're being hunted down and decided to get the hell out of town? Lambino's men searched their homes. Suitcases were untouched. No clothes missing. Travel items were intact. Franklin's car was parked a block away from the lab complex and Peterson's car was missing, so obviously they're traveling together. His office hadn't heard of his whereabouts either. Sounds to me like they've done one helluva good job making fools of your security people."

McKnight, figuring that at this point it didn't matter who eliminated Linda and John, as long as they were eliminated before they uncovered too much, preferred it be Morris. Besides, he thought, the more he could insulate himself from the dirty work, the better. Cooperating seemed the expedient thing to do, at least for now.

"A few hours ago we got a report of an unauthorized computer break-in," McKnight said, deciding that now was as good a time as any to break the news. "An omega file was accessed, which triggered an alert. The Vox security system traced it to a communications bunker near Quantico. When security arrived, they found Peterson's fingerprints all over the circuit panels."

Morris sat there stunned, not believing what he was hearing, his gaping mouth nearly swallowing his knuckles. "What else?" he asked, dropping his head into his hand.

"Intelligence isn't sure how much information they were able to download before security locked them out, but they're certain the files weren't accessed long enough. The Vox shuts the system down as soon as a trace indicates where a break-in has occurred along the line."

"I'm not so certain," Morris shouted. "Even if it took

the system a few seconds to pinpoint the origin of the break, that may have been long enough. They may have had enough time to study the file before it disappeared. I'm telling you they know something and they hauled ass. And if they *did* see something related to CONDOR and keep digging . . . hell, God knows what else they'll eventually find.'' Morris wiped his round face with a silk handkerchief and waited for something reassuring from McKnight.

''We have our computer people tracking every passenger on every flight,'' McKnight assured him. ''My security agents are stationed throughout the regional airports. No one gets in or out of Washington without our knowing it. Peterson is driving an Alfa Romeo with a vanity license plate that reads COMPUTE. Immediately after the break-in, we put out an APB to every law enforcement agency in the area, warning them that whoever's driving that vehicle is a wanted felon and that a government reward will be issued for his arrest.''

''And what about any of their coworkers?''

''We've got everyone under strict surveillance, in case they make contact. All phone lines at the lab complex, the computer research center, and their homes have been tapped. So far there's been no contact between anyone since their return from New Hampshire. My people searched every home and found nothing that would have linked them with Franklin. I think they're all clean, but we're keeping a monitor on them anyway, just in case.''

Morris took a deep breath and closed his eyes again. They bulged toadlike above fleshy pads. He clenched his teeth in anger as he envisioned everything unraveling because of two meddlesome fools he knew could never understand the concept of shifting global economics. The stupidity, he thought, the arrogance to think that anyone would know better than he how the system should work. He rubbed his eyes with his thumb and forefinger and spoke slowly and deliberately.

''What do your sources inside the White House say? I'm sure they have an opinion on the security violation.''

''They know, and they're concerned,'' McKnight said. ''It

wasn't simply a Pentagon computer break-in, you know. It was an *accessed* computer break-in. Omega file."

"Meaning?"

"Meaning that Peterson and Franklin probably broke into a Pentagon black project security file. It's a damn serious matter."

"Does the Pentagon know which file was accessed?" Morris asked somberly, knowing that any security breach would be met with a full and immediate investigation.

"That's the one good piece of news we have," McKnight said. "The damn security system worked so well that it shut the entire system down before the accessed file was ever logged. Apparently, an extra loop was programmed into the system so that it couldn't perform a trace and record the file at the same time. A glitch they hadn't anticipated until now."

Morris smiled for the first time since calling McKnight. "You're telling me they knew it was an omega file that was accessed but have no idea which one? They don't know? Is that possible?"

"That's right. There's probably a major ass-chewing going on right now as we speak."

"Thank God," Morris whispered as he fell into his chair and threw his head backward. "I trust you'll be giving me updates on your search for Franklin and Peterson?"

"Hopefully it won't be necessary too much longer. After the show of force we exhibited at Quantico, those two are not about to trust anyone. And as long as they think it's the government after them, it gives us time to locate them. I've got security people everywhere."

"I want them found," Morris growled. "I want them found and eliminated . . . soon."

"It'll be done."

"Call me tomorrow on my private line."

"I'm sure that . . ." McKnight heard the click. He hung up the phone and with disgust whispered, "Fat bastard. Thinks he's a goddamn four-star general."

The fat bastard, as McKnight liked to call him, *was*, for all practical purposes, a general. Not in the strict military sense, but in the sense that in reality the Vanguard, over the course of two decades, ultimately had been responsible for altering forever the direction of U.S. military policy.

Over the past few years, however, the relationship between the Pentagon's most secret operations branch and its long-time benefactors had grown strained, in particular between Gregory Morris and General McKnight, who was beginning to suspect that the Vanguard had become more interested in its own financial gains than its original goal of preserving America's national security. But strained as it was, the relationship had reached the breaking point when McKnight learned that it was the Vanguard who, two years prior to the Gulf War and solely for economic interests, was behind the U.S. transfer of biological weapons of mass destruction to Iraq. He'd since become privy to top-secret Department of Defense information claiming that thousands of Desert Storm soldiers had died since 1993 as a direct result of exposure to weapons manufactured by Universal Biomedical and distributed by the Vanguard through one of its shadow corporations.

Disgusted by the secret reports, McKnight had decided that Morris would be held accountable for his crime. With the mission to be launched in less than three weeks, McKnight, visualizing his own place in history, saw not only the return of America as the world's preeminent economic superpower, but the end of a group that had been corrupted by the very system it had vowed to destroy.

He opened the humidor on his desk, took out a cigar, and lit it, blowing puffs of thick white smoke upward toward the ceiling. He put his feet up and smiled, and though concerned about Dr. Linda Franklin, knew that she wasn't about to show her face to government officials she was certain would kill her.

It was only a matter of time, he thought. Only a matter of time.

chapter twenty-two

"What'll it be?"

"Excuse me?" Linda asked, paying more attention to the fleeting customers than she did the menu.

"Special today's grilled sea trout. What'll it be?" With pen ready, the shapely waitress examined a muddy couple who looked as if they'd just finished a sordid romp in the backwoods. She hovered above them impatiently, tapping her foot and chewing gum so hard it nearly slipped from her mouth. Then, catching it expertly between a set of puffy burgundy lips, she ruminated even faster, asking, "You want I should come back?"

"No," John said. "I'll have the special and a cup of coffee. How 'bout you, Linda?"

"The same. I'll take an iced tea with that, please."

"Sweetened or unsweetened?"

"Unsweetened."

"Salads with that?"

"None for me," John said.

"No thanks," Linda added.

The waitress flipped the order pad closed, stuck her pencil through a tight barrier of teased blond hair, and strutted away. John watched Maxine—that was the name on her tag—push a swinging door wide open and enter what looked like a kitchen from hell.

"Nice place you and Jack picked," John mumbled with directed sarcasm.

"It's perfect," Linda said. "A little dirty, maybe. But who in their right mind would even think of coming here?"

John looked around and had to agree. "Good point. I suppose no one who wants to stay healthy."

* * *

It had been more than two hours since Linda had left the phone message for Jack. Their food had arrived only seconds ago and was now looking up at them from thick plates chipped from heavy use: two grilled trout specials, floating in something that resembled a thin yellow sauce, one strong coffee that tasted like potting soil, one iced tea that was actually pretty good. They shared the iced tea and, after several refills, began to suspect that something had gone wrong, fearing that if the Feds were after *them*, they may also have gotten to Jack, who might even be in custody right now.

"Need another refill?" Maxine asked, appearing from nowhere with a pitcher of iced tea for the third time. Then, noticing that the trout was still swimming in its sea of congealed butter, untouched: "Somethin' wrong with the food?"

"We're both on low-cholesterol diets," John said. "And this looks a little too rich. We've decided just to skip dinner. We'll pay for the meals, of course."

"Of course." Maxine twirled around on her Reeboks and, in a huff, sauntered toward the kitchen.

"Real nice, John. A little too rich. Look around. Like this place could care less if anyone's on low-cholesterol diets."

As they both laughed, they heard the entrance bell on the door clang. They jerked their heads up nervously to see who the latest customer to risk his life would be.

"Thank, God. It's Jack," Linda said, waving her arm toward him and sliding over in her bench seat. Jack spotted her at once and headed straight for the table, pushing over ketchup bottles and knocking a fork from someone's hand as he did.

"Goddamn security people," he grumbled as he approached. "I had a helluva time shakin' them. Followed me for three goddamn miles before I finally ditched 'em." Jack pushed the table toward John to give himself enough room to squeeze in.

"It's nice to see you, too, Jack," Linda said as she put her arm around him and gave him an affectionate squeeze.

"Hey, I'm sorry, but I've been through hell trying to figure a way out of the city and over here without being followed."

"*You've* been through hell?" John could have leapt across the table and strangled Jack with his bare hands. "You don't know what hell is till you've spent a couple of hours dodging gunship helicopters."

"No shit? Helicopters? Man, what have you two been up to?"

"We drove out to . . ." Linda stopped and took another sip of her iced tea when Maxine approached the table again.

The buxom waitress threw a ripped menu in front of Jack and poured him a glass of water, the smell of fresh Wrigley's and cheap perfume hitting him square in the face. "Be back for your order in a minute," she said while chewing.

"Nice lookin' babe," Jack said, nodding his head in approval as he watched Maxine wiggle all the way back to the kitchen.

"Oh, please." Linda rolled her eyes and continued. "We drove out to Quantico and—"

"Quantico? Are you crazy?"

"John took us to an abandoned underground communications bunker. He hooked up a computer, broke into the Pentagon computer system, and accessed their files."

"I'm impressed. You find anything?" Jack's face twitched. He lit his pipe, despite the no-smoking signs plastered on every wall, and started puffing furiously.

"Psychochemical warfare, Jack. The whole damn thing's about psychochemical warfare. CONDOR, WORLD ORDER, they're both code names for some government mission."

"You sure it wasn't chemical or biological?"

"Positive."

"Damn, what else?"

"Unfortunately, even though John thought he bypassed encryption, the Pentagon tracked the break-in and cut off transmission. John thinks he remembers something he saw in the file. We were hoping you could figure it out."

Tearing a paper napkin from the dispenser, Linda slipped one of Jack's pens out of his pocket protector and wrote down 5-HTP-5-HT. "What do you make of it?" she asked.

Jack puffed on his pipe. "Shit. I guess it *would* make sense. That's why it would be psychochemical. But how?"

"What is it?" Linda asked.

"Serotonin."

"I don't understand," John said.

Jack reached over and pulled out another napkin. He jerked the pen out of Linda's fingers, drew a picture of a human brain and a series of chemical equations, then turned the napkin sideways so that John could see what he was about to say.

"Serotonin's a naturally occurring neurotransmitter produced in this part of the brain." He circled the brain stem, the part of the brain that connects the spinal cord to the cerebral hemispheres. "This is where most serotonin's made." He drew an arrow in the middle of the circle, where nerve endings that release serotonin originated, then projected outward to different parts of the central nervous system.

"Five-HT is an abbreviation often used for serotonin," he continued. "Five-HTP is the abbreviation for the brain chemical that's converted to serotonin, or five-Hydroxytryptophan." Jack pointed to the reactions he scribbled across the napkin.

Tryptophan→5-HTP→5-HT

"All these reactions occur within the brain itself because serotonin doesn't cross the blood-brain barrier. It's a—"

John put his hand on Jack's arm and cut him off midsentence. "I'm a computer guy, Jack. Neurotransmitter? Blood-brain barrier?"

"The nervous system is basically an electrical system," Jack explained. "One nerve cell lines up next to another like a series of extension cords. You can actually measure the voltage produced. When a nerve is stimulated, it generates a potential, just as a battery would. The electrical charge then runs the length of the nerve cell, except that the electrical cords aren't connected and the electrical signals can't just leap from one cord to the next. So when the signal reaches the end of a cell, the cell has to release a chemical that swims across the gap between the cells. Only then can it trigger another electrical signal. That's how nerve signals travel. Neurotransmitters are the chemicals involved in nerve transmission. Without them you don't generate nerve signals, period. And when they bind to receptors, not only do they generate electrical signals, they trigger emotions. Serotonin happens to be one of those chemicals."

"So you're tellin' me that my emotions are the end result of nothing more than brain chemicals attaching to receptors? Love, joy, sorrow, anger, all of them simply products of biochemical reactions?"

"Whether you like it or not," Jack answered. "Think about it. Think about how many people you've known whose behaviors changed as a result of a chemical imbalance brought about by even the simplest illness. Any change in brain chemistry—even the slightest—can alter our emotions. Love turns to hate, joy to sorrow or depression, tranquillity to anger, passivity to violence. In fact, I was working with a guy once who was studying how the brain's limbic system is affected when chemical signals are disrupted. He was experimenting with rats he'd been using for months . . . animals so docile you could pick 'em up and pet 'em like hamsters. When he walked into his lab the morning following some experiments he'd done the previous day, he opened up one of the cages and one of those suckers literally jumped out at him and started chewing on his lab coat. Never seen anything like it. Overnight, that rat had been transformed from a pet to a damn killer rat. Now *that's* what a change in brain chemistry will do to you."

"What about the blood-brain barrier?"

"It's nothing more than a system of blood vessels within the brain that keeps things out. Very few things get into the brain through blood vessels, including serotonin. Things like water, nicotine, and glucose can get in; things like proteins and even most antibiotics can't. So, if someone injected you with serotonin, let's say, it wouldn't get into your brain because it couldn't cross the blood-brain barrier. It would—''

Linda stopped him before he could finish and looked at the picture of the brain. She tapped it with her finger. ''I don't get it,'' she mumbled. ''It wouldn't matter how much serotonin you got, it wouldn't get to your brain anyway.''

''And if that's the case,'' John added, ''what does this have to do with psychochemical warfare? If serotonin's already found in the brain naturally, and if there's no way it can get into your brain through blood vessels, then what's going on?''

Linda stared at the drawings again. There had to be something they were missing, she thought. Something about those reactions. About serotonin. ''I'm not exactly sure how serotonin is linked to psychochemical warfare, but I do know that the government was doing work years ago with LSD. Figured if they could somehow get the enemy high on the stuff they could wipe them out, no problem. I always assumed MKULTRA was terminated back in the late sixties.''

''Projects like that never die completely,'' Jack said. ''They're just hidden from public view and from congressional inquiries. The brain is the last frontier. You think they would stop research on something that could alter behavior if there was a chance they could somehow pinpoint the behavior they want to control?''

''What does all this have to do with serotonin?'' John interjected.

''Jack, you've worked with neurotransmitters,'' Linda said. ''Could there be some kind of link?''

''Neurotransmitters like serotonin work only if they bind to their specific receptors, located on the surface of cell membranes,'' Jack said. ''If a chemical resembles a neurotransmitter, it can bind to the same receptor. That's the mechanism behind drug action. Heroin binds to our opioid receptors, nicotine binds to acetylcholine receptors, beta-blockers bind to adrenaline receptors. LSD happens to bind to serotonin receptors because the two molecules are structurally very similar."

"Damn," Jack whispered. "LSD and serotonin. You think there may still be some connection?"

"Don't think so," Jack answered. "The LSD research is over and long buried. We're all pretty sure of that. But I know for a fact there's still a helluva lot of brain research going on. Top-secret research. In fact, much of the new recombinant DNA work in the area is focusing on the development of naturally occurring compounds found within the brain. It's the next frontier. The neurotransmitter system, naturally, has to be a target for next-generation weapons research. Yeah, I can see why serotonin would be of interest, but I can't see how they'd pull it off. No way that *I* know of."

"What's the effect of serotonin in humans?" John asked.

"Violence, impulsive behavior, depression, suicide have all been linked to low serotonin levels. In fact, the real cutting-edge work in suicide is being done in brain biochemistry. Prozac, the most widely prescribed antidepressant drug, works by preventing serotonin's reuptake once it's produced. It reverses low-serotonin levels."

"So, if there's not enough," John asked, "or if something happens to block serotonin, we can become violent or suicidal?"

Jack puffed furiously. Linda looked up and stared at John as if he'd suddenly hit on the one possibility they hadn't considered: a reversal of the process.

"John, you may have something," Linda said. "If what Jack said is true, an agent that blocks serotonin production in the brain would be incredibly dangerous."

"Dangerous how?" John asked.

Jack leaned back against the diner seat and underlined the chemical reactions in front of him with the end of his pipe, staring at the napkin and for the moment ignoring John's question. When he finally spoke, he did so as if no one else was there with him.

"Serotonin's the key. You've hit on it, Linda. That's it. It must be it. Serotonin."

"What, Jack? What's it?" Linda grabbed hold of Jack's arm and shook him. "What are you thinking? Tell me."

"Back in the seventies, psychiatrists at the Karolinska Hospital and Institute in Stockholm discovered something about serotonin that sent shock waves throughout the medical community. I'm sure you've heard about it. They found that many of the patients who had abnormally low serotonin levels killed themselves, or at least tried to. There was a tenfold greater incidence in committed suicide among those with very low serotonin levels than those with normal levels. What was even more disturbing was that patients with the *lowest* serotonin levels killed themselves in the most violent manner, either by hanging or blowing their brains out or drowning themselves. The lower the level, the more violent the suicide. Since then, serotonin's been linked to all kinds of violent crime. The more studies they do, the worse it gets."

"Meaning?" John asked.

"Murder for starters. In one prison, they found that seventy-five percent of the murderers had low serotonin levels. And since we know that aggression and suicide are linked—suicide being an inwardly directed aggressive drive—it makes sense that murder is one of the strongest predictors for suicide. In England, for example, one study showed a suicide rate among murderers of thirty percent, an incredible number statistically. It's probably that high here."

"Damn!" John exclaimed. "It's hard to believe something so simple can change behavior that much."

"That's not all," Jack said. "Murderers aren't the only ones with low serotonin levels. Impulsively violent criminals are number one; arsonists, for example. Right up there with the leaders."

"If, somehow, we've managed to develop a way to alter brain chemistry, the effects would be devastating," Linda said. "Anyone not committing suicide could potentially become violent enough to kill."

"*Impulsively* violent," Jack emphasized, "which makes it even worse. Impulsively violent behavior is unpredictable, more easily triggered, more intense, more extreme and chaotic. In other words, you wouldn't even wanna look at these people the wrong way. It'd be a damn nightmare."

"The LSD research," John interrupted. "You think it's linked to any of this serotonin business?"

"I doubt it," Jack answered quickly. "LSD is one thing. Yeah, it was bad, but whatever's going on here will make LSD seem like kid's stuff, I guarantee it. If what I think is true, if brain serotonin's the target, this may be one of the most dangerous mind-altering agents anyone's ever developed."

There was deathlike silence around the table. Until now, the very idea of WORLD ORDER and psychochemical warfare seemed impossible, unreal, symbols on a computer screen and, at worst, some futuristic vision of how war might be waged in the next century, not now. All that had now changed.

Linda's mind was suddenly flooded with a seemingly endless list of worst-case scenarios: Suppose the agent went out of control? Suppose brain chemistry didn't change as predicted? Suppose an entire new and unknown set of chemical reactions was initiated? Suppose the agent fell into the wrong hands? Suppose, suppose, suppose. The possibilities were nightmarish indeed.

"Jesus Christ," John whispered, beginning to understand the full impact of what had just been proposed. He knew that if true, it was diabolically hideous. He felt himself getting sick. *Psychochemical warfare. WORLD ORDER.* The words rattled around in his head. "This is hard to believe. It's a nightmare. Our government would actually do something like this?"

"Think about it," Linda cut in. She leaned over and spoke softly. The dinner crowd was swelling and Maxine was growing curious about all the muttering. "Whoever's able to control what goes on inside a person's brain is going to control that person's behavior. That's all behavior is, remember, a bunch of chemicals that happen to be in just the right balance. Alter that balance and you create the ingredients for disaster.''

''But what's the sense of eliminating entire populations?'' John asked. ''It's crazy. Absolutely crazy.''

''Not if there's some way to control it,'' Jack said. ''The LSD project was meant to target a limited group. Same thing with ethnic weapons. That same scenario no doubt applies here. They can probably deliver this stuff however they want, to whomever they want; to a small group, to an entire population. It's all controlled. You wanna eliminate a group of fanatics or even an entire population causing real problems in the world? You somehow make them kill *themselves* or each other without having to risk one young soldier's life or firing one cruise missile. Wanna shift the balance of power? Just get one population so screwed up or so suicidal they can't even fight off an aggressive neighbor. Think about the damn possibilities. Iran, Iraq, North Korea, Libya, the Baltics, et cetera, et cetera. The list is endless. And the number of countries that would be on the hit list is frightening. Makes the way war is fought obsolete. You'd never have to send in troops, for Christ's sake. You could shape the destinies of entire nations simply by altering the behavior of its people.'' Jack slapped his hand on the table and shook the plates, startling Linda. ''Sorry. It makes my blood boil just thinking about it. We've just leaped into the next generation of weapons, and I'm scared as hell of what I'm seeing. I thought we learned our lesson in Iraq.''

''What's that supposed to mean?'' John asked.

Jack looked over at Linda, who nodded. ''We've isolated *Mycoplasma incognitus*—one of the main biological organisms used for germ warfare—in quite a few Gulf War veterans,'' he said.

''I didn't think biological weapons were used?'' John asked incredulously.

''No one did,'' Jack answered. ''The government's denying everything, of course, but we know what we found. What's worse, this strain of *Mycoplasma* bacteria also happens to have the HIV envelope around it, which means it was artificially produced."

"What! What are you saying?" John asked, not sure he wanted to hear the answer.

"It's a hybrid, so to speak," Jack said. "Larger than a virus, smaller than a typical bacterium, it buries itself deep in the cell. When it exits, it takes a piece of the cell with it and infects other areas of the body, specifically the joints. The HIV coat was used as a means for the bacteria to burrow itself into the cells. Whoever manufactured this decided to look to HIV as a carrier because it was known that many AIDS victims also have mycoplasma infection. There was a connection there that obviously proved useful."

"That's why so many Gulf War vets complained of aching joints and debilitating arthritis shortly after coming home," Linda added. "They're also coming down with unusual types of cancers that young, healthy men should never come down with. The stuff literally rained down on them when the scud missiles were blown out of the sky. Sad thing is, we knew a year before Desert Storm that those gas masks they were going to use would be rendered useless against *Mycoplasma* by hydrogen cyanide, which Saddam had stockpiled all over Iraq."

"Worse than that," Jack cut in. "The CIA issued a report a year before the invasion that Saddam *would* use biological weapons. Special vaccines and antidotes were grown several years in advance against bio agents we supposedly had no knowledge of. That's hard to explain. Also hard to explain is why most of the hard files on the Desert Storm illnesses and deaths were in the Murrah Federal Building in Oklahoma when it was bombed."

John then turned to Linda and said, "After what you told me this morning, I think you believe there's more to this HIV–Gulf War thing than we're being told."

"I know there is," Linda responded. "This whole chemical agent business you've been hearing about in the news is nothing more than a smoke screen."

"How do you mean?" John asked.

"Exposure to chemical or nerve agents will kill you or make you sick, but it doesn't explain how spouses, children, and relatives of Gulf War vets are getting infected. You *don't* infect someone else with chemical agents you've been exposed to. You *do* pass on biological agents. That's what's so sinister about them. It could go on for years."

"You folks gonna sit here all night?" Maxine's nasal voice caught them off guard, forcing Jack to quickly compose himself. "I got customers waitin'."

"Three coffees, please, and three apple pies," Jack ordered, giving Maxine a wink, then waited for her to walk away before looking back at John, who sat stone-faced in front of him, stunned at this latest revelation.

"What I want to know," Linda continued, "is where in the hell TIMBER WOLF comes in. The Pentagon omega file we broke into had nothing at all about it. If TIMBER WOLF is a secret Pentagon project connected with CONDOR, why wasn't it included in that file?"

"Here ya go, sugar." Maxine looked at Jack without glancing at the other two and slipped the check under Jack's saucer before turning on her Reeboks and rushing to another customer.

"We better finish up and get out of here before Maxine decides to join us," Linda said. "An hour and a half in this place is about an hour and fifteen minutes too long. What we need to find out is what kind of brain research is going on involving serotonin and genetic engineering, how the two are linked, and whether someone who's not supposed to got hold of it." She grabbed Jack's arm, then said, "Whoever's behind this probably doesn't suspect you're involved, since you haven't been seen with me since yesterday. John and I are the ones they'll be after. Until we know for sure who *it* is, we don't trust anyone, not even the government."

The three sat in silence, studying the drawings, thinking back to only four days ago when the worst thing they had to worry about was finding enough time to keep up with bureaucratic paperwork. As hectic as their lives had been to this point, they could at least count on being able to walk the streets freely without getting killed. TIMBER WOLF had changed all that.

"What are you proposing?" Jack asked. "There's no turning back now. We either uncover everything or you two spend the rest of your lives on the run."

"I think we need to get out of Washington for a while," John suggested.

"Get out of Washington?" Linda was surprised to find herself actually agreeing with the idea of leaving this hotbed they got themselves into. "But where?"

"I have a journalist friend in Maine. We went to school together at Michigan State. While there, we can kill two birds with one stone. Craig can help us dig up some information from news sources and we can lay low for a while and decide what we do next."

"I think you two should go ahead while I stay behind," Jack cut in. "If I skip town with you, I'll just get added to the list of suspects. And that's not gonna do you two any good in case you need me. If something comes down or if you need to contact me, you know how to do it."

"What do you have in mind, John?" Linda asked.

"We get some money and fresh clothes and head out to the airport. I'll contact Craig when we get to Maine. Jack stays behind as if he knows nothing and sets up base here. If anyone asks, Jack, you tell them the last you heard, Linda was talking about going to Virginia Beach for a few days but that you haven't seen or heard from her since yesterday. That'll lead them on a false chase for a few days and get you out of the spotlight. Meanwhile, you go to an out-of-the-way post office tomorrow morning and rent a large P.O. box. We'll need one in case we have to send you information or anything else from wherever we are."

John reached into his pocket and pulled out a pen and notebook, scribbling a series of numbers across the top. "Here's Craig Richardson's number. It's in code. Add one number to every other digit when you dial. Call me tomorrow from a pay phone and give me the address of the P.O. box. Check it every day, just in case."

"Unless you think we need to see you right away," Linda added, "always contact us by pay phone."

Jack folded the paper and shoved it into his shirt pocket, then grabbed the check, took out a couple of tens and threw them on the table. "Lemme get this. I owe you for last time."

"Thanks, Jack." Linda put her arm around his neck and kissed his bearded cheek. "Take care of yourself. And don't do anything to draw attention to what we're doing."

"Don't worry. Just keep in touch. I'll keep my eyes and ears open here and see what I can learn. You take care of yourselves. Now get outta here." Jack prayed silently that this was not the last time he would ever see them.

Linda and John walked out of the diner and ran across the gray, littered street to the Cavalier. Through the filth of the diner window they could barely make out Jack waving at them from the cashier's stand. John turned away and saw a tear roll down Linda's cheek.

"God, I hope he's okay," Linda said. "We've been through a lot together, you know, and I'd never forgive myself if something happened to him because of me."

"If he plays it straight," John said, trying to be as convincing as he could, "he should be okay. It's us they're after, remember?"

"I know. I'm just scared for him, that's all. It's easy to say he'll be all right while we leave him behind with people who wouldn't think twice about leaving him in an elevator the same way they'd left Adam."

John opened Linda's door, then ran around to his own, jumped in, and started the engine. As he pulled out, they both turned and took one last look at Jack before rounding the corner.

"I don't think we should worry about clothes or luggage or anything else until we get to Maine," John said. "We can use the ATM at the airport, get some money, buy our tickets, and be in the air as soon as possible."

Linda had no idea what lay ahead for them in Maine, or anywhere else for that matter. It certainly wasn't the way she had imagined her life. "What happens if it *is* the government, John? What happens if we end up running forever because we know too much?"

"Hey, don't think that way. We're gonna get to the bottom of this and come out of it just fine. And if we have to run for a while, at least we have each other and we'll make it somehow. It may not be here in D.C., but we'll make it. Besides, I can't think of anyone I'd rather be on the run with."

The tightly packed storefronts, porno shops, and dirty apartment complexes eventually gave way to government buildings and office suites. When they hit 1395 and crossed the Francis Case Memorial Bridge, they knew Washington National was only minutes away and that within hours they'd be taxiing toward the north runway and kissing D.C. goodbye.

"Maine is actually pretty nice this time of year," John said. "A little cold, but nice."

"I think I can get to like it," Linda responded, anticipating a long stay if they weren't successful with their search.

She looked up, watched a large 747 fly overhead, and for what seemed like the thousandth time thought about the crash. But she also thought about something else that had been bothering her ever since their last computer break-in. How did Peter know about project TIMBER WOLF? How could he have known to scribble the letters PTW if TIMBER WOLF was so secret it wasn't even in omega files?

The thought of Peter being involved in this was unimaginable, but possible. She couldn't shake the feeling that the man she adored and thought she knew so well might have been more than a government scientist and more than an innocent victim. The thought of it left her as cold as ice.

chapter twenty-three

Barely awake, Linda felt herself sliding across the cramped seat as the plane banked left then righted itself before starting its final descent through a deep gray curtain that swallowed it like an angry storm. She looked out groggily through the small rectangular window, exhausted from an ordeal that left her feeling as if every ounce of energy had been sapped from her body. Then, pressing her forehead against the fogged Plexiglas, she thought how unbelievable it was that in such a short period of time her life could have changed so drastically.

The McDonnell-Douglas DC10 dipped its wings and made a final, U-shaped approach toward Bangor, Maine. Wisps of dense gray clouds flashed past her face, eventually thinning, and finally disappearing with the sudden descent. The ground appeared for the first time in nearly two hours. The fasten-your-seat-belt sign suddenly blinked on, accompanied by the obligatory, monotonous voice of a pilot who sounded as if he'd recited the same speech enough times that he could have repeated it in his sleep.

"We hope you enjoyed your flight," the voice announced through the stillness of the cabin. "At this time, we're in our final approach to Bangor. Temperature on the ground is a pleasant fifty-two degrees with a sixty percent chance of precipitation. Passengers continuing on to Montreal will have a one hour layover and may deplane until our next departure. Those of you remaining in Bangor, have a nice stay, and we invite you to fly with us again. Thank you."

The voice clicked off. Turbulence suddenly rocked the plane as it decelerated and dipped again. A few thousand feet below, small patches of single-family homes could be seen tucked neatly between the canopies of mostly bare trees.

What she wouldn't do, Linda thought, as she stared down at it all; what she wouldn't sacrifice to have it to do all over again, to be given one final chance. She'd never wanted much in the first place. A nice home, kids, two cars, a couple of bicycles in the driveway, someone to share life with. Was it all down there, she kept thinking? Among the trees and the white steepled churches, the community centers and winding driveways?

In the distance, Linda spotted the outline of Bangor's skyline. She looked over at John, who was dead to the world and hadn't heard a word the pilot had said. She nudged him out of the deep sleep he'd settled into since they'd left Washington.

"John, we're almost there. Wake up."

John groaned softly as he rolled his head back and forth. He opened his eyes and almost painfully looked over at Linda. He rubbed his face with the palms of his hands and stretched his feet underneath the seat in front of him. "Man, was I tired," he mumbled. "Slept right through dinner and didn't even know it."

"You didn't miss much, believe me." Linda turned back to the window again. "Looks so peaceful down there. You were right. It *is* nice this time of year . . . in a rustic sort of way." *The grass always looks greener when yours is dying*, she thought.

"I used to come up here quite a bit years ago," John said, his eyes finally adjusting to the dim light of the overhead cabin. And as he stretched across to look out the window, he smiled fondly. "Fly fishing . . . camping . . . mostly to escape D.C., really. Never *could* stand Washington for more than a few months before having to get away."

Linda took John's hand and held it tightly as the DC10 continued its descent. Within minutes it touched down, then taxied to a small terminal gate at the far end of the airport. When it stopped, Linda took a deep breath and squeezed John's hand.

"Don't worry," John said in response to what he sensed

was Linda's apprehension. "When I talked to Craig, he told me there'd be a rental car waiting for me under the name Bill Ransom."

"Sounds like your friend has done this before."

"He was an investigative reporter. I guess he knows what to do when he has to. We'll be just fine, promise."

The rented maroon Ford Escort headed north on Highway 95. Sixteen miles from Bangor, it turned onto 16 and continued northwest past stretches of deep brown farmland that lay fallow beneath a dying late-winter sky.

Towns seemed to crop up from nowhere, all small, all looking as if they'd been erected at the turn of the century. Quaint churches—Episcopalian, Methodist, Catholic, with names like Saint Matthew's, Calvary Methodist, Our Lady of Fatima—claimed prominent positions along the main streets and advertised Sunday's scriptures—quote, chapter, and verse—across the glass-and-metal bulletin boards that sat angled on the corners of spacious front lawns. Spreading outward from the churches were Victorian and clapboard homes, a few of them perfectly manicured, others in disrepair or abandoned and overgrown with weeds. The towns, some of them not more than a few blocks in length, gave way to mile after mile of pristine forest interspersed with small family farms.

"Craig's place is about thirty minutes from here," John said. "Little town called Kennecut."

"You sure he's not going to mind us just dropping in like this?"

"Not Craig. He'll be happy to see me. When I talked to him on the phone, he couldn't wait. Said he'd have supper ready for us when we arrived."

"He must love living up here," Linda said.

"He does. Craig worked as a full-time investigative journalist with several newspapers and magazines in Boston and New York and could never get used to city life. He's an expert at digging up the most obscure news, finding missing stories, piecing together evidence based on scant news items.

He was always the one they'd call on if they needed something tracked down.''

''So what happened? Why's he up here now?''

''He just up and quit.''

''Why?''

''Burnout. Decided to go freelance. There were rumors—I'm not sure how true they were—that his life had been threatened because he was beginning to expose too much. Now he works out of his home, writing articles for newspapers and magazines on his own terms and likes it just fine. Makes a decent living. The less contact he has with the pressures of deadlines and editors the better he likes it. Last I heard he'd started work on a book.''

''And you're sure he might be able to help us?''

''If anyone can track down a lead, or at least head us in the right direction, it's Craig. I wouldn't have dragged you up here if I didn't think so.''

Linda, her pessimism not nearly as great as it had been yesterday, was thinking that each step she'd taken since New Hampshire had been more revealing, more frightening, but at least she knew they were on the trail and she now smelled a breakthrough. Craig Richardson, she prayed, would be the one to uncover the one critical piece of information that would point them in the final direction.

''At least no one would ever think to look for us up here,'' Linda said, leaning back and taking in the scenery moving past her. She could have forgotten about everything, could have gotten lost in the peace and tranquillity of this rugged Maine countryside. She hadn't smelled air this clean in God knows how long, and she couldn't get enough of it. The more she inhaled, the more her body craved it. Crisp, woody, light, the scent of pine tingled her nostrils, forcing her to take deep breaths as though her lungs knew it would be a long time before they felt anything like this again.

''Kennecut,'' John said. ''There's the sign.'' He slowed down and began looking for familiar landmarks. ''Craig's place is along Route 3, maybe two miles, if I remember right.''

It was more like four. John turned onto Route 3, a small, winding road that was paved well enough but that couldn't have been more than the width of one and a half cars. It bent and wound its way for nearly a mile before John turned off suddenly and pulled onto an open patch of grass that Linda assumed was a makeshift driveway. Nestled among a stand of tall pines stood a cedar-sided home, wrapped on three sides with a wide porch and topped with a steep peaked cedar-shake roof that blended perfectly with the bark of surrounding trees.

Before the Escort came to a stop, a bald, bearded giant rushed onto the porch, waving an arm the size of a tree limb. Craig looking rugged in his thick plaid shirt, blue jeans, and hiking boots. The wiry beard, running midway down his chest, was a foot wide at the bottom and as red as a Maine sunset.

"Glad you made it!" Craig shouted as he flew down the thick log stairs and approached the car like a lumbering Viking. He was trailed by a graying bullmastiff that Linda prayed didn't mind strangers. She stayed in the car as the beast stuck its wet face against the passenger side window.

"C'mon, Linda," John urged. "That's Max. He's harmless."

"He's the size of a small cow," Linda said.

John climbed out of the car and greeted Craig with a giant bear hug. "It's great to see you, my friend." He let go and turned to Linda. "This is Linda Franklin."

"Pleased to meet you, Linda." Craig extended a large hand, and Linda felt a gentleness that was well hidden by his robust appearance. "This is Max. He won't bother you. I keep him around to scare people off, that's all." Craig rubbed Max's head and thick neck with great vigor. "Please, come on in. You've gotta be exhausted from your trip." He then led John and Linda up the steps and into an elegant but comfortably rustic living room.

After what they'd just been through, Linda was relieved just to sink into an overstuffed colonial chair, face the gray stone fireplace, and for an exhilarating moment, drain everything from her mind but the rhythmic crackle of burning hardwood logs. Within minutes she felt comfortable enough to kick off her boots and bury her toes in the bearskin rug that spanned the floor between chairs.

"John, you've been awfully evasive about this trip," Craig said, rubbing his hands and extending them outward to catch the heat of the roaring fire. "I'm assuming you didn't want anyone to know you were coming for a reason?"

"Good assumption, Craig. I wish I could say the only reason we came up here was to pay you a visit, but I can't. We came up here because we're in real trouble and we could use some help. I'm not even sure how much you *can* help, but I was hoping you might at least head us in the right direction."

"Trouble? What kind of trouble?" Craig's bushy eyebrows lowered, his voice noticeably more serious. "Or should I ask?"

"We can't tell you everything because we're not even sure what's going on ourselves. But what we do know is beginning to scare the hell out of me."

"Uh-oh." Craig leaned forward and picked up a pack of Camels from the coffee table. "Maybe I don't wanna hear this." He snapped the pack forward, pulled out a cigarette with his teeth, and lit it, blowing smoke away from them. The mastiff dropped to the floor in front of his feet. "What the hell, go on."

By the time John had finished recounting the events of the last several days, Craig was working on his third smoke and shaking his head in total disbelief. "This has got to be the most incredible goddamn story I've ever heard. Brain chemicals? Mind control? World order? Psychochemical warfare? What in the hell have you two gotten yourselves into?"

"That's not the worst part," Linda interrupted, tempted to light up a Camel herself, though she'd never smoked in her life.

"You mean there's a worst part?"

"Afraid so," said Linda. "John hasn't told you about TIMBER WOLF."

"What's that, some sort of code?"

"I think so. We don't know what it means yet, but we suspect it might be an acronym of some kind. We're not sure if it's the government behind any of it or some other organization, but we believe it's a top-secret mission that involves this new technology."

"What makes you think it might be someone other than the government?" Craig asked.

"We found nothing on TIMBER WOLF in any of the top-secret accessed Pentagon files," Linda said. "The only place we ever saw it was in General McKnight's own personal file and in the message I found inside Peter's notebook. I think Adam Wesely was going to tell me what it was."

"That means Wesely must be involved somehow . . . or at least has knowledge of it."

"*Was* involved," John said. "He's been murdered."

"Murdered? Because of this? Man, you two *are* into something you shouldn't be into."

"Tell me about it," said Linda. "We think it's the reason my husband Peter was killed. They both may have been involved."

John locked his eyes onto Linda. It was the first time he'd heard her use the word involved when talking about the Tucson incident. It was always "he must have uncovered something" or "he saw something he wasn't supposed to have seen" or "he stumbled across," but never "involved." There was something in the way she said it, he thought. Nonchalant, unemotional, as if she'd finally resigned herself to the fact that Peter and Adam had both been a party to whatever it was that was now threatening her own life.

"Okay, I'm willing to do anything I can to help. Let's talk about it over supper."

Craig poured the Riunite and sat at the head of the oblong dining room table. He raised his glass, looking first at John, then Linda.

"To my good friend John . . . and to you, Linda. May you both find happiness once this is over . . . wherever it leads you."

Linda tipped her glass and took a sip of wine. Happiness would have to wait, she thought.

"Now, tell me how I can help," Craig said.

"We need you to tap into whatever databases you can access and see what you can come up with," John said. "The memos we found in Adam's filebox contained several news stories that didn't seem to be related to any of this, if someone were reading them independently. But because Adam had them filed away with other secret documents, we know they must have been linked somehow. We're just not sure how."

"That's probably true," Craig said. He managed a weak smile, barely exposing a set of yellowing teeth through the dense, flaming beard. If there was one thing he liked more than anything else, it was a hidden story waiting to be exposed.

An investigative journalist for the *New York Times* back in the 1980s, Craig had stumbled onto a major financial scandal involving several New York investment banks and the government of Mexico which, as everyone even back then knew, had been controlled for six decades by a corrupt family whose fortune was inextricably linked to Wall Street. With the tenacity of a bulldog and the exuberance of youth, he'd probed into records, transactions, and agreements between Mexican and U.S. government officials until he'd uncovered a trail of money leading directly to the U.S. administration itself. The story was a bombshell, destined to earn him a place in newspaper history and, no doubt, the Pulitzer prize.

To this day, no one knows why the story had been pulled so suddenly or who was behind the pressure to silence an investigation that would have exposed a large secret financial network. The threatening letters Craig had received stopped, oddly enough, when the investigation was squelched. Craig's principal source, without whom he could not have gotten as far as he had, was found in a hotel room, dead from a massive drug overdose. It was ruled a suicide, though Craig knew the man was as straight as an arrow and had three kids he'd been putting through college. It was shortly after that that Craig was reassigned, his belief in a free and open society irrevocably shattered.

"Well, the first thing we need to do is a news search," Craig said. "Scan local sources first, then regional sources. Unless it's a breaking story, or something with a narrow national interest, the mainstream news media or the networks won't necessarily pick it up. There are lots of stories on wire services, for instance, that don't get touched. You and I will never hear about them. Sometimes on purpose."

"On purpose?" Linda asked, somewhat perplexed.

"It's all big business, Linda. Big business and politics. Don't buy that crap about fairness and impartiality in the media."

"Meaning?"

"I worked at one paper years ago where the reporters were afraid to write stories about controversial issues unless they were ordered to do so or could put a slant on them. The slant always depends on who runs the paper or who owns it. Sometimes you're told that 'it's not something we want to cover because it might incite the wrong feelings' or 'we don't do those kinds of stories.' Now, you can tell me there's no such thing as media bias, but selectively *not* printing news because it doesn't go along with your own personal views or your own political agenda is blatant bias, as far as I'm concerned."

The veins along the sides of Craig's neck were suddenly expanding, the redness moving upward and settling like a bad rash over his entire face. "Political correctness," he mouthed disparagingly. "Make people talk or write a certain way and eventually they'll think a certain way; prohibit the use of words that offend a certain group and in time society will conform like mindless sheep to whatever standard happens to be the order of the day. It's a concept that was born with Hitler and Stalin and I thought died with Gorbachev.

Poor bastards all over the world are dying in front of tanks for the right to express themselves and we're doing our damnedest to stifle free speech. All because a bunch of assholes tell us they don't like what we're saying. I'm tellin' you, we're becoming a goddamn nation of morons and whiny parasites and we don't seem to care about shit any more."

"That happen a lot?" Linda asked. "Selectively not printing news they know *should* be reported?"

Craig nearly choked on his wine and shook his head as if anyone would be naive or stupid enough to believe it didn't. "Happens all the time," he answered. "Sometimes the word comes from the top; sometimes you're pressured into not writing a story. And sometimes the paper or the network is owned by interests that prevent you from doing your job as a reporter. Freedom of speech is all relative. You only have it if you own the paper or the network or if you mouth the opinion of whoever controls you. Try to use your position to inform too much and you're edited out or told to tone it down. It's like working for a pharmaceutical company and discovering something that could help treat cancer, but the head of the company tells you not to report it."

"That's a bit of a stretch, isn't it, Craig?"

"Who the hell do you think owns the media?" Craig exploded, nearly spitting the words into Linda's face.

"Tell me."

"Corporations, that's who. General Electric owns NBC and CNBC, Westinghouse owns CBS and TV and radio stations around the country, Disney owns ABC, the Dow Jones Company owns the *Wall Street Journal*. More and more of the media are being controlled by people who may not want you to get information that would go against their financial interests. Free press? Forget it. Even most local newspapers are corporately owned. Who the hell would run a controversial story if the major advertisers tell the network they'll pull their financial support if they go through with it? It's called the velvet hammer in our business. Hammer because it figuratively hits you right between the eyes, velvet because the threat is implied. The don't need to be too obvious about it because they know you'll toe the party line. You really think G.E. or Westinghouse is gonna allow NBC or CBS to report anything negative about NAFTA or GATT? No way. Look what's happened since that trade deal went through. Factories literally flying across the border for cheap labor. Towns being ruined. Pollution along the Texas border so bad you got record numbers of babies being born without brains, for Christ's sake. You hear anything about that? No. Because they don't want you to. The only place you'll get that news is from independent radio stations or from overseas news sources that can't believe we're not reporting this stuff. And then these jerks scratch their heads and wonder why they've lost credibility."

By the time he'd finished his tirade, Craig was wearing a look of utter disgust on his face. He knew from experience that many journalists had little interest in simply reporting news. They craved more. It was the reason they went into journalism in the first place. Misguided idealists and zealots he liked to call them, writing to persuade their readers into changing their points of view, needing desperately to be an integral part of some noble scheme for social change, insisting that everyone who read their articles think and feel not only as passionately about issues as they did, but in the same *way* they did. They were willing to do almost anything they could to achieve that goal by using the most powerful tool they had at their disposal—words on paper.

He put the goblet to his lips, threw his head back and, with a quick swallow, downed the last of his wine. "The pen is mightier than the sword, you know. It's as true today as it ever has been." He slurred his words just a bit.

He then poured himself another glass and Linda noticed a glaze beginning to settle across his eyes, betraying him. She knew instantly that pouring another must have been something he did quite often. She'd seen that look before, in court, when she looked into the eyes of the vile drunk who had killed her parents on the Long Island Expressway. She shuddered and looked away, pushing her own wine glass away as she listened.

"Nowadays, if you wanna find information, you've gotta dig. You can't depend on bleeding-heart journalists who refuse to report both sides of a story, and you can't assume everything's gonna be reported in the major press. They're a bunch of elitist assholes, same as all those economists and political science types you see on *Meet the Press* and all the network news shows. They graduate from the same damn Ivy League schools, are taught by the same liberal professors, learn to think in the same way, go to the same Washington parties and seminars, and all develop a kind of collective mind. Anyone not in lockstep with this elite little group is an idiot, not worthy to be heard. So what you have is a system run by people who have to conform to the group in order to climb the ladder. If you don't, you're out, bottom line."

"Is that why you got out?"

Craig nodded, a trace of sorrow emerging from the stonelike expression. "I got out of this business 'cause I got tired of putting up with it, tired of hearing that crap about certain stories giving the paper a certain tone that would cause them to lose advertising revenue or sources, even if the story happened to be true; tired of being told that a reporter's job is to present whatever damn information the paper feels will shape the attitudes and opinions of their reading public."

The sorrow turned quickly into anger as Craig narrowed his eyes and lit another Camel. "Pisses me off to think what a bunch of elitist assholes these people really are. Pisses me off even more that people allow themselves to be taken so easily. They won't even try to find out if they're getting the whole story. Won't listen to differing opinions. No one reads widely any more, so they all believe what Ken and Barbie on the national news tell 'em they need to hear. It's a goddamn sorry-ass state of affairs, and the networks all know it. They got us by the balls, so to speak, and we let 'em get away with it because we're stupid. Anyway, that was it. I quit right then and I haven't regretted it since."

Despite the glaze in those bloodshot eyes and the bitter memories it brought back, Linda sensed in Craig a determination to do whatever it took to get to the bottom of a story. He answered to no one, owed no one, and by the resoluteness in his crusty, almost obnoxious voice, seemed to relish the idea of uncovering secrets that lay hidden from public view by a media he abhorred and felt had long since abandoned its principles.

"When can we start?" Linda asked, almost impatiently.

Craig threw his head back, and when he'd finished the last of his drink, scooped a final portion of lasagna through the opening in his beard.

"I guess now's as good a time as any."

chapter twenty-four

Linda grimaced as she followed Craig, along with the drift of alcohol, to the far end of the house. It was a sweet, sickening smell, she thought, the kind that seeps from the pores and clings to the body like an ugly, ninety-proof shroud. She tried hard to pretend she didn't notice, or at least to make Craig believe she didn't. But when they reached Craig's office, she had to distance herself from it, allowing John to serve as a protective barrier between them.

"This is it," announced Craig, waving his outstretched hand like a slick salesman demonstrating fine furniture. "Everything I need, right here. If it's out there, I'll find it; if it's buried, I'll dig it up." He took a few steps back and leaned toward Linda, pointing to his nose with an index finger and tapped it. "Sometimes I can smell it . . . between the lines . . . the words. Sometimes it's implied, but it's always there. I know it's there, hiding, and I'll flush it out, guaranteed."

Linda glared into Craig's fiery, determined eyes. And though she despised alcoholics, despised being reminded once again that it had been someone just like him who'd swerved headlong into her parents, and under any other circumstance would have turned away in disgust, knew instantly, alcoholic or not, that this was their man, a hard-drinking, hard-nosed journalist who'd obviously not lost his love for old-fashioned muckraking. At least, she conceded reluctantly, he had *that* going for him.

Two IBMs, modems attached, sat next to each other on the far side of the large square room. Both side walls were covered with floor-to-ceiling shelves brimming with books, old newspaper files, directories, indexes, and encyclopedias and replete with almost every other kind of resource material an investigative reporter would need to do a search and dig up obscure facts.

"How do we start?" Linda asked, anxious to have this man get out of her face.

"How depends on exactly where you wanna begin. We can go back into files as far as you wanna go, and we can search for different topics under various databases. There are hundreds of databases, you know. Hundreds. Just about any name, title, date, newspaper source, citation, geographic region, and news item is available." He walked quickly over to one of the IBMs and switched it on. Linda noticed that the slur in his speech had all but disappeared, the glaze in his eyes miraculously cleared.

"There are a lot of databases available," he repeated, "for just about any news story out there, in just about any part of the world. We can retrieve a story buried so goddamn deep you'd never believe it was reported in the first place."

"Can we start with something linked to the news clips we found hidden in Wesely's cabin?" Linda asked. "The ones in those southwestern newspapers?"

"You got it," Craig said, whirling around and flipping through a large directory of databases lying on the desk next to his computer. "There." He stabbed at the middle of the page and read the description, underlining it with his finger. "Southwest Newswire. Regional news from the Southwest United States from 1984 to present. Updated daily. Just what you're looking for." He flipped to other sections of the directory and transcribed the file numbers of several other news databases. "Got it. Everything we need is here. All I need now are some key words, and we're in business."

His eyes were suddenly on fire, and whatever alcohol remained in his system seemed to have no effect on the adroitness of his fingers as they began punching keys, accessing files, and bringing up potential databases. "I'm accessing as many databases as I can to search for whatever information we're gonna need," he stated. "AP, UPI, Reuters, Knight-Ridder, Federal News Service. There. The first thing we can do is start with any UFO news stories originating in New Mexico during August 1988. I'd be willing to bet you're not gonna get anything out of the mainstream press. They leave it to the local rags to report this kind of shit."

Craig began punching keys again. The computer screen glowed as he inputted data furiously.

>>> ENTER FILES
>>> 30,108,211,258,260,261,492,609,611,649,660,695, 771, 772
Files entered. Enter your select statements
>>> ? UFO and New Mexico and August 1988
Your select statement is:
?sUFO and New Mexico and August 1988

Items	**File**	
2	**258:**	**AP News—July 1984–present**
5	**492:**	**Arizona Republic/Phoenix Gazette—1982–present**
2	**611:**	**Reuters—1988–present**
4	**660:**	**Federal News Service—1988–present**
6	**695:**	**Southwest Newswire—1984–present**

5 files have one or more items: file list includes 19 files
>>>? File

Craig was staring at the bottom of the screen. "Not much there. But at least we got nineteen news items, six from file six hundred and ninety-five on the Southwest Newswire.

Let's see what they tell us." His fingers hit the keyboard, punching in a request to access the file.

>>> File 695
File 695 entered: SWNEWS
SetItemsDescription
?sUFO and New Mexico and August 1988

13	**UFO**
212	**New Mexico**
327	**August 1988**
6	**UFO and New Mexico and August 1988**

"Okay, let's dig. I'm gonna ask the computer to access those last six stories."

Craig typed in the command. Linda watched the screen go blank, then listened as the disk drive churned loudly. Within seconds, the first story flashed in front of them. Nothing out of the ordinary. The same with the next and the next one after that, until . . .

"Look at that, John." Linda rammed her finger against the screen. "This could be it."

11247865 File 695: SWNEWS * Use format 9 for full text*

Local Rancher Eyewitnesses UFO Near Roswell
The Roswell Dispatch 09486R253 August 10, 1988
Availability: Full text on-line line count: 00015
Identifiers: Newsbrief; News

"It's not the same article we saw," Linda said. "Wesely's article was from the *Albuquerque Gazette*. Can we get the full text?"

"You got it," said Craig."

Craig typed in format 9 and waited. Linda stood motionless as she read the story carefully line by line.

11247865
Local Rancher Eyewitnesses UFO Near Roswell

***The Roswell Dispatch* August 10, 1988 p. 2**
ISSN: 0856-0014

By Richard Makkeson

Roswell, NM—One of the most unusual UFO sightings to date has been reported near Roswell, NM, by David Bruner, a local cattle rancher working in the Hope Valley area on August 9.

According to local officials, Bruner claimed to have observed a large silver craft with triangular wings flying slowly along the desert terrain at a very low altitude. Bruner reported seeing the craft stop, hover for several minutes, then take off with blinding speed.

"I heard this low hum as it cruised," said Bruner, "then an explosive thundering roar as it took off. It nearly dropped me to the ground." The following day Bruner found ten of his cattle dead from unknown causes.

A local scientist in the area reported seeing charred vegetation and burn marks in the soil beneath where Bruner claimed to have seen the craft stop and hover. "I believe him," said Dr. Kenneth Sims, a retired physicist from New Mexico State University. "There was definitely something out there, no doubt about it." Officials from the nearby Roswell Airbase and the Defense Department had no comment.

"I'll bet it's our craft," said Linda. "Everything fits. The shape, the maneuverability, the sound that was probably made by the propulsion system. Let's take a look at these other articles."

Craig printed out every news story the database search produced, each having basically the same information, each looking more as though it had to be CONDOR that was involved, they were all certain of that.

"What about that story on Joe Reed?" asked John. "Let's find out if there's anything out there on *him*."

Craig instinctively punched in the key words Joe Reed, New Mexico, and August 1988 in file number 492. Once again the computer responded, this time with only three stories; one they'd already seen from the Wesely file, the others dated four and ten days later.

"Let's print out the full text on these last two," Linda said, pointing to the second and third entry on the screen.

Craig commanded the computer to print, and as it did, Linda and John held their breath.

23753110
Missing Truck Driver Found Wandering in Desert
***Albuquerque Gazette* August 14, 1988 p. 4**
ISSN: 0666-1247
By Charles Timothy

Hot Rock, NM—A San Diego truck driver, missing since August 10, was found wandering along highway 17 near Hot Rock yesterday. The trucker, identified only as Joe Reed, was reportedly dehydrated but in stable condition except for some bruises and burn marks on the back of his head. He also suffered from what attending physicians diagnosed as temporary amnesia.

Reed was taken to St. Agnes Hospital, where doctors there said his amnesia had no doubt been caused by several injuries to his head. According to Reed, "The last thing I remember is driving along the highway and stopping when I saw this strange thing in the desert. Everything after that and up until yesterday is a blank."

The only other eyewitness to the incident, Dorothy Smith of Hot Rock, claims to have seen an unusual silver craft near the area hover close to the ground before taking off with incredible speed. Authorities are investigating the incident.

"Looks like a normal story about a guy who saw something he thought was a UFO and exhibited trauma-induced amnesia," Craig said. "Probably smashed his head against something while he was out there in the desert and wandered off in the wrong direction."

"Except for the burn marks," Linda said. "And the mention of the silver craft and—"

"My God, look at this," John cut in, his hand over his

mouth as he read the last article. "This couldn't be a coincidence."

Linda grabbed the computer paper and tore it from the printer. The blood draining from her face was enough to send a chill through Craig's body.

"I can't believe this," she said. "My God, he was right. Jack was right."

The three continued staring at the printout in front of them, hoping that what they were reading was either a mistake or a cruel coincidence that had nothing to do with CONDOR or WORLD ORDER or TIMBER WOLF. Maybe there was some other explanation, they all thought, something they hadn't considered or thought through.

16843780
Missing Trucker Found in Desert Commits Suicide
***San Diego News Journal* August 21, 1988 p. 7**
ISSN: 2246-0578

By Dianne Nichols

San Diego, CA—Joe Reed, a 44-year-old San Diego truck driver found on August 13 after wandering in the New Mexico desert for three days, reportedly committed suicide yesterday while recuperating at his home in La Mesa, according to local police investigating the incident. Preliminary autopsy reports confirmed that death had been caused by self-inflicted injuries sustained to his head by a 16-gauge shotgun.

Authorities in both San Diego and New Mexico are trying to link Reed's death with the apparent suicide of Dorothy Smith, the only other eyewitness to a UFO sighting that Reed had claimed he experienced three days before he was found. Smith's body, which was submerged in a full bathtub and had both wrists cut, was discovered by her daughter during a routine visit. Investigators are puzzled because both Reed and Smith had committed suicide exactly ten days following their encounter with whatever it was they had witnessed in the desert.

The FBI has been called in to investigate possible links between the two deaths and are not discounting foul play.

According to Lt. James Pickens, chief FBI investigator on the case, "The probability of a double suicide committed on the same day by two people with something this unusual in common and living five hundred miles apart at the time of death is too much of a coincidence." The investigation is ongoing.

"It's no coincidence," Linda muttered.

"What do you mean?" Craig flinched at how certain she was of that.

"The suicides. They're not a coincidence. Both Reed and Smith were unsuspecting victims of some horribly sick experiment. These people were nothing more than lab rats in a controlled desert environment."

"How can you possibly know that?" Craig asked, his surprise turning to stunned disbelief. "You know what the hell you're saying? What you're implying?"

Linda shot a furtive glance at John, who displayed the same somber reaction as she did.

"Yeah, I know exactly what I'm implying." She turned back to Craig. "Believe me, I wish it wasn't true, but John and I both know these UFO sightings have less to do with delusions and hysterics than with the fact that one of CONDOR's air bases is near Roswell. We've seen the damn thing, Craig, and it's no UFO. The descriptions fit. And before we left Washington, Jack gave us an eye opener about what the agent it was designed to carry is capable of doing. That fits, too."

"You mean suicide?"

"Unfortunately, that's only the tip of the iceberg. What happened to Reed and Smith may be a prelude to what entire populations can look forward to if this thing gets out of control. It all fits. The craft, the suicides. It's the ultimate way to wage war. Just sit by and let enough of the targeted population kill itself to create total chaos."

Craig leaned back in his chair and, as he read through the printout again, found it hard to comprehend that any of this could possibly be real. *Suicide. What they witnessed in the desert. Psychochemical warfare.* He was no scientist—in fact, he considered most scientists bizarre idiots and social misfits—but he now had no reason to disbelieve that what he was looking at was indeed linked to everything Linda and John had told him. The thought of it sickened him, frightened the hell out of him in a way nothing else ever had.

"If there *is* such a thing," Craig asked incredulously, "and it *can* do what you say, then what could anyone do about it and who the hell is safe anymore?"

"No one, I'm afraid."

"Well, then I think we should find out if anything like this has happened anywhere else besides New Mexico."

"Any ideas?" Linda asked.

"You mentioned Malaysia. Lemme pull up an Asia-Pacific database and search for anything that may have happened overseas."

Craig linked into the Asia-Pacific Newswire, typed in the select key words SUICIDE and MALAYSIA or INDONESIA or SOUTH PACIFIC, and waited for the computer to search through any news sources originating from the Pacific Rim.

"Okay, twelve items in file 30," he said, continuing to punch keys. "Let's see what we get."

The three sat riveted to the screen for what seemed like minutes, though it took only seconds for the computer to respond with two articles.

"Bingo," Craig said. "We only got two hits. Must not have been a key story."

"Either that or it was kept well covered-up," Linda added.

"Maybe. But more than likely these overseas stories weren't taken seriously by the major news wires or the mainstream networks. Let's see what we get."

Craig requested full text on both stories, punched return, and leaned back against his chair. "My instincts tell me we're gonna get something unusual. Happens a lot, you know. Some third world news report comes in that sounds so bizarre no one but the tabloids will touch it. Then once it's printed in the tabloids, nobody believes a goddamn word of it, and within a week the story dies, whether it's true or not. I've seen it happen. You'd be surprised how much stuff out there is really worth going after, but reporters either won't touch it or aren't allowed to pursue it.''

And then, as the screen flashed on, needlelike chills ran the length of Linda's spine as everything they had predicted was suddenly before their eyes.

36448801
Violence Mars Isolated Region of Singkep Island
***Singapore Free Press*, February 3, 1995 p. 11**
ISSN: 0113-7743
By Ngai Kulana

Singapore—A local missionary hospital on Singkep Island has reported ninety-seven cases of mass suicide and carnage in the remote northern area of Tanku River Valley. The tribe involved, numbering just over 100 individuals, had been virtually exterminated in what one confused doctor described as a bizarre religious ceremony, no doubt involving one of the many types of hallucinogenic herbs found in this mountainous region. The eight survivors, all men, described a sudden change in the behavior of the tribe, followed shortly thereafter by suicides and outbreaks of unexplained violence. Many of the victims have died from wounds inflicted by other tribe members. The few terrified survivors claimed to have seen low-flying aircraft sweep over the area a few days prior to the incident. A limited number of investigators and scientists have been allowed into the remote site to investigate. Local authorities have prohibited anyone from visiting the area until the government completes its investigation.

''Believe us now?'' Linda asked. ''There it is . . . the practice run for the next holocaust.''

Craig stared at the screen, shaking his head at what he was seeing. ''Shit, I had no idea,'' he muttered. ''No idea they would go this far.''

''Believe it,'' Linda said. ''Anyone who thinks this can't happen is either naive or has no idea what certain elements of our government are into or able to get away with.''

''Meaning?''

''I can't say. There are things happening that we can't talk about, let's leave it at that.''

And with that, Linda ran through the news story again, visualizing herself on that tropical island, imagining the terror she would experience as day by day, minute by minute, she'd feel her twisted mind slipping away, losing its ability to control behavior, metamorphosing into an uncontrollable weapon of self-destruction. And then she imagined what it would be like to face a population of killers, or to be a killer herself, to kill wantonly without thought or feeling, to lose whatever rational thoughts and human emotions she may once have had and suddenly desire nothing but death.

As she read the report a second time, Linda recalled a seminar she'd attended a year ago at Harvard University, given by a professor of bioethics whose theories of man's inherent aggression seemed, at the time, exaggerated. She was suddenly reconsidering her skepticism, thinking back to Dr. Klingman's premise that man, if left to himself without moral guidelines and laws, would kill wantonly, violently, and without remorse. The unspeakable cruelty of man against man in places like Bosnia, Haiti, Chechnya, Rwanda, and Somalia had supported his claim that man, without the tranquillizing effect of God in his life, was basically an evil creature. How much more evil would he be, she now wondered, if the part of his brain that controlled violence were somehow altered in a way that would release the natural evil in his soul? It was unimaginable; nightmarish beyond all comprehension.

She read and reread the story in front of her a half dozen times before turning from the screen in revulsion. ''Jesus, we've got to stop this,'' she whispered. ''It's gone beyond world order. It's world domination. Hell, just eliminate anyone who happens to be a monkey wrench in the global cog. Wanna get rid of a population that won't go along with U.S. policy? Don't nuke 'em; no need to; just fry their brains. Some group of independent-minded thinkers—God forbid anyone could ever be independent minded again—refuses to go along with the way the world political system is supposed to operate? Wipe the problem out. Better yet, just let them wipe themselves out. Much neater that way. Before you know it, the only ones left will be those who'll toe the party line. What a beautiful concept."

While Linda closed her eyes and rubbed them hard with her fingers, Craig was scratching his immense beard, glaring at the screen with the kind of quizzical look that usually indicated something was amiss. He smelled a hidden clue between those lines and was suddenly dissecting the words like a surgeon cutting into soft flesh.

"What is it, Craig?" John asked, having seen that look on many occasions before. "You see something, don't you?"

"Something's different about this piece. Don't you see it? It's not like the others. There's more here than meets the eye. Don't you see it?"

Linda jumped back into her position behind Craig's shoulder and looked at the screen for what seemed like the hundredth time today. "What? What do you see?"

"Couple of things. First of all, Singkep Island is off the coast of Malaysia. Malaysia is where you said the tropical research center was located. Second, and more important, these survivors reported seeing an aircraft. Not a *strange* aircraft. Not a UFO with shiny metal or triangular wings that hovered, then flew off at incredible speeds. None of that. Just a plain, low-flying aircraft. Nothing unusual about that. Seems to me, at least from what's been reported here, that CONDOR wasn't used in this case. Whatever it was these people were sprayed with was sprayed from a regular plane. And that leads me to two theories."

"What?" Linda grabbed Craig's chair and spun him around, staring directly into his bloodshot eyes.

"One, the government wanted to test the agent on a human population without having to risk using CONDOR, and they picked Singkep Island because it's isolated and they knew it would be easy to do. Or two—and this one you may not like, but I think it's probably the correct assumption—that whoever's behind this didn't have official access to CONDOR but needed to test the agent anyway. They may not even have had government backing to do it. A rogue government agency, maybe, or a group that has nothing to do with the government at all.''

''And that means the U.S. Tropical Research Center may not be a government facility at all,'' Linda said, ''but a civilian pharmaceutical or genetic engineering lab, just like we thought.''

She shook her head. Was this how it was all supposed to end? she thought, how technology ultimately crosses that fine line between creation and destruction and reaches the point of no return? Was this how the universal laws of nature would finally deal with misguided, arrogant life-forms who dare to reach beyond their mortal boundaries and attempt to alter, as though it were their own, the work of God?

''Linda?'' John squeezed Linda's arm and brought her back from her despair. ''You okay?''

''How can I be okay?'' she answered, barely able to speak. ''If we don't get to the bottom of this. . . .''

For the first time in days, Linda showed visible signs of breaking down. She looked worn and haggard. She'd tried to remain strong in the face of death, to think beyond the events that were now unfolding and beginning to look as if they would spin out of control. But as she thought of what lay ahead and how powerless she felt to change any of it, she slumped lifelessly into the easy chair next to the computer and buried her face in her hands.

chapter twenty-five

MARCH 19, 1996: 6:45 P.M.

This was the second time since the day of Peter's tragic accident that Linda could ever remember not being able to sleep all night. She'd barely spoken through breakfast, and she'd spent the better part of the day going over the printouts that had begun to look more and more ominous each time she'd dig through them.

It was all beginning to make some sense, though the players were still very much a mystery to her. Some group, she figured—she wasn't sure who or for what godawful reason—must have gotten its hands on a new biotechnology capable of threatening the life of every living soul on the planet. Adam Wesely's name kept flashing through her mind again and again as she tried convincing herself that perhaps he had been trying to lift his burden of guilt and was killed because of it. As she sat on the front porch steps, mesmerized by a Maine sunset that had set the sky on fire, Linda simply could not understand why any of this was happening.

''Linda?'' John walked across the porch and slid next to her. ''We can't give up, you know. We've got to go on, find out what's happening.''

''Why CONDOR?'' She put her head on his shoulder and continued staring into the flaming red sky.

''What do you mean?''

''I've been asking myself why the government would use something like CONDOR. Why not an F16 or a damn crop duster, for that matter?''

''Secrecy and security, I guess. You can't just fly over a major city . . .'' John stopped, suddenly realizing what he was saying.

"Unless you have the defense-evading capabilities of CONDOR," Linda finished, snapping her head up as if another piece of the puzzle had suddenly shifted into place. "They need CONDOR because the real target is not some backward island like Singkep but a major populated area that would have air defenses. But which one and why? My God, John, it could be anywhere. It could be the United States, Israel, Washington, New York."

"Linda, some guy named Pilofski's on the phone," yelled Craig from behind the screened porch door.

Linda jumped off the steps and ran into the house toward Craig's outstretched hand. She snatched the receiver from his fingers and pressed it to her ear, her heart racing.

"Jack! Where are you calling from?"

The voice on the other end, low and somber, was unlike the witty cackle she'd grown accustomed to. "Phone booth near Bennie's," he said. "It's the only place in this town I feel safe to talk anymore. Listen, I'm due at the lab for a meeting in less than an hour, so I can't talk long. Here's the scoop. Colonel Williams is dead—"

"What!" Linda yelled, nearly dropping the phone.

"Dead . . . heart attack, they say. I don't buy it for a minute. But that's not why I called. Everyone in Washington's looking for you. General McKnight's been over this place like a blanket since you disappeared. Has an all-points bulletin out for both of you. A few other goons I'd never seen before were spotted here as well. They located John's car in Virginia and they're doing their damnedest to track down the rental. If they locate it at Washington National, it won't take 'em long before they link the phony ID with airline tickets. And once they pinpoint your destination, they'll have more security people up there than they had in northern Iraq. It won't be long after that till they're knocking on Craig's door."

Linda's entire body shook so hard she fell into a nearby chair and grabbed the phone with both hands. She'd been so certain that ditching the Alfa would allow them at least *some* time to think things through without having to look over their shoulders. But now it was over, and she knew that whoever converged on Maine would eventually track the rented maroon Ford Escort to a couple of fugitives on the verge of uncovering everything.

"How close are they, Jack?"

"Don't know, but I wouldn't hang around Craig's place much longer if I were you. Were you at least able to get anything up there?"

"We sure did. And you were right. We found a pattern that would be consistent with a psychochemical agent, just as you described. The article on Joe Reed? Turns out he killed himself ten days later. Dorothy Smith, the only eyewitness? Same thing. Ten days later. We even found evidence of what has all the markings of a large-scale human experiment they did on an island near Malaysia. It was horrible."

"Malaysia. Figures. That's where it is, Linda. The U.S. Tropical Research Center is where they're makin' it."

"What's going on back at the lab?"

"Last coupla days have been hell around here, with McKnight's people interrogating everybody, looking through files, searching offices, tearing apart labs. You'd think they were looking for the Holy Grail. Never seen anything like it around here. From what I'd been able to pick up, something's going to happen real soon. We don't have a lot of time."

"You think McKnight had anything to do with Williams . . . or with Adam?" she asked, almost expecting it to be so.

"From the looks of it, I'd say McKnight's a major player. If you thought your colonel friend was bad, you haven't danced with this guy yet. He's worse, believe it or not. Williams was nothing more than a lapdog. I get the creeps just being in the same room with this guy. Like I said, he's on your trail and he's a ruthless son of a bitch. You'd better get the hell outta there, at least by the morning."

"Where, for Christ's sake? Where do we go from here?"

"I think that's obvious, Linda."

"Not to me."

"What about Malaysia?"

There was silence followed by, "Are you serious or just plain crazy?" Linda's incredulous outburst sent John rushing through the door. He stood in front of her and silently mouthed "What's going on?" as he looked quizzically into her terrified eyes. She shook him off and listened for Jack's response.

"I'm as serious as I've ever been, Linda. You have no choice, from what I can see. They want you dead, trust me. Stay where you are—or even in the States—and chances are pretty damn good they'll find you and you'll end up exactly like the rest. Peter, Wesely, now Colonel Williams. Find out what's going on in Malaysia and you might just break this wide open. You've got nothing to lose, maybe a helluva lot to gain. I'll do everything I can on this end."

Linda suddenly felt like a cornered animal with nowhere left to run or hide. She knew that Jack was right and that given enough time and enough manpower, McKnight would eventually get to her. "Okay, Jack. Give me a few hours to think this through and talk it over with John. I'll call you back some time this evening."

"Don't think about it too long," Jack said. "I'll be back here at exactly ten o'clock. You have a pencil to jot down the number?"

"Yeah, right here. Go ahead."

Jack could barely make it out through the grime, but recited it slowly to make sure Linda made no mistake. "There's one other problem," he then said.

"What's that?"

"Your passports. How are you going to get them?"

"That's not a problem," Linda said. "Don't ask me why I thought I'd need it, but I took my passport with me when I left home the other day. I told John to take *his*. Maybe I knew all along we'd end up having to leave the country."

"Great," Jack said. "I'll be waiting for your call, then."

"I know you'll be careful, Jack, but what if you're followed? What if they ask questions about why you're there?"

"Not to worry. After you guys left here yesterday, I had

another cup of coffee and a piece of pie. One thing led to another and . . . well, I sort of asked Maxine out.'' He said it with an almost embarrassing tone, then added, ''I can always say I came back to see *her*. She gets off at ten thirty.''

''Okay, good luck, Jack. I'll call you then.'' Linda cradled the phone and turned back to John, who could tell by her dour expression that some sort of plan had been made. ''We need to talk, John.''

John turned dour himself and nodded. ''I figured something was going on.''

''We have to leave. They found your car and Jack thinks they may be close to locating the Cavalier you rented and left at the airport. It's only a matter of time.''

''Damn. Jack have any suggestions?''

She had to force herself to say it but had to agree with Jack that there was no other way. ''Malaysia. It's the only way we'll get to the bottom of this.''

''Shit, I had a feeling where this was gonna lead. But how in God's name are we going to pull it off?'' John latched onto her arms with both his hands. ''We've been damn lucky so far. I don't know about this.''

''I think I have a way we can do it.''

''I sure hope so. Because if you don't . . .'' John stopped and pulled Linda to him, holding her tightly.

Jack had been pacing nervously around the shattered phone booth for ten minutes, lifting and replacing the cracked receiver every few seconds to make sure it was in position. He looked on as drunks picked through Dumpsters in the alley across the street. Not ten feet from where he stood, a bedraggled woman with no teeth was busy making a bed out of cardboard and discarded newspaper. To his right, in a filthy hallway across the street, a crack addict had just finished smoking a rock and, with only his feet hanging out the doorway, stretched out like a dead fish and within seconds was oblivious to the world around him.

''Jesus Christ, Linda, c'mon,'' he whispered, even more nervous now as he glanced at his watch and saw that it was

10:03. A skinny hooker with heroin written all over her wiggled past him in three inch heels and black fishnet stockings. She blew him a kiss, then teasingly flipped out her tongue as if *that* would make him nod his head and reach back for his wallet. He turned in disgust and stared again at the phone.

Two minutes later, a ring echoed through the narrow street like a cathedral bell. Jack vaulted into the booth and tore the receiver off the hook. "Hello?" he asked.

"Jack."

"Yeah. Thank, God."

"Listen, Jack. I have a plan. I can't go into detail now—it's too complicated—but here's what you do on your end."

"Go on."

"Tomorrow, call McKnight and tell him that you received a postcard from me and wanted to let him know I'm okay. Tell him that I'd arrived in Baltimore yesterday, that I'm visiting some friends who work at Johns Hopkins, and that I'll be back in Washington in a few days. If he thinks I'm in Baltimore, he'll send his troops there to scour the area. That'll at least buy us some time. Meanwhile, wait for us to Express Mail anything we get in Malaysia to the post office box you rented. You did rent one like we told you to, didn't you?"

"Yeah, yesterday. It's P.O. box 187755 in the 20059 zip code."

"Good. Let me write that down." Linda jotted the number on a slip of paper and handed it to John. "Check it every day. The minute you get something from us, make a few hundred copies. Keep one copy in the post office box and distribute the rest to every major news source and every senator in Washington. There's got to be people left in this country who'll be so shocked at this they'll launch a complete investigation. You got all that?"

"Got it. Good luck on your end."

"Thanks, Jack. Be careful."

"I better go. Lot of deals going down around here and I don't exactly look like I belong. Take care."

"Yeah. Take care."

Linda hung up and let out a deep sigh. The plan had been set, and she knew there'd be no turning back, regardless of what happened now.

"I suppose we should pack," she said. "We can head out to the airport first thing in the morning."

After they'd finished gathering whatever evidence could give them away, John and Linda spent their remaining night in Maine trying to catch up on the eight years since Peter's death. They walked for an hour in the moonlight, watched the stars disappear behind the gathering clouds, talked about marriage and family and about how much they regretted allowing their work to take over their lives. The next morning, as Craig watched from his porch, a tear trickling past his rugged face and onto his beard, they left Maine as secretly as they'd arrived.

chapter twenty-six

The United 747 flight from Los Angeles to Honolulu had taken off at 10:27 A.M. Pacific time. And after stopping to refuel in Guam, it continued over the turquoise waters of the East Indies and the southern tip of the Philippines until, at 1:02 P.M. Singapore time, it crossed the South China Sea and now took them along the northern edge of Borneo's jade coastline.

They'd tried sleeping as much as they could to adjust to the change in time zones, but it had been nearly impossible. Who could sleep, thought Linda, as she found herself gazing at mile after mile of tropical jungle and crystal blue water that lapped against beaches as white as the Colorado snow she'd seen when they'd passed over the Rockies. How easy it would be to get lost, to disappear from Washington forever, or at least to hide until it was all over or until someone else had found a way to expose the madness that was sending them halfway round the world.

The forest below them stretched endlessly for as far as the eye could see. Giant, bare-trunked hardwoods, ten or more feet in diameter, swept upward for more than a hundred feet before spreading into thickly gnarled branches above the black peat soil. Whatever light might otherwise have filtered through an unbroken canopy as dense as a thickly woven rug was sealed out, denying the tropical world beneath it the precious, life-giving rays of sun that allowed photosynthesis to exist.

Linda imagined life beneath that stiflingly humid and suffocating canopy; the unending darkness, broken only by an occasional clearing that allowed wisps of sunlight and hot wind to penetrate to the forest floor; insects the size of a man's hand; birds of every color and characteristic imaginable; the perpetual danger lurking beneath each plate-sized leaf and fallen, rotting branch; the silent glare of camouflaged, predatory eyes that followed each movement of prey—human or otherwise—from atop hidden, overhanging limbs that seemed to reach from nowhere and everywhere at once to snarl their unsuspecting victims like long and stealthy fingers.

What was so different between that and what she'd experienced in Washington? Linda pondered. Would a toxic plant, a poisonous insect, a snake be any different than a bullet to the head? Was this green, forbidding jungle any worse than her black asphalt one? Would she be in any more danger beating a path through the dense rain forests of Malaysia than she would be walking the violent killing fields of New York or Los Angeles or, for that matter, Washington, D.C.? The more she thought of it, the better she felt about being *there*, halfway around the world.

A half hour later, as Linda felt the 747 dip and begin its descent, she exchanged glances with John, who for the past several hours had himself traded bouts of restless sleep with silent stares that betrayed the apprehension he felt about this final trip. It was a long way from the car rental agency in Bangor, she thought, and she imagined herself there right now, slipping into a car, driving off to Bar Harbor, renting a cabin in the middle of nowhere and losing herself in the beauty she'd just left behind. Linda smiled weakly at the absurdity of such thoughts.

"Tired?" she asked John, trying to break the tense silence that had settled between them.

"Very. A little scared, too."

Linda turned back to the small window and continued viewing a stretch of water translucent enough to reveal massive coral reefs beneath its surface and schools of fish that weaved gracefully along the surface like endless streams of dark ribbon. In the distance to the right, Singapore rose from the horizon in a modern fusion of steel, concrete, and glass. It seemed so out of place, Linda thought, in the midst of an ancient land that even today paid homage to gods and cultures many thousands of years old.

The plane banked right, then leveled off, heading directly for a skyline that appeared sculpted against the far eastern heavens like a sea of crystal and jewels. The blend of American-style capitalism and Eastern philosophies seemed distinctly at odds in this ancient land; rice paddies juxtaposed with McDonalds parking lots, oxen grazing alongside rows of Mercedes. It was all so unreal, so exotically beautiful and unnatural at the same time. But though it was a city Linda could have imagined herself and John retreating into for as long as they had to, she knew it was far from their final destination. Kuala Lumpur, site of the U.S. Tropical Research Center, was almost two hundred fifty miles due north. And now, as she looked toward the northern horizon, a foreboding apprehension gripped her.

"I hope these customs people buy your story of us being writers, John." Her voice quivered as she anticipated the interrogation that was certain to be waiting for them the minute they stepped off the plane. "From what I've heard and seen, Singapore is definitely not the place to be caught lying to authorities or breaking the law." She was thinking the entire time of the government flyers they'd been issued and the in-flight movie they'd watched detailing Singapore law and describing the harsh punishments meted out to violators of even the most minor infractions.

"Look, if they need a reason why we're here, we just go with our plan and tell them we're working on a book about tropical rain forests. We rub it in about how beautiful and exotic this place is and how we absolutely love the people. These guys really get off on being liked and respected by Westerners. I guarantee you, within minutes they'll be tossing our passports back to us and grinning like Cheshire cats."

"You sound like you know," Linda said, a little surprised at John's knowledge of the local customs.

"Been to this area several times," he said. "Japan, Hong Kong, Taiwan, Singapore. Never seems to change, except for the modern buildings that keep going up. People stay the same. Nice for the most part. Friendly. They'll give you anything if they like you."

"I've been thinking, John. Maybe we should make a change in our plans."

"Meaning what?"

"I don't think we should fly into Kuala Lumpur. If anything went wrong, if somehow McKnight got wind that we were heading into Malaysia, the first place he'd send men would be the airport. And the last thing he'd expect would be for us to drive from Singapore to Kuala Lumpur."

"You may be right. Okay, we drive then."

With a deep grunt, the large, hunchbacked 747 bumped heavily against the runway, then rumbled as it slowed and made its turn into gate 73. Overhead baggage was removed, and within minutes a long line of passengers began inching its way along the aisles toward a sleepy pilot and three haggard stewardesses, who, despite the jet lag, managed somehow to break into accommodating smiles and forced thank-yous.

John bent down, retrieved the two carry-on bags he'd gotten from Craig, and handed one to Linda. The two then broke into the line of disembarking passengers, made their way to the front of the customs line, and found themselves face to face with two grim-looking uniformed men who ordered them to open their bags. John unlocked both bags and watched a pair of white gloves maneuver carefully among their clothes and other belongings.

"Reason faw being heah?" one of the customs agents asked with an accent that sounded like a mixture of British and Indian as he continued his search without looking up.

"Business," John responded. "We're writing a textbook on tropical rain forests. We'll be spending a week or so studying the local flora, mainly along the west coast." John waited for some sort of challenge, prepared to kiss butt if he had to in order to get through this ordeal as quickly as possible.

"Enjoy yaw stay. Nex please." The Cheshire grin never materialized. Instead, the customs agents looked ahead to the next passenger, seemingly more eager to get through the day than to catch foreigners in lies about their purpose. That, John figured, they would leave to local authorities who worked tirelessly to make Singapore one of the most crime-free places on Earth.

Linda tapped John and pointed to the car rental booth across from the massive airport walkway. It was barely visible through the human wall that flowed steadily this way and that like a swollen river. They managed to fight their way through the mass of humanity and stood wearily before a beautiful slender woman dressed in a blue-and-white Avis car-rental uniform. She smiled pleasantly. Through her perfect teeth, her San Francisco English was nearly as perfect. This, thought Linda, was going better than expected.

A half hour of paperwork and pleasantries later, the thin wisp of a beauty was directing Linda and John to the Avis parking lot, where a gray Toyota Celica was waiting for them. When they reached the car, they threw their bags into the trunk, climbed in, and as Linda unfolded on her lap a road map of Malaysia she'd purchased at the airport, John started the engine and headed directly toward the sign that read EXIT.

"This all seems too easy so far, John. A bad omen, maybe?"

"It won't be this easy once we get out of Singapore, believe me. The villagers get more wary and the officials more suspicious of conspicuous outsiders. We need to keep our NASA security IDs out of sight until it's time to execute the plan. The last thing we need is some nosy little cop calling the American embassy, asking a million questions about why two U.S. government scientists with top-secret clearances are sneaking around the country pretending they're writers."

"Right." Linda buried her nose in the map and, with her finger, followed the highway from Singapore to Kuala Lumpur. "When you get out of the airport, follow the signs north. There aren't too many other options, from what I can see."

They weaved their way out of the bustling airport, heading north through a city that looked more like it belonged on the east coast of the United States than in Southeast Asia. Silk merchants, grocers, open-market street vendors, electronics retailers on every corner, shops of every imaginable kind selling every product manufactured anywhere in the world, factories and suppliers, wholesalers and distributors, more restaurants than New York's Chinatown, and modern office buildings that towered above it all heralded Singapore as one of the new, undisputed giants at the crossroads of world trade. It was all there, crowded on acre upon acre of the most densely populated piece of real estate Linda had ever seen.

"Once we get through this maze," she said, studying the map that was now spread out across half the front seat, "we should be able to see some kind of sign for Kuala Lumpur. Depending on road conditions, we could be there in less than four hours."

"Try more like six," John said. "Even with good road conditions. And up ahead is one of the reasons why."

John slowed the Toyota to a stop in front of a red-and-white-striped border security roadblock that stretched ominously across the road. Two security police officers approached, one on each side of the car. At least *they* smiled, Linda thought.

"Step ow of cah, preeze," the senior officer asked as politely as a little boy would, ashamed of even having to make the request. "We check yaw trunk one minute and then you go."

John stepped out, unlocked the trunk, and watched the two go through their bags slowly, deliberately, feeling along every seam and every lining with their gloved fingertips, obviously looking for drugs or other contraband that these two rich-looking Americans might be smuggling across the border from Singapore. After a check of the bags, the two officers pulled up trunk carpeting, checked every crevice, removed hubcaps, and dug bony fingers between the seats. The promised one minute had become ten.

"Okay," the officer announced. "You go now. Which way you travel?"

"Kuala Lumpur," Linda shot back, anxious to get on with it.

"Follow road about faw hundred kilometer nawth."

"Thank you." *Thank God,* Linda thought. *Now let us through, dammit.*

Both security officers tipped their black, narrow-brimmed hats courteously and watched them drive off. John stared into the rearview mirror, and only after the curve in the road took them out of sight of the checkpoint did he feel comfortable enough to concentrate on the road ahead.

"Seems so different the farther we get away from Singapore," Linda said, looking out at the dark green Malaysian landscape and once again thought of Maine. "At least back there I felt like I was in a Western city. But this, this is something else. I feel as if I'm being pulled into some tropical maelstrom."

"Beautiful though, isn't it?"

"I have to admit it is. It's a shame we're not *really* here to study tropical rain forests. Right now I'd take that in a heartbeat."

As she said that, the air conditioner suddenly cut off, and

after a few minutes of obscenities, Linda decided it would be better to roll down her window and put up with the heat and humidity than to drive back and have to deal with the airport car rental agency and the checkpoint again. She settled into her seat and watched as thick gray clouds emerged like blankets of smoke from the jagged mountain peaks, blackening the deep green fields of sugarcane along the open road.

The air was even more unbearably hot and steamy than it had been back at the airport, the darkening clouds portending the arrival of rains that would soon add to the heavy, water-laden atmosphere that stuck to Linda and John like soggy plastic. Mid-April marked the beginning of monsoon season, which brought with it sudden squalls and unpredictable thunderstorms that rumbled through the valleys with such intensity that rivers would often rise twenty feet above normal in just a few hours.

Along the side of the road, they could see the tops of wide, pointed hats. One would occasionally pop up and reveal the gaunt, weathered face of a peasant tending his field. But mostly the hats and the hunched backs and the invisible faces remained fixed in place as if stuck in the drenched mud, unaware that civilization was cruising past them only a hundred feet away. It was a unique world for someone who'd never experienced it, a world seemingly caught in time and space, indifferent to what most people in developed nations considered even the barest necessities of life.

In the distance, beyond the lush fields, small villages, *kampongs*, spread out from the base of the mountains and broke through the mist like apparitions. There were no cars, no church steeples, no electrical lines or stores of any kind; just wood and palms, tethered into huts that swayed and leaned eastward in the strengthening wind. Next to desolate villages was an occasional emerald green golf course, complete with tennis courts and English Tudor clubhouse that trumpeted the once dominant influence of rich British tradition. And where jungles were cleared, settlements had sprung up adjacent to newly established plantations of palm and rubber trees.

The land had changed considerably since their encounter at checkpoint one. No longer the gentle, rolling plains and coastal swamps that characterized the southernmost tip, the terrain here was a mix of dense mountain jungle and rich, verdant farmland. The farms grew more scarce the farther north they drove, replaced by broad-leafed hardwood rain forest of such immense proportions that from where they sat, John and Linda could catch only glimpses of its magnitude. Countless epiphytic plants, deriving their nutrients from the moist air and abundant rainfall, draped from trees and other plants throughout the forest. From the main road, other side roads veered off and disappeared into the precipitous slopes where remote villages lay hidden beneath the tightly packed canopy.

It was something Linda had never even imagined. She felt awed, but at the same time terrified. *Was this the reason the Tropical Research Center was located here?* she thought. *To hide it like drug lords hide their cocaine laboratories in the jungles of Colombia? Or was there something else here, something else out there in that terrifying darkness?*

"Look, there's a sign up ahead," John said, breaking the suffocating silence that had made the heat in the Toyota even more unbearable. "Maybe it'll show us how much farther."

They had already been driving five hours. Violent rainstorms had forced them off the road twice in the past three hours. The large thermos they'd filled with water and ice back at the airport was nearly dry. And from what Linda could see from the car window, the Malaysian jungle that now enveloped them was growing thicker and darker with every mile.

"Thirty kilometers," John announced, reading the rusted sign as it zipped past them. "Thank God. I was beginning to wonder how much longer I could take this heat. Just our luck we came to Malaysia during the hottest month of the year."

Thirty kilometers, Linda repeated in her mind. Thirty kilometers. What in the hell have I gotten us into?

chapter twenty-seven

The unexpected late-night meeting was already running an hour behind schedule. General McKnight, who sat waiting anxiously for the last participant to arrive at a secret conference room somewhere on the outskirts of Washington, D.C., was growing increasingly impatient with the status of their ongoing search for Linda Franklin and John Peterson.

Scattered throughout what looked like a strategic war room were the men charged with the actual implementation of TIMBER WOLF. Wall maps, flight patterns, and illuminated charts of target areas surrounded them in a brightly lit display of military overkill.

The moment Colonel Jefferey Patterson walked in, General McKnight's mind shifted back to attention and he stood before the group, waiting for each man to take his seat.

"Good evening, gentlemen," he began. "As you well know, we've finalized the mission flight path and are on schedule for a target date of six April. We've just received the latest computer enhanced reconnaissance photos and medical reports from Singkep, and I can tell you the results were absolutely outstanding."

McKnight looked toward the back of the room and wasted no time. He snapped his fingers. The lights went out, and a slide projector lit up a screen positioned in front of the conference table. He pressed a button on the handheld remote, advancing the tray with steady clicks until a photograph of the Pacific Rim flashed onto the screen. He then turned and jabbed at the screen with the tip of a metal pointer and drew an invisible line southeast from Malaysia to a small island off the coast of Sumatra.

"The final kill assessment, taking all factors into consideration, approached one hundred percent. For those of us who'd been involved in Desert Storm, we know damn well that bomb damage assessments back then didn't come close to half that.''

McKnight continued to drag the pointer along the screen toward the northwest corner of Singkep Island. ''This, gentlemen, was the January twenty-fourth flight path taken to the target area right here.'' He stopped and circled a portion of Singkep jutting out from the main island.

Another press on the remote and the room blackened as the projector advanced and dropped in another slide of Singkep Island. McKnight resumed. ''As scheduled, our pilots swept the Tanku River and engaged a select target population of approximately one hundred individuals.''

''Any evidence that the pilots knew what they were dropping?'' Patterson asked.

''No. It was a routine training flight as far as they were concerned. The canisters were exchanged prior to take off, and the pilots discharged what they thought was innocuous fluid. As predicted, the agent surpassed all performance criteria.''

The room blackened again. The next slide zoomed into focus and brightened the screen with a spy plane close-up of a small deserted village. Square, palm-roofed huts, encircling what appeared to be an enclosure used for community gatherings, could be seen torn apart as if shredded by a violent storm that ripped through and left chaos in its wake. Several of the huts had been partially burned. Debris, food, clothing, and other unidentifiable objects were strewn about the central area as though someone or something had taken everything in the village and tossed it haphazardly into the enclosure.

''This photo was taken from one of our high-altitude reconnaissance planes,'' McKnight continued. ''The village, as you can see, appears to be in shambles. If you look closely at the bottom of the screen, you can spot several bodies clustered together in an area some hundred feet from the center of the village.'' With the tip of his pointer, McKnight circled six thin brown objects, barely visible against the bronze dirt of the jungle floor.

"This next slide—" McKnight hit the remote again—"is a magnified view of the bodies." He tapped each with a delicate flick of his pointer.

Another slide. Then another. The room fell into a deathlike silence except for the sounds of the projector and McKnight's deeply resonant voice as it expounded on the horror that was appearing on the screen.

"This next slide shows the river adjacent to the village. Eighteen bodies . . . there . . . against the bank. And up on the bank to the left . . . right there"—McKnight pointed to four more mutilated bodies. "Thick, gaping wounds are evident across the chests and abdomens on these two. This one's head is partially severed, and this one's head and face appear to have been smashed in."

For the next thirty minutes, slide after slide of reconnaissance photos flashed by, depicting an experiment that was successful beyond all expectations. The men remained grimly silent, caught off guard by the graphic photographs of innocent victims and the systematically callous descriptions of the sacrificed bodies as if they were little more than Texas roadkill.

"Lights, please." McKnight went on. "The remaining sixty-nine bodies were reportedly found scattered throughout the area within a mile of the village. Hospital autopsies, from what our people have been able to find out, showed no trace of anything that would indicate use of biological or chemical agents. Official reports concluded that the deaths were directly related to untraceable levels of several types of hallucinogenic plant toxins to which the individuals had been exposed prior to the incident. Which is, by the way, precisely one of the reasons Singkep was chosen. The Tanganese, descendants of Malayan Indians, are well known throughout that part of Southeast Asia for bizarre drug-enhanced religious practices, which at one time included animal worship, ritual human sacrifices, and self-infliction of wounds. It was an expendable population. Fortunately for us, that played right into our hands."

"Does this confirm mode of delivery?" Colonel Patterson asked. "Is efficacy as high as the previous run?"

McKnight nodded and pointed at a large chart positioned on the left side of the room. "Results have shown that, unlike an aerosol spray system, infecting the water supply guarantees total contamination with minimum delivery time. Our planes made a sweep of the river, making sure, based on calculations of water flow, that the agent was delivered far enough upstream to ensure contamination of the target area for at least three days. The biological agent, for some reason, can't survive in the soil as long as we'd expected and degrades quickly once exposed to the atmosphere. In water, however, its life span increases sixfold. The biggest advantage, other than extended life span, is that the entire population is affected maximally because everyone within the target area uses the same water supply. Since there's approximately a five-day incubation period before symptoms begin to develop, no one would suspect contamination before then, and virtually everyone would have been exposed to the agent by the third day. By that time, nothing could be done. Within ten days of infection, full manifestation of the agent will have occurred. CONDOR will essentially utilize this same basic protocol. Rather than contaminating rivers, though, it will be contaminating select water supplies in specific locations, which we can target much more discriminately."

McKnight pointed to the chart and circled satellite photos of reservoirs and lakes, then added, "We don't want to depopulate an entire country, after all, just enough of it to create the conditions necessary for destabilization."

"I'm still concerned about the agent's effectiveness once it leaves a contained water supply and gets into the population," Lieutenant Colonel Steven Phillips said. "An open river is one thing, getting it through a filtered or chemically purified water treatment facility is another. How will the agent's structure be altered as a result of water treatment?"

"The agent should not be affected by any kind of water treatment," McKnight answered bluntly.

"How can you be certain?"

"The cryptosporidium tests."

"Explain."

"If you remember back in 1993, half the population of Milwaukee—nearly half a million people—was infected with cryptosporidium, a parasitic microbe that managed to get into the city's water supply. As you know, nothing killed it, not even chlorine. We selected cryptosporidium back then because we knew that for the most part it wasn't fatal but that it would make people sick enough so we could accurately assess, from hospital records, how soon infection would spread after a treated, contained water supply was contaminated. It was a very well-coordinated domestic experiment that clearly demonstrated what we suspected all along. The results were dramatic. Very positive."

"And the agent? Same effect?"

"Yes. Tests showed no impact of even dual water treatment on molecular structure. Furthermore, we'd discovered that in most cases, the agent, for reasons we don't fully understand, somehow makes its way into the limbic system, that part of the brain most responsible for emotions and behavior."

During the past decade, studies had shown that disruption of electrochemical activity within the brain's limbic system causes explosive rage and episodes of extreme violence. Neuroscientists at leading universities around the country, for example, had demonstrated that a normally calm and evenly dispositioned individual could easily be turned uncontrollably violent simply by altering the electrical charge produced by an electrode implanted in a certain area of that person's limbic system. The agreement among experts now is that the limbic system is the single most effective site within the brain for triggering violence in human beings.

"Combined with the agent's primary function," McKnight said, "this was an unexpectedly positive side effect. Our scientists were stunned, to say the least. At this point, do any of you have specific questions or concerns regarding the efficacy of the biotechnology?'' McKnight, seeing there were none, continued.

''Gentlemen, I'll be brief. First of all, I'd like to say I'm very impressed by the dedication and commitment each of you has shown. You can all be proud of that. Your final orders will be delivered by April fourth.'' And as McKnight made his way around the conference room table to shake the hand of each man individually, the red telephone emitted a short buzz and began to blink. He turned and reached across, punching the flashing button and picking up the receiver in one swift motion.

''McKnight here.''

''General, I have the information on Franklin and Peterson.'' The voice on the other end was quick and erratic.

''Go on.'' McKnight listened without interruption, nodding his head and tapping his finger heavily against the conference room table for nearly five minutes before giving the order to carry on and keep him abreast of further developments.

On the other end, Pilofski hung up and choked back his emotions. Recruited three years ago after McKnight had uncovered documents alleging that his father had been a Nazi collaborator in Poland during World War II, Jack knew full well that playing both sides was becoming increasingly dangerous. And as he thought of Linda and John somewhere in the dense jungles of Malaysia, he began to question his ability to pull it off. But like everyone else who had ever been trapped or coerced into cooperation by McKnight, he had little choice.

McKnight replaced the receiver and cleared his throat. ''That was one of our inside intelligence people,'' he announced. ''Franklin and Peterson are in Baltimore. He received a postcard from her saying that she's staying with some friends in the Johns Hopkins area. She may know someone there, a colleague, a former schoolmate. After we adjourn, I'll order my team up there to investigate.''

"Do they suspect anything they shouldn't?" Colonel Patterson asked.

"They know about Desert Storm," McKnight said.

"I'm sure they do. What's the latest we have on *that*?"

"At last count, almost ten thousand dead; maybe another three hundred thousand infected, including spouses. Reports from overseas, especially Israel, are not good."

"All because *someone* decided it was in their best financial interests to deal with Baghdad," Patterson said with a tone of derision. "No link has been established, I assume?"

"No, thank God."

McKnight, keenly aware of the importance that Middle East oil played in the stability of the Vanguard's worldwide economic network, suspected from the outset that Desert Storm would be launched irrespective of what some in the government knew all along. Benefit versus risk, the final analysis had concluded. After all, it was rationalized, how can the lives of even a thousand insignificant soldiers be compared to the risk of allowing Iraq to control the flow of oil to the free world? No, he knew that the possibility of exposure to known germ warfare agents supplied by Universal Biomedical would not even be a factor when we prepared to launch sorties across the deserts of a country that harbored more types of U.S. developed biological weapons than any other nation on Earth.

"Universal knew damn well what it was doing when it sold them those weapons," McKnight said, his face as somber as the mood of everyone in that room who'd held Universal responsible for killing more veterans than Saddam Hussein. "Knew damn well what the consequences would be."

"Anything else?"

"They know everything except what TIMBER WOLF is about, as we suspected. They're the ones who broke into Pentagon files and they assume it's the government behind it all."

"So as long as they still believe that," Patterson added, "as long as they're certain it's U.S. Intelligence or the Pentagon, they'll remain hidden and keep their mouths shut."

"We don't take that chance," McKnight responded. "I want those two found and neutralized. The sooner the better."

"When will you hear from your contact again?" Patterson asked.

"Franklin is supposed to call him within the next day or two to send him any further information or evidence they may find. I can't imagine what that might be. He's then supposed to take it to authorities. Instead, he'll turn everything over to us for analysis and appropriate action."

"And once his usefulness is over?"

"All three will have to be eliminated at one time. We'll have no need of him any longer. Loose ends tied up in one clean sweep, so to speak."

"Unless there's something out there," Patterson interrupted, leaning forward and squeezing his fingers nervously. "Something you may have overlooked."

"There's nothing. Absolutely nothing. I'm sure of it."

chapter twenty-eight

Along the outskirts of Kuala Lumpur, row upon row of eighty-foot rubber trees stood erect like rigid soldiers at attention. Each tree, dotted identically with a clay cup that hung limp from wire ties and was positioned beneath a set of V-shaped incisions, oozed what looked like white streams of thick latex tears. Men and women, who seemed as old and weathered as the trees themselves, could be seen gathering one of Malaysia's principal agricultural exports.

Closer to the city, traffic had become much more congested. The asphyxiating fumes of gasoline, incense, and open-market cooking oil lingered beneath the heavy layer of air and fused into a sickening blend of near toxic vapor. Squalid villages and squatter camps along the highway gave way to attractive bungalow suburbs, surrounded by brilliantly colored displays of lush, tropical vegetation. Straddling the confluence of the Kelang and Gombak rivers, the city itself was encircled by emerald green hills on three sides. Modern high-rise apartments and glass office buildings thirty or more stories high crowded the bustling downtown skyline and offered proof of Malaysia's new role in international trade and commerce.

Despite this new role, religious and cultural symbols were evident everywhere. A magnet for Southeast Asian immigration, Malaysia was at once Muslim, Buddhist, Hindu, Christian, Taoist, and pagan; a country with a diverse mix of Malay, Chinese, Indian, and European, as well as countless races that claimed as their heritage onetime headhunters, cannibals, and primitive tribesmen who until recently had only rarely crossed paths with the likes of modern man. Kuala Lumpur, however, remained a largely Chinese city with a population of more than one million busy residents.

As Linda gazed out at this sprawling, attractive city, she couldn't help notice the jarring blend of old and new. Deluxe hotels and shining stadiums stood next to ancient Moorish temples. Recently erected air-conditioned restaurants sat cheek-by-jowl with open-air street vendors peddling assortments of reptiles, amphibians, insects, and bats as casually as Western vendors would sell hot dogs and soft pretzels. While the outskirts of the city were crowded with Chinese shop houses, squatter's huts, and Malay stilt *kampongs*, the inner city was a futuristic model of architectural design and organization, a mecca for international business and industry that was growing with an unbridled vitality even its city planners and political leaders had found truly amazing.

John stopped for a traffic light and, in amazement, watched several old, thin-boned women weave frantically through the stalled traffic like young athletes. Spread across their fragile shoulders, long, flat sticks bowed from the weight of intricately woven baskets that swung precariously from each end and overflowed with fresh fish and vegetables. When the light turned green, the women scurried like rabbits, barely avoiding oncoming Volvos, Hondas, Toyotas, and Mercedes, the countless motorcycles, mopeds, and scooters, and the ubiquitous bicycles that danced and flirted with everything on the street.

"Wow, I didn't expect anything like this," Linda said, surprised at how crowded and busy but at the same time how modern, diverse, and exotically wonderful it all was.

"What did you expect, Kennecut, Maine?" John laughed.

"No, but I didn't think it would be so modern . . . so American."

John waved his hand, pointing at some of the buildings. "Kuala Lumpur's one of the most vibrant and rapidly growing cities in Southeast Asia. Look around. Except for the Malay and Chinese signs, if you didn't know better, you'd think you were in San Francisco. A lot of American companies are closing down their manufacturing plants and moving here."

John stopped at another traffic light and looked ahead to the next large intersection. "I'm gonna pull into that gas station down the street. Afterward, we can get something to eat before we find a hotel."

After filling up, John handed the diminutive gas station attendant several of the Malaysian dollars he'd exchanged at the Singapore airport for his American. He waited for change, then drove across the street into the parking lot of the Golden Dragon, a Chinese restaurant flanked by two gilded lions guarding an ornate, pagoda-style entrance.

They climbed out of the car and walked quickly through a stifling heat that made their lungs burn. Then, as John swung open the heavily carved entrance door, they were hit by the first blast of cold since before their air conditioner had quit on them nearly four hours ago.

The hot sweat clinging to Linda's body began to evaporate, making her stop dead in her tracks and close her eyes as she reveled in the rejuvenating quality of cool, dry air.

"Christ, this feels wonderful," she said. "I didn't realize how hot it was out there till now."

John grabbed Linda by the arm and pulled her through the inside restaurant door. They were greeted immediately by an exuberant, tuxedoed maître d' of Chinese ancestry and a young Malay waitress who couldn't have been a day over fifteen. The five-foot tall girl picked up two menus, tucked them beneath her skinny arm, and pointed toward the end of an aisle. She then turned and guided John and Linda past dimly lit faces that stared up at them suspiciously and into a darkened room that looked more like an opium den than a modern restaurant. She stopped at a table for two, placing the menus on each side, then walked away.

"Nice atmosphere," Linda said. "You think they even want us to see the menus . . . or the food?"

"Would you rather be back at Bennie's?"

"Good point. Let's order."

"Number five okay? Rice, fried pork, vegetables?"

"Sounds good. Right now I'd eat the rats I saw those street vendors out there selling."

John reached over and took Linda's hand in his. The light from the glass-enclosed candle barely illuminated her face, exaggerating her worn and tired appearance. And as he stared into her beautiful eyes and saw the look of profound sadness, almost anguish, he'd not seen before, he found himself cursing Peter, whose involvement—whatever it was—he was certain had been responsible for his own untimely death.

"I can't think of anyone I'd rather be here with than you," he said, then lifted her hand and placed it against his lips, kissing it gently.

Linda responded with a weak smile. "How do you know so much about this place?" she asked, allowing John to continue holding her hand as she watched his face.

"I already told you," John answered. "I've been to this part of the world several times."

"But you never said why," Linda said. "Exactly what was it that you'd come here for?"

"C'mon, what is this?" John asked. "I traveled to conferences, meetings, took a few pleasure trips. You sound as if you're having doubts. Are you?''

Linda slid her hand from his and said, ''I'm sorry. It's just that the last few days have been a nightmare, and I guess this whole affair is getting to me, that's all.'' Then, her face turning stone serious, ''If there's anything you're keeping from me because you're trying to protect me, don't. We're past that, John, and we're in this together. No more secrets, okay?''

John nodded, pinching the bridge of his nose and rubbing it as if suddenly hit with a splitting headache. ''I don't know if this is the right time or place to tell you . . . but there's a reason I've been avoiding your questions about Peter. Maybe why I've been avoiding *you* all these years.''

''I figured as much,'' Linda said. ''Please, John. I need to know.''

''It's true that Peter and I did some work together,'' John said. ''It's also true that I didn't know exactly what he was doing, just that we had top-secret security clearances to do it. But when I analyzed some of his coded data, the cryptonym MKULTRA kept coming up.''

''What!''

''Jack was right. Apparently some of MKULTRA's subprojects had continued secretly even though the program was terminated. I'm sorry, Linda, but I think Peter was involved in it. Exactly how, I don't know, but he was. I knew how you felt about that kind of work, and I never wanted to tell you, never wanted to be the one who gave his secret away, especially since he'd died and there was no point to it.''

''Are you telling me that all this could be linked to the CIA or to MKULTRA? That we're *still* experimenting with mind control and Peter was a part of it?''

''It could be,'' John said. ''I'm really sorry that he got caught up in all this.''

''I'm sorry, too,'' Linda said, then stared at her hands as though reflecting on everything Peter had ever told her and thinking that it was all a lie. ''I guess that would explain finding the CIA memo and why Peter was so evasive about it. I'm glad you told me. For a while I didn't know whether you were telling me the truth and why you seemed to be keeping things from me."

"Do you trust me now?" John asked, once again taking hold of her hand.

"Yes," Linda answered, her heart heavy, but glad that her suspicions about John were finally allayed. "Completely."

When their dinner arrived, they ate as though they'd gone without food for days. Every few minutes or so, the young waitress appeared from out of the darkness and, in barely understandable English, interrogated them pleasantly about their meal. Between the intrusive visits, John and Linda went over their plan several times, and when all was said and done, they agreed that unless they could locate Dr. Abraham Vijan and search his home for the evidence they needed, none of it would be possible.

When the waitress came by for what seemed like the hundredth time, John requested every telephone directory she could find for Kuala Lumpur and its surrounding suburbs, hoping that Dr. Abraham Vijan's name would be listed in at least one of them. Obligingly, she bowed, rushed back to the kitchen, and emerged a minute later.

"Here she comes," Linda said, following the waitress back to the table with her eyes and noticing only two directories in her hand. Linda grabbed both, handing one to John and tearing open the other. She flipped through the pages and ran her finger down narrow columns, looking for one Abraham Vijan, an uncommon-sounding name she hoped was really not the Malaysian equivalent of a Smith or Jones.

"John, look!" Linda turned the directory toward John and pointed to the bottom of the page. "Vijan, Abraham Dr., 17 Sempora. That's it. It's gotta be."

"That's it, all right," John said. "We can get a city map later and figure out where Sempora is. But I think we should try to get to Vijan's house earlier tomorrow morning than we'd planned—maybe five o'clock—to make sure he doesn't slip off to the research center before we get there."

John waved his arm and signaled for the check, anxious

for them to find a hotel where they could shower and rest. The jet lag had long since taken its toll on both of them, and since they had no idea what tomorrow would bring, they realized that what they needed more than anything else was at least eight hours of hard sleep.

The concierge removed two bags from the trunk and placed them on a luggage cart in front of the large glass doorway of the twenty-two-story Kuala Lumpur Embassy Hotel. John drove the Toyota into the underground parking deck while Linda followed the cart into an enormous circular lobby. The place was incredible, she kept thinking. More marble than a Greek temple, more sparkling glass-and-mirrored walls than a Las Vegas casino. Certainly more people sauntering about with gold and diamond jewelry than anywhere outside of Palm Beach or Beverly Hills.

The images of rotting villages just twenty miles south seemed to her almost impossible next to this gaudy splendor. Two worlds, separated by a system in which people were either members of a tiny middle and upper class or forever banished into the most degrading squalor one could imagine. But as Linda gazed in awe at the crystal chandeliers, the gold trim and silk drapes, the gleaming black-and-white marble floors, it all made sense. She knew that Malaysia, precisely because of its division between rich and poor and the willingness of peasants to work for slave wages, was emerging as one of the Pacific Rim countries to which American corporations were flocking like vultures for the express purpose of establishing industrial labor camps. With women and children willing to make hundred-dollar sneakers for fourteen cents an hour, why wouldn't they? she thought.

"You get our room?" John asked, startling Linda, whose eyes had been glued to the ostentatious display of wealth surrounding her.

"No, I was just looking around, trying to figure out how we could be in the middle of all this after what we saw a couple of hours ago. Seems so unfair."

"Unfair? Kind of like Park Avenue and Harlem. Happens in the United States, too, you know."

"No, John. In the States, *anyone* can make it if they really want to and work hard enough. Kids from Harlem go on to Harvard and Yale with little more than the clothes on their backs because they want it badly enough. Not here. The kids back there in those awful slums are lucky if their parents make enough money in our American factories to feed them, much less send them to school. Hell, most of them are probably forced to go to work when they're eight years old. It's obscene, as far as I'm concerned. Factories move here from the States and use slave labor, all the while putting entire communities back home out of work and onto welfare. I'm telling you—"

"May I help you?" The desk clerk's voice was almost condescending in its tone as it interrupted Linda's lecture on industrial immorality.

"Yes," John said. "Room for three nights, please."

"Single or double?"

"Single."

"Two nights' room fee in advance." The desk clerk hardly made eye contact, remaining aloof, as if working at this particular hotel was a career reserved for the privileged few. It no doubt was.

"Fine." John took out his wallet and pulled out a pair of Malaysian hundreds.

"Fill this out, please." The desk clerk slid a hotel registration form toward John and turned to find the key to room 1518. He turned back, handed John a pair of keys, and extended a bony finger across the lobby. "Take the elevator, make a right, then walk down the hall. Number 1518 is on the left." He then rang the bell in front of him, gave John his change, and went back to his computer as if nothing had transpired between them. A boyish-looking bellhop dressed in tropical khakis and white straw hat, immediately rushed to their side and grabbed the luggage cart.

The trip from the front desk to the gold elevators was like a walk through Caesar's Palace. No amenity was overlooked, no expense spared. Furriers, jewelers, gift shops, and restaurants lined both sides of the chandeliered hallway adjacent to the front desk. Throughout the sumptuous lobby, a maze of plush white sofas and dark leather chairs were arranged perfectly and occupied by important-looking men in silk suits and sophisticated bone-thin women wearing elbow-length white gloves and puffing French cigarettes while pretending all the while they were oblivious to the stream of activity around them. The antique furniture was rich mahogany, the floor, Italian marble of exquisite quality. Large tropical plants stretched thirty feet upward, giving the whole place the look of an exotic, tropical museum.

The bellhop led John and Linda through the open elevator doors and took them fifteen floors up. When they emerged, they turned right and sank an inch into the carpet as they walked another hundred feet and stopped in front of 1518. The bellhop then opened the door, carried the bags inside, and stood at attention with his hand positioned for a tip. Linda stepped into the luxury suite overlooking the modern downtown skyline, while John slipped the bellhop money and shut the door behind him. He took ten steps back and dropped onto the bed, exhausted. Linda lay down next to him and put her arm around his waist.

"All I want to do is sleep," she whispered.

"I'll put in a wakeup call for three-thirty," John said. "That should give us enough time to get ready and leave here by four-thirty. Thirty minutes should be plenty of time to find Vijan's place."

"What about a map?"

"You stay here. I'll go down to the lobby and pick one up . . . and a few breakfast items for tomorrow morning. We can make coffee here—" John pointed to the complimentary Mr. Coffee on the table next to the TV—"and eat in the car on the way."

As John got up and walked to the door, Linda sat up wearily and stared out the window at the Kuala Lumpur skyline and the mountainous jungles beyond. She didn't know what to expect out there, whether they would even be successful in locating the secret research center hidden somewhere deep in that tropical rain forest, and even if they did, whether their plan to get past security would even work. But she knew there was no alternative, no turning back, no way she could ever return to Washington unless she exposed the plot and whoever was behind it. She fell back onto the queen-sized bed, too weak to even think about it any longer, and within minutes fell into a deep sleep.

chapter twenty-nine

There was nothing even remotely like it back in the States. The blend of exotic, heavily spiced foods, acrid temple incense, and the blood of freshly butchered wildlife lingered in the heavy air and permeated the concrete and asphalt around them. Even at 5:30 A.M., well before the raucous street vendors began gathering in the city's teeming marketplaces and the sun rose to turn leftover or discarded animal flesh into dried, wrinkled leather, the previous day's fading stench was still there, waiting to be mixed with the pungent aromas of a new business day.

Linda turned on the interior car light and held open the map on her lap while John drove slowly and searched for street signs that would lead them to Sempora. They'd gotten lost three times already and were on the road almost half an hour longer than they'd expected. The gray streets were beginning to see life here and there but were still pretty much deserted. The fear of Malaysian police spotting a lone car driving around town at that hour made them anxiously cautious, but their plan was simply to explain that they were trying to make their way to the Subang International Airport early enough to avoid traffic and catch a flight into Singapore and back to the States.

"Keep going on this street until you get to Kanlong," Linda said, her eyes fixed on the street map spread before her. "Look for Muar, make a right, then . . . let's see . . . go about a mile." She followed a thin line with her index finger. "Sempora looks like a small dead-end street in a section called Kenney Hill."

John continued to drive cautiously, making sure he didn't do anything that would attract undue attention. With street vendors becoming increasingly active with the approach of sunrise, maneuvering had become more difficult. Already the smell of fish was making the air seem heavy. The cacophony of car horns was noticeably more frequent. Bicycle traffic, which began as a trickle, had become a tidal wave. Rush hour, obviously, had come upon them as if someone had thrown a switch.

"There's Muar," John said, relieved that at least they were on the right track. He made a right and checked his odometer. "Almost there. What time is it?"

"Nearly six. I hope we didn't miss him."

A mile and a half later, John made another right onto Sempora, a wide, perfectly manicured street in what seemed, thus far, to be one of the most exclusive neighborhoods in all of Malaysia. "This must be Kenney Hill. Nice. Real nice."

"Looks like Dr. Vijan has done well for himself," Linda said with enough sarcasm to make her wince at the splendor around her. "The government doesn't pay its top U.S. scientists *this* well. I can see why he'd sell out and move to what has got to be the Beverly Hills of Southeast Asia." And as she said that, the name Vijan was suddenly flashing through her mind as though she'd heard it somewhere before.

"We've gotta be working for the wrong side," John said. "Look at some of these homes. They're incredible."

John slowed the car and drove past Moroccan-style mansions, English Tudors, marble villas with swimming pools spanning the length of their backyards, ornate fountains, and acre upon acre of landscaped gardens. Thick wrought-iron gates, many encircling entire perimeters of vast complexes, protected the shiny Rolls-Royces and Mercedes that sat side by side at the end of winding driveways. Servants, draped neatly in sparkling white uniforms, had begun arriving at the grand entranceways. Gardeners were already busy at work and, like trained surgeons, could be seen clipping and sculpting and trimming hedges and tropical plants into perfectly shaped arrangements.

To Linda and John, it all had the feel and appearance of an exclusive realm of the very rich, the Malaysian elite. And as they continued their drive past millionaires' row, they knew full well that Dr. Vijan's presence among that elite crowd was by no means an accident.

"There it is, John. Number seventeen."

"Wouldn't you know it. The head of an obscure jungle research center living in a multi-million-dollar mansion."

"I'd say something stinks worse than the fish over here." Again, Linda repeated the name Vijan in her mind, and again she was hit with the unsettling feeling that somehow she knew who this man was.

They drove past a palatial white villa, complete with marble statues that lined the circular driveway. A Roman fountain, positioned on the spacious lawn in front of the house, sprayed blue-lit water from its alabaster base.

"We're too conspicuous," Linda said. "If we wait in the car for him, we'll look like sitting ducks out here. This is a dead-end street. There's only one way in or out."

"What then?"

"There was a blue Mercedes parked in Vijan's driveway. Let's wait for him on Muar. When we see his car come out of Sempora, we tail him."

John nodded in agreement, then drove down to the cul-de-sac and turned around. Once back on Muar, he slid inconspicuously between a group of parked cars on the side of the road and cut the engine off.

They waited for what seemed like hours, though it was only thirty-five minutes later that a dark blue Mercedes 560 SEL pulled out of Sempora and headed exactly where they'd expected it would: east, toward the rugged mountainous interior. John waited a few seconds until the Mercedes turned the corner, then started the engine and pulled out.

It was already 6:45 A.M., and in Malaysia it was the time of day when traffic would soon begin to fill the winding roads. Linda felt less anxious, since the growing congestion was already making it impossible for anyone to suspect they were being followed. She leaned back comfortably and stared at the blue Mercedes ahead of them, not surprised, after seeing his palatial home, why a man like Abraham Vijan would get involved in something like this.

As they headed farther east, climbing steadily into some of the densest rain forest in all of Southeast Asia, the terrain became noticeably different. They'd heard that in some parts of the country, the only passable travel routes were by river and, that even today, as much as 70 percent of Malaysia was still jungle. Driving along a road that seemed to be heading straight into that 70 percent only dispelled any doubts they had about *that* statistic. They were also nervously aware that some of those jungle regions still harbored Communist guerrillas, remnants of a once-menacing terrorist army that relied on the impenetrability of the forests to lay hidden from Malayan government troops. Could it be that this was the army chosen to protect the research center? That like the guerrillas of Central America or the ruthless soldiers in the cocaine fields of South America, these guerrillas were the shadowy warlords who'd kill anyone threatening an operation that funded their very existence? The thought of *that* made them even more wary and apprehensive as they looked at the gloomy darkness on each side of them and saw invisible danger lurking behind every tree.

"We've been driving for nearly an hour, John. Either he's taking us on a wild goose chase or this place is in the middle of nowhere. I'm beginning to get worried. Where the hell—" Linda grabbed hold of John's arm. "Slow down."

They watched the Mercedes turn north onto what looked like a private road and stop in front of a ten-foot-high razor-wire fence that protected an enclosed concrete security structure. They saw Vijan's hand, holding a security pass, emerge from the blackened Mercedes window, then retract as the fence opened slowly to allow the car through.

"I guess this is as far as we go," Linda said. "At least we know where it is when we come back. Let's head back to the city."

"Phase two?"

"Right."

By 9:10 A.M., John and Linda were once again fighting the increasingly congested traffic of Kuala Lumpur. Clutched in Linda's hand was Dr. Vijan's home telephone number; in her purse, a small 35mm camera and several rolls of film.

"Let's do it over there," John said, turning the corner and driving down a quiet street until he came to a telephone booth. "Good luck," he added as he watched Linda step out of the car.

Linda closed herself in the phone booth, deposited some coins, and dialed Vijan's number. Three rings later, a thin voice came on.

"Good morning. Dr. Vijan's residence."

Linda prepared herself for phase two. She took a deep breath and responded with, "Good morning," trying as best she could to imitate the Chinese accent she'd practiced much of the morning. "This is Kwan, calling from the Research Center. Dr. Vijan requested that I call and remind you that one of his assistants is supposed to be arriving this morning to transcribe some research papers."

"This morning? I didn't—"

"Yes! This morning. Didn't you remember? Dr. Vijan will be very upset if—"

"Oh, yes, yes. I remember now." The voice was quick and apologetic.

Servant jobs, especially cushy maid jobs in that section of town, were more prized than gold. Linda knew that losing it because of something as stupid as forgetting an appointment was not something this poor Malay servant was about to do. Besides, since only a few people knew of Dr. Vijan's involvement with the Research Center, Linda was certain the maid would assume the phone call had to be legitimate.

"Who should I ask is coming?" the maid asked politely.

"Her name is Mary Baldwin. She'll introduce herself to you when she arrives. Be sure to allow her complete access."

"Shall I assist her in anything?"

"No. Dr. Vijan gave her specific instructions. This is very important. Make sure you maintain strict security."

"I understand."

"Thank you."

Linda hung up and gave John a thumbs-up sign as she ran around and jumped into the car.

"She bought it?" John asked, forcing a weak smile.

"All the way. I think I scared her enough so that she'll keep her mouth shut and let me do whatever I want."

"You sure?"

"Yeah, pretty sure. Now let's see if everything works."

From her purse, Linda removed two tiny rectangular boxes. A three-foot wire extended from one of them and looked like a hearing aid. The other box, a transmitter, she handed to John. She inserted the earpiece from the first, got back out of the car, and jogged across the street.

John pushed the button on the transmitter and spoke into it. "Linda, if you can hear me, turn around and give me a signal."

Linda turned immediately and gave John another thumbs-up. She ran back to the car.

"All set," she said. "Drop me off and wait at the entrance of Sempora, out of sight. If you see *anyone* driving into the street, follow the car. If it pulls into Vijan's driveway, signal me right away and drive up to the side of the house. I'll take whatever I have, sneak out the back, and run around the house to the car."

"Try to work as fast as you can," John pleaded. "You sure you have enough film?"

"Ten rolls."

"I hope to God you don't need that many."

John parked the Toyota along Muar in the same place he'd parked it earlier. Linda, meanwhile, walked the length of

Vijan's driveway and climbed the eight steps that led to a lavish entranceway. She rang the doorbell, then waited for the door to swing open and the maid to appear.

When it did, the tiny maid stood fixed in place and asked, "Yes?"

"I'm Mary Baldwin," Linda announced in the most official-sounding voice she could muster.

"Oh, yes, from the Research Center." The middle-aged woman looked at Linda, then past her and, with suspicion spreading across her wrinkled face, saw that there was no car in sight.

"Yes. Kwan must have told you I was coming. My driver had to run an errand. He'll pick me up shortly." Linda watched the suspicious expression vanish as quickly as it had appeared.

"Please, come in. Would you like something? A refreshment, perhaps?"

"No, thank you, nothing. I'm on a busy schedule and need to get started right away, if you don't mind. Dr. Vijan needs me to work on some reports. Would you please show me where he keeps them?"

"Of course." The maid escorted her quickly from the foyer, past a spiral staircase, and through five rooms that Linda was certain had to have been replicated from the British Royalty issue of *Architectural Digest*. There was no way, she thought, that Vijan, even as head of the U.S. Tropical Research Center, could afford anything remotely close to this.

"Right through here, please." The maid extended her arm and waited for Linda to walk through a marbled hallway and into Dr. Vijan's private mahogany-lined library. "You'll find everything you need in here. I'll show you out whenever you're finished."

Linda closed the door and listened for footsteps as they faded across the wooden floor of the adjacent room. She slipped the wire from out of her blouse and inserted the ear piece. Then, dashing to the far end of the room, she zeroed in on the oak filing cabinet that sat next to Vijan's desk. She opened the top drawer and quickly thumbed through page after page of requisitions, invoices, purchase orders, guidelines, forms, so on. Nothing there of any use or significance. The next drawer produced similarly disappointing results.

And then, as she dropped to her knees, about to open the third, her eyes were immediately drawn left, focusing on the bottom of a wall tapestry that stopped an inch from the floor and revealed an obvious break in the molding.

"My God," she whispered, then rushed to pull back the heavy tapestry and expose what looked like a hidden closet behind it. She opened the door, felt for the light switch, and walked into a small cubicle she figured had to have been concealed for a reason. Then, gently nudging the door closed behind her, she removed the camera from her purse, placed it carefully on top of the two drawer filing cabinet positioned against the wall. She held her breath as she wrapped her fingers around the upper handle and pulled open the drawer marked "A–M."

Fifteen minutes of thumbing through file after file of alphabetically arranged papers and documents had revealed nothing of any apparent importance. She pushed the drawer closed, then pulled open the bottom one, hoping to find something there. And when she pried apart the file marked P, she let out a soft gasp as she held in her fingers a three inch thick subfile marked "Psychochemical Agent Research."

Linda fumbled for her camera, nearly dropping it to the wooden floor. She clenched her teeth and froze, her head cocked toward the door, listening for the maid. Gathering herself, she placed the contents of the file folder on the floor in front of her and readied her 35mm. She looked at the first document and began shaking, confused by what she was seeing, but managed to steady her hands enough to shoot two photos of what she could only assume was the genetic code for the agent.

1 ACTGACCAGATCGATCGACCCAAAGCTCCGGATAGGCGAATTGGAACTGAAGTA
55 CTAGGACACAGCTAGCTAGGATCGATCGATCGGATAGGGATCGACATAGGATCG

109 TAGACAGGCTAGACATCGATAGCTTAGAGATCGACAGATAGACCCAGCTGAGAT
163 GGGACATACAGATCGCGATAGACCCAGCTAGACAGATTAGATCGACAGATAGAG
217 GACTGGATAGCACCAGAATCGACCAGATAGAGGATCGATAGGGATATTGACAGT
271 CATAGACCAGAATAGCTAGATCGGACAGATAGACAGATCGGAGATCGACAGTAG
325 TTAGACCAAAGCTCTTAGACAAGCCCAGATCGGATAGACAGATTAGAAGATCCGC
379 AAGATTCCGAAAATCGACAGATTCGCCTAGACAGATAGCTAGACAGATAGACCGA
433 GATAGCTAGAAATTCGGCCTAGACACCAGATAATAGACAGATAGAGTAGGACATA
487 TTTATAACAGGAAAAACAGATCGACAGATACAGATAGACCAGATCACAGGGATAG
541 CAGATAGACCAGAATCGACATAGACAGATAGGACAGTAGACGATGACCAGATGA
595 CCCCGATAAAAAGGGCTCGACACCAGAAATCGACAGATAGACAGATTAGACAGA
649 TTTACAAACAGGCTCTCGGACAGAATCGACAGATCGGCTAGACAGGATAGCAGAT
703 GGACAGGATAGCAGAAATCGACAGATCGACAGATCGACCAGATCGACC

The next document and the next and the one after that were everything Linda had hoped for, each more revealing than the last, each a critical prelude to the next, every one a vital piece of evidence that together with the others would not only expose a new and horribly deadly weapon but would also expose everyone involved in the project.

With little time to stop and examine or absorb it all, Linda shot and advanced film with frenzied speed. There were names, dates, budget codes, contacts, suppliers, copies of secret transactions between General McKnight and Dr. Vijan, satellite photos of cities, target areas and reservoirs, details of how the agent could be delivered most effectively, and test results of monstrous human experiments, conducted with the full knowledge of McKnight and members of his team.

And if that weren't enough, Linda, as she came to the end of the files, was now looking at the complete documentation of exactly how the agent had been produced and how it altered brain chemistry. She stopped for a moment to study the diagrams of molecular structures, biological pathways, and a new type of genetic engineering technology, unaware that she had already been there more than two hours.

At that moment, John had spotted a black airport limousine turning onto Sempora. He started the car and followed, sweat dripping down his forehead, his finger ready on the transmitter button as he watched the limousine glide into

Vijan's driveway. Looking on anxiously, he watched a burly chauffeur step out and open the back door. Panic turned to fear as the limousine disgorged an older woman dressed in what looked like the latest Paris fashions and weighed down with enough jewelry to ensure her drowning if she tripped and fell into the fountain next to her. The chauffeur then unlocked the trunk and pulled out a pair of Gucci suitcases.

John pressed the transmitter button frantically. "Linda, get the hell out of there, fast. I think Mrs. Vijan just pulled into the driveway."

In near panic, Linda stuck the files back into the bottom drawer as neatly as time would allow, then pushed it closed. She gathered her camera and film, shoved it all into her purse, slipped out the door, and edged her way around the tapestry, replacing it carefully against the wall. When she turned, the maid, with a look of anger and suspicion, was staring straight into her eyes from the middle of the room.

"Please explain what you were doing in that back room before I call the research center. Not even Dr. Vijan's staff is allowed in there." The front doorbell suddenly rang and echoed through every room in the mansion. "That would be Mrs. Vijan returning from Singapore. Perhaps you can explain to her."

It was time for the rest of plan B.

"Listen," she said sternly. "I just took photographs of everything in there. Top-secret things that people would kill for. But before I did that, I planted an envelope with money in it somewhere in this room, along with a letter thanking you personally for your cooperation in betraying Dr. Vijan and looking forward to working with you again in the future for even more money. You whisper one word and I'll say that you're working for us. As proof, I'll point out exactly where I saw you hide the envelope with all that money and the letter when you heard the doorbell. By this afternoon, you'll either be back in a rat-infested *kampong* eating rice once a day, if you're lucky, or more likely, you'll be dead once Dr. Vijan finds out what you've done to him. Your choice."

The anger on the maid's face vanished instantly, replaced by a look of sheer terror. And when Linda saw tears pooling in the poor woman's eyes, she knew she had won. "Well?" she demanded even more sternly now.

The doorbell rang again. They both turned toward it.

"If I agree and let you leave," the maid asked frantically, "what happens if Dr. Vijan accidentally locates the letter?"

"It's very well hidden. He won't find it, I promise. I'll call you tomorrow and tell you exactly where it is. You'll get the money anyway and you get to keep your nice job and your life. You can't lose. Whaddya say?"

"Quickly, out this way," the maid said at once. "I won't say a word. Please don't report this. Please. I beg you."

"Deal."

While the maid rushed to greet Mrs. Vijan in the foyer, Linda slipped out a back door, ran alongside the house toward the Toyota, and jumped through the open passenger-side door. With a quick spurt, the car lunged forward and sped toward Muar. Linda took a quick glance backward and saw that all was quiet. She breathed a sigh of relief and closed her eyes tightly.

"Well, did it work?" John asked as he turned left onto Muar and stepped on the gas.

"Like a charm."

"Are you going to call the poor woman eventually and tell her it was all a bluff . . . that there *is* no money and no letter?"

"I won't have to. You won't believe what I got in there. Once Jack gets this film and distributes the prints, Vijan'll be dead anyway, along with everyone else. They'll all be saying good-bye to seventeen Sempora."

"Tell me everything."

"Can it wait till we get back to our hotel room? I need to sort it all out in my mind. Right now let's see if we can find a post office somewhere in town. The sooner this film's in Washington the better."

Linda reached under the front seat and pulled out a square box. She wrapped eight rolls of film in thick paper, sealed the box with four layers of packing tape, and addressed it to Dr. Jackson Pilofski.

chapter thirty

''Have your security people come up with anything?'' Morris asked.

''Negative. We've checked with relatives, colleagues, acquaintances. Nothing's turned up.'' McKnight, bracing himself for what he figured would be a vicious verbal onslaught, found instead that the voice remained surprisingly calm.

''I was afraid of that,'' Morris answered. ''And that's exactly why I had my own team do an independent investigation.''

''You what?''

''Lambino's computer people did a search and identified two individuals—Mary Baldwin and Frank Tippett—who'd boarded a United flight 4730 out of New York heading for Los Angeles the morning of the twentieth. The same couple then went on to Honolulu, Guam, Singapore, and the final destination, Kuala Lumpur. Not a coincidence, I'm afraid. The date, the origin of flight, the final destination all point to Franklin and Peterson.''

''Jesus Christ,'' McKnight spit. ''They're in Malaysia. How the hell did they know?'' McKnight threw his head back and closed his eyes, incredulous that anyone could be lucky enough to have slipped through his network of security people so easily but now realizing that Malaysia was precisely where they would eventually end up. ''How in the hell did they find out?''

"I always worried about a smoking gun, Ben. Obviously you must have missed the one damn thing that was able to link the crash with CONDOR and ultimately with the facility in Malaysia. Look, I don't really give a shit what kind of research we're currently doing over there; what I'm concerned about is whether Franklin traces funding of CONDOR and this program back to us. And if that information is somewhere in Malaysia, I wanna know."

"I'll arrange for security to fly out immediately."

"No, not this time," Morris bellowed. "We're taking over security on this one. Lambino and two of his best army intelligence people are already on their way." There was derision in Morris's voice as he added, "They'll keep it as nonmilitary as possible to avoid arousing suspicions." What he felt like saying was that he'd grown weary of McKnight's pitiful incompetence and, if not for the fact that he needed him to ensure the integrity of the Pentagon's CONDOR program, would have eliminated the fool as well.

"What's your plan?" McKnight leaned forward in his chair, placing his forehead in his hand, fearful that Morris would learn too much.

"Lambino and his men should be arriving in Kuala Lumpur sometime early tomorrow morning. Once they begin their search, it shouldn't be too difficult to find them. Lambino was given specific instructions to locate the two, maintain surveillance, follow them back to the States, but not to make a move until they've set foot back in Washington. He's to contact us at each stop along the way and report on exactly where they are and when their flight will land in D.C. You'll be at Vanguard headquarters waiting for Lambino and his men. In order to avoid any suspicions or any trouble at the airport, Pilofski will lead Franklin and Peterson to an area where Lambino will make the arrest. Have you tried making contact with any of your people in Malaysia recently?"

"Yes, just today, with the head of the facility. We've been trying to get through but the telephone lines are down in that damned jungle. Storm or something. Who the hell knows."

"Have you tried his home?"

"I got hold of his answering machine and left a message for the staff to be on full alert for anything out of the ordinary," McKnight lied, thinking of the real message he'd left, which warned Vijan to watch for unfamiliar Americans with security clearances who might try to gain access to the research center or to his home and to remove all documents related to the Vanguard and transfer them to another location.

But McKnight, at that moment, was unaware that his urgent message had already been intercepted by a terrified maid who'd erased it at once for fear it would lead to a search of the library and the discovery of an incriminating letter that would leave no doubt of her implication in espionage. He paused for a moment and wiped the beads of sweat from his lips, though he seemed calm, even overly confident, as he realized that he finally had them. This wasn't the United States, after all. It was unfamiliar territory. Malaysia of all places. He imagined the two of them frightened and confused, fish out of water, wandering about like typical American tourists and sticking out among a sea of Asian faces like sore Caucasian thumbs. Morris's intelligence team, he was absolutely certain, would find them as easily as he'd find a pair of white diamonds in a coal field.

"Has anyone tried to make contact with the White House?" Morris asked. "Or anyone in Congress?"

"We've been monitoring every call coming in," McKnight responded. "Nothing to indicate any unusual or damaging communication. Certainly nothing from overseas. Looks clean."

"And Pilofski. What have you heard from him?"

"He hasn't made contact with us since yesterday. Still waiting for word from them, I guess."

Morris fell silent. General McKnight heard the deep breathing and suspected that the mind beneath that fat skull was busy at work. Morris continued, "We'll have to string him along till the end."

"Meaning?"

"He delivers to you whatever it is he's expecting from Dr. Franklin. When we get the word from Lambino about the flight into Washington, you give Pilofski the word that we're making the arrest at the airport and that we need him along as insurance, so to speak. He'll lead the two of them out to the parking lot to a prearranged area where a car will be waiting. Lambino will take care of the rest."

"Why not get rid of Franklin and Peterson in Malaysia and Pilofski as soon as we get the evidence?" McKnight asked. "Why take the chance of letting them back into the States? Risk having them get lost again? Lot of jungle out there to bury the bodies, you know."

"Because, General McKnight," Morris answered, annoyed and frustrated at the idea that McKnight would be that stupid, "we have a situation here that requires our thinking three moves ahead. Franklin and Peterson don't suspect what Pilofski's doing. In fact, they're relying on him to receive the evidence they'd gathered and supply that evidence to proper channels. Pilofski, on the other hand, has no idea we're using him as expendable bait and planning to eliminate him as well. If evidence is already en route—and it very well may be—and if some sort of arrangement had been made for them to contact Pilofski at a certain time, from a certain place, he'd grow suspicious if no contact were made. He may stall handing over any or all of the evidence until he's sure that he's not being double-crossed. If he suspects *anything*, if Franklin tips him off because she happens to get wind of a setup, he could pull the plug, make a run for it himself and ruin everything. No, we have to allow Franklin and Peterson to go ahead with it and think that everything is running like clockwork, that this mission of theirs is nearing completion. And we have to make absolutely certain Pilofski's convinced that helping us get to Franklin will guarantee that his father doesn't spend the rest of his life rotting away in some rat-infested prison. If we do that, we get it all: the evidence, Franklin and Peterson, Pilofski. If we don't . . . well, we may all be looking for real estate property in Malaysia ourselves, now won't we?"

It was McKnight's turn to fall silent as he thought through the consequences of any evidence falling into the wrong hands. He considered the possibility that everything he'd worked for was threatened because of his inability to find that one note, that one letter or document, that one slip of paper that would have, if not for the fact that Pilofski was working for them, sealed his fate. After thirty-five years in the army and after witnessing firsthand the workings of the system both inside and outside Washington, the pathologic loyalty had grown into frenzied patriotism, and the frenzied patriotism into a paranoia that slowly ate at him like a cancer through otherwise healthy flesh. His belief that the government was selling out, that corruption in Congress and the Senate was so rampant that the national security of the country was threatened, fueled a passion that lately bordered on insanity. He'd become a man seemingly without a country. A man who believed with all his heart that the world he knew was inexorably coming to an end. He couldn't care less about Morris or the rest of the Vanguard now; couldn't care less if every damn one of the greedy sons of bitches lost everything they had. What he worried about now was that *his* mission was being endangered by two people who had no idea what they were doing and, because they didn't, threatened the very security of the United States. So great was his rage that if he had Franklin before him now, he would have killed her with his bare hands. He thought ahead to the end of the search, to the next few days, visualizing taking the gun out of Lambino's hand and blowing Linda Franklin's highly developed but naive brains out himself.

"Everything will be in place," McKnight said. "I'll report on Pilofski as soon as we get word from him and let him know exactly what we expect."

"Good. The sooner we wind this problem down the better. I don't particularly like having to explain to my people why these two loose cannons, regardless of whether they can do anything at this point or not, are still out there. I'll expect a call from you the minute you hear from Pilofski."

Morris hung up and reached across the desk, punching the intercom button.

"Yes, Mr. Morris?" his administrative assistant answered.

"Get me Bradly from army intelligence right away," Morris ordered.

A minute later, Morris snatched the phone and pressed the button for line one. "Brad, Morris here. I need a favor. There's a Dr. Jackson Pilofski with NASA's Division of Biotic Investigation. You should have a complete dossier on him with recent photographs in your files. Put a couple of men on him immediately and make sure he doesn't take a shit without you or me knowing about it. He's supposed to receive a package of information from someone in Malaysia, either at his home or at a post office box somewhere. Make sure he delivers it to McKnight. If he tries to deliver it to anyone else, if you see him trying to take it anywhere other than to whom he's supposed to, take him into custody immediately and bring him directly to us."

"Yes, sir. We're on it."

"One more thing," Morris added. "There are people here asking a lot of questions about why recently discharged soldiers are coming down with diseases they shouldn't be coming down with. I'm concerned about that. I'm also concerned that Israeli intelligence is not gonna sit on this once word gets out that civilians in Jerusalem and Tel Aviv are dying of the same damn thing. I hope your people have enough sense to keep a lid on this and make sure everything stays buried."

"Everyone from the administration on down realizes it was a mistake dealing with Baghdad. As far as we're concerned, that's history. No one ever has to know what happened, Mr. Morris. No one. We took care of it. The records are gone, that's all that matters."

"Thanks, Brad. Keep me apprised of everything." Morris hung up and lit a thick cigar. Like a chess grand master with an uncanny eye for detail and an instinctive ability to see beyond the immediate, he was three moves ahead and had just positioned himself to go in for the kill.

He blew smoke into the air in front of him and spread his

face into an evil grin. He knew full well that in this country, more than any other, money was power, and that his power reached farther and was infinitely greater than anyone could ever imagine.

chapter thirty-one

The nearest post office was in Petaling Jaya, a sprawling suburb originally settled by the indigent squatters of Kuala Lumpur but now one of the most industrialized and prosperous cities in all of Malaysia.

On the six-lane highway that stretched seven miles from Petaling Jaya to the capital city, hunger had forced them to stop and fill up on local fruit, rice, and the ubiquitous fish that seemed to make its way onto every plate along the Malaysian byways they'd traveled. Despite the exasperating traffic that crept at a snail's pace, they had made it there by 11:00 A.M. and had been assured repeatedly by the obliging Malay clerks that the package would be delivered in Washington, D.C., no later than noon eastern standard time within two business days. What this meant was that Jack would not receive the film until Wednesday the 23rd and would not have copies to distribute until Thursday morning the 24th. The hitch, thought Linda, as she tried to think of everything that could possibly go wrong, was that she'd have to spend at least four more miserable days in what was beginning to feel like a waking nightmare.

The wide, modern road had taken them through the broad expanses of rubber plantations, past the famous Malaysian tin mines, among the world's largest and most productive, and alongside immense industrial complexes that housed everything from electronics and pharmaceutical firms to international film production companies. Industry, it seemed from inside the car window, had catapulted Malaysia from a backward, third world nation onto the doorstep of the twenty-first century. Closer to town, smaller businesses cropped up everywhere, shouldering the roads and ubiquitous dwellings, competing for whatever sidewalk spaces remained and blending almost seamlessly into one other as though one massive flea market.

Traffic had become a living nightmare. The heat and the humidity, trapped inside the Toyota like a thick fog, grew into a sauna. The smell of incense, a blessing if one wanted to neutralize the gagging stench of raw fish and rotting garbage that sat piled in back alleys and side streets, was overpowering enough to make the inside of Linda's nose burn and her eyes water. And as John battled the continuous stop and go of vehicles that seemed to come at them from every direction at once, the tension that had been tempered only briefly by their success at finding Vijan's top-secret files was now turning into fear at the thought of having to drive back to the U.S. Tropical Research Center in less than ten hours.

"How much longer?" Linda asked, her eyes sweeping back and forth from one side of the street to the other.

"About a mile, I think," John answered. "Once we get into Kuala Lumpur, it shouldn't take us long to get back to the hotel."

"I get the shower first," Linda insisted with a wry smile, then wiped her face with the damp cloth napkin she had lifted from the roadside vendor.

"And then you can fill me in on the details of what it was you saw," John said.

Linda's smile disappeared quickly. She looked straight ahead, staring into space, her arms folded across her stomach as if suddenly she had taken ill. "If we don't expose this, John, something terrible . . ." She fell back against the headrest and shut her eyes.

John watched a tear slip from beneath her eyelid and fall to her cheek. "Tell me what you saw," he asked, then reached over and squeezed Linda's hand tightly. "Tell me."

"I was so busy shooting film—making sure I got it all as quickly as possible—that I couldn't read everything. But what I *did* see was horrible, especially the documents on the psychochemical agent." She held her arms against her stomach as though about to throw up, taking a deep breath instead. "It was everything we suspected . . . and more."

"What does it all mean? And what does TIMBER WOLF have to do with any of it?"

"There was nothing about TIMBER WOLF or CONDOR, only statements alluding to a date of April sixth. Apparently, something's about to happen on that day or shortly after."

"The sixth? That's less than three weeks away," John said, nearly making the car swerve into oncoming traffic as he looked over at Linda. "What's going to happen? Where? By whom? Is it the government? Did it say?"

"There were lots of documents referring to psychochemical warfare and the people involved, but nothing to identify the specific region or regions that would be targeted. I just don't know." Linda shook her head, straining to recall something that had been gnawing at her. "I know that name, John. I know it."

"What name? Vijan?"

"Yeah. I'm not absolutely sure, but I believe I'd seen his name in a classified report on some recombinant DNA germ warfare research that at the time was being conducted at a private pharmaceutical firm heavily funded by the CIA or the Department of Defense."

"What the hell is he doing here, then?"

"Who knows? Money, maybe. Funding could have dried up. The public outcry against that kind of research, combined with all the military budget cuts, could have forced him to offer his services on the open market. If the guy has no scruples, and if the price was right—"

"From what I've seen," John interjected, "the price was right."

"And obviously he's working for someone with enough financial clout to pull this off."

"Damn. It has to be the U.S. government if they're going to use CONDOR."

"I'm not so sure, but I know General McKnight's involved up to his neck."

"What was in the files about *him*?"

"There were secret communications between McKnight and Vijan, along with pages of names, affiliations, documents, bank statements, and indirect funding sources funneled through McKnight to the research center from some organization called Vanguard. From what I saw, this group is involved with the military in some way—it may even *be* part of the military—and is diverting massive amounts of funds for some reason. And if it could do that, it probably has enough influence to do whatever the hell it wants. Seems to me these people are running the damn show, John."

"Christ, it sounds like whoever's pulling the strings here is selectively directing government military policy." John thought about the prospect of that and winced. "Good God, it may be worse than we thought. How the hell do we know whom to trust, who's involved, who we can go to with information?"

"I'm hoping Jack can get this to people inside the government, people who haven't been bought, if that's possible. Out of our list of key people who should be getting the evidence by Friday, there's got to be enough of them who'll take a look at this and be so shocked they'll have to break it wide open."

"Maybe plastering it over the national media all at the same time will force some of those guys to open their damn eyes and make them realize what the hell's going on. What did you find out about the agent?"

"The biotechnology they've developed for this is incredible," Linda said, shaking her head in disbelief. "If I didn't see it with my own eyes, I wouldn't have believed it possible."

As Linda thought back to exactly what she'd seen, she was at once impressed and appalled by the scope of the science that had been achieved. She didn't think it possible, but there it was. For years it had been suspected by some in Congress that scientists at both military and private labs were racing furiously to establish a lead in recombinant DNA weapons research. Pentagon files, alluding to psychochemical warfare and the secret biological agent that would achieve something called world order by altering brain chemistry, certainly confirmed that. But actually to have seen the details, the descriptions, the actual research notes and documents, the diagrams of the new genetic engineering technology, was akin to having peered through a blackened window and suddenly witnessing the future of civilization on the brink of an unspeakable catastrophe.

"I spent most of my time looking at protocols for the genetic engineering system," she continued. "Apparently, they'd been able to isolate a gene that produces a critical precursor molecule. When combined with a peptide found in the brain, it inhibits 5-HTP decarboxylase, the enzyme that triggers the production of serotonin. That's the key, John. But the incredible thing is that what they isolated is not a human gene at all."

"What, then?"

"You remember when we were up at your place, talking about the DNA research that was being funded by the Department of Defense?"

"Yeah."

"Well I'd forgotten about something. Back in 1984, Fort Detrick scientists had applied to the Office of Recombinant DNA Activities for permission to insert genes from cobra neurotoxin and cardiotoxin into *E. coli* bacteria. The stated aim at the time was to produce large amounts of snake toxins. They claimed the work was needed strictly to manufacture antivenin for defensive purposes. The scuttlebutt, though, was that it was offensive weapons research, pure and simple."

"What's that have to do with this?"

"Remember that day at your place, when I told you about the novel recombinant DNA research Peter had told me about?"

"Yeah."

"What I didn't tell you was that I visited that lab right before it was shut down for security reasons. I learned that it was doing the same controversial work as this, manipulating genes to produce deadly toxins. What they've isolated here, John, is a gene located on chromosome number four, from tropical sea snakes."

"Sea snakes! That's why Malaysia. This must be where they get them."

"Yeah, it's perfect. The gene itself codes for a coenzyme that activates the production of snake neurotoxin. By itself the coenzyme's harmless, but when it attaches to one of the carbons in 5-HTP decarboxylase, it inhibits the production of brain serotonin. The entire supply of that gene is right here, and the research center is hidden deep in the jungle of a country most Americans don't know anything about."

"What's the link? How's the technology work?"

"That's where the *new* biotechnology comes in. It's a dual recombinant binary system. Nothing like it's ever been done."

"A what?"

"A sophisticated method of engineering a bacterium so that it operates at two levels in the brain. In other words, it's not just a simple recombinant DNA mechanism; it's a two-step process. Step one is getting the chemical—which is initially produced by the gene—to go through the blood-brain barrier and into the brain; step two is to combine that chemical with another chemical—in this case a naturally occurring brain peptide—in order to produce the binary compound that then does the damage. Until now, it wasn't possible to get most molecules through the blood-brain barrier."

"Until now? And how's *that* done?"

"With the bacterium itself. It's unbelievable. Somehow—and this is even more incredible than the actual genetic engineering—they've been able to develop a new strain of bacteria by manipulating different parts of the bacterial DNA until it mutated or evolved in a certain way. They did it by exposing them to very specific environmental mutagens like ultraviolet radiation, X rays, electromagnetic fields, or any combination of those. We've known for some time that theoretically it's possible to cause genetic change by altering various environmental conditions. It's called site-directed mutagenesis. The mutagen acts specifically on the targeted gene to introduce specific nucleotide deletions, insertions, or substitutions, which then cause the altered gene—or designer gene as it's called—to produce a new protein. Until now, it's never been proved that you can selectively do that . . . to actually make any specific protein you want simply by forcing the bacteria to evolve in a certain direction."

"It's like God playing around with evolution until He has it right," John said, shaking his head.

"Right. These guys were literally trying to direct the universal laws of nature, and in this case they actually succeeded. They forced something to mutate exactly the way they wanted. It may have been done accidentally, but more likely they went through years of trial and error until they achieved the precise nucleotide change in the DNA sequence. I saw it, John. The genetic code for the protein is roughly seven hundred fifty base pairs long. Once that was accomplished, the mutated bacteria were isolated, engineered with the sea snake gene, allowed to reproduce, and used as the vector that would then inject the chemical into the brain. What an incredible breakthrough."

"But how does the chemical actually get through to the brain?" John asked. "You said yourself that very few things get through the blood-brain barrier."

"The specific protein these evolved bacteria release is a type of glycoprotein that breaks through the capillary membrane walls of the blood-brain barrier. It's like having an army of microscopic bugs drilling through to your brain. All that's needed is a crack, a slight weakness in the capillary wall for the chemical to find its way through. And when it does, it's all over."

"What else was in Vijan's file?"

"I didn't have time to read through a lot of it," Linda said. What I saw was enough. The genetic code, amino acid sequence, schematic diagrams, HPLC and electrophoretic analyses of the glycoprotein, results of its ability to penetrate the blood-brain barrier, results of the agent's effects in laboratory animal experiments, methods of dispersal. Everything, John, including the final test results of that terrible human experiment on Singkep Island.''

John shook his head in disbelief. ''Singkep. So it *was* the agent. What are these bastards planning to do with it?''

''If it's possible to find one positive thing in all this—''

''Positive?'' John interrupted. ''You can find something positive?''

''From what I was able to read—and I'm not even certain of it—the bacterium has a limited strike capability; it doesn't do well outside the incubation vats or outside the human body. It can't be sprayed into the soil because any exposure to air or to other factors in the soil kill it within twelve to twenty-four hours. So the mode of attack is through water contamination. Apparently, the bacterium's life span in an aquatic environment is roughly seventy-two hours, as long as the temperature is between forty and a hundred degrees. Above or below that and it begins to degrade rapidly. It's a one-shot deal. The selected water supply is targeted and contaminated, and it's hoped that enough of the population drinks it within that time period to produce a mass effect. Within a few days, the ecosystem purges itself naturally of the contaminant or, if necessary, is recontaminated. The Singkep population was killed because its only source of drinking water—the river—was the mode of infection.''

''If that's the case, why couldn't the pathologists detect anything in any of those Singkep victims? Wouldn't there be traces of the bacterium in the body?''

''Unfortunately no. There'd be no evidence because once the bacterium's degraded, it leaves no visible signs of it's presence anywhere, no fingerprints that would point to anyone.''

''How?''

''That's also ingenious. Several days after infection, the

body responds to the bacterial attack with a natural increase in body temperature. And once a person's temperature rises above a hundred degrees, the bug is wiped out by antibodies, but not until enough of the chemical has already gotten into the brain to begin the process of disrupting serotonin output. Everything's gone, turned into innocuous elements and molecules and microscopic bits of organic matter that simply blend into the brain tissue and disappear; almost as if you shot someone with a gun, then watched the bullet vanish. This has got to be the perfect weapon, John—invisible, terminal, untraceable—and in the wrong hands, one of the deadliest and most effective means of waging war the world has ever known.''

''I have a feeling you were right about it not being the government at all. What if McKnight is in this on his own, using his power and influence with the Pentagon to gain access to military hardware like CONDOR?''

''Exactly. Whatever it is he's up to, he needs the military—or at least part of it—and he damn sure needs CONDOR, no question. It's the motive, though, that's still a mystery to me.''

''You know what I think, Linda. McKnight could be using the military without its knowledge, maybe conducting some kind of secret campaign under the guise of a government operation. We might be worrying about the wrong people.''

''I'm not willing to bet my life on it just yet. Until we see Jack, until he tells me himself that it's over, I won't feel safe from anyone.''

''There's the city limits sign,'' John said. ''Thank God. Never thought I'd be glad to see Kuala Lumpur again.''

John made it through the convoluted maze of city streets that once again led them to the familiar surroundings of the Kuala Lumpur Embassy Hotel. After parking the car, they retraced their steps through the lobby, into the elevator, up to their floor, down the hall, through the door of their suite, collapsed onto the bed, and stared silently at the ceiling.

John put his arm around Linda and held her tightly against him. She looked past him with a kind of grim stare and felt a suffocating sense of dread at the very idea that in less than eight hours they would either be dead or they'd be witnessing firsthand the inside of a top-secret facility that was at the very core of a new and hideously deadly military weapon.

chapter thirty-two

By 8:05, the night sky above the city had grown as black as new coal, and as Linda gazed out the hotel window, trying hard to visualize the outline of the mountains to the east, she rehearsed over and over in her mind exactly how their next two hours would be played out. She knew there'd be no room for error, that it had to be nothing short of perfect, and that any mistake by either of them could cost them their lives. The thought of that sent a wave of cold nausea through her fatigued body.

John had just finished digging through his wallet for the fifth time, making certain there was nothing tucked between the folds that would give away his identity in the event of a routine search. Linda, after examining her counterfeit Pentagon security card, was now studying the forged authorization letter she'd typed on a sheet of Dr. Vijan's own letterhead stationery taken from his desk when she had first entered the library.

The signatures, Linda was satisfied, looked authentic. Having practiced them often enough after studying Vijan's letter to McKnight, and the few signed Pentagon memos she'd taken from Adam's file, she knew they were near perfect forgeries. They had to be. After spending the last seven years dealing with the incessant paranoia of the intelligence community, Linda was well aware of standard security procedure. Signatures of all specially classified personnel were keyed into a computerized security system that could identify unique handwriting characteristics and use them as flags in the event of a security breach. Any trained intelligence agent would, simply by using a computer scan, be able to spot insignificant deviations in a forged signature.

"Almost ready, John?" she asked.

"Not really, but what the hell. It's now or never, I guess."

Linda folded the letter into an envelope and placed it carefully into her purse, along with her Pentagon security card. She checked her thin miniature camera one last time, to make sure the film was in and the battery fully charged. She slipped it down into her pantyhose where the legs met, sandwiching it between two maxi pads that she'd stained with red ink, figuring that would be the last place anyone would think or care to look. Two small rolls of film were already taped beneath her breasts.

"Okay, it's eight-fifteen," John said. "We'll try to get there no earlier than ten. Hopefully, by that time the place'll be pretty much deserted, except for security. You have what you're supposed to say down pat?"

"Yeah. You have the spray?"

"Right here." John held up his keys. Attached to the key ring was a small replica of a rubber tire, filled with concentrated pepper spray. "Good for at least three squirts. Hope we won't need it."

"Okay, I guess we should get going."

As they walked through the door, Linda glanced back into the comfortable security of their hotel suite, thinking all the while how much easier it would be to forget the research center and simply end their mission right then and there. They could wait it out, she figured; hope that Jack would receive the evidence and do what he needed to do on his end, then pray that what she'd uncovered in Vijan's files would be enough to bring McKnight to his knees and the new biotechnology to a fitting end.

But, despite the burning nausea that bore into the pit of her stomach the minute she stepped into the hallway, she knew that unless they recorded the technology behind the project, their investigation, regardless of how successful it had been thus far, would be incomplete at best. They had little choice. With a finality that gave the maid she noticed across the hall a sudden jolt, Linda slammed the door and marched directly toward the elevator with a determination that surprised John.

"Damn, it's so dark," Linda whispered. "You think you can find it again?"

They'd been driving for over an hour. Linda was squinting through the windshield, straining to identify any of the natural landmarks they had seen earlier that morning but which now blended into a blackness so deep that even the beams from the car lights seemed to disappear into the dense forest as if they'd been swallowed.

"I'm pretty sure we're almost there," John said, his face pushed forward and his breathing so deep he formed a moist fog against the windshield. "I remember it being about a mile or two from that river we just crossed. The road going up to the research center should be on the left, just around this curve coming up."

John drove slowly, switching on his high beams and slowing down as he made the approach to a narrow tree-lined road that looked more like a one-way tunnel into hell. "There, that's it," he said, then switched back to low beams and turned left. The sentry station was dimly lit, but he saw three guards inside, their shadowed heads turning toward the light of the approaching vehicle.

Neither John nor Linda uttered a word. Suddenly their plan, which they'd gone over enough times they knew it backward, seemed inadequate, though they both knew that on this night, at least, they had to rely on *it* rather than instinct.

One of the security guards, a hulk of a man with a wide flat nose and square chin, stepped outside and stood in the middle of the road, a muscular arm raised. Green military fatigues were stretched tightly across his chest. The black helmet blended perfectly with the blackness of his slanty eyes. The other two sentries followed behind him, their fingers pressed tensely against the triggers of automatic weapons.

John stopped and threw the car into park, praying that everything would not come apart in the next sixty seconds. Taking a deep breath, he readied himself and whispered, ''Good luck, Linda. In case anything goes wrong, I want you to know I've always cared for you . . . more now than ever.''

''I knew that,'' Linda answered, her voice trembling noticeably. ''Why else would you have followed me here?''

''Step out of the vehicle, please.'' The enormous guard looked Malaysian but spoke with a near-perfect American accent. ''Identification, please.''

John flashed the security guard his Pentagon ID card, then watched a hand twice the size of his swallow it. Linda walked briskly around to the driver's side, presenting hers as if following standard protocol. Then, with a few deep breaths that made her feel as if her chest were being crushed, she knew it was time to implement their mission.

''Dr. Mary Baldwin,'' Linda announced as nonchalantly as she could. ''Special science investigator and project director for General Benjamin McKnight, Pentagon. We arrived from Washington this morning after being issued special orders to do a random, unannounced inspection of the facility. There was not to be any prior notification. Not even Dr. Vijan was to know when we were to arrive. In order to prevent interference, no one is to be apprised of our presence until we've completed the inspection. All surveillance cameras and monitoring equipment in the lab need to be shut down during the inspection.'' Linda hoped the official tone of her voice did the trick.

The guard studied the photographs on the ID cards. The cold stare on his face wasn't the least bit reassuring.

''I have an official memo signed by Dr. Vijan and cosigned by General McKnight, issuing a directive for research center personnel to allow access to the inspection team.'' Linda took the official-looking letter from the envelope and presented it to the guard, who then brought it close to his face.

Dr. Abraham Vijan, Ph.D.
17 Sempora
Kuala Lumpur, Malaysia

To: Security Personnel, U.S. Tropical Research Center
From: Dr. Abraham Vijan, Ph.D.

Re: Facility Inspection

Please be advised that Drs. Mary Baldwin and Frank Tippett have been authorized, with my full knowledge and permission, access to the U.S. Tropical Research Center's genetic engineering facility for the purpose of conducting a random inspection. Under no circumstances should their inspection be announced, impeded, or hindered in any way. Monitoring during their visit will be restricted to nonlaboratory areas. Failure to comply with the directive set forth in this document will be regarded as breach of security and a violation of our inspection policy.

Dr. Abraham Vijan, Ph.D.   General Benjamin McKnight

Abraham Vijan   B McK

Linda watched as the guard read and then reread the letter twice, looking at the words and signatures as if trying to identify something he thought should or should not be there. She knew, when they'd made their plans, that these security people would play by the book. Because of their almost pathologic fear of breaking military security procedures and their inflexibility in thinking through situations themselves, she was confident they could easily be manipulated into doing exactly what she expected.

"I might as well warn you," she said sternly. "This is a very important part of a very important top-secret project. We've been sent here halfway round the world from Washington, D.C., to do this. Any deviation from security protocol, any change in procedure will not be looked at very favorably, especially by General McKnight. In fact, there'd be hell to pay. Read the letter. I'd hate to see any of you get charged with a criminal military violation because you couldn't follow a simple command.'' Linda realized it was touch and go at this point as she stared the guard down with a menacing face that was meant to strike fear in his large heart.

''One minute, please.'' The guard seemed almost apologetic. He carried the letter into the security building and slid it into a computerized scanner that in seconds would compare their signatures with a master file containing the signatures of everyone who would be in a position to authorize an inspection of this kind.

Linda listened to the hard drive churning, sounding as if it were readying itself to spot the forgery and spit it out like a piece of counterfeit trash. She glared at the red and green lights that sat like a pair of mismatched evil eyes on top of the scanner, and she imagined the red one suddenly flashing on and the guard rushing toward her with his weapon drawn.

John, meanwhile, placed his hand in his pocket and gripped the pepper spray container lightly between his fingers in the event the wrong light *did* come on. Red was as good as dead, he said to himself, visualizing what he would do next in the event something went wrong. Never in his wildest dreams had John ever imagined he'd be doing anything like this.

A sudden buzz rang out, sending a jolting tremor through Linda's entire body. She clenched her jaw and felt her teeth rattle, then held her breath as she shot a glance at the scanner and saw that a light had indeed flashed on. Green! They'd done it. The forged signatures had enough of the key characteristics incorporated into them that the computer calculated the statistical probability of a forgery as not significant.

The guard punched a button and watched the letter slide out, handing it back to Linda, along with a metal security pass that was dangling from the end of a long silver chain. "Here you go, ma'am. Wear this around your neck and use it to gain access to the labs in sector four. That's the genetic engineering facility. I'll call ahead. A security guard at the front of the building will direct you to the area."

He threw a switch and stepped aside as the gate before them opened slowly. John and Linda got back into the car and drove through, noticing for the first time the red letters that warned DANGER—HIGH VOLTAGE. As Linda turned back, she saw the gate close and realized that, for better or worse, they had just been sealed inside a fortified compound with ten thousand volts between them and the outside world.

chapter thirty-three

General Benjamin McKnight swung around and, with a sharp flick of his thick wrist, pushed the flashing red button. "Yeah, McKnight here."

"General, it's Lambino."

"Where are you?"

"Guam. We're an hour behind schedule but we'll be arriving in Kuala Lumpur at two fifteen. Something goin' on? I just checked in with Mr. Morris and he told me to contact you right away."

"Yeah, listen. We've been able to get a fix on those aliases we gave you through our international computer search network."

"You know where they are?"

"The downtown Kuala Lumpur Embassy Hotel, room 1518. They're driving a silver Toyota Celica, rented in Singapore, license number BC412. We traced the flight from Washington to Singapore, then temporarily lost them when they changed travel plans and rented the car. Showed up at the Embassy Hotel some six hours later. It has to be them."

"Right. Any info on what they've been doing since arrival? Contacts made? Communications to Pilofski?"

"Negative. We suspect they've been lying low until they decide how they're going to gain access to the research center. Morris gave you the map, didn't he?"

Lambino unfolded a local map of the region and fingered the area. "Yeah, got it right here."

"Good." It's about an hour northeast of Kuala Lumpur," McKnight said as Lambino quickly followed the red line through a dark green stretch of map that identified several hundred square miles of tropiçal rain forest. "We don't know how the hell they're planning to do it, or when, but we suspect they've been able to get hold of classified security IDs, which they believe will give them access to the facility. There's no other way the fools could possibly get through."

"Have you been able to make contact with the research center?" Lambino asked.

"Not yet. Goddamn lines are still down. But we're sure it's too soon for them to have tried anything."

"What makes you so certain?"

"We would have heard by now," McKnight answered. "Entrance by any nonregular or even authorized visiting personnel, for any reason, at any time, must be reported immediately to both me and to Dr. Vijan, the head of the facility. It's security protocol. No such word's been issued at this point."

"And there's no other way they could slip through without us knowing?"

There was momentary silence as McKnight imagined the consequences if they could. But there was no way, he thought. Absolutely no way. Security was too tight, too rigid, too foolproof. "Our intelligence people are convinced the only way Franklin would be able to get inside is to use her position with NASA, maybe try to fool them into believing she's a visiting scientist working for me or the Pentagon. With her expertise in molecular biology, she'd be able to pull it off, no doubt about that. But like I said, we'd have known within the first five minutes and sent word of that to Dr. Vijan.''

''What makes you think she won't try to get access when no one's around?''

''Impossible. Can't be done and she knows it. If anything, she's not stupid. She realizes that if she tries to break inside that compound after hours, security would be over her like flies on shit. No, I can't think of any way she'd even consider a move that bold. She'll wait, maybe till tomorrow. By then you'll have arrived, and as soon as you do I want you to contact research center security and go over the details of what's going on. If the lines are still down, send one of your men up there. Give security their photographs but tell them *not* to make an arrest. Instruct research center personnel to escort them to the dummy lab, then allow Franklin to access the false information. She'll leave the area thinking she got away with it. We want her set up to think she can return safely to Washington with everything she came to Malaysia for.''

''Anything else?''

''Yes. Don't do anything that'll give you away. You're not to make a move that'll expose you or your men. Follow their every move, tail them back to Washington, make sure we know exactly when their flight is scheduled to arrive, then assist in making the arrest at the airport as you've been instructed. If they even suspect we know, they'll alter their plans and we could end up losing whatever evidence they've been able to gather up to this point. We *don't* take that risk, understood?'' McKnight leaned forward on his elbow and waited for a response.

''Perfectly,'' Lambino answered. ''We stay invisible until we arrive at Washington National.''

''Reassure me. How do three of you *stay* invisible for twenty hours while you follow them all the way back to Washington?'' McKnight tapped his finger nervously on his desk, needing to hear Lambino say it.

''None of us will ever be seen together. Standard procedure. Tomorrow, one of my men remains at the hotel while

Franklin and Peterson are out of their suite and plants bugs inside their phone and in their room. He'll remain at his station twenty-four hours a day, listening for any calls they make to the airlines. When they call, we immediately make the same reservations. We board the same flight out of Kuala Lumpur—or Singapore, if that's where they're flying from. At the second layover—probably Hawaii—one of my men gets off and takes a military flight to Washington, arriving earlier, then waits for us at the final destination gate. My other man gets off at the first stateside layover—California, most likely—and switches flights as well, eventually joining his partner in Washington. I remain behind with them for the remainder of the trip. Before the last leg of the flight, I switch to a first-class seat that I've already reserved and reboard some time after Franklin and Peterson get back on the plane. Since I won't be in coach after changing to first class, they'll assume I've gotten off at the last stop. I then get off the plane in D.C. before they spot me and wait to follow Pilofski to a car that'll be waiting in the prearranged area of the parking lot.''

''Splendid.'' McKnight was impressed. It all seemed to be going so right for him and so wrong for Franklin. A few more days, he thought. A few more days. ''I want you to contact me as soon as you arrive at the Embassy Hotel.''

''Yes, sir.''

McKnight cradled the phone and immediately picked it back up to call Jack Pilofski. He stuck a Marlboro between his lips, lighting the end with a gold Zippo, then pulled it out abruptly when he heard the voice on the other end. ''Jack. Good, you're home.'' He formed the words with thick smoke blowing into the phone. ''I just got off the line with Lambino.''

''Lambino?'' Jack asked, stunned that it was Lambino he was calling about. ''What the hell's goin' on? Why's *he* calling already? Did he come up with something?''

The tension in Jack's voice was apparent, and the general, picking up on it, said, ''He didn't, but we did.''

''What does *that* mean?'' More surprise.

"We found them, Jack." McKnight, again sensing apprehension in the questioning, wanted to make sure that Jack understood exactly where his loyalties ought to lie. "Intelligence located Franklin and Peterson in Kuala Lumpur. It's over. We'll turn over your entire dossier, including all the documents pertaining to your father, when the mission is complete, not before. I'm sure both of you will be happy when that part of his life is once again his. Is that agreeable?"

"Yeah . . . sure."

"Something wrong, Jack?"

"No . . . no. I, ah, I'm just surprised you located them so quickly. Where are they?"

"Embassy Hotel, downtown. We have agents on the way. We suspect Franklin will make an attempt to infiltrate the research center within the next day or so and may very well be planning on breaking into Vijan's home. If she has, you'll probably be receiving whatever it is she found *there.* I want that information as soon as you receive it, understood?"

"Yeah, I understand."

Jack suddenly felt the knot in his stomach swelling. Everything was happening so damned quickly. He thought back to the years he'd worked with Linda, regretting now that she'd ever laid eyes on that craft in Brittan. For he knew that once she had, once she'd decided to pursue the investigation, it would've only been a matter of time before she'd become entangled in a web from which there'd be no way out. But as much as it hurt him to see Linda in such danger, he realized that he had to follow this through, using himself as the decoy to get her into the hands of an organization that would stop at nothing to see her dead.

"And you guarantee me—absolutely guarantee me—that once I deliver Franklin and Peterson to you, you'll keep your end of the deal."

"Jack, you have my word on that. You'll go on with your life as if nothing happened. In fact, your life will be better than you'd ever have imagined it, I promise." McKnight grinned sarcastically and took a long drag of his cigarette.

He thought how foolish these so-called intellectuals really were, how naive they had to have been to think that a loose end that big would ever be allowed to remain dangling so freely. "I promise you, Jack," he repeated.

"Okay."

"Good. Now listen carefully. When Franklin makes contact with you—and she probably will within the next day or two—I want you to warn her that there are agents on the way, that intelligence has been able to locate her whereabouts, and that once they arrive—probably within the next twenty-four hours—she'll be picked up along with Peterson. That should reassure her there's no one in Malaysia yet. By then our people will be in position. They'll have established surveillance, and Franklin will think she's dodging another bullet and assume that she'll be safely on her way out of Malaysia before anyone arrives. Tell her you need to know their arrival time so that you'll be there with a car waiting for them at the airport. Meet them at the gate and lead them directly to us. I'll go over the final details with you when you've received the information from Franklin and meet with me. You got that?"

"Got it. I'll contact you as soon as I hear anything."

"Very well. Carry on, then."

McKnight hung up and lit another cigarette. His obsessive paranoia had made him suspect everything, including Jack's intentions. But he had a fail-safe security network in place and at that very moment, Jack's phone was being monitored, and he was under continual surveillance by two of Morris's best men. If anything *did* arrive from Dr. Linda Franklin, there was no possible way he'd be able to take it anywhere but to McKnight himself.

chapter thirty-four

The Toyota wound sharply through several hundred feet of dense jungle road, stopping at another, larger security checkpoint. The bold red letters stood out against a white metal sign illuminated by two spotlights that emerged from the ground in front of it.

Warning
U.S. Tropical Research Center
High-voltage Security Zone
Authorized Personnel Only

"That's it," Linda said, staring beyond the formidable ten-foot security gate to a hexagonal two-story concrete building.

"Look. Over there." John pointed to the right, where a team of security guards was patrolling the inside of the compound with attack dogs.

Flood lights, positioned at twenty-foot intervals along the periphery of the building, transformed the stark night into day. Adjacent to the security gate rose a fifty-foot steel tower housing a massive searchlight that shone across the entire compound every few seconds like a lighthouse beacon.

A sentry, pulled abruptly from his security hut by a snarling German shepherd, approached the car with quick steps. The searchlight above him suddenly turned, its intense beam flooding the inside of the car with a blinding light that made Linda squint. John placed his hand above his eyes and strained to see the face that was now bending down and glaring at them through the driver-side window.

"This what you need to see?" Linda asked, holding up

the security pass given to her at the front gate.

The guard straightened up and waved his arm toward a second checkpoint farther ahead. The gate slid open just enough for the car to drive through. Without a word between them, the guards stood by with weapons ready, glaring intently as John accelerated forward. And as the gate rumbled closed behind them, the sickening hum of ten thousand volts filled the humid air, reminding them in no uncertain terms that any slipup would seal their fate.

"Talk about security," John said. "Place looks like a maximum-security prison."

"God, I hope those goons back there don't decide to break security protocol and call Dr. Vijan."

"If they do, we're dead, you know that. There's no other way out of here, so let's work fast and get the hell back out as soon as we can."

John followed the road another hundred feet to the front entrance of the research center and pulled into a reserved space assigned to Abraham Vijan, Ph.D. Seeing no other vehicles, he turned the key and listened as the engine fell silent. He and Linda then sat facing a facility much larger than either had expected. From what they could see, it spanned at least three acres and, though tucked away in some of the most impenetrable rain forest in Southeast Asia, looked every bit as impressive as any private research lab they had seen anywhere in the world.

"Ready?" Linda asked tentatively.

"Yeah, let's do it."

They slid out of the car, and as they walked to the front door, they were approached by another security guard who took the pass that Linda was now holding out in front of her.

"Sector four," he said. "Genetic engineering, right?"

"Right," Linda answered, confident now that after getting this far into the secret compound, the rest would fall into place. "Can you show us the way to the lab, please?"

"Of course. Follow this way."

Her instincts proved correct. Obligingly, the guard led them up the steps, pushed a metal card into a wall slot, and punched four numbers in rapid succession. A sharp click rang out, followed by a rush as the heavily reinforced door slid open.

"This way," he said, turning and leading them through a massive lobby before stopping in front of one of five stainless steel doors, above which an illuminated sign read SECTOR 4. He slid the metal card into another slot, pushed a different set of four numbers, and once again watched as a door slid open. "Through here, please."

The brightly lit corridor of labs stretched for what seemed like a hundred yards at least. Not a soul was in sight. Perfect. They walked for nearly two hundred feet, turned left, and faced yet another door, this one displaying a sign that told them at once they'd reached their final destination.

CAUTION

BIOLOGICAL HAZARD AREA
Radioactive Isotopes in Use
Security Clearance Required

"This will require both security cards," the guard said. "Insert yours there," he instructed, pointing to a slot on the wall next to the door. As Linda did, he inserted his card simultaneously into an adjacent slot and punched a series of letters and numbers. The door slid open, revealing an inner chamber that all three then proceeded into.

"Your security card will now access the lab," the guard continued. "Today's code is eight four eight three. When you're finished in the lab, reenter the chamber, insert your card into the inside slot, and push this." He touched a large red button on the wall. "Only research center personnel have security cards that will open the outer door to the lab. I'll need to come back and escort you out. Please leave all loose belongings, including jewelry, in the basket outside. You may retrieve them after your inspection.''

The guard immediately stepped back into the hallway, waited for John and Linda to remove their belongings, then threw a switch. The door closed in front of Linda's face, literally sealing them inside a steel-and-concrete tomb with only one way in or out. She turned, unlocked the entrance to the lab with her card, and with a shudder that made her feel as if a cold wind had suddenly pierced her flesh, stepped into an enormous research facility she knew was at the heart of a biotechnology that, if allowed to continue, would change the world forever.

''Look at this,'' Linda said. ''I can't believe it. It's a replica of one of our genetic engineering labs in Washington. What the hell's going—''

''C'mon, Linda,'' John interrupted. ''You've seen one lab, you've seen 'em all. It's a modern research facility with state-of-the-art technology.''

''No, John. Not like this. There's something going on, something really familiar about all this.''

''Like what? It's a lab, that's all.''

''Dammit, John. I'm telling you, I've seen this lab before. Not just any genetic engineering lab. *This* lab. It's exactly like the recombinant DNA lab I told you about, the one I was allowed access to before it was shut down.''

''I remember. But you never told me why it was shut down.''

''It was originally set up to do defensive germ warfare research, to stay one step ahead of the Soviets and develop antibiotics and antidotes for newly developed recombinant DNA pathogens. There was no explanation why they shut it down. Unofficial word was that the research had changed focus to offensive biological weapons and the whole unit was moved to an undisclosed location, I suppose to keep it hidden from the public.''

''Malaysia?''

''God, I hope not. But it's almost as if someone's been

able to duplicate every detail, every piece of equipment, everything.''

John scanned the lab slowly from end to end, as if that would give him some insight into what Linda was seeing, then stared directly into her eyes. He took her arm. ''Linda, c'mon. How could it be? How could two labs on opposite sides of the world possibly be identical . . . unless—''

''Unless it's not a coincidence?'' Linda shot back. ''Unless this *is* a government lab or unless someone on the inside knew?''

John turned back and scanned the lab again. ''If it's not a government lab, what do you think's going on?''

''Dr. Vijan, that's what's going on. We've got ourselves a damn traitor who must have sold out . . . who with the help of someone back at the complex had information smuggled out piece by piece until an entire lab was replicated that could produce the psychochemical agent. Don't you see? There's got to be another reason besides sea snakes why this place is here in Malaysia. Hell, they could've smuggled sea snakes into the country by the shipload. It's gotta have something to do with Dr. Vijan.''

''But why Vijan?'' John asked.

''I'll bet if you ran his name through CIA or classified Pentagon computer files, you'd find that at one time he worked for us, maybe during the very early stages of recombinant DNA research, then decided he was too good to work for government. Maybe he needed money—lots of it—to finance the breakthrough research he was working on, and he got it. All he needed besides that was an inside contact, a knowledgeable accomplice who'd keep feeding him everything the United States was doing to refine the technology. Without that, he probably couldn't do it.''

''So you're saying that this renegade scientist, with the help of some slime back in Washington, set up a research facility that's producing the same agent we are? Jesus Christ, with all our security it's impossible.''

''Why? They did it with the atomic bomb, didn't they? With nerve gas, bacteriological weapons, chemical weapons.

What's different about this? As long as you have greed or hunger for power or misguided zealots with good intentions, you'll have transfer of technologies, often to the highest bidder. There's nothing new about security breaches, especially nowadays, when the reward for doing so far outweighs the penalty for getting caught.''

''You think Peter found out about all this?'' John asked as sensitively as he could without dredging up old feelings again. ''That he was too much of a threat to risk keeping alive?'' He knew that Linda wanted to remember Peter as a hero, not as some casualty whose life was snuffed out in a bizarre desert explosion.

Linda shut her eyes for a moment. She needed to believe that Peter had not died in vain because of some freak accident but because he'd sacrificed his life so the world would never experience the monstrous consequences of what they were about to find. ''Yeah, I do,'' she said solemnly, shaking her head. ''And I believe that note in his lab book proves it.''

Linda turned and gazed around a lab half the size of a football field. Sophisticated research work zones dotted the lab complex like rows of NASA mission control stations. Giant stainless steel fermentation vats, inside of which the genetically engineered bacteria were isolated and grown, rose twenty feet upward, dwarfing everything beneath them. Pipes and wires covered the vats like thick metal intestines. Countless gauges positioned along the pipes precisely regulated the pH and temperature of fermentation medium, as well as the concentrations of other chemicals that maintained the life-giving atmosphere necessary for the delicate bacteria to reproduce. Beneath the vats, motors the size of small cars churned continuously, propelling the giant blades that stirred the bacteria in their slushlike fermentation vats.

To the left, in a special glass-enclosed section resembling a zoological research park, specially designed tanks bubbled with the sea snakes from which genetic material was extracted and used as the primary source of the biological agent. In another room, racks of cages sat filled with the laboratory mice used in the testing of the final product. To the right, Linda spotted canisters that looked similar to some she had seen at the Brittan crash site which she assumed were part of CONDOR's delivery system.

For the next two hours, Linda and John worked nonstop, searching, examining, and documenting everything they thought could be used as evidence against Vijan, McKnight, and whoever else was involved in this monstrous experiment.

"It feels like we've been here all night," John yelled from across one of the lab benches. "I think we better get out of here before someone gets suspicious and decides to make a security check, maybe even give Vijan a call."

"Okay, I think I have enough. Let's get out of here before our luck runs out." She then returned the camera and film to their original hiding places, followed John to the interior door, and watched as he hit the security buttons. When she entered the chamber, Linda threw the inside switch and punched the red security button. As she did, she suddenly found herself shaking as if cold water had been thrown on her.

The two minutes it took for the security guard to return to sector four felt more like an hour. Linda visualized the entire plan unraveling before her eyes, the security guards swooping down on them like wolves on unsuspecting prey. As the other door slid open, she tried to look calm and unemotional, as if nothing out of the ordinary had just happened.

"Did you find everything in order?" the security guard questioned as John and Linda stepped into the hallway and prayed that he would treat them as unsuspectingly as he had two hours ago. He did.

"Yes, everything was fine," Linda responded with an air of professional aloofness. "We'll have a complete report to Dr. Vijan first thing tomorrow morning."

They silently thanked God that it all seemed to be running like clockwork. The guard led them back through the tunnel-like corridors and eventually into the lobby. Then, only steps from the front entrance, he stopped abruptly when he noticed a flashing red light on the sector four security panel. Linda's heart nearly jumped through her chest.

"I'm afraid I can't allow you out." The guard turned and glared at them suspiciously. "Security sensors indicate some kind of malfunction inside the genetic engineering lab. You'll have to wait here while we check it out. I'm sorry."

Linda's eyes widened as she watched the guard reach for a phone. "John, he's calling for backup. Do something."

As the guard raised the phone, about to press the alarm button, he was instantly overcome by an incredible burning in his eyes that dropped him to the floor in excruciating pain. John stood over him, put the pepper spray container back into his pocket, then tore the handcuffs from the guard's belt while Linda removed his firearm. John cuffed the guard and took the security card from the chain draped around his neck.

"Tell me the number or I'll blow your head off." John took the gun from Linda's hand and placed it against the guard's temple. "Now!"

"Three four four five," he yelled, his eyes wide with fear.

"Let's go." John leaped to his feet, pushed the card nervously into the slot, and punched the numbers. The door opened with a loud swish. "Hurry, Linda. Now."

They ran to the car and jumped in. John backed out of the parking space and drove as slowly as he had coming in so as not to attract undue attention to their sudden departure. They approached the security gate and eased to a stop. The enormous guard looked through the window, then at the backseat, and waved for them to drive through the electric fence that another guard was now opening.

A few more feet, Linda prayed. A few more feet and they'd be clear of everything. The Toyota inched forward and brushed by three more guards, each lined up with attack dogs at their side, each watching intently as the unfamiliar American faces drove by.

The second John saw the rear bumper clear the fence, he eased steadily down on the gas peddle and turned the corner, letting out a long sigh of relief. ''Thank God,'' he whispered. ''Should be no problem getting out now that—''

But before he could finish his sentence, John's heart nearly stopped as he heard the explosive wail of sirens screaming through the compound.

''Jesus Christ!'' Linda yelled. ''It wasn't supposed to happen like this.''

''Shit! Now what. How the hell do we get through the main security gates?''

''Quick, pull over. Jeeps coming!''

John nearly turned the Toyota on its side as he pulled off the road and crashed along an embankment behind a dense stand of trees. He turned off the lights and watched two Range Rovers speed toward the facility, their blue lights flashing. When he felt certain no other guards were on their way, he turned the lights back on and floored the gas pedal. The damaged vehicle sputtered for a minute, then managed to accelerate enough for them to get back on the road.

Within seconds, the security station came into view. John slammed on the brakes and brought the Toyota to an abrupt halt. ''Linda, take over.''

''What!''

''Take over. They left a guard stationed at the security gate. There's no way we're getting through. Pull up to the fence and start yelling frantically. Get out of the car and tell the guard that I was trapped in an explosion and that you need to call for help. Lure him into opening the gate. I'll take care of it from there.'' With that, John jumped out of the car and began running along the tree-lined road toward the security station.

Linda threw the Toyota into gear, began driving toward the fence, and stopped ten feet short of the high-voltage sign on the fence. ''Please! Help me,'' she yelled, throwing herself from the car and running toward the guard. ''My partner's been trapped in some kind of explosion. Don't you hear the sirens? Please, I need help!''

The guard, who'd been left alone while the two others

drove to the lab complex, ran out and stared suspiciously through the fence. "No one allowed through," he said. "There's been a security breach."

"Please, at least let me use the phone. I'll leave the car here so you know I can't go anywhere. Please."

The guard thought for a second, reached in and threw the switch, then drew his firearm as he watched the double-doored security gate swing open toward her. "Okay, let's go."

Linda rushed through the gate. *C'mon, John. Where the hell are you?* She turned her eyes right, then left, looking desperately for any movement in the bushes or trees that would at least let her know John was somewhere nearby. *C'mon, dammit.*

The security guard kept his gun trained on her and was about to throw the gate switch when the bottom of one of John's black boots suddenly caught her eye. As it moved stealthily across the top of the flat roof of the security station, Linda knew she had to move fast. Forget the damn plan, she thought. Go by instinct.

"Ow!" Linda dropped to the ground as if she'd sprained an ankle, giving John a chance to move into position. The guard knelt down beside her and placed his weapon on the ground next to her. The second he did, Linda felt a thunderous vibration as both of John's boots came crashing onto the middle of the guard's back. Though in pain, the guard instinctively reached for the gun. Linda rolled toward it, groping for it, then snatched it away at the last minute from his extended fingers. She held it up to his face while John removed the handcuffs from the guard's waist, twisted his arms behind his back, and snapped the cuffs on in one swift motion.

"Let's go." John pulled the guard to his feet and shoved him into the security building, latching the door from the outside. "C'mon. Let's get the hell outta here."

They raced to the car, threw the doors open, and got in. John stomped the accelerator to the floor. In seconds, they blew past the security building and were racing toward Kuala Lumpur, fleeing for their lives. Behind them, through the heavily lined rain forest canopy, the distant sirens faded, then were swallowed by the black night.

chapter thirty-five

Malaysia, though modern in many ways, more recently had become a country in which the population, fearful of violent reprisals and brutal death squads, asked few questions. So it was little wonder that a place like the U.S. Tropical Research Center could exist in such secrecy and that what had occurred there only two days ago may as well have occurred in another country.

But back in Washington, General Benjamin McKnight had been notified within an hour of the incident and was now anxiously awaiting word from Jack Pilofski about the evidence he was to receive from Franklin and Peterson. Twenty-four hours earlier, he had received confirmation from Kuala Lumpur that Lambino had arrived, was establishing surveillance, and had everything else under control.

The one thing that concerned General McKnight at that moment, however, was Pilofski's solemn assurance that he would turn over everything he was to receive from Dr. Linda Franklin. He knew damn well that the security breach had involved Franklin and Peterson, and he figured that if they had been clever enough to have pulled *that* off, they surely were clever enough to have gotten away with enough evidence to bring down everyone connected with the project. The two questions that continued to rattle through his mind were how and exactly when they would get that evidence to Pilofski.

The two agents assigned to Jack had already wired his

apartment and phone. They had followed him each morning and afternoon to the post office box he'd rented at Linda's request and had run a computer search on everyone he'd come in contact with, including a waitress named Maxine Drumright, who'd spent the last two nights in his bed and who would also have to be eliminated as a possible security risk.

One of the agents, George Luppin, a hulking figure with a flattened nose, had been glaring sleepily through his side of the windshield for the past four hours when he saw Jack rush out the door of his apartment building.

"Hey, Frank, get up." Luppin shoved an elbow into his sleeping partner's ribs. "There he is."

Frank Craven pulled the baseball cap up from his face and squinted through the mucus in his dark eyes. "Okay, let's move. Make sure you give him enough lead time."

They watched Jack cross the street, get into a VW bus, and pull out of the parking space. The minute it turned the corner, Luppin cranked the ignition and followed, making sure he stayed far enough behind to avoid detection.

"He's goin' back to the post office," growled Luppin. "Predictable little bastard."

"Yeah. Better check in with McKnight." Craven picked up the car phone, punched some numbers, and stuck the receiver to his ear. "Yeah, this is Frank Craven. Lemme talk to General McKnight."

"One moment, please." The secretary placed Craven on hold for a few seconds before McKnight's booming voice came on.

"Frank, what's up."

"We've got Pilofski on the road again. Looks like he's goin' to the post office. Maybe today we get lucky."

"Okay. That means he hasn't gotten anything yet. Just make sure you follow him into the building, and if he gets anything, see to it he doesn't try to mail it."

"Will do. Check back with you as soon as we get there."

"Right."

Craven listened for McKnight to hang up, then placed the

car phone under the dash, staring straight ahead at the back of the VW bus. "There he goes. He's pullin' in. Give him a chance to get out of the van."

Luppin slowed to a crawl, waiting for Jack to park and leave the van, then stepped on it and pulled up in front of the post office entrance just as Jack was opening the door to go in. Craven jumped out and followed him in, walking to a table near the post office box section where he pretended to fill out postal forms, all the while keeping his eyes focused squarely on Jack.

He looked on as Jack reached into his pocket, pulled out a small key, then made a 180-degree sweep of the area before inserting it into the box. Craven dropped his eyes quickly and continued filling out forms when Jack turned toward him. When he lifted his head, he watched Jack remove a small package, tuck it under his arm, and with a smile on his face race out of the lobby and toward his van.

Craven followed, pausing at the door, then throwing it open as Luppin pulled up in the car. "He got it. Let's move." Craven slid onto the front seat, yanking the car phone from its cradle, and punched up McKnight's number again.

"General, we're on the move."

"What do you have?"

"He got it."

"A package?"

"Yeah. A small box."

"Box? Small was it? Damn! It's not what I expected. You sure that was it?"

"Yeah. I'd say it was film or—"

"Of course!" McKnight yelled into the phone, making Craven's head snap sideways. "Film. She must have photographed everything. That's it. Is he on his way here?"

"Doesn't look like it."

"Whaddya mean?"

"Looks like he's headin' back to *his* place," Craven said, then asked, "You want us to detain him?"

"Hell no! Follow him back to the apartment and see what

he does next. Stay out of his way, unless he makes a move to go anywhere other than to meet me. You got that?''

''Got it. We're a few blocks from his apartment right now. We'll maintain surveillance and check in when he makes his next move.''

''See that you do. Screw up—lose that package—and I'll have both your asses.''

Craven heard the sharp click and dropped the phone onto the seat next to him. ''Damn. McKnight's got a bug up his fat ass over this one. The guy must be carrying one helluva piece of info.''

Luppin coasted past Jack's apartment building and made a U-turn at the intersection, pulling into a parking space he'd spotted across the street and halfway down the block. He cut the engine, took out a pack of Winstons, and snapped it until one peeked out. He shoved it in Craven's direction. ''Might as well kick back and wait,'' he said, then pulled out the car lighter and pointed it at Craven's face. ''There's gotta be a reason he stopped here before goin' to see McKnight. I don't like the feel of this. Somethin's goin' down. I know it.''

''Relax,'' Craven shot back. ''He's probably gonna inspect the stuff to make sure he has what McKnight's lookin' for, that's all.''

''Maybe.'' Luppin took a long drag and blew a tight smoke ring against the windshield. ''Maybe. I'm not so sure I trust the fat little bastard, though.''

''The fat little bastard knows damn well what'll happen if he tries anything funny. He's not stupid. And like everybody else, he's lookin' out for himself. You heard what the general said. We stay out of his way.'' Craven then leaned back against the headrest and closed his eyes.

Forty-five minutes after Jack had returned to his apartment, there was still no sign of him. This time *Luppin*, growing edgy at Pilofski's unexpected detour, grabbed the car phone and called McKnight.

''Listen, General. Pilofski's been up in his place now for almost an hour. No sign of movement yet and I'm startin' to worry. Anything from your people listening in on him?''

"Negative. He hasn't made any calls. He may be inspecting the evidence before handing it over. Don't know why the hell it would take him so long. Give him another thirty minutes, then call me back."

"Right. We've got . . . wait, there he is." Luppin hit Craven's thigh with the back of his hand. "He just walked out of the building with a briefcase."

"Briefcase?" McKnight asked, making sure he'd heard right. "You don't see the original package?"

"No. It may be in the briefcase, I don't know. He just pulled out. We're on our way."

"Okay, listen. Don't lose him. If he stops anywhere and tries to give that briefcase to anyone, nail him, then bring him and whomever he gives that briefcase to directly to headquarters."

Luppin hung up and drove several blocks, pulling over when Jack stopped alongside a pay phone. He watched Jack get out of the van, drop a quarter into the change slot, and dial a number. "He's calling his contact," Luppin said. "Probably arranging to deliver whatever he has. McKnight better know about this."

As soon as Jack hung up, Luppin snatched the car phone and called McKnight back. "General, he just made contact. He's—"

"I know," McKnight interrupted. "It was me he was contacting. I'm on my way to meet him at the Lincoln Memorial. Maintain surveillance and watch for any detours he might take. I don't know what's going on here, but I want him to think he can do anything he wants. We'll see what the briefcase is all about."

McKnight paced nervously among the fluted columns of the Lincoln Memorial, looking out from behind one every few seconds to see if Jack was anywhere in sight. He lit a cigarette, and as he glanced at his watch for the fiftieth time, his attention was suddenly diverted by the sound of a sharp voice.

"General. Why don't we go somewhere not so congested."

General McKnight twisted his lips into a forced grin and extended his hand. "Good to see you, Jack. I presume you have what we've been waiting for?" He cast his eyes down at the briefcase in Jack's other hand.

"It's all here," Jack told McKnight, keeping his hand firmly at his side as though not wanting to touch the man. "Just as I told you it would be."

Though he kept thinking that the package he knew Jack had received was nowhere in sight, McKnight continued to smile, realizing that any slip of the tongue, any mention of a package, would give him away and cause Jack to suspect immediately that he was being stalked. No, he knew he had to allow Jack to tell him about the package himself. "Did she send documents, papers?" he asked innocently. "What exactly do we have?"

"Not here."

Jack led McKnight down the steps and around the back of the memorial to a less-populated grassy area. He veered left and sat down on a wooden bench. McKnight followed and looked anxiously in both directions. Jack snapped the gold latches and swung the top of the briefcase open, revealing a stack of eight-by-ten black-and-white photographs. He slid the open briefcase onto McKnight's lap.

"She sent me a shit load of film in a small box," he said. "One of my expertises is photography, so I have a darkroom set up in my apartment. As soon as I received the package of film, I developed it. Didn't want to risk losing any of it. There were eight rolls. Everything's here, including the negatives. Enough evidence to put an end to everything and bring down the entire organization. I hope you're satisfied."

McKnight looked hurriedly through the photographs, then closed the briefcase and snapped it shut. He extended his hand again. "Good work, Jack. I'll have to admit I had my doubts, but you've proved yourself a very valuable asset to us."

''Don't forget our deal,'' Jack shot back, ignoring McKnight's obviously phony compliment.

''Certainly not.'' McKnight had to refrain from laughing in Jack's face at the sound of those words. ''You'll be well rewarded as soon as you've completed your end of the assignment. Now, did Franklin include a number where she could be reached?''

''Yeah, this is it.'' Jack shoved a hand into his jacket pocket, pulled out a sheet of paper and unfolded it, displaying it to McKnight. ''She wanted me to contact her at 8:00 P.M. Washington time the day I received the package. That's a little less than five hours from now. According to the note, one of them will always be in the room, waiting for my call.''

''Good. You know what to do.''

''Perfectly.''

McKnight took the note, examined it front and back, and handed it back to Jack. Then, with a nonchalance that surprised even himself said, ''Vijan's people told us that the two of them were inside the facility for about two hours—more than enough time to get whatever they needed. Apparently they managed to forge some papers with proper authorization and get through security. Very industrious, but futile, I'm afraid. Of course we had to shut down the facility.''

''How does that affect the mission?'' Jack asked.

''It doesn't,'' McKnight answered.

''Meaning?''

''We have other means of production, and we have enough of the agent stored to carry on.''

''Where?''

''That, Dr. Pilofski, is more highly classified than what you have in that briefcase.'' McKnight's yellow teeth broke through his lips as he grinned from ear to ear, confident that by April sixth, the second American revolution would begin and the course of history would be changed forever.

''Is that all, General?''

''When you talk to Franklin, make damn sure you're convincing enough to get her on a flight back here by tomorrow. We need to eliminate these people before final countdown begins. I don't want anything interfering with the launch.'' McKnight stood up, looked around, and spoke without looking back at Jack. ''Stay here until I leave the area. Then go back to your place and make the call. We'll be in touch.''

McKnight walked off. Jack remained huddled on the bench, the note blowing back and forth between his fingers like a distress flag on a sinking ship. When he saw McKnight slip out of sight, he, too, left. And when he got back to the van and took off for his apartment, Luppin and Craven followed, making sure that Jack stayed loyal and played by the book till the very end.

chapter thirty-six

Linda dove into her purse, wrapping her finger carefully around the trigger of the gun she'd taken from the research center security guard. She stared at the door as it vibrated again from the soft knock, then pulled out the gun and slid it beneath a pillow, her hand close enough to slip it out if needed.

John, meanwhile, tiptoed quietly to the peephole and looked out into the hallway. He turned back, nodded his head, then opened the door slowly as the bellman wheeled in a linen-draped cart with the breakfast they had ordered over thirty minutes ago.

''I could eat a horse,'' he said after escorting the bellman back to the door and rushing to the serving platters positioned on each side of the table. ''What time is it, anyway?''

''Almost eight.'' Linda stared at her watch and thought about the twelve-hour time difference between Kuala Lumpur and Washington. ''Seven forty P.M. Washington time, to be exact. Jack must have gotten the package hours ago and should be calling here any minute. God, I hope everything went okay.''

''So do I,'' John said, then stabbed a piece of sausage and put it to his lips. A thin stream of grease squirted onto his chin as he bit into it. ''You sure he's clever enough to avoid being followed for an entire week?''

''Jack's one of the shrewdest guys I know,'' Linda answered, trying hard to convince herself of that. ''He's brilliant, incredibly observant, and suspicious to a fault. If anyone can spot an intelligence agent and ditch him, or at least fool him, Jack can.''

''I hope you're right. We've put all our faith in him. Hell, we've put our lives in his hands and that's beginning to worry me.''

Linda glanced nervously at her watch again. ''We'll know soon enough,'' she said. ''If he doesn't call, he either hasn't received the package, which is doubtful, or—''

''Or what?'' John asked.

Linda hated to admit it, but the possibility existed that despite every precaution, Jack, God forbid, had somehow slipped up and got caught. She finally verbalized it. ''Or . . . he *did* get the package but something happened to him when he left the post office.'' Then, as if discounting that scenario, said, ''It's almost time. He'll be calling any minute.''

The last five minutes had felt as if time had come to an unbearable standstill. Linda found herself glued to her watch, shifting her eyes continually from *it* to the phone, then back to her watch again, the second hand sweeping across the numbers in excruciating slow motion. She was suddenly thinking the unthinkable, that regardless of her faith in Jack's ability to outsmart any intelligence agent he'd be up against, this time he'd be dealing with a different breed—a breed that would sooner slit his throat than blink an eye.

''It's three minutes past, John. I'm starting to worry. Jack's usually very punctual when—'' Linda dropped her fork and leaped from the chair as a loud ring suddenly exploded through the room. Reaching over, she tore the receiver off the hook. "Hello?"

"Linda, it's me, Jack."

"Jack! I was beginning to think . . . God, it's so good to hear your voice. I'm glad you're okay." She had tears in her eyes as she spoke. "You got the package?"

"Sure did. Man, that stuff you sent me was dynamite. Good work. Damn good work."

Jack, well aware that everything they were saying would be monitored, recorded, and immediately reported to General McKnight, had to measure every word he said. The slightest mistake, the tiniest slipup and Jack knew it would all be over. "Listen," he continued as convincingly as possible. "You've gotta pack up and get ready to get the hell out of Kuala Lumpur. They know where you are."

Linda stiffened, turning and staring at John with a look of horror that made him stop chewing and freeze over his plate. "My God," she whispered. "How?"

"They had their computer people poring through airline flights and analyzing passenger lists twenty-four hours a day till they tracked you two down in Singapore. That was a good move, by the way. It threw 'em off base for a while, but not long enough. Otherwise they would've gotten to you by now. They know, Linda, and once they get to Kuala Lumpur, it won't take these guys long to find you. You've gotta get out as soon as you can."

The blood rushing to her head so quickly she nearly passed out, Linda dropped her head into her hand and slumped on the edge of the bed. She could hardly force the words from her lips. "Were you able to make copies of the stuff yet?"

"Not yet," Jack said. "I developed the film as soon as I got it, but I didn't want to risk taking it out of the apartment just yet. I'm going to the lab tonight to make copies. By this time tomorrow, everyone who should have the evidence in their hands will."

"Good." Linda's demeanor changed slightly and, despite the fact that no action had been taken thus far, gave John a halfhearted thumbs-up sign. ''Be careful, Jack. It's far from over.''

''You don't have to tell me that. Make your reservations as soon as you get off the phone and call me back at the number I'm gonna give you with the flight schedule. Got a pen?''

''Yeah, go on.''

Jack recited the phone number, then said, ''I'll be here waiting. I'll meet you at the airport with a car and let you know what's going on. As soon as you get off the plane in D.C., look for me. If I'm waving, it means everything's cool. If my arms are folded across my chest, then something's gone wrong and I'm there to let you know that you'll need to make a run for it.''

''Okay. I'll call the airport as soon as I hang up. Call you right back.'' Linda pushed down on the button several times, released it, then dialed the hotel operator for airline information.

Three floors down in room 1211, Max Grishaw sat at the edge of the bed, listening through headphones and recording every word. ''She bit,'' he muttered into a microphone. ''Flight 7888 to Singapore, departing at 8:14 P.M. from gate seventeen, Subang International Airport.''

Lambino, who'd stationed himself in the hotel lobby, pushed on his earpiece with an index finger and listened as Grishaw went down the list of flights and layovers. He pulled a small microphone from his vest pocket, cupped it in his immense hand, and placed it discreetly up to his mouth. ''Okay, tell Sid to get up and make the necessary reservations,'' he lisped. ''Keep monitoring while I stay down here, just in case.'' He then tucked the microphone safely back into his pocket and remained sitting in one of the lobby's plush chairs, a *London Times* covering a portion of his face.

''Gregory Morris, please. This is General McKnight.''

''Ben.'' The voice came on instantly. ''I've been waiting for your call. Any word from Pilofski?''

''Yeah. He supplied us with photographs of documents

and sensitive papers they could only have gotten from our research facility in Malaysia. The documents, unfortunately, tie me directly to CONDOR."

"Anything there implicating us?" Morris probed, hearing something in McKnight's voice he found profoundly discomforting.

"You can rest assured," McKnight answered with a lie. "There was nothing about Vanguard."

"And Pilofski? He turned over the film intact? Undeveloped? With the package still sealed?"

"He developed it all in his apartment and turned over the photographs. He was followed the whole time. No other contacts were made."

There was an uncomfortable stretch of silence as Morris thought through the remote possibility that some of the film could have contained *something* that even indirectly would lead to him. "You're certain you got it all, Ben?"

"Luppin and Craven followed him from the post office back to his apartment where he remained for over an hour developing the film. They then tailed him directly to the Lincoln Memorial, where he met me with the evidence. As soon as he left his apartment, the other surveillance team went over and searched it thoroughly. It was clean. No evidence of anything anywhere."

"Good. Did you send the photographs to headquarters?"

"Already done."

"Fine. Has Pilofski set them up?"

"Everything's in place. They've already made their flight reservations back to Washington. Pilofski's arranged to meet them with a car as soon as they arrive at the airport. Lambino and his men have their flight plans ready. We should have Franklin and Peterson in hand within twenty-four hours. Their flight arrives at 12:46 A.M., and there'll be few witnesses around the parking area at that hour."

"Excellent," Morris said. "Keep me updated."

"We'll let you know what's going on. I don't foresee any problems."

McKnight sounded off like a man confident in his ability

to do anything he wanted to anyone he chose. He knew that in a little more than two weeks TIMBER WOLF would finally become reality and, as far as he was concerned, Franklin and Peterson had just been relegated to nothing more than loose ends about to be tied up.

At 2:40 P.M., as she made a final sweep of the hotel room, Linda continued replaying her conversation with Jack, trying to put her finger on what it was that had bothered her so much. Maybe it was the sound of his voice, she thought. A nervous apprehension she'd detected between words that were suspiciously distant coming from someone who had never been distant to her before. Strange, uncomfortable images suddenly flashed through her mind. Thoughts of subversion and betrayal surfaced, making her wonder if going back to Washington was really the wise thing to do.

"You okay, Linda?" John asked, sensing her uneasiness.

"I'm not sure." She continued to scan the room, searching for anything that might be found and give their next move away.

"What's wrong? You've been over this place three times in the last hour. You've hardly said a word since Jack called."

Linda stopped her search and sank into one of the chairs next to the window. "I had this feeling that something was terribly wrong the entire time I was talking to him. I've worked with Jack for years, and it didn't sound like the same guy I know."

"Of course something was wrong," John said, trying to ease her suspicions. "For Christ's sake, the poor guy's not used to being smack in the middle of a game of life and death. He just received a box of film that's about to expose something that could threaten the stability of the entire planet and you expect him to get on the phone and talk to you as if you two are discussing plans for a beach trip? Get real, Linda. To him, you probably sounded as whacked out as he did. No, not probably. Believe me, right now you *do* sound as whacked out as he did. The question is, do you trust him?

Trust him enough to do what he's asking you to do?''

Linda relented and nodded in agreement, though torn between her need to trust Jack with her life and her usually reliable instincts to be more cautious than ever before. ''I suppose you're right,'' she submitted. ''He would've given me some signal that he was being coerced or that something was wrong.''

''John walked over to Linda and kissed her gently on the forehead. ''I think after what we've been through, I can't blame you for overreacting. C'mon, this isn't the time to start second-guessing or having second thoughts. We need to go.''

''You're right. Besides, if they think we're still in Malaysia, it'll just buy us more time. Let's go home.''

Lambino had already checked out of the hotel and, along with Grishaw, was now waiting in the lobby while Paxson, the third member of the team, positioned himself outside the hotel with the car. With his eyes barely above the business section of the *London Times*, Lambino followed Linda and John visually from the elevator to the front desk. He watched intently as they checked out, collected their luggage, and walked across the lobby to a door leading to the underground parking lot. With only one car entrance in or out, Lambino knew they wouldn't be able to drive off without being seen.

When he saw the door close behind them, Lambino threw the newspaper down, looked over at Grishaw, who'd been standing in a phone booth with a receiver against his ear, and with a nod of his head toward the front exit, rushed out to the waiting car.

''Okay, they'll be coming out any time,'' Lambino said as he slid his large frame into the front seat and ripped the false mustache and eyebrows from his face. ''Don't pull out right away. Give 'em some room.''

Within minutes, the front end of the Toyota appeared from the parking-lot tunnel. It eased onto the street and turned right. Lambino kept his hand up as a sign for Paxson to stay put, then dropped it when he saw the Toyota well down the street. ''Let's move,'' he ordered. ''Stay far enough behind to keep an eye on 'em. As soon as we get to the airport, we disperse. No one so much as looks at anyone else. You both have your orders and flight schedules. We'll regroup in Washington, where Pilofski and Craven will have cars waiting, make the arrest, and drive to headquarters."

As he said that, the Toyota ahead of them made a sharp left and headed west, following the sign to Subang International Airport.

"All right, we're nearly there," Lambino announced. "As soon as we pull into the terminal area, drop me off. Keep following Peterson, ditch the car, and get rid of everything but carry-on luggage. You know the plan."

The air traffic control tower was suddenly in sight. Lambino watched John take the entrance ramp that directed him to the departure gates and, as soon as they reached the first airline terminal and pulled up to the curb, pushed the car door open and jumped out. "Meet me at the flight departure gate," he ordered. "And don't let 'em out of your sight." He slammed the door and lumbered through the automatic doors.

There was enough traffic flow and noise in the airline terminal for Lambino's men to take advantage of the one thing John and Linda had counted on to avoid detection—crowds and confusion. They weaved between pillars and strolled through corridors like tourists, one wearing a casual sports jacket and Dockers, the other a Par Four golf shirt and Levi jeans, both expertly blending into the hordes as if travelers on vacation. And when they'd reached gate seventeen, they sat inconspicuously on opposite sides of the passenger waiting area, taking occasional but unnoticeable glances at the two scientists who sat facing the window overlooking the runway.

Max Grishaw was the first to get up. He walked back down the terminal hallway and entered the men's rest room. He stood in front of a stained urinal and unzipped his pants, looking directly at the tiled wall in front of him while next to him Lambino flushed the urinal and slipped an airline ticket into his jacket pocket.

When Grishaw returned to the waiting area, Paxson got up and retraced his partner's steps. And after locking himself into a stall, he sat on the toilet and began tapping his right foot until a boarding pass slid along the floor between the stalls. He picked it up and strolled casually back to the waiting area.

"Flight 7888 to Singapore will be boarding in five minutes," the voice on the intercom announced. "Those flying first class will board now. We hope you've enjoyed your stay in Kuala Lumpur and wish you a safe return home. Please come and visit our beautiful country again."

"Yeah, right," Linda whispered. "In my nightmares, maybe."

Lambino approached the gate and remained a safe distance away, knowing that the less he was seen the less noticeable he would remain. Then, only after he saw that Linda and John had boarded, did he walk into the waiting area and board the plane.

Paxson had already seated himself in first class. Grishaw was well hidden in row thirty-five, next to a window that he could turn to in the event that anyone walked back to the rest rooms and looked in his direction. And Lambino, who'd made sure he was the last to board, was now squeezing into a window seat seven rows in front of Linda while she buckled her seatbelt and fumbled for a flight magazine in the pocket of the seat in front of her.

As the engines whined to an ever-growing crescendo, pushing the jet toward the runway, Linda grabbed John's hand and whispered, "I love you, John." She raised his hand to her lips, kissed it, and not wanting to let go, held it tightly against her cheek.

"When this is over," he responded, "I don't think I'll ever look at life the same way."

Linda kissed his hand again. She felt herself being pushed against the seat and watched from the window as the ground below them grew smaller and the skyline of Kuala Lumpur faded beneath the thickening clouds.

And as she pressed her head against the back of the seat and felt a sense of relief at finally leaving Malaysia, Lambino closed his eyes and, for the first time since arriving in Kuala Lumpur, fell comfortably asleep, knowing there was nowhere for any of them to go.

chapter thirty-seven

The black limo sped past armed security guards and across the vast, 400-acre compound that was home to the Universal Biomedical Research Corporation. Minutes later, making a sweeping right into a circular driveway, it slowed to a stop directly in front of an enormous glass-and-steel-framed pyramid. The chauffeur slid out, rushed to the back door, opened it quickly, then stood stiffly at attention as General Benjamin McKnight stepped out in full dress uniform.

"That'll be all," McKnight ordered. "I've arranged for someone else to drive me back to Washington later."

"Yes, sir."

The chauffeur slipped quickly back into the car, rolled the tinted window shut, and drove off at once. McKnight turned and marched up a set of white marble steps, taking from his jacket pocket the specially encoded key that would allow him access to the building. He made an about-face and checked the area one last time. Then, turning back and inserting the key into a metal panel located at eye level on the side of the glass door, McKnight waited for security confirmation. A yellow light above the panel flashed on. Immediately, he pushed the heavy glass open and entered the building, proceeding directly across a circular lobby to another glass door, where the security ritual had to be repeated.

McKnight stepped through the door and, as if he'd traveled the route so often he could have continued blindfolded, marched twenty paces straight ahead and turned left into a science library whose walls were lined floor to ceiling with new textbooks and conspicuously unblemished journals. Going directly to the *Journal of Pharmacology,* he pulled volumes twenty-five and twenty-six from the shelf, then reached into the empty space with a second key. As he turned it, the bookshelf to his left swung open three feet. He replaced the volumes, slid through the opening, pulled the bookshelf closed behind him, and entered a hidden elevator.

Inside, a computer screen flashed red digital letters, instructing him to press his left hand firmly against the handprint identification monitor to his right. As he did so, an inner door slid closed. With a high-pitched whine, the elevator began its rapid descent to an underground control center five stories beneath the earth.

The layover in Hawaii had lasted nearly two hours. Sid Paxson had already departed, reboarded a military flight, and was now on his way to Washington via an alternate route that was to arrive from Atlanta at 11:41 P.M., sixty-five minutes before John and Linda were scheduled to touch down. Grishaw had departed immediately upon landing at Los Angeles International Airport. *His* alternate military flight was to arrive in D.C. via Pittsburgh at 12:04 A.M.

Lambino, who had managed to stay out of sight for much of the trip, was now boarding first class on flight 2237 leaving Cincinnati and due to arrive in Washington at 12:46 A.M. And in less than two hours, all three, who until now had been nothing more than inconspicuous passengers on three different flights heading for the same destination, would be in the vicinity of gate fifty-five, watching cautiously as Jack Pilofski escorted two unsuspecting scientists to the last such meeting they would ever have.

As flight 2237 accelerated down the lighted runway and lifted itself from the stretch of black asphalt, Linda felt the plane shift and buckle as it cut through the unstable atmosphere of a gathering storm. It was ironic, she thought, that the final leg of their flight should start in such turbulence. She watched the lights of Cincinnati International Airport disappear quickly as ominously dense clouds engulfed the plane and tossed it about like a plastic toy.

"I hope it's not like this all the way into D.C.," Linda said, throwing her head backward and shutting her eyes to relieve the nausea that was now overtaking her. "I feel like throwing up already."

"We'd better get some rest," John said, settling back into his seat as well. "We'll be in Washington in a few hours and we don't know what to expect." He slid his fingers in between Linda's and squeezed them gently. "How'd Jack sound when you talked to him back at the airport?"

"Okay, I guess. He said the plans haven't changed. He'd already rented a car when I talked to him and he'll be meeting us at the prearranged area when we arrive."

"Any trouble with the hotel reservation?"

"Uh-uh. And at least the Holiday Inn at Key Bridge is close enough so we can keep in contact with Jack. It's also far enough out of the way so we don't run into anyone we shouldn't. God, I pray we don't."

John looked around to see if anyone was alert enough to listen in, then asked, "Did you get a sense that he found anything especially revealing when he developed the film? Anything specific about what this is all about or what it's going to be used for?"

"Only references, nothing to establish the connection between *it* and psychochemical warfare or WORLD ORDER or who it was that was supplying the money for the research. I still have a feeling there's a connection . . . that the government developed this thing and now it's out, and God only knows who has it."

"So what's Jack's assessment?" John asked. "He have any?"

"From what he saw, he's certain the evidence we sent him would at least be enough to lead us to who or what's behind all this. Hopefully, we can stop it before April sixth."

"Christ, I hope so. Seems no matter where you look, it

all points to General McKnight, CONDOR, and ultimately to this TIMBER WOLF thing. I have a feeling that what we have here is something so sinister it's gonna shock the hell out of us. But more than knowing *what* it is, I want to know who, besides the government or the Pentagon, is powerful enough to be able to carry out human experiments and eliminate entire populations with total impunity."

John shook his head in disbelief as he felt anger welling up inside him. "I've gone beyond wanting to find out what's going on, Linda. I wanna see these bastards hang."

"No more than I do," Linda shot back.

The plane dropped suddenly as if yanked from below. Linda snapped her head around and stared at the rotating wing light as it illuminated the thick clouds that battered the window incessantly and left broken streaks of water behind. With each passing moment, the storm grew more violent, the plane seemingly less able to handle the continuous pounding it was taking. No longer worried about just turbulence, Linda now imagined the plane's underbelly being ripped open from end to end. What a way for everything to end, she thought. To come so close, then die in a damn plane crash less than a hundred miles from home.

Her head was again jarred sideways by another pocket of violently turbulent air. "Hell, maybe it's better this way," she whispered, trying to calm herself down. "Who'd be fool enough to be out in this weather, anyway? It'll be a perfect cover."

"Perfect or not, I'm not going to feel completely safe till Jack has it plastered on the front pages of every paper in the country. Getting it on all the major networks wouldn't hurt either."

"Jack'll pull it off," Linda said. "He's never let me down yet, and I don't believe for a minute he'd let me down now, especially now, as close as we are." Linda slid her arms across her stomach as the plane shook and the lights blinked on and off for several seconds. "No, he wouldn't let me down now," she repeated. "Not Jack." She closed her eyes and within minutes, despite the intensity of the storm, fell into a fitful sleep.

McKnight stepped away from the elevator and into an eerily silent conference room that was empty except for the lone figure that stood with his hands clasped behind his back, facing the wall-to-wall map of the world.

As McKnight walked briskly toward him, Christopher Doyle spoke softly without turning. "It's almost here, isn't it?" he said. "Almost time. Never thought I'd finally see the day when it would all begin."

Doyle turned slowly and followed General McKnight with deep-set eyes until the two stood side by side, gazing at the map as though relishing the inevitable transformation of a world they both knew was on the verge of a new political, social, and economic order.

Each man—one a military leader whose patriotic fervor was matched only by his desperate willingness to do anything to save his country, the other a career politician who'd long ago predicted the collapse of America's global dominance—had spent the last two decades witnessing the gradual but inevitable march of the United States toward societal and political bankruptcy, a nation they were convinced was on the brink of impending doom. But it was their singular vision of the tragic and precipitous decline of America's economy that lead McKnight and Doyle to join forces and eventually pledge allegiance to their common goal of saving the greatest nation in the history of the world from those who would destroy her.

"What's the latest word from the field?" Doyle asked, pointing to a set of chairs that faced one another. They both sat.

"Our last contact with them confirmed that Franklin and Peterson are on the final leg of their journey to Washington as we speak," McKnight answered. "They don't suspect a thing. Pilofski should be at the airport right now to join in making the arrest. We should have them all back here within the next hour or two."

"All three?" Doyle's head snapped firmly to attention. "You're bringing Dr. Pilofski here as well?"

"We thought it best this way," McKnight said. "He's being brought here to be eliminated along with Franklin and Peterson, and that meant getting all three of them here."

"I certainly hope this is the end of it."

"It will be." McKnight slipped a cigarette into his mouth and lit it. He blew smoke toward the ceiling and narrowed his eyes. "What's the feeling in the White House these days?" he asked in a casual manner, as if that even remotely mattered at this point. "Do we need to worry about the president and his willingness to keep CONDOR flying?"

"Not at all," Doyle answered confidently. "In fact, the administration's pretty damned upset over new intelligence reports coming in from Southeast Asia."

"Concerning?"

"Heroin, arms smuggling, terrorist organizations."

"So the new reports *are* as bad as what we've been getting," McKnight said.

"Worse," Doyle answered grimly, his eyes softening, then growing moist for a second before he composed himself. "The bastards aren't satisfied with current levels. They're trying to drown us in the stuff. And getting it here is easier than it's ever been."

The reports, which some experts were saying grossly underestimated the problem, concluded that massive shipments of drugs were beginning to flow into the country like water through a broken dam and were getting larger by the month. Experts along the two-thousand-mile Mexican border, though maintaining confidentiality due to the sensitive nature of ongoing trade deals, had been warning U.S. government officials for the past several years that once NAFTA took effect, the border would become more porous than ever. Mexican drug lords, who at one time were subordinate to the Colombian drug cartels, were now powerful enough to run distribution centers that smuggled twenty billion dollars of cocaine alone into the United States this year. By conservative estimates, some 700 tons of cocaine were being grown annually, 200 tons were awaiting shipment across the porous border, and God only knew what the real numbers actually were. Heroin was another matter altogether.

But not only was the DEA powerless to stop the flow of cocaine, they had evidence to show that a new form of heroin was now being smuggled, so pure that it could be snorted like cocaine and so highly addictive that lifetime dependency was a certainty. The Justice Department itself had predicted that the violent crime rate, as a direct result of what they called "narco terrorism," would go through the roof, creating an economic burden far exceeding anything projected thus far. To make matters worse, the CIA had gathered documented evidence that Asian and South American governments had actually formed an alliance that was secretly financing a drug distribution network in the United States rivaling anything in history.

Reports had also circulated that radical groups in every region of the world were waiting in the wings to get in on the action, the latest entry into the market being South Africa. Christopher Doyle knew better than anyone that an invasion from every corner of the globe was imminent, and that by the end of the decade, according to all current projections, an epidemic of drug use would literally explode through the next generation's workforce. What industry couldn't legitimately justify closing its factories in America, he thought, with the future so bleak. He knew the president had no choice. There was too much at stake.

"The president is not about to pull CONDOR, believe me. He's got to go forward with the test flights and have CONDOR fully operational as soon as possible."

McKnight took another drag and smashed his cigarette into an ashtray, satisfied that Doyle was thinking *his* thoughts, expressing *his* feelings about the direction in which America was heading. It was a second American revolution, as far as he was concerned, a war to bring industry back and once again return the country to a greatness it had long forgotten. He turned and looked up at the map, following, as he had done so often, the flight path of CONDOR's first mission. His voice was low and somber. "It seems so ironic, doesn't it, Chris?"

"What, that something as insignificant as a flower could destroy the greatest nation on earth?" Doyle answered. "We're such damn fools."

"In more ways than one, I'm afraid," McKnight announced. "We all thought World War II was the end of it. But it was a different world back then. Simpler. So much simpler. So much more predictable. Things could have been so different if it weren't for the damn fool bleeding hearts, building up everyone else, giving away our technology, teaching the bastards who tried to destroy us everything they needed to know to outpace us. And before we knew it, they were doing exactly what they said they would: defeat us, not militarily but economically, scoffing at us while they watched us crumble beneath our own stupidity. It's about time we go back and undo those tragic mistakes."

McKnight leaned forward and looked at Doyle with a scowl on his face that revealed the contempt and revulsion he had for every administration he felt had sold out. "You can have your goddamn Serbs, Muslims, Somalis, and Russkies. As far as I'm concerned, they can keep killing each other off until there are none of the bastards left. Me? I wanna see us take back what's ours. That's how nations become what they are. Industry. Without it they shrivel up and die or remain third-world hellholes. We're dying right now, my friend, and it doesn't matter how powerful we've been in the past. Unless we take it all back, it's over. I'm not ready to see us thrown onto the ash heap of history. Not while I'm alive, and not without a damn fight."

Doyle nodded in agreement. A political insider who'd witnessed the growing involvement of foreign governments in a rampant drug trade he envisioned the effect that that would have on every aspect of the economy and, consequently, on America's power and influence around the world. He knew damn well that McKnight was right. He also knew that economic power was inextricably linked to political and military dominance and that without it America's continued role as leader of the free world was essentially over. He wasn't ready to admit that America's best days were behind her, and he felt it a duty to ensure that that would not happen in his lifetime.

"I've got to get back to Washington," Doyle said. "I'm due at a meeting with the man in the White House within the hour. Let me know how things go later."

McKnight nodded and looked Doyle squarely in the eye. There was something behind that stare, he kept thinking. He didn't know why or how, but there was something there, something not right, something he couldn't quite put his finger on. He forced a smile and let it pass.

While Doyle got up and walked toward the elevator, McKnight remained behind, a security precaution meant to ensure that no two high-ranking members were ever seen entering or leaving headquarters at the same time.

McKnight then reached over and picked up the top-secret folder that was lying on the table next to him. He opened to page two and reviewed the list of the ten Asian cities that had been targeted as the world's heirs to nearly every industry following the collapse of the American economy. McKnight's eyes focused on the code, then the flight path, and finally on the list of cities as if burning them indelibly in his mind:

CODE: 0000612084
Flight Path: 05/04/06/07/68/19/22/03/81/40

Code	City/Country	Strike Path Sequence
T + 0	Taipei, Taiwan	5
I + 0	Inchon, South Korea	4
M + 0	Macau, China	6
B + 0	Bangkok, Thailand	7
E + 6	Kuala Lumpur, Malaysia	8
R + 1	Singapore, Singapore	9
W + 2	Yokohama, Japan	2
O + 0	Osaka, Japan	3

L + 8	**Tokyo, Japan**	**1**
F + 4	**Jakarta, Indonesia**	**10**

He saw in those ten letters and those names, not cities or buildings or people, but a growing malignancy that threatened to destabilize the entire future of America's way of life, its economy, and its historic place as the leader of a free world. He saw in those letters a disaster the likes of which no generation had seen this century.

He closed the folder and looked at his watch: 12:35 A.M. He thought ahead to the historic events that were about to unfold, lit another cigarette, and pictured in his mind the rubble of Hiroshima and Nagasaki, the squalor of Bangkok and Jakarta, and how peasants who ate little more than a bowl of rice a day were out producing middle-class Americans who drove two cars, bought homes in the suburbs, sent their kids to the best colleges in the world, and who'd spent a lifetime believing that *no one* beats American workers. *No one*. How very appropriate, he thought, that Tokyo would be the first, and Jakarta, the newest member of Asia's cadre of economic predators, would be the last to be hit by TIMBER WOLF'S stealthy but lethal power.

When ten minutes had elapsed, he left the conference room and returned to the circular lobby in the main part of the building aboveground. And after seeing that Christopher Doyle had already departed, he exited the building and walked around to a small secured warehouse where, in less than two hours, the capture of Franklin and Peterson would be accomplished and the final countdown to TIMBER WOLF would begin.

chapter thirty-eight

The intercom directly above her crackled with static, forcing Linda's eyelids open as the plane prepared for final descent into Washington International. Since taking off from Subang, her journey had been filled with terrifying nightmares of Malaysia and premonitions that made her skin crawl. Thoughts of Peter had resurfaced over and over in her fatigued mind; the entire history of her life, from her miserable childhood to the death of her parents to the tragedy near Tucson had flashed before her like sickening photographs she wished would disappear forever from her memory.

The past week seemed unreal, a bizarre dream from which she was only now beginning to awaken. Surely this would all come to an end, she thought in her semiconsciousness, the second she felt John's warm, comforting arms wrapped around her. Instinctively she reached over and felt for him, groping for what for a groggy second she knew to be his hand, then quickly recoiled when the pilot's voice came on and slapped her abruptly back into cold reality.

"We're beginning our final approach into the Washington, D.C., area at this time," the monotone voice announced. "We apologize for the turbulent flight, and we certainly hope your stay in our nation's capital is a pleasant one. Again, thanks for flying with us."

The voice cut off. Linda found herself staring at the fasten-your-seat-belt sign and trying to will herself into consciousness. At this point, she didn't know whether or not she was ready to face the reality of being back exactly where they had started.

"Linda? You awake?" John rubbed Linda's arm gently. "We're almost there." He looked at his watch and rubbed the sleep from his eyes. His body felt as if it had been overdosed with Novocain. "Twelve-forty. Hope to God Jack's waiting with a smile on his face."

Linda remained silent. A chill ran through the length of her body as she remembered the sound of Jack's voice and the feeling she'd had that something was terribly wrong. But it was too late, she thought. In just six minutes they'd be touching down, and only then would she discover whether her suspicions and anxiety were nothing more than worn nerves gone bad.

The storm had abated enough for Linda to catch glimpses of glimmering streetlights and the brightly illuminated buildings of Washington below. There was a kind of relief in knowing that at least she'd be back on familiar ground. But as she felt the plane descending and watched the city beneath her grow larger and more brilliant, she envisioned being swallowed by a total blackness from which there was no way out. Her breathing accelerated. A nervous trembling overcame her. Her clothes grew damp and clung uncomfortably to her body as if she had been suddenly transported back into the steaming jungles of central Malaysia. And then, after all they had gone through, Linda suddenly realized that her whole life—everything she had ever accomplished, everything she had ever lived for—had come down to this: a single meeting at an airline terminal that would determine whether she lived or died and how she would spend the rest of her life.

Linda gripped both armrests as flight 2237 touched down with a deep rumble and screeched against the wet runway. The plane slowed to a crawl, then turned off and taxied Twelve steadily toward gate fifty-five. Twelve forty-eight A.M. Two minutes behind schedule, she thought. Jack would be there, she prayed, hair bouncing with excitement, waving his arms and signaling that everything was okay.

When the plane grunted to a stop, Lambino stood up and, with no glance back, rushed quickly out of first class and disappeared into the airline terminal. Linda and John, meanwhile, gathered their on-board luggage and walked tentatively along the narrow aisle toward the front of the plane. Ignoring the halfhearted smiles of weary stewardesses, they stepped into the jetway tunnel and began a slow and anxious walk with no guarantee of what they'd find at the other end.

John extended his hand and took hold of Linda's as the two approached the end of the walkway and peered out. At 12:52 A.M., there wasn't much sign of life, but what Linda *did* see made her heart skip a beat. She ran to Jack, throwing her arms around his neck, forgetting for the moment that she was back in Washington and feeling in that tender embrace a warmth that assured her it was all finally coming to an end. But when she loosened her grip and lifted her head from Jack's shoulder, she saw a hint of sadness in his eyes that made her pull away.

"What's wrong, Jack?"

"Nothing," he answered. "I was worried about you . . . and I'm glad to see that you made it back, that's all." Then, like Judas himself, he kissed her cheek as though he knew he was kissing it for the last time.

"You have no idea how good it is to see you, Jack." Her smile returned, and she wrapped her arms around him again. "Let's get our bags and make it out of here. You have the car?"

"Yeah. I parked it as far out of the way as I could. Let's go."

Not more than twenty yards away, Sid Paxson, dressed in a neatly starched navy blue pilot's uniform, stood hunched over with a phone to his ear, watching every move from the corner of his eye and listening to the conversation that was being picked up by the hidden microphone in Jack's lapel. Max Grishaw had stationed himself near the rental car, waiting and listening in as well. And Lambino, who'd raced to the baggage claim area upon deplaning, was now strategically positioned for the final few minutes of surveillance before the arrest was complete.

Linda took John by the elbow and, as she pulled Jack along with her other arm, rushed confidently from the terminal gate as if nothing could possibly go wrong now. Paxson turned away, cradled the receiver, and gave the threesome enough leeway before trailing cautiously behind.

"They're on their way," he whispered into the small microphone cupped between his fingers.

"Got it," Lambino responded into his own microphone, his finger pressed against an earpiece. "Max, you read?"

"Yeah, I read you," Grishaw replied instantly. "I'm less than twenty-five yards from the car."

"Okay. Let Pilofski get behind the wheel and hold his position before you make your move. Don't do anything to scatter them. We'll make the transfer to the other vehicle as soon as we get there."

"Right."

Grishaw replaced his microphone and checked his weapon one more time. He made a visual sweep of the parking lot and was satisfied that not a soul was anywhere within a hundred yards of the arrest area. And as he slid the .45 back into his shoulder holster, he visualized ahead to his part of the assignment on this particular mission: a single bullet to the back of Pilofski's head as he walked unsuspectingly out the warehouse door.

"So tell me, Jack," Linda asked once they were clear of the airport terminal and well on their way to the deserted parking lot, "how soon is it all going to break?"

"Can't say, Linda. Could be tomorrow. Could be next week. We won't—"

"That's not good enough," Linda interrupted angrily. "It can't be next week. That may be too late. It's got to be sooner. Weren't you able to distribute the evidence to everyone we agreed on?"

"Everyone. We just have to wait and allow the documents to go through all the proper channels. They need to verify a few things, you know, make sure it's all legitimate."

"And still no clue as to what TIMBER WOLF is all about?"

"Not yet. But I'm sure there will be."

Linda noticed that Jack seemed particularly uneasy, his

voice shaky, almost quivering to the point of breaking. The sudden knot in the pit of her stomach warned her again that something was going on. As they approached the car, the knot grew into a sharp pain, then intensified when Linda thought she caught a moving shadow or something dark skulking among the parked cars. She took a few more steps and stopped, pulling John toward her. There it was again.

''Someone's over there,'' she whispered, clutching tightly to John with her hand and pointing toward a group of cars with her chin. ''It's moving . . . following us.'' She turned to Jack and saw him looking in the direction where she thought she'd seen it. ''You see it too, Jack?''

''No, there's nothing there. It's your imagination. Let's go.''

More movement. From the left this time. ''There it is again,'' Linda said, almost in a panic now. ''I want to go back to the terminal. Now.''

''I saw it, too,'' John said. ''Something's going on. I have a real bad feeling all of a sudden.''

As he said that, the dark shadows seemed to cross the parking lot and close in on them from every direction. Linda and John instinctively dropped their bags and started running back toward the terminal. Jack trailed behind, trying to keep up, calling after them. The three dodged rows of parked cars, and were not more than thirty yards into their sprint when they stopped dead in their tracks and suddenly found themselves looking directly down the barrel of a gun.

''Relax, Dr. Franklin,'' Lambino said, attempting to sound as nonthreatening as possible, while at the same time pointing the weapon squarely at her chest. ''You're perfectly safe. General McKnight wants to ask you a few questions regarding your New Hampshire crash site investigation, that's all.''

''So why the gun, then?'' Linda snapped. ''That supposed to reassure me?''

''Security. It's necessary. Orders, you know. I'm sure you understand.''

A black Town Car pulled up, driven by Sid Paxson. Max Grishaw appeared out of the blackness and, with one hand tucked inside his jacket pocket where the .45 was holstered, opened the back door with the other.

"Shall we?" Lambino pointed to the door with a fat palm up and waited for the three scientists to settle into the backseat before he and Grishaw climbed in and sat in the bench seat facing them. "Let's go, Sid." He knocked on the glass partition and turned back to Linda. "Please don't try to resist. Our orders are to bring you safely to General McKnight. I'm sure you'll want to cooperate and settle this as expeditiously as possible." He smiled as he held the gun on his lap, finger curled tightly around the trigger.

"Yeah, I suppose we have a choice whether we'd like to cooperate or not," Linda said, more brazen now that she figured there was nothing more to lose.

Lambino smiled again, seemingly amused by Linda's bravado, but didn't answer. His eyes shifted continuously from Linda, who sat opposite him, to John, who sat next to her and held her hand tightly in his.

The Town Car stopped briefly at the parking lot attendant's booth. Paxson handed the attendant a twenty, waited for change, then followed the exit signs to 395 South. Once safely on the deserted highway, the car sped nonstop toward Springfield, Virginia, where General Benjamin McKnight was anxiously awaiting their arrival.

chapter thirty-nine

"Exactly where is it you're taking us?" Linda demanded, at last breaking the deathlike quiet that had made the last thirty minutes seem more like a funeral drive.

Her question elicited no response from any of the men seated opposite her. Instead, they each sat expressionless, purposely averting their eyes and looking out at the road on either side.

A few minutes later, following another prolonged stretch of silence that had Linda convinced their meeting with General McKnight was more than simply a government debriefing, the Town Car turned sharply into the driveway of the Universal Biomedical Research Corporation. Linda glanced at her watch. Funny, she thought, that at 1:42 A.M. they'd be arriving at a pharmaceutical company. Her suspicions intensified as they drove another hundred feet to a secluded warehouse adjacent to the main building.

"This is it," Lambino announced tersely. "Where General McKnight has arranged to meet with you."

As the limo pulled up alongside the gray concrete warehouse, Grishaw and Paxson jumped out and stood by guardedly, looking right, then left, and waiting for the rest to get out. A massive steel door rolled halfway open, the interior floodlights illuminating the faces of Craven and Luppin, who now emerged and flanked the opening like overweight sentries in expensive Armani suits.

"This way, please." Lambino again extended a large hand, this time toward the opening, then followed them into the warehouse.

Linda was suddenly hit with the gut-wrenching conclusion that, although every aspect of the operation thus far had involved what appeared to be nonmilitary personnel, General McKnight would surely have selected professional soldiers to carry out his orders. What she feared now was that McKnight was acting not on orders from the Pentagon or the White House but in concert with a shadowy military organization far more powerful than even she had realized. She was sorry that she'd ever gotten off that plane in Washington.

Once inside, Lambino ordered everyone to march straight ahead. "That's far enough," he demanded. Craven slid the door closed behind them and locked it.

Linda made an about-face and looked Lambino squarely in his unblinking eyes. Behind him, she saw that Craven and Luppin had posted themselves on either side of the impenetrable door while Max Grishaw positioned himself in front of it and between the two. Sid Paxson, feet apart, hands clasped in front of him, stood guard twenty feet off to the right.

Linda and John were now surrounded, feeling as helpless as convicted felons at their own executions and, by the looks and presence of McKnight's people, were perceptive enough to know that the setup had been well planned and orchestrated with the help of someone who knew everything.

"Dr. Franklin."

The deep voice, resonating from in the immense warehouse, made Linda's head snap around in search of its origin. Squinting, she caught sight of a shadowed figure emerging from the bright floodlights to her left, walking slowly toward her, his hands placed casually behind the small of his back.

"We finally meet," he growled softly with a thick Georgian accent. "You caused us considerable grief." And as he said that, he walked past Jack and greeted *him* in a way that nearly tore Linda's heart out. "Well done, Jack. Well done."

Linda's eyes tore away from McKnight and turned now to the man she thought was the closest friend she'd had since Peter died. But rather than feeling anger or hatred, she felt a deep sense of betrayal and a revulsion. She looked away and shut her eyes, tears streaming down her cheeks as she searched the depths of her soul for a reason, any reason, why someone she'd loved like a brother would do this to her. She took a deep breath, wiped her tears away, then faced McKnight to ask him what she believed would be the final question she would ever ask.

"Why? Why are you doing this?"

McKnight shook his head as though he couldn't believe she didn't know. He ordered Lambino and the other men to the other side of the warehouse, away from earshot, then looked Linda straight in the eye with a look that sent a tremor through her very being. She had every right to know, he figured. Despite his cold heart, this fastidious military man, with an unrelenting hatred for anyone who got in the way of his mission to save the country, had a deep admiration for guts. And Linda, in her own amateurish way, had been able to get farther than even *he* thought she could, against the best in world.

"Because, Dr. Franklin," he said softly enough for the others not to hear, "this country's on the verge of total collapse . . . economic catastrophe . . . social decay of biblical proportions."

"I don't understand."

"There's not much to understand," McKnight countered disparagingly. "We're being destroyed by foreign governments we know are flooding our streets with new drugs, while at the same time our industrial base is being eroded day by day. We're being transformed from a nation that had produced everything it ever needed to survive into a nation that'll produce nothing. We can't even build a goddamn weapons system without Japanese microchips, for God's sake. By the next decade, our warplanes will be built by the South Koreans. Our goddamn *war*planes!"

He looked at her blank expression with growing scorn. "You have no idea, do you? No idea whatsoever. People like you, Dr. Franklin—naively idealistic—have allowed all this to happen. While politicians and social architects like those damn idiots in Congress and the White House are moving this country toward anarchy and economic ruin, formulating trade policies and social programs that work only on paper and in their own minds, you're oblivious to everything around you. And then you have the audacity to try and interfere with us, with a mission that will bring back our industrial base and protect America's future—America's vital national security, not to say anything of its way of life."

"But you can't just—"

"Can't?" McKnight interrupted. "Can't? In less than ten years, ninety percent of all high-tech products will be controlled by Asia. Low-tech jobs are being transferred to Mexico and Latin America at an unprecedented rate. Services like computer programming, banking, and communications are going to India, Ireland, and God knows where the hell else. Everything this country has built is disappearing, and we're heading toward bankruptcy because no one wants to open their eyes and see what's coming."

"And building a wall around this country is going to make it better?" Linda posed, trying to understand the man's motivation and perhaps find a way out of her predicament.

"What do we do with our people when there are no more jobs for them, Dr. Franklin? Put 'em all on welfare? What do we do when they start rioting in the streets because they can't afford a car or three meals a day? Fill up our prisons? And then what do we do when our tax base is so small that we accumulate enough national debt to make it impossible to ever pay off? You know damn well that the owners of that debt are gonna call it in. What do we do then? Say 'we're sorry, but how 'bout taking all our oil and mineral reserves instead? How 'bout our national parks or the revenues from our highway system?' Maybe give 'em Hawaii or Guam? We can't go on like this. From an economic and national security standpoint, it's suicide."

"You're crazy," Linda said. "You can't possibly think you'll get away with this."

McKnight smiled and shook his head. The smile quickly gave way to a pained look that, more than anything, revealed the disgust he felt toward her and her ilk. "Get away with it? People like you, Dr. Franklin, make me want to puke, because you sit back as if you don't give a shit or are too inept to realize it, and then you watch it all happen. Didn't you suspect a revolution was coming? Were people like you stupid enough to think we'd allow this country to be dismantled piece by piece by the likes of those fools in Washington? We tried our damnedest to change things from within, to work with the system, to try and make these people understand. Apparently it wasn't enough. Nothing seemed to be enough. So now we're being destroyed by leaders who either don't know what the hell they're doing or don't care that what they *are* doing is goddamn treason."

He then turned away and nodded. "Desperate times require desperate measures, I'm afraid."

Lambino immediately walked over and positioned himself

behind Linda, screwing a silencer into his .45 and holding it at his side until the order would officially be given.

"I can't say I'm sorry to have to do this," McKnight continued. "There's too much at stake. Too much to do." He nodded at Lambino again, who now lifted his gun and placed it a few inches from Linda's head.

Linda grabbed John's hand and pulled him toward her, nearly collapsing in his arms. Everything around her was suddenly moving in slow motion. Images of death, more ugly and vile than any she'd ever experienced, swirled through her mind. She then closed her eyes and readied herself to take the bullet that would end her life. And as she held her breath, expecting to feel the sharp sting of metal tearing through her head, a shot rang out and echoed violently through the emptiness of the warehouse.

Linda tensed as if frozen in place, thinking that it had been John who got it first, releasing his hand instantly and waiting for him to drop limply to the floor. Her eyes shut tightly, she prayed that the next second would be quick enough so that it would all be over in an instant.

But then, two more rapid shots were fired, followed by a series of thuds. She opened her eyes. Her mouth dropped open as she saw Lambino stretched out on the floor next to her in a growing pool of blood.

"What the—" She turned in Jack's direction and saw him holding a gun tightly in his hand. Spinning to her right, she then saw Paxson pointing *his* gun at Craven, whose hands were lifted in an act of surrender, and Grishaw and Luppin, who themselves were now lying dead on the warehouse floor, guns held loosely in their limp fingers.

It had all happened in a few seconds.

And then, as McKnight tried to reach into his jacket, a gun suddenly appeared and was pressed against his temple.

"Don't try it, fat boy," Jack said. "I've been waiting a long time for this and I wouldn't think twice about putting a bullet through your big head."

"You have no idea what the hell you're doing!" McKnight yelled, his face twisting into the appearance of Satan himself. "You idiot! You've ruined everything. Don't you realize that? Everything. You're a fool. A goddamn fool."

"Yeah, yeah, call me whatever you want, just don't call me anymore. And I wouldn't be expecting any of your friends to bail you outta this one. It's over, General. It's been nice. Real nice."

Linda felt her knees buckle as she watched Jack remove a .38 from General McKnight's jacket and hand it to her. Dazed, she took it, still speechless. Jack then slid a small transmitter out of his sock and placed it to his lips.

"You guys pick up our signal?"

"Yeah, we got you," the voice coming from the transmitter responded. "Everything okay down there?"

"Everything's fine," Jack answered, looking over at Linda and breaking into a smile. "A little too close for comfort, but fine. We'll hold 'em till you get here. Look for Universal Biomedical Research Corporation."

"No shit! I wouldn't have suspected that's where it was."

"We're in the warehouse adjacent to the main building."

"Got it. We're on our way."

Jack shoved the microphone into his pocket and twirled McKnight around, pushing him over to Craven and ordering them both to the floor while Sid Paxson kept a gun trained on them. When he turned and walked back to Linda and John, he let out a heavy sigh of relief and said, "I guess I owe you one hell of an explanation."

A weak nod was about all Linda could manage, though she felt like grabbing Jack by his neck and strangling him for what he'd just put them through. Sensing that, Jack took hold of Linda's hands and pulled her into his arms, rubbing her back gently and allowing her a few seconds to compose herself. And for the first time since leaving Washington, Linda felt a security she didn't believe she'd ever experience again, but at the same time she felt a deep pain in her heart because she sensed that Jack was about to tell her something she didn't want to hear.

"You're going to tell me Peter was involved in all this, aren't you?" she asked, releasing herself from Jack's embrace and leaning against a wooden crate behind her. "And I suppose you're also going to tell me you've been in on this from the start."

"I'm sorry, Linda. I know this will be hard to accept or believe, but you need to know."

"I'm listening." Linda stared past Jack without expression as he began recounting what to her was an almost impossible tale of intrigue and deception.

"What you stumbled across was a plot to reestablish world order with psychochemical weapons," Jack explained. "McKnight, along with a group of self-proclaimed, so-called patriots, decided to take matters into his own hands, to reverse what he saw as America's inevitable economic and social decline. He figured the only way to do that—since *we* weren't doing anything about it—was to decimate the populations responsible for it."

"The man's a damn psychopath," Linda whispered as she turned toward McKnight and glared at him.

"A brilliant one at that," Jack added. "He used everyone and everything at his disposal to divert funding for his mission."

"What about the research center?" Linda asked.

"McKnight and his people truly believed we were on the brink of a national disaster. Their plan was to turn the tables and destroy the workforces of the nations that were going to replace America as the new home to the world's industries. By diverting millions—and with the government, that's not hard to do—they were able to smuggle out and replicate a technology that could literally wipe out entire populations. And because of their military positions, they could easily use CONDOR to do it. To them, it was no different than using nuclear weapons in defense of national security. This *was* a matter of utmost national security."

"And that's where Peter comes in?" Linda asked, the look in her eyes a telling sign of how painful she knew the answer would be.

"Peter was a brilliant scientist who unknowingly and unfortunately got caught up in something he was totally unprepared for. He was recruited by Adam Wesely."

"Adam," Linda mouthed, shaking her head, not surprised at anything at this point.

"Yeah. Adam had a daughter, you know, a North Vietnamese daughter. He loved her very much. Kept in contact with her and wanted desperately to bring her to the States. But the fact that he knowingly associated with and had relations with a Vietcong during the height of the war would have destroyed his career and his life. Trumped-up charges that as an officer he collaborated with the enemy didn't help either. They set him up to look like a damn spy. May as well have put a bullet in his head. One of his assignments was to recruit a top scientist, someone close to him that he could keep an eye on and who had access to the top-secret biotechnology you uncovered in Malaysia, someone who unknowingly but willingly had an affair with a phony KGB agent who threatened to expose him if he didn't cooperate."

"Peter."

"I'm sorry, Linda. Peter was able to smuggle out plans of the technology for Dr. Vijan piece by piece until a duplicate laboratory was set up for complete production of the genetically engineered agent. Vijan himself was one of the top U.S. government scientists working on the project during its early development. He was a genius, but an arrogant and greedy bastard who wanted recognition and desperately wanted money. Wesely saw that as a good combination, and he promised him both. Didn't take much for Vijan to defect. Problem was he defected before the critical portion of the work was complete and he needed an inside man who could get him what was required to duplicate the new biotechnology."

Linda wiped the tears from her eyes, trying to keep from breaking down. "What about Adam? Why did he have to die?"

I suppose he'd finally had enough and didn't feel he had anything to live for anymore. He couldn't live with himself any longer and was about to turn himself and everyone else in. That's when they killed him."

"Even if Peter *was* being blackmailed . . . even if he *did* have an affair, he wouldn't be a part of anything like this if he knew what this technology would be used for."

"Believe me, he didn't know. Very few individuals knew about CONDOR, much less psychochemical warfare. It was so secret that most of the top scientists working on the project didn't know exactly what the applications would ultimately be. They assumed their work was defensive in nature, that it would lead to antidotes against new recombinant biological weapons being developed at the time by the Soviets. The government got suspicious when a standard security check showed that Peter had deposited a large amount of money in a Swiss bank account. They suspected he was selling what he thought could be used simply for medical and pharmaceutical purposes. By then it was too late. Much of the biotechnology had already been transferred. That's when I came in. I couldn't very well admit to you that an intelligence agent with a Ph.D. was brought in to track it down, to find out where it had gone. I know we became best friends, Linda, but I couldn't take the chance."

Linda buried her face in her hands and rubbed her eyes, trying to comprehend something that to her was incomprehensible. "I never even suspected," she whispered. "Never had a clue. Why did he have to die?"

"He found out."

"About what?"

"About McKnight's involvement in CONDOR and TIMBER WOLF. Peter accidentally stumbled across some documents containing details of something we're only now beginning to uncover. He was shocked to find out that he'd been recruited to work on what was the successor project to MKULTRA."

"So it *is* true. John was right."

"Peter couldn't believe what he'd done," Jack continued. "What he was involved in. He found out that TIMBER WOLF was an acronym for cities targeted for attack by CONDOR."

"My God, April sixth."

"Yeah. When he confronted Adam with the evidence, he was told that he was in so deep there was no way out. Besides threatening to kill *him*, they threatened to kill *you*, Linda. You. That's why he kept quiet. To protect *you*. You've got to understand that."

"Then why Arizona? Why the accident?"

"With the eighty-eight CONDOR crash, McKnight saw a perfect opportunity to eliminate someone who knew too much. They figured Peter's work was done. They got what they needed out of him. I'm sorry, Linda. Peter did what he had to do to keep you alive, but he had no idea that his actions would have had such profound consequences. He was a good man."

"Then why the hell did it take so long to get these bastards? Why eight years, Jack?" Tears streamed down her face now.

"When Peter died, it was as though everything shut down. Everyone went underground. They already had most of what they wanted. Vijan took care of the rest. I tried everything to get the goods on Adam, on the organization behind all this, but it was futile. So the government had to try something bold."

"Bold?"

"That's right. They planted some false KGB information about my family that would make me a prime candidate for blackmail and coercion. Fortunately, McKnight bit. He used the information to recruit me as an informant and eventually to get to you. Meanwhile, as a double agent, I continued trying to find anything that would lead me to their secret lab and to this place. There was nothing until Brittan, New Hampshire. And when you began linking the two crashes and started uncovering evidence, we knew we finally had the break we were looking for. The only problem was keeping you alive and safe and figuring out a way to use you to find out where the secret labs were and where Vanguard headquarters was located. Until we found that, we had nothing."

"So you used me. Dr. Franklin, unsuspecting secret agent. I can't believe how convincing you were. I could have been killed. You strung me along like a kid on a damned scavenger hunt.''

''Had to, Linda. They were going to kill you, believe me. There was no other way.''

''No other way? You couldn't trust me enough to let me in on everything from the start?''

''I couldn't blow my cover, and I had to allow your investigation to take its course. Hell, at times I felt like I was up for the Academy Award. We knew about the biotechnology and the possibility that it was going to be used, but we didn't know how or when or that it was CONDOR they were going to use to deliver the agent. We needed you to set the trap.''

''I could've been killed in Malaysia or at the airport, for Christ's sake!''

''No,'' Jack reassured her. ''I was always there for you if anything went wrong. Sid was there with you in Malaysia and would've stepped in if something went wrong or if you were in any kind of danger. I swear to you, Linda, I knew for a fact they wouldn't risk killing you until they were absolutely sure you turned over every piece of evidence you found.''

''What about the film? How did you develop it and make copies without anyone knowing?''

''We knew I was being watched and followed. So when I brought the film back to my apartment, I developed it, then copied it next door in an apartment we secured for just that purpose. After I left for my meeting with McKnight, they searched my apartment and found nothing but the developing equipment. One of our men spent the rest of the day Xeroxing the evidence. The president himself is probably studying a copy right now. It's over.''

Jack saw the trace of a smile beginning to grow on Linda's face. He reacted with his own. ''That's better,'' he said. ''It's been a helluva ride, hasn't it?''

''The president himself?'' Linda asked.

Jack nodded. ''The evidence you sent us was all there, but the last piece of the puzzle was finding out where the secret headquarters was located. We've been looking for this place for years and needed you to lead us to it. It's a gold mine of evidence."

At that moment, Linda heard the sound of choppers overhead and the screeching of brakes outside the warehouse.

"Sounds like the cavalry's here," Jack said. "Mission accomplished. You're a hero, Linda."

"And what about you? Do you just go back to the lab with me and continue on as if none of this ever happened?"

Jack suddenly lost his smile and shook his head, turning away and looking out at the open warehouse as he spoke. "Afraid not, Linda. I won't be going back, and neither will you."

"What do you mean?" Linda flew off the wooden crate and grabbed Jack's arms, twisting him around. "What do you mean not going back?"

"We received word that several of McKnight's people have disappeared. They'll blame you for this, Linda, and they'll hold you responsible for killing the mission."

"So what now? And what about you?"

"Until we find them—if we ever do—you won't be safe for a single moment. Me? I've gotta disappear for a while."

At that moment, the warehouse doors flew open. Agents poured in and spread out in every direction, their weapons drawn. One of them walked directly to Jack and extended his hand. "Great work, Jack. We've got an army next door tearing that building apart, gathering enough evidence to put these guys—and maybe a few senators—away for life. We just got word that our security teams around the country are rounding up most of those involved. Our people in Malaysia have located the other lab. The plan was nearly flawless, Jack, except for some of McKnight's key people, the slippery bastards. I'm sure they're out of the country by now."

The agent then turned and offered his hand to Linda. "We owe you a great deal, Dr. Franklin. Sorry we had to do it this way, but we had no choice. It was a matter of grave national security. The president has ordered this investigation classified top-secret umbra. It never happened. As far as you're concerned, there's no such thing as CONDOR or a psychochemical agent. And you've never set foot in Malaysia in your life. Naturally you're bound to secrecy by your national security oath for the remainder of your life or until such time—if there is a time—that the information is made public. Of course you know that. You'll be supplied with a new identity, plastic surgery, if you like, a lifetime salary. We'll make arrangements for you to settle in whatever part of the world you'd like. Jack here will help with those arrangements as soon as we process you. There's a car waiting to take you to a temporary facility.'' He said that as indifferently as if he'd said it a hundred times before. Probably had.

As the agent turned and went back to his team, Jack walked over to John and shook his hand. He smiled and, with a sadness in his voice, said, ''Have a good life, my friend. You're a good guy and I'm glad I got to know you. You're damn lucky they considered you a bit player who happened to get sucked into this through no fault of his own. Otherwise you'd be on your way out of Washington yourself.''

''Will I ever see you again?'' John asked.

''Maybe our paths'll cross again when we least expect. Then we can talk about old times.'' He slapped John on the side of the arm and turned back to Linda, who had tears in her eyes.

''There's something you're not telling me, Jack,'' she whispered as she looked deeply into his eyes and knew at once that there was. ''I know it. Tell me, please.''

Jack hesitated for a moment. But the sadness that now overcame him would not be enough to weaken him into revealing what else he knew. ''There's nothing more,'' he said. ''Hey, c'mon. Could be worse. You could still be in Malaysia.''

She tried to force a laugh but found it too difficult to hold back the tears that came pouring from her eyes. She hadn't expected this. Not in a million years. Not after what she'd been through. ''Always joking,'' she said. ''Even to the very end. Give me some time alone with John.''

''Sure. Take all the time you need.''

Linda couldn't believe her life had come to this. That in less than two weeks, she'd gone from brilliant scientist and senior NASA investigator, her whole future ahead of her, to a fugitive with no guarantee that she'd ever be able to show her face again. She'd lost one love already, albeit an unfaithful one, and as she looked over at John, she realized that once she left Washington she would probably never see him again.

''I can't believe this is happening,'' she said, sobbing. ''After all this . . . after everything we've done, gone through . . . I can't believe I'm losing you. I wish they'd have killed me.''

''What the hell are you talking about?'' John asked.

''Didn't you hear? It's over. My career . . . my life . . . us. They want me to disappear, maybe permanently. We may never see each other again.''

''You've gotta be kidding.'' John took hold of Linda's arms and shook her gently. ''You actually thought I'd go back to my life and let you get away from me? Just like that? Leave me behind in this rotten excuse for a city? No way, sweetheart.''

Linda's face flushed, then broke into a wide grin as she threw her arms around John and kissed him. She stroked his face and stared into his eyes, no longer caring about what might lie ahead, knowing only that John was willing to give up everything he had for her.

''What will we do, John? Where will we go?''

''I happen to know of this beautiful little place up in Maine. White picket fence, porch, nice church down the street to get married in, enough land for a couple of kids to run around on. Maybe not as exciting as traipsing halfway round the world, but—''

''Sounds absolutely perfect,'' Linda interrupted. She wrapped her arms around John's neck and kissed him tenderly, knowing she'd found in John the love she so desperately longed for ever since her life had ended in that Arizona desert so long ago.

They stood facing each other, and in an instant they both realized that, more than anyone else, *they* were responsible for creating a new world, a better world, but that ironically the price they would now have to pay for their noble efforts was separation from everything they'd known for the rest of their lives.

They had each other, and that was all they needed, all that mattered. They walked together through the warehouse door and looked back at Jack. And as if they knew they would never see him again, they turned and, with a final wave good-bye, vanished quietly into a cold Virginia night.

chapter forty

Jack stood for a moment in the emptiness of that vast space, reflecting nostalgically on the past eight years and thinking how empty his life suddenly had become. There it was, just like that. Since coming to Washington, Linda had been the closest thing to family he had left, and now even *she* was gone. Then remembering what it was like before he'd met her, the emptiness gave way to the bitterness of knowing he might never see her again. So much for happy endings.

He watched his friends walk through the steel door and disappear from sight, then made an about-face and marched quickly to the far end of the warehouse. He slipped through a back door and was met immediately by a dark sedan that pulled up and came screeching to a halt in front of him. The black door swung open. Jack stepped in and settled into a seat next to Christopher Doyle.

"Good work, Jack. Damn good work. We couldn't be

more pleased. The president sends his congratulations . . . anonymously, of course.''

''Of course. Thank you, sir.''

''Has everything been arranged for Dr. Franklin?''

''Yes, sir. Peterson decided he'll be going with her. I'm glad about that. I'm sure they'll be okay wherever they decide to go.'' And then, resting his head against the back of the seat, ''That was the hardest goddamn thing I ever had to do, lying to Linda like that. There's no possibility we can tell her the truth?''

''What, that Dr. Franklin's still alive? Hell no.'' Doyle's eyes widened into dark saucers at the very possibility. ''He knew the deal going in. He disappears without a trace, forgetting everything he knows about CONDOR and the agent, and Linda Franklin stays alive. She's the best insurance policy we have.''

''And there's no other way?''

''As long as she's alive—and that's precisely why she *has* to be protected—Peter Franklin stays dead, receives immunity, and keeps his mouth shut. No, let's not even open the goddamn book on that one, Jack.''

''What about your boy, McKnight? You know damn well he's the one who had Wesely killed. Damn near killed all of *us*. How are you gonna ensure he's not heard from again?''

''He's served his purpose well,'' Doyle answered, looking straight ahead and breaking into a smile before turning serious again. ''A casualty of a cruel war we all know too well. And thanks to Dr. Franklin, a perfect scapegoat for future U.S. government covert operations. Damn fool was so obsessed with taking out half the planet, he never suspected a thing . . . went too far. A man like McKnight is too dangerous to have around. He knows too much and can't be trusted. No, I think we can make sure he's never heard from again. Besides, we can't take the risk that this Gulf War thing will come out and interfere with our upcoming mission. Hell, can you imagine what the reaction would be if it were made public that the government sat by and knowingly allowed Iraq to buy weapons of mass destruction we weren't even supposed to be making ourselves? And worse, that we sent troops, knowing all along that every damn gas mask used in Desert Storm would be useless against those weapons? It won't matter a goddamn that most of us had no idea what was going on. All hell would break loose. No, I wanna be dead long before any of *that* ever comes out."

"And the lab?"

Doyle glanced down at his watch. "Stealth bombers will be overhead in approximately thirty minutes. There'll be a fire storm in that jungle the likes of which no one in those parts has ever seen. They'll be lucky to find a brick intact."

"You believe the diversion was completely successful?" Jack asked.

"Flawless," Doyle answered without hesitation. "Not even our people at the Pentagon have any idea. By this time tomorrow, everyone from the Joint Chiefs of Staff on down will think it's over. Letting McKnight think his mission was safely under way definitely helped our overall strategy. I have to admit, it was brilliant. Allow McKnight to divert funds for his research center, let him think he's using CONDOR for his own purposes, then blame *him* for what's coming, should that become necessary. It's perfect."

"And the president?"

"It's a no-brainer, Jack. The president's willing to do whatever it takes—and I mean *whatever* it takes, even if it means sacrificing himself in the process, to see this through. He's already given the order for countdown, and he's prepared to be held accountable for the consequences. Naturally, he'd like to stay out of the loop as much as possible from this moment on . . . for deniability purposes. The operation will be conducted and coordinated from Red Devil Mountain."

Jack looked out the sedan's darkened window, took a last glance at the Universal Biomedical Research Center, and thought back to everything he and Linda had gone through. It all seemed like such a charade, such a lie. He felt like crying, but kept it in. He turned back to Christopher Doyle, who was pouring himself a scotch on the rocks, and asked, "Is everything still on schedule?"

"It was damn close, Jack. Damn close."

Doyle then held out a manila folder, which Jack took and removed from it a top-secret memo.

* * * * * * *

Top Secret—Eyes Only

* * * * * * *

Eyes Only **Copy One of One**

SUBJECT: WORLD ORDER/CONDOR MISSION TARGETS
DOCUMENT PREPARED: MARCH 18, 1996

* * * * * * *

At 0500 hours, 2 April 1996, attacks will be launched simultaneously from the Roswell and Desert Flats air bases on all designated target areas. CONDOR from Roswell will deliver agent to selected drug regions and financial centers in Afghanistan, Iran, Pakistan, Burma, and Cambodia. The Desert Flats crew will follow up with attacks on Colombia, Bolivia, Venezuela, Peru, and Argentina. Raids will continue for ninety-six hours to ensure complete depopulation of all targeted areas linked to the growth, production, and distribution of narcotics into the United States.

Simultaneous covert operations will be conducted by special forces in Medellin, Bogota, Cali, Panama, Mexico City, Tijuana, Guadalajara, Islamabad, Kabul, Rangoon, and Bangkok. Assassination of every major drug lord operating from those cities should complete the disruption of all drug flow.

At this time, all assets are being identified for seizure. If necessary, follow-up attacks will be ordered on areas reporting less than 100 percent success rates. All known existing drug traffic routes will be sealed, and remaining drugs in the pipeline confiscated. The Department of Defense is on standby at all embassies in target areas. The

National Guard is on alert and will be called out to maintain order once drug flow into the country ceases. A total communications blackout is in effect immediately.

* * * * * * *

Top Secret—Eyes Only

When Jack finished reading, he stuck the memo into the folder and handed it back to Doyle, a look of gloom spreading across his face.

"Jack, I know how you're feeling," Doyle said, seeing the anguish in Jack's eyes. "Forget it. Let it go. We'll handle the Gulf War thing in our own way. We're discouraging any scientific inquiries and investigations, and hopefully the epidemic will begin to kill itself off as the last of the infected veterans die. I hate to sound so damn callous, but this is better than allowing a major foreign policy blunder to affect the future of this country."

"There are treatments out there. You know it and I know it. And the poor bastards are being sacrificed for the sake of a mission, for the sake of national security."

"Not just a mission, Jack. World order. It's not like we're killing innocent people. We're eliminating the scum of the earth. I don't give a shit if they're starving peasants, presidents, or kings. These people are directly responsible for destroying this country, for poisoning our children and devastating our economy. The very fabric of our society is being torn apart, for Christ's sake. Asia, from what CIA tells us, is using drugs to systematically cripple us from within. South America doesn't give a shit and would just as soon watch us collapse as a nation than see us maintain hemisphere dominance. And the entire Mexican government, as you damn well know, is nothing more than a front for three quarters of the drugs flowing into the country. It's a goddamn invasion from two fronts, and I'm afraid our people in Washington have known about it for a long time. Used it very effectively, I might add, whenever they needed a large infusion of cash for one of their goddamn secret operations. Didn't faze 'em a bit that they were sacrificing Americans in the process."

"I always thought it would've been the economy that triggered this," Jack said.

"Hell, it's bad enough we're losing our economy," Doyle spit back. "Add drugs to the equation and we're dead as a society."

"And what makes you think eliminating that part of the equation is gonna do anything to reverse the overall trend? Deindustrialization, as far as Washington and Wall Street are concerned, is a foregone conclusion. We're losing it faster than we ever thought possible, and while we wage our savage war on drugs, every industry we have is crumbling away."

"One step at a time, Jack. One step at a time. Phase two of WORLD ORDER is on standby, and we'll damn sure use it if we have to. In the meantime, anything that would undermine this mission is to be kept absolutely classified, even if it means withholding information that might save a few lives but, in the process, create a situation in which our going forward is compromised."

Doyle then looked out the window and, with a melancholy that settled across his face, stared deeply into space and remembered his own son, who, at the hands of the murderous scum he was seeking revenge on now, had died from an overdose at the innocent age of sixteen. He had sworn, at the moment he laid his eyes on the casket, that he would never rest until this war was finally won.

"Twenty years I've stood by, Jack, watching us lose the war on drugs, watching the most productive workers in the world become goddamn zombies, watching children die—watching my own son die—witnessing the crime rate skyrocket to proportions unthinkable in civilized society. I wondered when in the hell we were really going to do something about it. Thought that maybe the nineties would have slapped some sense into them. It didn't. And so this is it, Jack. No more games. All out war. No prisoners. No survivors. Just a guarantee that we finally win. Everything else will fall into place. Our economy, our society, our freedom from those who'd see us die as a nation. So you know as well as I do that the next week will determine whether America lives or dies, whether we continue to be the greatest nation and economic superpower in the world or end up becoming a wasteland. Do you understand what this means, Jack?''

As the sedan drove through the compound gates and toward Washington, D.C., Jack's only thoughts were not of America or of a final, devastating war that would once and for all put an end to what many knew was the greatest scourge on the face of the earth, but of Linda and Peter and how he had it in his power to tell them everything but couldn't.

This was war. The greatest war ever to be waged by the greatest nation on earth. A war he knew in his heart would reverse the decline of America's society and decide the economic future of America well into the next century. A war to be waged with the same ferocity that all wars must be waged if absolute victory is to be achieved. As codeveloper of an agent that was about to wipe out entire populations, he knew the devastation that targeted nations would experience only days from now.

Tears formed in his eyes. He looked straight ahead at the Lincoln Memorial in the far distance, at the Washington Monument beyond it, and knew that, for better or worse, no matter what happened, no matter what this new world order would ultimately accomplish, neither he nor his country would ever be the same again.

''Yes, sir, I understand,'' Jack said. ''I understand perfectly.''

epilogue

DECEMBER 24, 1998

Winters in Maine were typically hard and bitter. This one, by anyone's measure, was certainly no exception. In fact, the previous two summers in Caribou had been followed quickly by the shortest autumns in recent memory, providing no more than fleeting transitions from delightfully warm springs that painted the picturesque countryside with brush stokes of vivid color to winters so grim and violently cold it seemed as if the polar icecaps themselves had drifted several hundred miles south and settled on Maine's northernmost doorstep.

It had been more than two long years since Linda and John left everything behind them and disappeared into the government's most secret witness protection program. But unlike the programs offered by the Justice or the State Departments, this one guaranteed refuge in an invisibly harsh world so far apart from the rest of society that it seemed as if the witnesses, for want of a better description, were literally sucked out of existence. Normally, those who'd been offered such protection were allowed to have jobs, but little else. Contact with neighbors was permitted, but participation in anything other than such innocuous activities as the PTA or garden club was strictly forbidden. The lower the profile the better, even if that meant living the sheltered life of a recluse.

John had opened a small grocery store about a year ago and that, along with a generous stipend offered by the government, was enough to allow them a comfortable living. Linda, who even before the start of their exile, had grown tired of the rigors of her career and the demanding role of senior scientist for a top-secret agency, had taken a position as assistant librarian at the local branch of Caribou's tiny library. The pay was pitifully meager, but the solitude, which she found almost intoxicatingly serene, and the companionship of her many books, were enough to satisfy her needs. And as long as she knew that John would be home waiting for her and that she could find instant comfort in the embrace of his loving arms, nothing else seemed to matter.

Townsfolk in those parts were nice enough, though they kept mostly to themselves and expected as much from their laconic neighbors. Sundays were usually occupied by daylong church picnics and family get togethers. The rest of the week was taken up by work and occasional evenings at the local bowling alley, movie theater, or bingo hall. Rarely did an event stir the excitement that a local parade or the appearance of a campaigning politician would. In Caribou, more than any other place in America, it seemed, people were down to earth. No one thought to ask questions, nor figured it was their business to pry into anyone's private life, and that was exactly why Caribou had been chosen in the first place.

Shortly after they'd taken up residence in this town of nearly ten thousand, Linda and John began hearing occasional stories on the evening news of civil wars in regions of the world where drugs were a major cash crop. Most of the stories were purportedly nothing more than rumors or vague eyewitness accounts from less than reliable sources. But there'd also been leaked reports of entire villages destroyed, their inhabitants driven to murder by violent rampages, cartel leaders killed, supply lines disrupted as a result of a dramatic rise in regional conflicts. It seemed that everywhere one looked, there was evidence of widespread but suspiciously targeted violence that had created an enormous vacuum in the world's heroin and cocaine networks.

What was even more surprising, albeit pleasantly so, was that the sudden increase in this phenomenon was accompanied by a concomitantly rapid American economic resurgence. Crime rates had fallen precipitously two years in a row; productivity was at the highest level in decades; industrial plants were returning to the States in record numbers; welfare rolls were shrinking at the same time employment was rising; and school systems were reporting a significant decline in violent crime and truancy. It was almost as though someone had finally realized that, although a number of factors are responsible for how a society evolves, the wholesale destruction of the drug trade would contribute so much to the rebirth of an entire nation.

The government, only recently, had also admitted that a series of mysterious illnesses, collectively termed Gulf War syndrome, was real and caused by exposure to biological agents sold to Iraq by a rogue pharmaceutical company named Universal Biomedical. Reports confirmed that those responsible for the transfer of weapons had either escaped from the United States, died, or were being held for prosecution under the 1972 Biological Weapons Convention, which prohibited the development, production, and stockpiling of biological and toxin weapons. The United States government, it was concluded, had absolutely no information regarding the production, sale, or transfer of any such weapons systems to Iraq at any time. It was also learned that many of the Gulf War veterans infected with *Mycoplasma incognitus*, the bacterium that was an integral part of the germ warfare program, could be treated successfully with doxycycline, essentially putting an end to whatever suspicions there had been regarding U.S. government involvement.

On the evening news, anchor-man Brent Scanlan was just about to cut away to the last commercial when Linda nearly dropped her coffee at the sound of a knock at the door. Despite being away from Washington for more than two years, the threat of somehow being discovered was still very much on her mind. She placed her coffee cup on the lamp stand, eased off the couch, and proceeded cautiously to the door. She pushed the curtain aside ever so slightly, looked out the side window, and for a brief moment, stood frozen in place, staring at the figure waiting on the front porch and finding it hard to believe her eyes.

"John, come in here, quick!" she yelled back toward the kitchen.

John rushed into the foyer with a handgun clenched in his fingers just as Linda was opening the door. He watched in disbelief as she ran out onto the porch and nearly jumped into the outstretched arms of Jack Pilofski.

"My God," she said, "I never thought I'd ever see you again. What are you doing here?"

"Figured three Christmases in a row without seeing you would be unforgivable." Jack loosened himself from her grip, then reached down and picked up a box that was wrapped neatly in silver and green and topped with a large red bow that Linda just knew he had to have tied himself. "Merry Christmas," he said with a smile and a reminiscent look in his eyes that made Linda begin to weep.

Linda took the box from his hands while John greeted Jack with a bear hug that lifted him two inches from the porch floor. "Come on in you son of a gun," he said, putting Jack down and leading him into the house. "Lemme get you some coffee. You look half frozen."

When his coat was off, Jack blew into his cupped hands to remove the chill and looked around approvingly at the warm home that Linda had made for herself. He nodded and said, "I love it, I really do. You did really good, despite . . ."

"Thanks, Jack. We're doing just fine, if that's what you're concerned about. Are you? Is that why you're here?"

"No, I'm—"

And before he could answer, he looked over at John who was coming in holding a tray with three cups of coffee. Trailing right behind John was the loveliest two year old he had ever seen. "Don't tell me," he said, a grin exploding across his face.

"That's Rachel," Linda answered. "Beautiful, isn't she?"

Jack bent down and picked up the little angel, kissing her cheek like he would a niece he'd suddenly discovered and fallen in love with the instant he looked at the deep green eyes and silky brown hair that reminded him so much of her mother. When he put her down, he grabbed a coffee cup and made his way to a La-Z-Boy next to the fireplace. Linda and John followed, anxious to hear news from Washington, even more anxious to know exactly why it was that Jack was here. Rachel climbed onto Linda's lap and laid her head serenely against her mother's bosom.

"Good news and bad news," Jack said, taking a quick sip of hot coffee and placing the cup gently on the saucer next to him.

"Tell us the good news," John said as he positioned himself behind Linda and placed his hands on her shoulders. "I'll let you know if we even want to hear the bad news."

"Fair enough. You'll be happy to know that McKnight's key people have been located. After the raid in Virginia, many of 'em scattered. Took a while to track 'em down but we got 'em. McKnight, of course, was court-martialed, convicted of murder, treason, et cetera, then died mysteriously about a year later. Suicide they say. It's always suicide, it seems. Three senators and five congressmen are currently serving life sentences. A few more may be indicted if the evidence holds up. Maybe you heard about it."

Linda nodded her head. "What about CONDOR?"

"Last I heard it's been mothballed. Groom Lake, Nevada, probably. When or if it's ever gonna be commissioned is anyone's guess. My best guess is that it's being saved for next century's star wars. It'll be a while before it's let out again."

"Again?" Linda asked. "You mean after the New Hampshire crash, don't you?" She'd suddenly remembered the recent news reports and felt a cold shudder at the possibility that CONDOR may have been used after all. She stared directly into Jack's eyes, praying that his answer would reassure her.

"Yeah," Jack lied, though he knew Linda was bright enough to suspect what he'd really meant. "There's no way we'll have to go through any of that again."

"So what does it all mean? And why did you come up here, other than to see me, of course?"

"What it means is that you're free to leave here and come back any time you want. The probability of a threat to you or your family is no longer a factor." He looked directly into

Linda's eyes. "It's over. The government's offering you a rather substantial reward for everything you've done for the country. You could go on with your life from here on without fear."

Linda sat stunned, unable to comprehend the sudden turn of events that were about to change her life once again. "What about John?" she asked.

"Gets his old job back, no questions asked, if he wants it." He looked up at John, whose face was exhibiting the same disbelief as Linda's. "You, my friend, can give up your grocer's apron for a super computer. They could always use someone with your skills and brains in Washington. God knows, they need it. After everything you've been through, it's the least our government can do."

"And the bad news?" Linda asked. "You said something about bad news."

That was the one thing Jack regretted most about coming up to see her. With a new openness infecting Washington, Jack had been able to convince the powers that be that Linda had every right to know about Peter. He wasn't sure whether it was the new openness that caused this change of heart or simply the fact that Peter had died of liver cancer six months ago and there was nothing more to lose. It pained him to think how Linda would react to the shocking revelation that Peter had been alive all along and that she had lived more than ten years of her life—part of that life as John's wife—believing her husband was dead. But it was his call. If he didn't tell her, no one else had the authority to do so, and she would spend the rest of her life thinking that Peter had died a noble death in the Tucson crash.

Jesus Christ, he was thinking. *Why? Why?*

"Tell me, Jack," Linda prodded. "What's the bad news?"

Jack let out a deep sigh, looked up at John, then down at Rachel, who'd fallen asleep in Linda's arms. And seeing no sense in hurting Linda again, said, "The bad news, Linda, is that you'll have to leave all this. So whaddya say?"

Linda closed her eyes for a moment, then opened them. Tears fell onto her cheeks. And as she looked into Jack's eyes, she saw something that frightened her as nothing else in the two years since leaving Washington had. Something she knew that Jack was hiding and was not about to share with anyone, not even her.

John walked around to Linda's side and put his arm around her neck. "Linda? It's up to you," he said. He then bent down and kissed her on the forehead and added, "I gave it all up to come with you. I suppose it wouldn't be so bad going back."

Linda turned her gaze away from Jack and looked deeply into the eyes of a man who'd sacrificed everything he ever had, for her. She shook her head, then turned again to Jack with a smile on her face that seemed puzzling to someone who'd just offered her the chance to begin a new life all over again.

"Sorry, Jack," she said, "But we belong right here. If I never see Washington again it'll suit me just fine. If that's okay with John."

She looked up at John, who kissed her lips and realized that leaving Washington was not a sacrifice at all but the best thing that ever happened to both of them. She turned back to Jack and said, "You're welcome to come and visit anytime you want. There'll always be a bed upstairs and a place at the table for you. Rachel will have to start calling you Uncle Jack."

Jack nodded and looked at Linda and Rachel. There were tears forming in his own eyes now. He envied Linda, glad that she chose to stay and glad that she would never be part of something he wished to God he could forget. "I'd like that," he whispered, choking back the tears. "I'd like that very much."

Then, as he took another sip of coffee and felt the warmth of the fire against his back, he wondered why he'd even offered them a return trip to Washington in the first place. Everything they had ever wanted or cared about was right there in that living room. And somehow, from the moment he stepped inside that cabin, he'd known what Linda's answer would be even before he asked.

afterword

Is the concept of a psychochemical agent or of psychochemical warfare really that farfetched? Certainly if we know anything about molecular biology and the incredible strides made in the field of neuroscience, we know that manipulation of brain chemistry has not only become possible but, in many cases, is easily accomplished. One need only examine the scientific literature and the plethora of recently declassified government documents to uncover case after case of activities the Department of Defense would rather the public know nothing about.

Since World War II, and despite the 1972 Convention on the Prohibition of the Development, Production, and Stockpiling of Biological and Toxic Weapons, the United States, under the guise of national security, has been heavily involved in the research and development of chemical, biological, and psychological agents. In fact, during the past decade, funding for the next generation of biological agents has been steadily ongoing, with as many as 120 universities having been engaged in biological weapons research. And according to sources close to Washington, some of the more illicit research is masked or cleverly disguised, resulting in the illegal diversion of billions of dollars that would otherwise be destined for biomedical research.

Thanks to this often clandestine partnership between government and the private sector, advances in molecular biology have allowed scientists the freedom to develop synthetic viruses and bacteria and produce deadly mutant strains of existing microorganisms. Current arsenals include everything from naturally occurring venoms and toxins to genetically altered combinations of viruses and bacteria, spliced together to create entirely unique and vaccine-proof organisms. The insidious side effect of this kind of development is obvious. With nuclear weapons technology beyond the financial reach of most nations, the danger of terrorists acquiring more easily accessible and transportable agents, such as biologics, looms larger than ever.

The earliest known biological agents were simple infectious pathogens, microscopic organisms that attack the body's defenses, causing physiological breakdown, disease, and in many cases, death. Since the 1970s, however, the stakes have been raised, the search for more "effective" offensive capabilities taking military scientists into an area many hoped they would never be allowed to tread but feared they have already: genetic engineering.

Surrounded by clouds of secrecy, the focus of current research has been not only on "ethnic weapons" that could target specific populations because of differences in population genetics but also on agents that could be altered through recombinant DNA and to which there are no known cures or treatments. The gloves, so to speak, have long been removed. The vast array of possibilities when it comes to molecular biology is, without question, staggering.

On June 9, 1969, for example, Dr. D. M. MacArthur, deputy director of research and technology for the Department of Defense, appeared before the House Subcommittee on Appropriations and requested from Congress 10 million dollars for the research and development of a new infective microorganism that would have no known immunological defense and would be resistant to any current therapeutic process (see appendix). Asked by Democratic Congressman Robert Sikes of Florida if work on this project was not yet being done because of a lack of funding or a lack of interest, Dr. MacArthur replied, "Certainly not lack of interest." He went on to testify that within as little as five to ten years it would be possible, through molecular biology, to make such a new microorganism.

Work on this new agent began in 1970 at Fort Detrick, the government's top-secret biological warfare facility, under the code name MKNAOMI, the successor to MKDELTA, (a CIA project established for the purpose of using biochemicals in clandestine operations), MKULTRA (a secret research program designed to develop methods and agents to achieve mind control), and MKSEARCH (a project intended to develop the capability to manipulate human behavior in a predictable manner through the use of drugs and biological agents) (see appendix). A retrovirologist working for the government had developed various AIDS-like viruses for the National Cancer Institute (which had taken over Fort Detrick) and the Cell Tumor Biology Laboratory.

The decade that followed saw the field of genetic engineering progress to the point that virtually no idea for the manipulation of genes was off-limits or deemed improbable. Entirely new species of organisms could be developed. Cross-species viruses were produced by combining foreign genes, then incubating the viruses in human tissue. The splicing of human genes into bacteria had become almost commonplace. And the promise of revolutionary products, medicines, and disease-resistant plants had become more than simply theory or hypothesis. It was very much reality.

But amidst the euphoria, there had always existed a dark side: the possibility that a technology promising the world so much would someday be used to create—either on purpose or by accident—the ultimate weapon of mass destruction. Recombinant DNA, a novel technique that allows one to combine the genetic material from two separate organisms, could easily be misused and lead to global cataclysmic events. In fact, according to some experts, precisely that scenario may already have occurred during the Persian Gulf War. The individuals attempting to warn the public and expose what could very well be the first such example of the dangers of this new biotechnology have been either ignored, discredited, or silenced.

Shortly after joining Operation Desert Storm, Captain Joyce Riley, an air-evacuation nurse for the 32nd Air evac squadron began seeing illnesses that young, healthy GIs should not have been experiencing: joint pain, debilitating arthritis, chronic fatigue, memory loss, and strange abdominal and pancreatic cancers, rare in twenty-five-year-old individuals (which was the mean age of affected persons). Captain Riley soon began to suspect that a number of these Gulf War soldiers had been exposed to some sort of chemical and/or biological agent. It wasn't until she herself had contracted what is now referred to as Gulf War syndrome, or GWS, that she stumbled onto what was to be a shocking trail of government duplicity and deception.

Returning to the States, Captain Riley met with Dr. Garth Nicolson, professor and chairman of the Department of Tumor Biology at the University of Texas M.D. Anderson Cancer Center. Dr. Nicolson's daughter, a Blackhawk helicopter crew chief with the 101st Airborne Division, had herself been infected and had subsequently infected the entire Nicolson family. A Nobel prize nominee and world-renowned cell biologist, Dr. Nicolson decided to investigate what to him was more than simply the beginnings of a coincidental epidemic. What he soon discovered was a nightmare beyond even his own expectations.

With enough expertise to unravel the molecular structure of whatever it was that had infected his family, as well as the hundreds of veterans whose blood he'd sampled, Dr. Nicolson developed a technique he called "gene tracking." Armed with this new technique, he'd learned not only that the microorganism responsible for many Gulf War illness symptoms was *Mycoplasma incognitus* (one of the microbes used in developing germ weapons), but also that *this* particular strain of mycoplasma was man-made and had incorporated into it 40 percent of the HIV protein coat, making it extremely pathogenic.

In conversations with Dr. Nicolson, I learned of reports that as many as one million individuals had been infected in Southern Iraq alone. The epidemic, which Nicolson claims has been covered up by the U.S. government for legal, economic, and political reasons, is spreading rapidly into Pakistan and other surrounding areas; and he fears that unless something is done, a worldwide crisis will soon erupt. Because of this mounting evidence, various institutions have been pressured by the CIA and the Defense Department to limit or abandon mycoplasma research and to curtail public statements regarding Desert Storm illnesses or the link between genetically engineered biological agents and Gulf War syndrome.

Given some of the main symptoms of GWS (joint pain, muscle spasms, debilitating arthritis), and the fact that this mycoplasma first burrows itself deep into the cell, exits, then travels to another area of the body such as the synovial joint, it's conceivable that HIV had been used in order to facilitate the entrance of the microorganism through the cell membrane. Skeptics who refuse to believe that anyone would purposely manipulate HIV in this manner should know that for more than a decade now, HIV has been studied by academic and military scientists for its effectiveness in a new role: as a retroviral package and vector to deliver genes into cells.

In the 1990 issue of *Current Topics in Microbiology and Immunology*, for example, Dr. P. O. Brown states that retroviruses such as HIV have been widely used as vectors for genetic engineering and are likely to be the first vectors used for introducing foreign genes into cellular chromosomes. Moreover, the *Journal of Virology* and the international journal *Cell* have published detailed articles describing new gene therapy techniques in which parts of the human immunodeficiency virus type I (HIV-1) are altered and packaged as a delivery system for DNA components into human cells.

Could HIV have been used in the manufacture of biological weapons for precisely this purpose? Could a relatively benign mycoplasma have been genetically modified into a highly invasive and pathogenic microorganism? Certainly the technology was there. And based on the government's track record of research into other weapons systems, why wouldn't they make use of an ideal vector that would transport deadly microorganisms into cells?

One compelling piece of evidence shows this may be the case. A concerned Defense Intelligence Agency (''DIA'') agent confided to Dr. Nicolson that a leading "mycoplasma expert" from the Armed Forces Institute of Pathology in Washington, D.C., flew suddenly to Israel during Desert Storm to meet with a senior researcher in the field of mycoplasma research. While there, they allegedly had discussed the types and origins of biological agents used during the Gulf War.

According to Captain Riley, who now heads up the American Gulf War Veterans Association, more than 15,000 Gulf War vets have died, as many as 250,000 are sick, many of them infected with a synthesized microorganism that is easily treatable with the antibiotic doxycycline (*Journal of the American Medical Association*, Feb. 22, 1995: Vol. 273 (8): 618–19). Captain Riley has further obtained evidence that some of these biological agents had been produced in the United States, by individuals working with U.S. intelligence, that the mycoplasma agent had initially been tested on death-row inmates (350 prison employees later contracted GWS), and that the Department of Defense knew well before sending troops to Kuwait that Gulf War soldiers exposed to chemical and biological agents would not be protected against them, despite the wearing of gas masks and/or other protective garb. Interestingly, it was reported in a journal that in 1984, several key Texas Department of Corrections health officials were abruptly replaced by military officers having no health training.

For his part, Dr. Nicolson, despite his claims of repeated interference by the U.S. government, continues to offer information about free blood testing and treatment for any Gulf War veteran who suspect's that he or she may be infected and/or has infected members of his or her family (see appendix).

The reports by Senator Donald Riegle (May 25, 1994) and Senator John D. Rockefeller IV (December 8, 1994) conclude that Gulf War syndrome is real, despite statements by the U.S. Army to the contrary; that the Department of Defense is lying about the use of chemical and biological agents in Iraq; that research into and development of biological agents is ongoing; and that Gulf War soldiers had been used as human guinea pigs in a mass experiment. Moreover, the United Nations Special Commission on Iraq has found that the Iraqi biological program was actually initiated in 1986. During their inspections, UN investigators uncovered evidence that Iraq, with technology secretly provided by the United States government, may have created genetically altered and undetectable microorganisms using *E. coli* and recombinant DNA components that had been licensed for export by the U.S. Commerce Department to various Iraqi agencies, including the Iraq Atomic Energy Commission (see appendix). Why does the U.S. government continue to deny involvement? Possibly because, after convincing the American public that it had no knowledge of biological weapons use, to admit so would be to admit that it had known all along and still allowed Gulf War vets to suffer and die rather than breach national security or reveal military secrets.

What other weapons systems are currently being developed or ready for implementation? Is altering brain chemistry, as proposed in this novel, so inconceivable? Is the idea that government officials would purposely subject American citizens to experimental drugs or weapons systems and allow them to die rather than confess involvement so outrageous? After all, the Department of Defense, along with the CIA, had given hallucinogenic drugs such as LSD and quinuclidinyl benzilate (code-named BZ) to thousands of ''volunteer'' soldiers, many of whom as a result experienced extreme erratic behavior, some even attempting suicide. According to Dr. Sidney Gottlieb, a former CIA agent, ''The program was designed to investigate whether and how an individual's behavior could be modified by covert means'' and was justified because ''it was felt that in an issue where national survival might be concerned, such a procedure and such a risk was a reasonable one to take.''

More recently, according to a September 28, 1994, U.S. General Accounting Office report and a December 8, 1994, United States Senate report on military research and veterans' health, the Department of Defense and other national security agencies had knowingly exposed hundreds of thousands of military personnel to potentially dangerous substances, often in secret. Medical research involving the testing of nerve agents, experimental antidotes, psychochemicals, and irritants were often classified, much of that research remaining classified even today. And according to Senator John D. Rockefeller, Persian Gulf War veterans given unproven investigational vaccines and drugs had been ordered (under threat of military Code of Justice Article 15 or court-martial) not to discuss their treatment or symptoms with anyone, not even medical professionals needing critical information in order to counteract adverse reactions—this despite the Nuremberg Code, which makes it a criminal violation to prevent soldiers from refusing experimental or unapproved drugs or treatments.

Is there once again a cloud of secrecy, this time regarding the use of genetically engineered biological agents? Are veterans and their families becoming sick and dying needlessly? Senator Riegle believes so. Senator Rockefeller certainly believes so. And Dr. Nicolson, who had first discovered the cover-up and whose information packages are routinely intercepted by government agents, has learned firsthand of the desperate measures the Department of Defense will take in order to keep secret the truth behind our military's recombinant DNA research and development program. An all-out effort is currently under way to block academic grants, stifle critical research, reject publications dealing with Gulf War syndrome, silence public speakers, and discredit anyone attempting to investigate the matter.

But despite being told that biological agents were not used and that there is no such thing as Gulf War illness, despite the attempts at silencing veterans, government officials, and frustrated researchers, a growing epidemic will eventually force the Clinton administration to admit what should have been admitted by the previous administration. And with that, unfortunately, America will come to grips with yet another grim reality: that hundreds of thousands of brave men and women had willingly offered themselves up to defend their country, only to be told that their lives have once again been sacrificed—but without consent—for the sake of "national interests."

With our knowledge of molecular biology and brain chemistry, can psychochemical warfare be far behind? Have we crossed the final threshold and entered an invisible new world we didn't expect and were ill prepared for? Are we on the brink of developing new classes of unspeakable weapons? We may, in fact, have done so already. And with science advancing so rapidly it's hard for most individuals to even comprehend, it may be only a matter of time before today's fiction becomes tomorrow's unimaginable reality.

DEPARTMENT OF DEFENSE APPROPRIATIONS FOR 1970

HEARINGS

BEFORE A

SUBCOMMITTEE OF THE

COMMITTEE ON APPROPRIATIONS

HOUSE OF REPRESENTATIVES

NINETY-FIRST CONGRESS

FIRST SESSION

SYNTHETIC BIOLOGICAL AGENTS

There are two things about the biological agent field I would like to mention. One is the possibility of technological surprise. Molecular biology is a field that is advancing very rapidly, and eminent biologists believe that within a period of 5 to 10 years it would be possible to produce a synthetic biological agent, an agent that does not naturally exist and for which no natural immunity could have been acquired.

Mr. SIKES. Are we doing any work in that field?

Dr. MACARTHUR. We are not,

Mr. SIKES. Why not? Lack of money or lack of interest?

Dr. MACARTHUR. Certainly not lack of interest.

Mr. SIKES. Would you provide for our records information on what would be required, what the advantages of such a program would be, the time and the cost involved?

Dr. MACARTHUR. We will be very happy to.

(The information follows:)

The dramatic progress being made in the field of molecular biology led us to investigate the relevance of this field of science to biological warfare. A small group of experts considered this matter and provided the following observations:

1. All biological agents up to the present time are representatives of naturally occurring disease, and are thus known by scientists throughout the world. They are easily available to qualified scientists for research, either for offensive or defensive purposes.

2. Within the next 5 to 10 years, it would probably be possible to make a new infective microorganism which could differ in certain important aspects from any known disease-causing organisms. Most important of these is that it might be

refractory to the immunological and therapeutic processes upon which we depend to maintain our relative freedom from infectious disease.

3. A research program to explore the feasibility of this could be completed in approximately 5 years at a total cost of $10 million.

4. It would be very difficult to establish such a program. Molecular biology is a relatively new science. There are not many highly competent scientists in the field, almost all are in university laboratories, and they are generally adequately supported from sources other than DOD. However, it was considered possible to initiate an adequate program through the National Academy of Sciences-National Research Council (NAS-NRC).

The matter was discussed with the NAS-NRC, and tentative plans were made to initiate the program. However, decreasing funds in CB, growing criticism of the CB program, and our reluctance to involve the NAS-NRC in such a controversial endeavor have led us to postpone it for the past 2 years.

It is a highly controversial issue, and there are many who believe such research should not be undertaken lest it lead to yet another method of massive killing of large populations. On the other hand, without the sure scientific knowledge that such a weapon is possible, and an understanding of the ways it could be done, there is little that can be done to devise defensive measures. Should an enemy develop it there is little doubt that this is an important area of potential military technological inferiority in which there is no adequate research program.

BIOLOGICAL TESTING INVOLVING HUMAN SUBJECTS BY THE DEPARTMENT OF DEFENSE, 1977

HEARINGS

BEFORE THE

SUBCOMMITTEE ON HEALTH AND SCIENTIFIC RESEARCH

OF THE

COMMITTEE ON HUMAN RESOURCES UNITED STATES SENATE

NINETY-FIFTH CONGRESS

FIRST SESSION

STATEMENT OF STEPHEN WEITZMAN, M.D., DEPARTMENT OF MICROBIOLOGY, SCHOOL OF BASIC HEALTH SCIENCES, HEALTH SCIENCE CENTER, STATE UNIVERSITY OF NEW YORK, STONY BROOK; J. M. JOSEPH, PH.D., DIRECTOR LABORATORIES ADMINISTRATION, MARYLAND STATE DEPARTMENT OF HEALTH AND MENTAL HYGIENE; GEORGE H. CONNELL, PH.D., ASSISTANT TO THE DIRECTOR, CENTER FOR DISEASE CONTROL, ATLANTA, GA.; MATTHEW MESELSON, PH.D., CHAIRMAN, DEPARTMENT OF BIOCHEMISTRY AND MOLECULAR BIOLOGY, HARVARD UNIVERSITY

Dr. WEITZMAN. Thank you, Senator. I am pleased to be here today to be given the opportunity to testify on what I consider a very, very important subject, and that is biological warfare research that has been and is still being conducted in this country today.

I studied these two volumes of unclassified Army reports, the one dated February 24, 1977, and this will probably be the main source of my comments on the history, nature, and the extent of production and testing biological simulants.

Reviewing the Army report leads to a consideration of two things. First it raises the question about the morality and safety of several large-scale tests that the Army conducted on civilian population without informed consent. The second point involves an examination of the military and political limitations and problems inherent in pursuing biological warfare research.

The most disturbing aspects of the Army's biological warfare program in 1950–69 concerns the open-air tests conducted on a number of U.S. cities between 1950 and 1966. In particular the San Francisco test has received a lot of attention since it first appeared in the newspapers in November of 1976. In addition, the Army spent about a dozen pages defending the test. Since the San Francisco open-air test seems to be the center of controversy, I would like to discuss it in some detail and use it as a model for examining a number of problems inherent in doing biological warfare research.

Office of the Scientific Director
The Institute for Molecular Medicine
P.O. Box 52470, Irvine, California 92619-2470
Phone (714) 476-0204 Fax (714) 757-0419

November 4, 1996

Mr. Andrew Goliszek
852 Terrace Dr.
Lexington, NC 27295

Dear Mr. Goliszek;
I have attached some information, reprints and preprints on Gulf War Illness (GWI) and the possible use of Chemical/Biological Weapons (CBW) during Operation Desert Storm and the possible testing of these agents in selected prisons before the Gulf War. For your information, we have found so far that about one-half of the GWI patients (and 2/2 British ODS veterans) have an invasive mycoplasma infection that can be successfully treated with antibiotics, such as doxycycline (Nicolson, G.L. and Nicolson, N.L. Doxycycline treatment and Desert Storm *JAMA* 273: 618-619, 1995; Nicolson, G.L. and Nicolson, N.L. Diagnosis and treatment of mycoplasmal infections in Persian Gulf War Illness-CFIDS patients. *Int. J. Occup. Med. Immunol. Tox.* 5: 69-78, 1996) (200 mg/d for 6 wk per course; several courses are usually required, similar to Lyme Disease), Cipro (1,000-1,500 mg/d) or Zithromax (500 mg/d). We have developed new diagnostic procedures (Gene Tracking and forensic PCR) for analysis of the types of mycoplasmas found in GWI, and these may also be useful and informative for soldiers with GWI-CFIDS and some civilians with CFIDS (These diseases are essentually the same--Nicolson, G.L. and Nicolson, N.L. Chronic fatigue illness and Operation Desert Storm. *J. Occup. Environ. Med.* 38: 14-16, 1996).

Currently we are using a test called Gene Tracking to identify unusual DNA sequences unique to mycoplasmas in blood leukocytes (Nicolson, N.L. and Nicolson, G.L. The isolation, purification and analysis of specific gene-containing nucleoproteins and nucleoprotein complexes. *Meth. Mol. Genet.* 5: 281-298, 1994). We have adapted forensic PCR procedures for the accurate determination of invasive mycoplasmic infections, and this may be useful for clinical labs that are struggling with antibody approaches for detecting mycoplasmas. What is interesting about these mycoplasmas is that they contain retroviral DNA sequences (such as the HIV-1 *env* gene but not other HIV genes), suggesting that they may have been modified to make them more pathogenic and more difficult to detect. We have been working with a support group of Texas Department of Criminal Justice employees that were apparently exposed to the same unusual mycoplasma before ODS, possibly during a Defense Department-supported vaccine testing program in selected state prisons here in Texas. One of the biotech companies involved in this TDC study (in Houston, TX) had US Army contracts to study mycoplasmas (this is indicated in their publications on the subject) and has been named in lawsuits as selling or supplying CBW to Iraq.

We have been able to assist thousands of soldiers recover from a life-threatening disease that is caused by invasive mycoplasma infections. This would explain the appearance of GWI in immediate family members and other close to Gulf War veterans with GWI. For our service to our Armed Forces, Nancy and I were recently made honorary full Colonels of the Special Forces for our assistance in helping Airborne and Special Forces soldiers recover from GWI. We have learned that 6,000-12,000 US soldiers have died of infectious diseases and chemical exposure in Operation Desert Storm. I suspect that this is being hidden from the American public for political, economic and legal reasons.

Sincerely,

Garth L. Nicolson, Ph.D.
Scientific Director and Research Professor
The Institute for Molecular Medicine
P.O. Box 52470, Irvine, CA 92619-2470
and
Professor of Pathology and Laboratory Medicine
Professor of Internal Medicine
The University of Texas Medical School at Houston

HUMAN DRUG TESTING BY THE CIA, 1977

HEARINGS

BEFORE THE

SUBCOMITTEE ON HEALTH AND SCIENTIFIC RESEARCH

OF THE

COMMITTEE ON HUMAN RESOURCES UNITED STATES SENATE

NINETY-FIFTH CONGRESS

FIRST SESSION

MK-ULTRA were approved, after personal review, including briefings by the Director of the Agency, Mr. Dulles.

It is well known that another CIA Director, Mr. Helms, approved the destruction of the MK-ULTRA records in 1972. This has made the task of reconstructing those events very difficult—both for the CIA and for interested Senate committees. What is clear now, from the witnesses we have heard and will hear, and from the few records that have been found, is the following:

1. When MK-ULTRA was phased out, it was replaced by MK-SEARCH. MK-SEARCH represented a continuation of a limited number of the ULTRA projects. It is now clear that the records of this project have also been destroyed. In fact, the records of all drug research projects available to the Director of the Technical Services Division of the CIA were destroyed at the same time.

"Did they involve experimentation?" The Admiral indicated, "No, sir." Senator Kennedy: "None of them?" And then, Admiral Turner said. "Let me say this: That these programs are code names for the CIA participation in what was basically a Department of Defense program."

So, we inquired from the Department of Defense about their knowledge and understanding of these programs, and for a complete report. Last evening, we received the correspondence from the General Counsel's Office from the Department of Defense, and we will make the letter a part of the record.

[The information referred to may be found on p. 157.]

Senator KENNEDY. In the letter—and I will read just the relevant parts:

I have enclosed a copy of memoranda and copies of the documents retrieved by the DOD. It appears from the available documents that the projects MKSEARCH, MKORPHAN, and MKCHICKWIT were directed, controlled, funded by the Central Intelligence Agency, and much of the participation of the military departments was solely as a conduit of funds from the Central Intelligence Agency to outside contractors.

And then, in the operative memoranda for the Secretary of Defense, prepared within DOD, on page 2, it continues:

It appears from the document that these three code word projects of the Central Intelligence Agency, identified by the Director in his testimony as basically Department of Defense projects, were, in fact, planned, directed, and controlled by the Central intelligence Agency.

GENERAL COUNSEL OF THE DEPARTMENT OF DEFENSE
WASHINGTON, D.C. 20301

September 20, 1977

MEMORANDUM FOR THE SECRETARY OF DEFENSE

SUBJECT: Experimentation Programs Conducted by the Department of Defense That Had CIA Sponsorship or Participation and That Involved the Administration to Human Subjects of Drugs Intended for Mind-control or Behavior-modification Purposes

On August 8, 1977 you requested that the Office of General Counsel coordinate a search of Department of Defense records to determine the extent of Department of Defense participation in three projects identified by the Director of Central Intelligence on August 3, 1977 as including the administration of drugs to human subjects for mind-control or behavior-modification purposes. In addition, you requested that the search attempt to identify any other project conducted or participated in by the Department of Defense in which there was any Central Intelligence Agency involvement and which included the administration of drugs to human subjects for mind-control or behavior-modification purposes. That search was conducted during the period August 15, 1977 through September 15, 1977 and covered the records of the Military Departments from 1950 to the present.

The results of the search indicate that there were three such programs in which the Army participated over the period 1969 to 1973; five such programs in which the Navy participated over the period 1947 to 1973; and no such programs in which the Air Force participated. In four of these eight programs the Department of Defense participation was limited to channeling funds to outside contractors in order that the sponsorship of the Central Intelligence Agency be covered. In two of the remaining four programs there was no testing on human subjects. Four of the programs were terminated in the 1950's or early 1960's and the remainder were terminated in 1973.

It appears from the documents that the three codeword projects of the Central Intelligence Agency identified by the Director in his testimony as basically Department of Defense projects were, in fact, planned, directed and controlled by the Central Intelligence Agency. Each of these projects and the participation of the military services is described below.

I. <u>Codeword Projects Identified by the Central Intelligence Agency</u>

In testimony on August 3, 1977, before a joint session of the Senate Select Committee on Intelligence and the Senate Subcommittee on Health and Scientific Research, the Director of Central Intelligence reported that the Central Intelligence Agency had located a number of boxes of documents, consisting largely of financial records, relating to experiments using human subjects in which drugs were tested for mind-control and behavior-modification purposes. The Director testified that it appeared that three of the projects described by these documents—projects designated MKSEARCH, MKOFTEN and MKCHICKWIT—were Department of Defense programs with which the Central Intelligence Agency had had some contact. The Director also described three other projects—designated MKULTRA, MKDELTA and MKNAOMI—which were primarily Central Intelligence Agency projects but which might have had some Department of Defense involvement.

It appears from the available documents that these projects cover subject matters as follows:

MKDELTA: This was apparently the first project established by CIA in October, 1952, for the use of biochemicals in clandestine operations. It may never have been implemented operationally.

MKULTRA: This was a successor project to MKDELTA established in April, 1953, and terminating some time in the late 1960's, probably after 1966. This program considered various means of controlling human behavior. Drugs were only one aspect of this activity.

MKNAOMI: This project began in the 1950's and was terminated, at least with respect to biological projects, in 1969. This may have been a successor project to MKDELTA. Its purpose was to stockpile severely incapacitating and lethal materials, and to develop gadgetry for the dissemination of these materials.

MKSEARCH: This was apparently a successor project to MKULTRA, which began in 1965 and was terminated in 1973. The objective of the project was to develop a capability to manipulate human behavior in a predictable manner through the use of drugs.

MKCHICKWIT or CHICKWIT: This was apparently a part of the MKSEARCH program. Its objective was to identify new drug developments in Europe and Asia and to obtain information and samples.

MKOFTEN or OFTEN: This was also apparently a part of the MKSEARCH project. Its objective was to test the behavioral and toxicological effects of certain drugs on animals and humans.

Beginning on August 4, 1977, Army and Navy investigators undertook a search of the boxes of Central Intelligence Agency records identified by the CIA code words OFTEN and CHICKWIT in order to locate documents relevant to possible Department of Defense involvement in these projects.

On September 7, 1977, the Agency permitted DoD representatives to search additional boxes containing MKULTRA records. Both sets of materials consisted of approvals of advances of funds, vouchers and accounting records relating to these projects.

PROJECT MKULTRA, THE CIA'S PROGRAM OF RESEARCH IN BEHAVIORAL MODIFICATION

JOINT HEARING

BEFORE THE

SELECT COMMITTEE ON INTELLIGENCE

AND THE

SUBCOMMITTEE ON HEALTH AND SCIENTIFIC RESEARCH

OF THE

COMMITTEE ON HUMAN RESOURCES UNITED STATES SENATE

NINETY-FIFTH CONGRESS

FIRST SESSION

There are roughly three categories of projects. First, there are 149 MKULTRA subprojects, many of which appear to have some connection with research into behavioral modification, drug acquisition and testing, or administering drugs surreptitiously. Second, there are two boxes of miscellaneous MKULTRA papers, including audit reports and financial statements from intermediary funding mechanisms used to conceal CIA sponsorship of various research projects.

Finally, there are 33 additional subprojects concerning certain intelligence activities previously funded under MKULTRA but which have nothing to do either with behavioral modifications, drugs and toxins, or any closely related matter.

We have attempted to group the activities covered by the 149 subprojects into categories under descriptive headings. In broad outline, at least, this presents the contents of these files. The following 15 categories are the ones we have divided these into.

First, research into the effects of behavioral drugs and/or alcohol. Within this, there are 17 projects probably not involving human testing. There are 14 subprojects definitely involving testing on human volunteers. There are 19 subprojects probably including tests on human volunteers and 6 subprojects involving tests on unwitting human beings.

Second, there is research on hypnosis, eight subprojects, including two involving hypnosis and drugs in combination.

Third, there are seven projects on the acquisition of chemicals or drugs.

Fourth, four subprojects on the aspects of the magician's art, useful in covert operations, for instance, the surreptitious delivery of drug-related materials.

Fifth, there are nine projects on studies of human behavior, sleep research, and behavioral change during psychotherapy.

Sixth, there are projects on library searches and attendants at seminars and international conferences on behavioral modifications.

Seventh, there are 23 projects on motivational studies, studies of defectors, assessments of behavior and training techniques.

Eighth, there are three subprojects on polygraph research.

Ninth, there are three subprojects on funding mechanisms for MKULTRA's external research activities.

Tenth, there are six subprojects on research on drugs, toxins, biologicals in human tissue, provision of exotic pathogens, and the capability to incorporate them in effective delivery systems.

Eleventh, there are three subprojects on activities whose nature simply cannot be determined.

Twelfth, there are subprojects involving funding support for unspecified activities con

ducted with the Army Special Operations Division at Fort Detrich, Md. This activity is outlined in Book I of the Church committee report, pages 388 to 389. (See Appendix A, pp. 68–69).

Under CIA's Project MKNAOMI, the Army assisted the CIA in developing, testing, and maintaining biological agents and delivery systems for use against humans as well as against animals and crops.

Thirteenth, there are single subprojects in such areas as the effects of electroshock, harassment techniques for offensive use, analysis of extrasensory perception, gas propelled sprays and aerosols, and four subprojects involving crop and material sabotage.

Fourteenth, one or two subprojects on each of the following: blood grouping research; controlling the activities of animals; energy storage and transfer in organic systems; and stimulus and response in biological systems.

Finally, 15th, there are three subprojects canceled before any work was done on them having to do with laboratory drug screening, research on brain concussion, and research on biologically active materials.

Now, let me address how much this newly discovered material adds to what has previously been reported to the Church committee and to Senator Kennedy's Subcommittee on Health. The answer is basically additional detail. The principal types of activities included in these documents have for the most part been outlined or to some extent generally described in what was previously available in the way of documentation and which was supplied by the CIA to the Senate investigators.

For example, financial disbursement records for the period of 1960 to 1964 for 76 of these 149 subprojects had been recovered by the Office of Finance at CIA and were made available to the Church committee investigators. For example, the 1963 Inspector General report on MKULTRA made available to both the Church committee and the Subcommittee on Health mentions electroshock and harassment substances, covert testing on unwitting U.S. citizens, the search for new materials through arrangements with specialists in hospitals and universities, and the fact that the Technical Service Division of CIA had initiated 144 subprojects related to the control of human behavior.

For instance also, the relevant section of a 1957 Inspector General report was also made available to the Church committee staff, and that report discusses the techniques for human assessment and unorthodox methods of communication, discrediting and disabling materials which can be covertly administered, studies on magicians' arts as applied to covert operations, and other similar topics.

XVII. TESTING AND USE OF CHEMICAL AND BIOLOGICAL AGENTS BY THE INTELLIGENCE COMMUNITY

Under its mandate the Select Committee has studied the testing and use of chemical and biological agents by intelligence agencies. Detailed descriptions of the programs conducted by intelligence agencies involving chemical and biological agents will be included in a separately published appendix to the Senate Select Committee's report. This section of the report will discuss the rationale for the programs, their monitoring and control, and what the Committee's investigation has revealed about the relationships among the intelligence agencies and about their relations with other government agencies and private institutions and individuals.

Fears that countries hostile to the United States would use chemical and biological agents against Americans or America's allies led to the development of a defensive program designed to discover techniques for American intelligence agencies to detect and counteract chemical and biological agents. The defensive orientation soon became secondary as the possible use of these agents to obtain information from, or gain control over, enemy agents became apparent.

Research and development programs to find materials which could be used to alter human behavior were initiated in the late 1940s and early 1950s. These experimental programs originally included testing of drugs involving witting human subjects, and culminated in tests using unwitting, nonvolunteer human subjects. These tests were designed to determine the potential effects of chemical or biological agents when used operationally against individuals unaware that they had received a drug.

The testing programs were considered highly sensitive by the intelligence agencies administering them. Few people, even within the agencies, knew of the programs and there is no evidence that either the executive branch or Congress were ever informed of them. The highly compartmented nature of these programs may be explained in part by an observation made by the CIA Inspector General that, "the knowledge that the Agency is engaging in unethical and illicit activities."

---

3. MKNAOMI

MKNAOMI was another major CIA program in this area. In 1967, the CIA summarized the purposes of MKNAOMI:

(a) To provide for a covert support base to meet clandestine operational requirements.

(b) To stockpile severely incapacitating and lethal materials for the specific use of TSD [Technical Services Division].

(c) To maintain in operational readiness special and unique items for the dissemination of biological and chemical materials.

(d) To provide for the required surveillance, testing, upgrading, and evaluation of materials and items in order to assure absence of defects and complete predictability of results to be expected under operational conditions.[9]

Under an agreement reached with the Army in 1952, the Special Operations Division (SOD) at Fort Detrick was to assist CIA in developing, testing, and maintaining biological agents and delivery systems. By this agreement, CIA acquired the knowledge, skill, and facilities of the Army to develop biological weapons suited for CIA use.

---

[9]Memorandum from Chief, TSD/Biological Branch to Chief. TSD "MKNAOMI: Funding. Objectives, and Accomplishments." 10/18/67. p. 1. For a fuller description of MKNAOMI and the relationship between CIA and SOD.

SOD developed darts coated with biological agents and pills containing several different biological agents which could remain potent for weeks or months. SOD also developed a special gun for firing darts coated with a chemical which could allow CIA agents to incapacitate a guard dog, enter an installation secretly, and return the dog to consciousness when leaving. SOD scientists were unable to develop a similar incapacitant for humans. SOD also physically transferred to CIA personnel biological agents in "bulk" form, and delivery devices, including some containing biological agents.

In addition to the CIA's interest in biological weapons for use against humans, it also asked SOD to study use of biological agents against crops and animals. In its 1967 memorandum, the CIA stated:

> Three methods and systems for carrying out a covert attack against crops and causing severe crop loss have been developed and evaluated under field conditions. This was accomplished in anticipation of a requirement which was later developed but was subsequently scrubbed just prior to putting into action.

MKNAOMI was terminated in 1970. On November 25, 1969, President Nixon renounced the use of any form of biological weapons that kill or incapacitate and ordered the disposal of existing stocks of bacteriological weapons. On February 14, 1970, the President clarified the extent of his earlier order and indicated that toxins—chemicals that are not living organisms but are produced by living organisms—were considered biological weapons subject to his previous directive and were to be destroyed. Although instructed to relinquish control of material held for the CIA by SOD, a CIA scientist acquired approximately 11 grams of shellfish toxin from SOD personnel at Fort Detrick which were stored in a little-used CIA laboratory where it went undetected for five years.

4. MKULTRA

MKULTRA was the principal CIA program involving the research and development of chemical and biological agents. It was "concerned with the research and development of chemical, biological, and radiological materials capable of employment in clandestine operations to control human behavior."

In January 1973, MKULTRA records were destroyed by Technical Services Division personnel acting on the verbal orders of Dr. Sidney Gottlieb, Chief of TSD. Dr. Gottlieb has testified, and former Director Helms has confirmed, that in ordering the records destroyed, Dr. Gottlieb was carrying out the verbal order of then DCI Helms.

MKULTRA began with a proposal from the Assistant Deputy Director for Plans, Richard Helms, to the DCI, outlining a special funding mechanism for highly sensitive CIA research and development projects that studied the use of biological and chemical materials in altering human behavior. The projects involved:

> Research to develop a capability in the covert use of biological and chemical materials. This area involves the production of various physiological conditions which could support present or future clandestine operations. Aside from the offensive potential, the development of a comprehensive capability in this field of covert chemical and biological warfare gives us a thorough knowledge of the enemy's theoretical potential, thus enabling us to defend ourselves against a foe who might not be as restrained in the use of these techniques as we are.

The annual grants of funds to these specialists were made under ostensible research foundation auspices, thereby concealing the CIA's interest from the specialist's institution.

The next phase of the MKULTRA program involved physicians, toxicologists, and other specialists in mental, narcotics, and general hospitals, and in prisons. Utilizing the products and findings of the basic research phase, they conducted intensive tests on human subjects.

One of the first studies was conducted by the National Institute of Mental Health. This study was intended to test various drugs, including hallucinogenics, at the NIMH Addiction Research Center in Lexington, Kentucky. The "Lexington Rehabilitation Center," as it was then called, was a prison for drug addicts serving sentences for drug violations.

The test subjects were volunteer prisoners who, after taking a brief physical examination and signing a general consent form, were administered hallucinogenic drugs. As a reward for participation in the program, the addicts were provided with the drug of their addiction.

LSD was one of the materials tested in the MKULTRA program. The final phase of LSD testing involved surreptitious administration to unwitting nonvolunteer subjects in normal life settings by undercover officers of the Bureau of Narcotics acting for the CIA.

The rationale for such testing was "that testing of materials under accepted scientific procedures fails to disclose the full pattern of reactions and attributions that may occur in operational situations."

According to the CIA, the advantage of the relationship with the Bureau was that:

> test subjects could be sought and cultivated within the setting of narcotics control. Some subjects have been informers or members of suspect criminal elements from whom the [Bureau of Narcotics] has obtained results of operational value through the tests. *On the other hand, the effectiveness of the substances on individuals at all social levels, high and low, native American and foreign, is of great significance and testing has been performed on a variety of individuals within these categories.* [Emphasis added.]

3. The Surreptitious Administration of LSD to Unwitting Non-Volunteer Human Subjects by the CIA After the Death of Dr. Olson

The death of Dr. Olson could be viewed, as some argued at the time, as a tragic accident, one of the risks inherent in the testing of new substances. It might be argued that LSD was thought to be benign. After the death of Dr. Olson the dangers of the surreptitious administration of LSD were clear, yet the CIA continued or initiated a project involving the surreptitious administration of LSD to non-volunteer human subjects. This program exposed numerous individuals in the United States to the risk of death or serious injury without their informed consent, without medical supervision, and without necessary follow-up to determine any long-term effects.

Prior to the Olson experiment, the Director of Central Intelligence had approved MKULTRA, a research program designed to develop a "capability in the covert use of biological and chemical agent materials." In the proposal describing MKULTRA Mr. Helms, then ADDP, wrote the Director that:

> we intend to investigate the development of a chemical material which causes a reversible non-toxic aberrant mental state, the specific nature of which can be reasonably well predicted for each individual. This material could potentially aid in discrediting individuals, eliciting information, and implanting suggestions and other forms of mental control.

C. Covert Testing on Human Subjects by Military Intelligence Groups: Material Testing Program EA 1729, Project THIRD CHANGE, and Project DERBY HAT

EA 1729 is the designator used in the Army drug testing program for lysergic acid diethylamide (LSD). Interest in LSD was originally aroused at the Army's Chemical Warfare Laboratories by open literature on the unusual effects of the compound. The positive intelligence and counterintelligence potential envisioned for compounds like LSD, and suspected Soviet interest in such materials, supported the development of an American military capability and resulted in experiments conducted jointly by the U.S. Army Intelligence Board and the Chemical Warfare Laboratories.

These experiments, designed to evaluate potential intelligence uses of LSD, were known collectively as "Material Testing Program EA 1729." Two projects of particular interest conducted as part of these experiments, "THIRD CHANCE" and "DERBY HAT", involved the administration of LSD to unwitting subjects in Europe and the Far East.

In many respects, the Army's testing programs duplicated research which had already been conducted by the CIA. They certainly involved the risks inherent in the early phases of drug testing. In the Army's tests, as with those of the CIA, individual rights were also subordinated to national security considerations; informed consent and follow-up examinations of subjects were neglected in efforts to maintain the secrecy of the tests. Finally, the command and control problems which were apparent in the CIA's programs are paralleled by a lack of clear authorization and supervision in the Army's programs.

MATERIAL FOR THE RECORD

MKSEARCH, OFTEN/CHICKWIT

MKSEARCH was the name given to the continuation of the MKULTRA program. Funding commenced in FY 1966, and ended in FY 1972. Its purpose was to develop, test, and evaluate capabilities in the covert use of biological, chemical, and radioactive material systems and techniques for producing predictable human behavioral and/or physiological changes in support of highly sensitive operational requirements.

OFTEN/CHICKWIT

In 1967 the Office of Research and Development (ORD) and the Edgewood Arsenal Research Laboratories undertook a program for doing research on the identification and characterization of drugs that could influence human behavior. Edgewood had the facilities for the full range of laboratory and clinical testing. A phased program was envisioned that would consist of acquisition of drugs and chemical compounds believed to have effects on the behavior of humans, and testing and evaluating these materials through laboratory procedures and toxicological studies. Compounds believed promising as a result of tests on animals were then to be evaluated clinically with human subjects at Edgewood. Substances of potential use would then be analyzed structurally as a basis for identifying and synthesizing possible new derivatives of greater utility.

The program was divided into two projects. Project OFTEN was to deal with testing the toxicological, transmisivity and behavioral effects of drugs in animals and, ultimately, humans. Project CHICKWIT was concerned with acquiring information on new drug developments in Europe and the Orient, and with acquiring samples.

There is a discrepancy between the testimony of DOD and CIA regarding the testing at Edgewood Arsenal in June 1973. While there is agreement that human testing occurred at that place and time, there is disagreement as to who was responsible for financing and sponsorship. (See hearings before the Subcommittee on Health and Scientific Research of the Senate Human Resources Committee, September 21, 1977.)

INTELLIGENCE ACTIVITIES

SENATE RESOLUTION 21

HEARINGS

BEFORE THE

SELECT COMMITTEE TO STUDY GOVERNMENTAL OPERATIONS WITH RESPECT TO INTELLIGENCE ACTIVITIES

OF THE

UNITED STATES SENATE

NINETY-FOURTH CONGRESS

FIRST SESSION

The CHAIRMAN. Now, my first question is, why did the Agency prepare a shellfish toxin for which there is no particular antidote, which attacks the nervous system and brings on death very quickly? Why did the Agency prepare toxins of this character in quantities sufficient to kill many thousands of people—what was the need for that in the first place, long before the Presidential order came down to destroy this material?

Mr. COLBY. I think the first part of the answer to that question, Mr. Chairman, is the fact that the L-pill, which was developed during World War II, does take some time to work, and is particularly agonizing to the subject who uses it. Some of the people who would be natural requesters of such a capability for their own protection and the protection of their fellow agents, really do not want to face that kind of a fate. But if they could be given an instantaneous one, they would accept that. And that was the thought process behind developing the capability.

Now, I cannot explain why that quantity was developed, except that this was a collaboration that we were engaged in with the U.S. Army, and we did develop this particular weapon, you might say, for possible use. When CIA retained the amount that it did, it obviously did it improperly.

The CHAIRMAN. This quantity, and the various devices for administering the toxin which were found in the laboratory, certainly make it clear that purely defensive uses were not what the Agency was limited to in any way. There were definite offensive uses. In fact, there were dart guns. You mentioned suicides. Well, I do not think a suicide is usually accomplished with a dart, particularly a gun that can place the dart in a human heart in such a way that he does not even know that he has been hit.

Mr. COLBY. There is no question about it. It was also for offensive reasons. No question about it.

The CHAIRMAN. Have you brought with you some of those devices which would have enabled the CIA to use this poison for killing people?

Mr. COLBY. We have, indeed.

The CHAIRMAN. Does this pistol fire the dart?

Mr. COLBY. Yes, it does, Mr. Chairman. The round thing at the top is obviously the sight, the rest of it is what is practically a normal .45, although it is a special. However, it works by electricity. There is a battery in the handle, and it fires a small dart.

The CHAIRMAN. So that when it fires, it fires silently?

Mr. COLBY. Almost silently; yes.

The CHAIRMAN. What range does it have?

Mr. COLBY. One hundred meters, I believe; about 100 yards, 100 meters.

The CHAIRMAN. About 100 meters range?

Mr. COLBY. Yes.

The CHAIRMAN. And the dart itself, when it strikes the target, does the target know that he has been hit and about to die?

Mr. COLBY. That depends, Mr. Chairman, on the particular dart used. There are different kinds of these flechettes that were used in various weapons systems, and a special one was developed which potentially would be able to enter the target without perception.

The CHAIRMAN. And did you find such darts in the laboratory?

Mr. COLBY. We did.

The CHAIRMAN. Is it not true, too, that the effort not only involved designing a gun that could strike at a human target without knowledge of the person who had been struck, but also the toxin itself would not appear in the autopsy?

Mr. COLBY. Well, there was an attempt——

The CHAIRMAN. Or the dart.

Mr. COLBY. Yes; so there was no way of perceiving that the target was hit.

The CHAIRMAN. As a murder instrument, that is about as efficient as you can get, is it not?

Mr. COLBY. It is a weapon, a very serious weapon.

The CHAIRMAN. Going back to my earlier question, Mr. Colby, as to the quantities of this toxin that had been prepared, can you conceive of any use that the CIA could make of such quantities of shellfish toxin?

Mr. COLBY. I certainly can't today, Mr. Chairman, in view of our current policies and directives.

The CHAIRMAN. Well, even at the time, certainly, the CIA was never commissioned or empowered to conduct bacteriological warfare against whole communities; and quantities of poison capable of destroying up to the hundreds of thousands of lives—it seems to me to be entirely inappropriate for any possible use to which the CIA might have put such poison.

The Director of Central Intelligence
Washington D.C. 20505

The Honorable Daniel K. Inouye, Chairman
Select Committee on Intelligence
United States Senate
Washington, D.C. 20510

Dear Mr. Chairman:

During the course of 1975 when the Senate Committee, chaired by Senator Church, was investigating intelligence activities, the CIA was asked to produce documentation on a program of experimentation with the effect of drugs. Under this project conducted from 1953 to 1964 and known as "MK-ULTRA," tests were conducted on American citizens in some cases without their knowledge. The CIA, after searching for such documentation, reported that most of the documents on this matter have been destroyed. I find it my duty to report to you now that our continuing search for drug related, as well as other documents, has uncovered certain papers which bear on this matter. Let me hasten to add that I am persuaded that there was no previous attempt to conceal this material in the original 1975 exploration. The material recently discovered was in the retired archives filed under financial accounts and only uncovered by using extraordinary and extensive search efforts. In this connection, incidentally, I have personally commended the employee whose diligence produced this find.

Because the new material now on hand is primarily of a financial nature, it does not present a complete picture of the field of drug experimentation activity but it does provide more detail than was previously available to us. For example, the following types of activities were undertaken:

a. Possible additional cases of drugs being tested on American citizens, without their knowledge.

b. Research was undertaken on surreptitious methods of administering drugs.

c. Some of the persons chosen for experimentation were drug addicts or alcoholics.

d. Research into the development of a knockout or "K" drug was performed in conjunction with being done to develop pain killers for advanced cancer patients, and tests on such patients were carried out.

e. There is a possibility of an improper payment to a private institution.

The drug related activities described in this newly located material began almost 25 years ago. I assure you they were discontinued over 10 years ago and do not take place today.

In keeping with the President's commitment to disclose any errors of the Intelligence Community which are uncovered, I would like to volunteer to testify before your Committee on the full details of this unfortunate series of events. I am in the process of reading the fairly voluminous material involved and do want to be certain that I have a complete picture when I talk with the Committee. I will be in touch with you next week to discuss when hearings might be scheduled at the earliest opportunity.

I regret having to bring this issue to your attention, but I know that it is essential to your oversight procedures that you be kept fully informed in a timely manner.

Yours sincerely,

STANSFIELD TURNER

February 9, 1994
Statement of Senator Donald W. Riegle, Jr.
Arming Iraq: Biological Agent Exports Prior to the Gulf War

On September 9, 1993, I released a report which suggested that "Gulf War Syndrome," that disabling and sometimes fatal collection of illnesses afflicting thousands of veterans with debilitating muscle and joint pain, memory loss, intestinal and heart problems, fatigue, running noses, urinary and intestinal problems, twitching, rashes, and sores, could have resulted from exposure to chemical and biological warfare agents, either from direct exposure or from the downwind fallout of the coalition bombings of Iraq.

My initial inquiry focused on exposure to chemical agents, due to the many reports of chemical alarms sounding before and during the war and the compelling accounts of eyewitnesses to events which appear to be best explained as chemical agent attacks. Since that time, a number of researchers have contacted my office with a more disturbing proposal.

These researchers believe that the symptoms experienced by these veterans may be the result not only of exposure to chemical warfare agents and other environmental hazards, but possibly also as a result of exposure to biological warfare agents.

This is an extremely serious issue with serious consequences, but it may explain the alarming and growing evidence that the illness appears to be spreading to the spouses and children of the affected veterans.

All government agencies and institutions, including the U.S. Congress, have a responsibility to uncover every available lead which might assist medical researchers in discovering the nature and scope of these illnesses. This Administration must defend the health and well-being of its people, especially those who have been willing to lay down their lives for the United States. It has been nearly three years since these young men and women began suffering, and too many have died.

The Senate Committee on Banking, Housing, and Urban Affairs, which I chair, has oversight responsibility for the Export Administration Act. Pursuant to this Act, Committee staff contacted the U.S. Department of Commerce and requested information on the export of biological materials to Iraq during the years prior to the Gulf War.

After receiving that information, we contacted a principal supplier of these materials to determine what, if any, materials were exported to Iraq which might have contributed to an offensive or defensive biological warfare program.

Records available from the supplier for the period from 1985 until the present show that during this period, pathogenic, meaning "disease producing," toxigenic, meaning "poisonous," and other materials, were exported to Iraq pursuant to application and licensing by the U.S. Department of Commerce. Records prior to 1985 were not available, according to the supplier. These exported biological materials were not attenuated or weakened and were capable of reproduction. Thus, from at least 1985 through 1989, the United States government approved the sale of quantities of potentially lethal biological agents that could have been cultured or grown in large quantities in an Iraqi biological warfare program.

I find it especially troubling that, according to the supplier's records, these materials were requested by and sent to Iraqi government agencies, including the Iraq Atomic Energy Commission, the Iraq Ministry of Higher Education, the State Company for Drug Industries, and the Ministry of Trade.

While there may be legitimate needs for pathogens in medical research, closer scrutiny should be exercised in approving exports of materials to countries known or suspected of having active and aggressive biological warfare programs.

Iraq has long been suspected of conducting biological warfare research, in addition to its chemical and nuclear warfare research programs.

Indeed, according to the Department of Defense's own report to Congress on the Conduct of the Persian Gulf War, written in 1992: "By the time of the invasion of Kuwait, Iraq had developed biological weapons. Its advanced and aggressive biological warfare program was the most advanced in the Arab world."

NEWS

DONALD W. RIEGLE JR., MICHIGAN CHAIRMAN

PAUL S. BARBANES, MARYLAND
CHRISTOPHER J. DODO, CONNECTICUT
JIM SASSER, TENNESSEE
RICHARD C. SHELBY, ALABAMA
JOHN F. KERRY, MASSACHUSETTS
RICHARD H. BRYAN, NEVADA
BARBARA BOXER, CALIFORNIA
BEN NIGHTHORSE CAMPBELL, COLORADO
CAROL MOSELEY-BRAUN, ILLINOIS

PATTY MURRAY, WASHINGTON
ALFONSE M. D'AMATO, NEW YORK
PHIL GRAMM, TEXAS
CHRISTOPHER S. BOND, MISSOURI
CONNIE MACK, FLORIDA
LAUCH FAIRCLOTH, NORTH CAROLINA
ROBERT F. BENNETT, UTAH
WILLIAM V. ROTH, DELAWARE
PETE V. DOMENICHI, NEW MEXICO

STEVEN B. HAUS, STAFF DIRECTOR AND CHIEF COUNCIL
HOWARD A. METHELL, REPUBLICAN STAFF DIRECTOR

U.S. SENATE COMMITTEE ON BANKING, HOUSING, AND URBAN AFFAIRS, WASHINGTON, D.C. 20510-6075

FOR IMMEDIATE RELEASE February 9, 1994

CONTACT: Tammy Boyer 202-224-9208

RIEGLE UNCOVERS U.S. SHIPMENTS OF BIOLOGICAL WARFARE RELATED MATERIALS TO IRAQ PRIOR TO GULF WAR: WANTS INVESTIGATION OF LINK TO GULF WAR SYNDROME

WASHINGTON, D.C.—Senator Donald W. Riegle, Jr., took to the Senate floor this morning to make an important disclosure that biological warfare related materials were exported from the U.S. to Iraq prior to the Persian Gulf War. Noting that Iraq has had a long-standing biological warfare program, Riegle expressed concerns that unexplained symptoms suffered by Persian Gulf War veterans and increasing evidence of transmission to family members upon their return home from the war, may be the result of exposure to biological contamination while serving in the Persian Gulf.

"I am deeply troubled that the United States permitted the sale of deadly biological agents to a country with a known biological warfare program," Riegle said today. "Now we have new evidence to assist medical researchers in the possible causes of Gulf War Syndrome. Several of these biological agents cause, among other things, fever, vomiting, chest pains, pneumonia, and inflammatory skin disease, all of which are symptoms present in thousands of Gulf War vets and their family members."

Riegle asked today that the Department of Defense and Department of Veterans Affairs establish disability compensation for these veterans consistent with their degree of disability regardless of their ability to arrive at a definitive medical diagnosis.

Riegle also asked the Department of Health and Human Services, the Department of Veterans Affairs, and the Department of Defense, including their newly formed task force addressing this issue, to study the reported transmission of these illnesses to the spouses and children of these veterans, and assess what, if any, public health hazard exists, and to report back on his request no later than March 31, 1994.

As Chairman of the Senate Committee on Banking, Housing, and Urban Affairs, which has oversight responsibility for reauthorization of the Export Administration Act, Riegle called for hearings to investigate the export of these materials and the possible link to Gulf War Syndrome. "I think we need to change our policy on the export of these materials to assure that such deadly agents don't fall into the hands of countries with known biological warfare programs," Riegle said.

The United States and Iraq are signatories of the 1972 Biological Warfare Convention which restricts the use and proliferation of biological warfare agents. Following the Persian Gulf War, UN inspectors confirmed that Iraq was conducting biological warfare research. According to the Pentagon's official report to Congress on the Conduct of the Persian Gulf War, written in 1992: "By the time of the invasion of Kuwait, Iraq had developed biological weapons. Its advanced and aggressive biological warfare program was the most advanced in the Arab world. Large scale production of these agents began in 1989 at four facilities near Baghdad. Delivery means for biological agents ranged from simple aerial bombs and artillery rockets to surface to surface missiles."

BACKGROUND MATERIALS AVAILABLE
PLEASE CALL 224-9208 FOR REQUESTS

OFFICE OF THE SECRETARY OF DEFENSE
WASHINGTON, D.C. 20301

3 NOV 1996

MEMORANDUM FOR: SEE DISTRIBUTION

SUBJECT: Identification and Processing of Sensitive Operational Records

1. The DEPSECDEF and the ASD/HA have expressed concern about potential sensitive reports or documents on GulfLINK. They have directed that the declassifiers identify such documents and forward them to the Investigation Team prior to release on GulfLINK. The purpose of this procedure is not to stop any declassified or unclassified documents from going on GulfLINK, but to allow the Investigation Team time to begin preparation of a response on particular "bombshell" reports. These responses could be provided to Dr. White and Dr. Joseph, or used in response to White House queries.

2. Realizing that a fair amount of judgment must be exercised by your reviewers in this process, request you task your teams to use the following criteria in selecting sensitive documents.

a. Documents that could generate unusual public/media attention.
b. All documents which seem to confirm the use or detection of nuclear, chemical, or biological agents.
c. Documents which make gross/startling assertions, i.e., a pilot's report that he saw a "giant cloud of anthrax gas."
d. Documents containing releasable information which could embarass the Government or DOD. Statements such as "we are not to bring this up to the press" fit this category.
e. Documents which shed light on issues which have high levels of media interest, such as the November 1995, Life article on birth defects among Gulf War Veterans' children.

All such reports should be flagged for the Investigation Team and sent directly to them by the fastest available means, e.g. E-mail, fax, mail, or courier.

3. The Investigation Team will make two determinations on each flagged record. One will be whether or not the subject requires further research, and the other will be who, if anyone, would receive the results of the research. As soon as these steps are expedited, the Investigation Team will notify the operational declassifier that they have completed their part of the process and that the document can be forwarded to DTIC for placement on GulfLINK. The Investigation Team will also notify the declassifiers when particular incidents or units are no longer considered potentially sensitive. In those cases, the declassifiers should stop flagging or highlighting reports on that incident or unit. The results of the Investigation Teams' investigations ultimately will be put on GulfLINK.

4. You are requested to ensure that your declassifiers follow the FOIA standards in the review, redaction, and release of health-related operational records. This will ensure that there is some consistency in operational records of the services and commands that are being made available to the public on GulfLINK. It also facilitates the use of FOIA and privacy exemption codes in the redaction of documents.

PAUL F. WALLNER
Staff Director
Senior Level Oversight Panel
Persian Gulf War Veterans' Illnesses

DISTRIBUTION:
Chief of Military History, USA
Director of Current Operation, J-33, JCS
Deputy Director, J-3, USCENTCOM
Director of Plans, XOX, USAF Air Staff
Director, Naval Historical Center
Director, USMC Historical Center
Air Force Declassification and Review Team

cc: DEPSECDEF
ASD/HA
USEC/Army
PASD/AE
DIA/DR
PASD/IS/C31

PERSIAN GULF WAR ILLNESSES: ARE WE TREATING VETERANS RIGHT?

HEARING

BEFORE THE

COMMITTEE ON VETERANS' AFFAIRS
UNITED STATES SENATE

ONE HUNDRED THIRD CONGRESS

FIRST SESSION

NOVEMBER 16, 1993

Printed for the use of the Committee on Veterans' Affairs

U.S. GOVERNMENT PRINTING OFFICE

51–631 CC WASHINGTON: 1994

F. HALLUCINOGENS

Working with the CIA, the Department of Defense gave hallucinogenic drugs to thousands of "volunteer" soldiers in the 1950's and 1960's. In addition to LSD, the Army also tested quinuclidinyl benzilate, a hallucinogen code-named BZ.[37] Many of these tests were conducted under the so-called MKULTRA program, established to counter perceived Soviet and Chinese advances in brainwashing techniques. Between 1953 and 1964, the program consisted of 149 projects involving drug testing and other studies on unwitting human subjects.[38]

One test subject was Lloyd B. Gamble, who enlisted in the U.S. Air Force in 1950. In 1957, he volunteered for a special program to test new military protective clothing. He was offered various incentives to participate in the program, including a liberal leave policy, family visitations, and superior living and recreational facilities. However, the greatest incentive to Mr. Gamble was the official recognition he would receive as a career-oriented noncommissioned officer, through letters of commendation and certification of participation in the program. During the 3 weeks of testing new clothing, he was given two or three water-size glasses of a liquid containing LSD to drink. Thereafter, Mr. Gamble developed erratic behavior and even attempted suicide. He did not learn that he had received LSD as a human subject until 18 years later, as a result of congressional hearings in 1975. Even then, the Department of the Army initially denied that he had participated in the experiments, although an official DOD publicity photograph showed him as one of the valiant servicemen volunteering for "a program that was in the highest national security interest."

According to Sidney Gottlieb, a medical doctor and former CIA agent, MKULTRA was established to investigate whether and how an individual's behavior could be modified by covert means. According to Dr. Gottlieb, the CIA believed that both the Soviet Union and Communist China might be using techniques of altering human behavior which were not understood by the United States. Dr. Gottlieb testified that "it was felt to be mandatory and of the utmost urgency for our intelligence organization to establish what was possible in this field on a high priority basis." Although many human subjects were not informed or protected, Dr. Gottlieb defended those actions by stating, ". . . harsh as it may seem in retrospect, it was felt that in an issue where national survival might be concerned, such a procedure and such a risk was a reasonable one to take."

Persian Gulf War Veterans

Almost 50 years after World War II veterans were exposed to unethical research, the Department of Defense again failed to comply with the well-established ethical requirement that all soldiers and civilians make an informed choice of whether or not to use investigational medical treatment.

1. *Military personnel were not given the opportunity to refuse investigational drugs.*

When the Department of Defense began preparations for Desert Shield and Desert Storm in 1990, officials were extremely concerned about the need to protect U.S. troops against chemical and biological weapons that were believed to have been developed by Iraq. However, the DOD lacked drugs and vaccines that were proven safe and effective to safeguard against expected weapons, such as soman and botulism.

[H.A.S.C. No. 103-27]

USE OF CHEMICAL WEAPONS IN DESERT STORM

HEARING

BEFORE THE

OVERSIGHT AND INVESTIGATIONS SUBCOMMITTEE

OF THE

COMMITTEE ON ARMED SERVICES HOUSE OF REPRESENTATIVES

ONE HUNDRED THIRD CONGRESS
FIRST SESSION

HEARING HELD
NOVEMBER 18, 1993

U.S. GOVERNMENT PRINTING OFFICE

WASHINGTON: 1994

76-568 CC

Mr. Chairman, there is a dirty little secret behind the Pentagon's reluctance to deal fully and openly with the mystery ailments afflicting thousands of Gulf War veterans. It is shameful that it has taken the tragedy of sick and dying Gulf War veterans to expose and focus attention on this dirty little secret.

But the truth is that a full and open investigation would reveal that our military leaders have not really prioritized protecting America's soldiers against chemical and biological weapons.

I make these statements with sadness and only after serious deliberations, after a few years in Congress working with chemical and biological defense issues. I would like to add in passing that this controversy is an outside-the-Beltway issue. It is somewhat like a savings and loan problem in that national leaders have avoided the issue like the plague, and until recently national media ignored it. Sick and dying veterans, their families, and local news media have forced the inside-the-Beltway crowd to finally address the problem, and the Department of Defense has yet to face it fully and openly.

The DOD's statements are deliberately circumspect; and they use careful qualifying phrases, wiggle words, and pledges to investigate this mystery further. But their bottom line message is clear.

"There is no plausible connection between the Czech report and the symptoms being experienced by some Gulf War veterans."

"There is no medical nor epidemiological documentation to link the unusual and ill-defined symptoms reported by some Persian Gulf War veterans to exposure to GB or HD."

"In conclusion, there is no reasonable linkage between these incidents and those Gulf War veterans reporting persistent health problems."

I am not making an official claim that Iraq attacked our troops with chemical or biological weapons; and I am not charging the Defense Department with lying to us. I am not going to use the word cover-up, although many outside the Pentagon are doing so. But the Defense Department is stonewalling sick and dying Gulf War veterans with its virtual denials.

These veterans have mysterious health problems and they are not getting satisfactory answers from the Pentagon. Military officials say they have no confirmed accounts or evidence of chemical or biological exposure, and veterans are coming out of the wood-work swearing to names, dates and places. The DOD and these veterans must have fought in two different wars.

I intend to demonstrate later in today's hearing as a Member of the Oversight and Investigations Subcommittee that the DOD's statements of no "known" connection between possible exposure and the mystery ailments is an unsatisfactory basis for its virtual denial of any connection. I intend to show that there is some scientific basis contradicting the DOD's position.

Fortunately, the Department of Veterans Affairs has begun the painful process of dealing with this issue and getting these veterans the help they need and deserve. However, Mr. Chairman, our job on the

Oversight and Investigations Subcommittee of the House Armed Services Committee gives us the responsibility and obligation to find out what is going on with the Department of Defense regarding this mystery ailment controversy.

IS MILITARY RESEARCH HAZARDOUS TO VETERANS' HEALTH? LESSONS FROM WORLD WAR II, THE PERSIAN GULF, AND TODAY

HEARING

BEFORE THE

COMMITTEE ON VETERANS' AFFAIRS
UNITED STATES SENATE

ONE HUNDRED THIRD CONGRESS

SECOND SESSION

MAY 6, 1994

Printed for the use of the Committee on Veterans' Affairs

U.S. GOVERNMENT PRINTING OFFICE

83-530 CC WASHINGTON: 1995

IS MILITARY RESEARCH HAZARDOUS TO VETERANS' HEALTH? LESSONS FROM WORLD WAR II, THE PERSIAN GULF, AND TODAY

FRIDAY, MAY 6, 1994

U.S. SENATE

COMMITTEE ON VETERANS' AFFAIRS

Washington, DC.

The Committee met, pursuant to notice, at 10 a.m. in room SD-106, Dirksen Senate Office Building, Hon. John D. Rockefeller IV (Chairman of the Committee) presiding.

Present: Senators Rockefeller, Mitchell, Daschle, and Jeffords.

Also present (staff): Jim Gottlieb, chief counsel/staff director; Diana M. Zuckerman, professional staff member; Patricia Olson, congressional science fellow; and John Moseman, minority staff director/chief counsel.

Chairman ROCKEFELLER. This hearing will come to order. I welcome everybody.

OPENING STATEMENT OF CHAIRMAN ROCKEFELLER

A few months ago, Americans were shocked to learn that our Government had intentionally exposed thousands of U.S. citizens to radiation without their knowledge and without their consent. Although many of us expressed horror at the apparently unethical behavior of our Government, we all were relieved to hear that such experiments had been stopped long ago.

We'd like to think that these kinds of abuses are a thing of the past, but, sad to say, the legacy continues. During the Persian Gulf War, hundreds of thousands of soldiers were given experimental vaccines and drugs, and today we will hear evidence that these medical products could be causing many of the so-called "mysterious illnesses" that those veterans are now experiencing. And for several decades, and continuing today, the testing of chemical and biological agents at U.S. military facilities has put soldiers and civilians at risk.

Today's hearing will examine the results of an intensive 6-month investigation conducted by this Committee's staff, particularly staff members Diana Zuckerman and Patricia Olson. The investigation focuses on Persian Gulf War veterans, but extends from World War II-era veterans to the present. So, while we're focusing on the Persian Gulf War, this is a pattern which has gone on for a long, long time.

The results of our investigation showed a reckless disregard that frankly shocked me, and I think will shock all Americans.

TABLE 1

BIOLOGICAL FIELD TESTING
ANTI-PERSONNEL
BIOLOGICAL STIMULANTS
INVOLVING PUBLIC DOMAIN

LOCATION OF TEST	DATE(s) OF TEST	SIMULANT / AGENT USED
Washington, DC	18 Aug 1949 26 Aug 1949 12–13 Dec 1949 11 Mar 1950	SM
USS Coral Sea anchored in Hampton Rds, & USS K.D. Bailey at sea off entrance to Hampton Roads, VA 1 trial at anchor, 16 trials at sea off the entrance	1–21 Apr 1950`	BG SM
San Francisco, CA	Sep 1950	SM BG
Port Hueneme, CA	10 Sep–24 Oct 1952	BG
Panama City, FL	Mar–May 1953	SM BG
Off-shore, between Port Hueneme and Point Mugu, CA, near Santa Barbara	17-27 Aug 1954	BG
Pennsylvania State Highway #16 westward for one mile from Benchmark #193	7 Jan 1955	BG
Kittakinny and Tuscarora Tunnels, Pennsylvania Turnpike	Aug 1955	BG
Offshore Hawaii	Jan–June 1963	BG
Vicinity Ft. Greeley, Alaska	Dec 1963–Jan 1964	BG
Central Alaska	Jan–Feb 1965	BG FP
National Airport & Greyhound Terminal, Washington, DC	May 1965	BG
Oahu, Hawaii	May–June 1965	BG
Off California Coast (San Diego)	Feb–Mar 1966	BG
Hawaii	Apr–May 1966	BG
New York, NY	7–10 Jun 1966	BG
Hawaii	Jan–Mar 1968	BG SM
Oahu, Hawaii	Apr–May 1968	BG
Dugway Proving Ground, Utah	1945 Jul–Nov 1949	BG BG
Camp Cooke, California	1955	BG FP
Edgewood Arsenal, MD	1959	BG
Key West, FL	1952	SM
Off California Coast (San Clemente)	Aug–Sep 1968	BG

The following is a detailed listing of biological materials exported to Iraq by the United States prior to the Persian Gulf War. Source: The Riegle Report; United States Senate, 103rd Congress, 2nd Session, May 25, 1994.

Date: February 8, 1985
Sent to: Iraq Atomic Energy Agency
Materials shipped:

1. Ustilago nuda (Jensen) Rostrup

Date: February 22, 1985
Sent to: Ministry of Higher Education
Materials shipped:

1. Histoplasma capsulatum (ATCC 32136) Class III pathogen

Date: July 11, 1985
Sent to: Middle and Near East Regional A
Materials shipped:

1. Histoplasma capsulatum (ATCC 32136) Class III pathogen

Date: May 2, 1986
Sent to: Ministry of Higher Education
Materials shipped:

1. Bacillus anthracis Cohn
   (ATCC 10)
   Batch # 08-20-82 (2 each)
   Class III pathogen
2. Bacillus subtilis Cohn
   (ATCC 82)
   Batch # 06-20-84 (2 each)
3. Clostridium botulinum Type A
   (ATCC 3502)
   Batch #07-07-81 (3 each)
   Class III pathogen
4. Clostridium perfringes
   (ATCC 3624)
   Batch # 10-85SV (2 each)
5. Bacillus subtilis
   (ATCC 6051)
   Batch #12-06-84 (2 each)
6. Francisella tularensis
   (ATCC 6223)
   Batch # 05-14-79 (2 each)
7. Clostridium tetani
   (ATCC 9441)
   Batch #03-84 (3 each)
   Highly toxigenic
8. Clostridium botulinum Type E
   (ATCC 9564)
   Batch #03-02-79 (2 each)
   Class III pathogen
9. Clostridium tetani
   (ATCC 10779)
   Batch # 04-24-84S (3 each)
10. Clostridium perfringes
    (ATCC 12916)
    Batch #08-14-80 (2 each)
    Agglutinating type 2
11. Clostridium perfringes
    (ATCC 13124)
    Batch #07-84SV (3 each)
    Type A, alpha-toxigenic
12. Bacillus anthracis
    (ATCC 14185)
    Batch #01-14-80 (3 each)
    G.G. Wright (Fort Detrick)
    V770-NP1-R. Bovine Anthrax
    Class III pathogen
13. Bacillus anthracis
    (ATCC 14578)
    Batch #01-06-78 (2 each)
    Class III pathogen
14. Bacillus megaterium
    (ATCC 14581)
    Batch # 04-18-85 (2 each)
15. Bacillus megaterium
    (ATCC 14945)
    Batch #06-21-81 (2 each)
16. Clostridium botulinum Type E
    (ATCC 17855)
    Batch #06-21-71
    Class III pathogen
17. Bacillus megaterium
    (ATCC 19213)
    Batch # 3-84 (2 each)
18. Clostridium botulinum Type A
    (ATCC 19397)
    Batch # 08-18-81 (2 each)
    Class III pathogen
19. Brucella abortus Biotype 3
    (ATCC 23450)
    Batch # 08-02-84 (3 each)
    Class III pathogen

20. Brucella abortus Biotype 3
    (ATCC 23455)
    Batch # 02-05-68 (3 each)
21. Brucella melitensis Biotype I
    (ATCC 23456)
    Batch # 03-08-78 (2 each)
    Class III pathogen
22. Brucella melitensis Biotype 3
    (ATCC 23458)
    Batch # 01-29-68 (2 each)
    Class III pathogen
23. Clostridium botulinum Type A
    (ATCC 25763)
    Batch # 8-83 (2 each)
    Class III pathogen
24. Clostridium botulinum Type F
    (ATCC 35415)
    Batch # 02-02-84 (2 each)
    Class III pathogen

Date: August 31, 1987
Sent to: State Company for Drug Industries
Materials shipped:

1. Saccharomyces cerevesiae
   (ATCC 2601)
   Batch # 08-28-08 (1 each)
2. Salmonella choleraesuis
   (ATCC 6539)
   Batch # 06-86S (1 each)
3. Bacillus subtillus
   (ATCC 6633)
   Batch # 10-85 (2 each)
4. Klebsiella pneumoniae
   (ATCC 10031)
   Batch # 08-13-80 (1 each)
5. Escherichia coli
   (ATCC 10536)
   Batch # 04-09080 (1 each)
6. Bacillus cereus
   (ATCC 11778)
   Batch # 05-85SV (2 each)
7. Staphylococcus epidermidis
   (ATCC 12228)
   Batch # 11-86S (1 each)
8. Bacillus pumilus
   (ATCC 14884)
   Batch # 09-08-80 (2 each)

Date: July 11, 1988
Sent to: Iraq Atomic Energy Commission
Materials Shipped:

1. Escherichia coli
   (ATCC 11303)
   Batch # 04-875
   Phase host
2. Cauliflower Mosaic Caulimovirus
   (ATCC 45031)
   Batch # 06-14-85
   Plant virus
3. Plasmid in Agrobacterium Tumefaciens
   (ATCC 37349)
   Batch # 05-28-85

Date: April 26, 1988
Sent to: Iraq Atomic Energy Commission
Materials Shipped:

1. Hulambda 4x -8, clone: human hypoxanthine phosphoribosyl-transferase (HPRT)
   Chromosome(s): Xq26.1
   (ATCC 57236) Phage vector;
   Suggested host: E. Coli
2. Hulambda 14-8, clone: human hypoxanthine phosphoribosyl-transferase (HPRT)
   Chromosome(s): Xq26.1
   (ATCC 57240) Phage vector;
   Suggested host: E. Coli
3. Hulambda 15, clone: human hypoxanthine phosphoribosyl-transferase (HPRT)
   Chromosome(s): Xq26.1
   (ATCC 57242) Phage vector;
   Suggested host: E. Coli

Date: August 31, 1987
Sent to: Iraq Atomic Energy Commission
Materials Shipped:

1. Escherichia coli
   (ATCC 23846)
   Batch # 07-29-83 (1 each)
2. Escherichia coli
   (ATCC 33694)
   Batch # 05-87 (1 each)

Date: September 29, 1988
Sent to: Ministry of Trade
Materials Shipped:

1. Bacillus anthracis
   (ATCC 240)
   Batch # 05-14-63 (3 each)
   Class III pathogen
2. Bacillus anthracis
   (ATCC 938)
   Batch # 1963 (3 each)
   Class III pathogen
3. Clostridium perfringes
   (ATCC 3629)
   Batch # 10-23-85 (3 each)
4. Clostridium perfringes
   (ATCC 8009)
   Batch # 03-30-84 (3 each)
5. Bacillus anthracis
   (ATCC 8705)
   Batch # 06-27-62 (3 each)
   Class III pathogen
6. Brucella abortus
   (ATCC 9014)
   Batch # 05-11-66 (3 each)
   Class III pathogen
7. Clostridium perfringes
   (ATCC 10388)
   Batch # 06-01-73 (3 each)
8. Bacillus anthracis
   (ATCC 11966)
   Batch # 05-05-70 (3 each)
   Class III pathogen
9. Clostridium botulinum Type A
   Batch # 07-86 (3 each)
   Class III pathogen
10. Bacillus cereus
    (ATCC 33018)
    Batch # 04-83 (3 each)
11. Bacillus cereus
    (ATCC 33019)
    Batch # 03-88 (3 each)

Date: January 31, 1989
Sent to: Iraq Atomic Energy Commission
Materials Shipped:

1. PHPT31, clone: human hypoxanthine phosphoribosyltransferase (HPRT)
   Chromosome(s): Xq26.1
   (ATCC 57057)
2. Plambda 500, clone: human hypoxanthine phosphoribosyltransferase (HPRT)
   Chromosome(s): 5 p14-p13
   (ATCC 57212)

Date: January 17, 1989
Sent to: Iraq Atomic Energy Commission
Materials Shipped:

1. Hulambda 4x-8, clone: human hypoxanthine phosphoribosyltransferase (HPRT)
   Chromosome(s): Xq26.1
   (ATCC 57237)
   Phage vector; Suggested host: E. coli
2. Hulambda 14, clone: human hypoxanthine phosphoribosyltransferase (HPRT)
   Chromosome(s): Xq26.1
   (ATCC 57540)
   Cloned from human lymphoblast
   Suggested host: E. coli
3. Hulambda 15, clone: human hypoxanthine phosphoribosyltransferase (HPRT)
   Chromosome(s): Xq26.1
   (ATCC 57241)
   Phage vector; Suggested host: E. coli

Date: November 28, 1989
Sent to: University of Basrah, College of Science
Materials Shipped:

1. Enterococcus faecalis
2. Enterococcus faecium
3. Enterococcus avium
4. Enterococcus raffinosus
5. Enterococcus gallinarium
6. Enterococcus durans
7. Enterococcus hirae
8. Streptococcus bovis (etiological)

WRITTEN TESTIMONY OF
Dr. GARTH L. NICOLSON and Dr. NANCY L. NICOLSON
COMMITTEE ON GOVERNMENT REFORM AND OVERSIGHT
Subcommittee on Human Resource and Intergovernmental Relations
UNITED STATES HOUSE OF REPRESENTATIVES
April 2, 1996

Dr. Garth Nicolson is the David Bruton Jr. Chair in Cancer Research and Professor at the University of Texas M. D. Anderson Cancer Center in Houston and Professor of Internal Medicine and Professor of Pathology and Laboratory Medicine at the University of Texas Medical School at Houston. Among the most cited scientists in the world, having published over 400 medical and scientific papers, edited 13 books, served on the Editorial Boards of 12 medical and scientific journals and currently serving as Editor of two (*Clinical & Experimental Metastasis* and the *Journal of Cellular Biochemistry*), Professor Nicolson has active peer-reviewed research grants from the U.S. Army, National Cancer Institute, American Cancer Society and National Foundation for Cancer Research. Dr. Nancy Nicolson is trained in molecular biophysics and is the President of the Rhodon Foundation for Biomedical Research of Kingwood, Texas. She has published over 25 medical and scientific papers and has delivered over 60 international and national scientific presentations.

In our studies *a large portion of the GWS patients that we have tested have an unusual mycoplasmal infection in their blood, but we have found that this infection can be successfully treated with multiple courses of specific antibiotics, such as doxycycline (200 mg/day for 6 weeks per cycle), ciprofloxacin (1500 mg/day for 6 weeks per cycle) or azithromycin (500 mg/day for 6 weeks per cycle)*. Multiple treatment cycles are required, and patients relapse often after the first few cycles, but subsequent relapses are milder and they eventually recover their health. In our published study approximately one-half of a small random group of GWS patients were mycoplasma-positive (14/30), and most (11/14) recovered after multiple cycles of antibiotics, and a few (3/14) are continuing antibiotic therapy. None of 21 healthy controls were mycoplasma-positive. In our earlier study on 73 Desert Storm veterans and their immediate family members who had the GWS-CFIDS signs and symptoms, 55 had good responses with doxycycline (100-200 mg/day for 4-6 weeks per cycle), and after multiple courses of antibiotic eventually recovered. The frequency of recovery increases with each cycle of antibiotic therapy. Although the numbers of patients in these studies are limited, the studies were conducted without any support whatsoever from the Department of Defense or Veterans Administration.

We consider it quite likely that many of the Desert Storm veterans suffering from the GWS-CFIDS symptoms may have been infected with slowly proliferating microorganisms, including pathogenic mycoplasmas and quite possibly other bacteria, and such infections, although not usually fatal, can produce various CFIDS signs and symptoms long after exposure. This would also explain the apparent contagious nature of GWS-CFIDS in veterans and the appearance of similar symptoms in their immediate family members. Fortunately, these infections can be successfully treated by multiple cycles of specific antibiotics.

There were several potential sources of chronic biologic agents in the Persian Gulf. First, deployed soldiers were given multiple inoculations of sometimes questionable vaccines in unproven immunization schemes such as those that were given all at once. Some of these vaccines could have been contaminated with small amounts of slow growing microorganisms. Second, the Iraqis were know to have extensive stockpiles of "weaponized" biological agents and the potential to deliver these agents offensively, even at long range in modified SCUD-B (SS-1) missiles. Third, many of the storage and factory facilities where chemical and biological agents were housed were bombed immediately up to and during the Desert Storm ground offensive, possibly releasing plumes containing these agents high in the atmosphere to be carried downwind to our lines. These and other possible routes of potential exposure must be carefully examined, not categorically dismissed by high level Defense Department personnel in Washington with little first hand knowledge of the conditions on the ground in the Persian Gulf Theater of Operations.

We believe that Congress holds the key to the solution of GWS. This and associated disorders (CFIDS) must be studied and solutions found using the peer-reviewed grant award system, such as that used by NIH. GWS cannot be left to the Department of Defense or the Department of Veterans Affairs, because they have not shown themselves to be especially effective or responsive to the health problems of our Gulf War veterans.

about the author

Andrew Goliszek, Ph.D., has been the principal investigator and coinvestigator on several grants from the National Institutes of Health, the most recent being a four-year grant involving neuroendocrine and cardiovascular functions. He is a professor and biomedical researcher at North Carolina A&T State University, where he has taught bioscience, human anatomy and physiology, endocrine physiology, and other biological subjects. He has written numerous nonfiction articles and several nonfiction books. *World Order* is his second novel. Both *World Order* and his previous novel, *Rivers of the Black Moon*, reflect Goliszek's keen insight into the medical and political crises that face modern humanity. He and his family live in the Piedmont region of North Carolina.